Praise for Joseph D. McNamara

"We never tire of McNamara's ingenuity, his eye for authentic detail, and his ability to make a wild and rip-roaring cop story sound to us like real life."
—*San Francisco Chronicle*

"He knows the territory and he can portray the exhilarating and the seamy sides of police work. He also can spin a pulse-throbbing tale with accomplished skill."
—*Kansas City Star*

"McNamara has the magical touch. He knows how to grip his readers with human emotion and raw action."
—*Ocala Star-Banner*

"McNamara handles it all in a hard-boiled style akin to Raymond Chandler and Ed McBain."
—*Richmond Times-Dispatch*

"A master of the genre . . . McNamara knows policing inside out, and when that expertise is mated with a crisp plot and well-drawn characters, the result is exciting and pleasurable."
—*The Chattanooga Times*

By Joseph D. McNamara:

SAFE & SANE (nonfiction)
THE FIRST DIRECTIVE*
FATAL COMMAND*
THE BLUE MIRAGE*
CODE 211 BLUE*

*Published by Fawcett Books

Books published by The Ballantine Publishing Group are available at quantity discounts on bulk purchases for premium, educational, fund-raising, and special sales use. For details, please call 1-800-733-3000.

CODE 211 BLUE

BLUE

Joseph D. McNamara

FAWCETT GOLD MEDAL • NEW YORK

A Fawcett Gold Medal Book
Published by Ballantine Books
Copyright © 1996 by Joseph D. McNamara

http://www.randomhouse.com

Library of Congress Catalog Card Number: 96-96360

ISBN 0-449-14894-7

Manufactured in the United States of America

First Edition: September 1996

10 9 8 7 6 5 4 3 2 1

PART ONE

Betrayal

Chapter One

Kevin McKay loved watching the first stirrings of this neighborhood the tourists would never see. The smell of a coffee factory. The murmur in various dialects of people on the way to work. The small fabric companies, sewing shops, and wholesale shippers crowded into functional commercial buildings. Big trucks nuzzling against loading docks just a couple of blocks from rare, low-rent housing. Asian and Latino workers buying their green cards, driver's licenses, and social security cards from whoever was selling. The easy rhythm of San Francisco. For more than a century a variety of poor people had sought out a living and raised families on these streets. Like the tides of the bay, there was a certain comfort to it.

A group of children on their way to grade school got off a Muni bus and clowned with each other. The boys made runs at the girls' books. The girls screamed and giggled in mock fear as they fought them off. Kevin remembered when Molly McGee, a whole year older, had taught him to play doctor in a park not very far from where he and Joey Demanto now sat. But that was before the shrubbery was used for rapes, murders, and dope sales. As Kevin watched, a boy in faded jeans dashed forward and faked a pass at a blond girl's book bag, at the last moment gently tugging her ponytail instead. Inside the shabby, battered car, he chuckled. The rules of courtship were timeless.

"You talk to yourself, you laugh to yourself. It's shrink time, baby," Joey said.

"Three more hours. Think Big Billy will show?"

Joey sighed. "Everybody knows Billy hasn't been around in a month."

The two detectives had been sitting on Tim's Bar and Grill for almost an hour. They'd watched mechanics and drivers from the nearby bus yard, a few postal workers from the depot across the street, and a uniformed cop stop for their morning wake-ups—probably a shot and a beer.

"I don't get it," Joey said. "What are all those donkeys doing inside a bar this time of day?"

"Telling wop jokes and lying to each other about hitting electras or scoring with beautiful rich women from Nob Hill," Kevin replied, meanwhile trying unsuccessfully to reach the itch in the middle of his back.

Inside Tim's, where the local bookie knew all the first names of the bar patrons and how much they were good for, a character like Big Billy would be a major part of the scene. Being connected enough to buy little tinfoils of Billy's nose joy had become as much a status symbol as having a credit line with the bookie, or being able to borrow a double saw-buck from the bartender. That's why they sat watching.

Kevin scratched his arm, itchy under the flannel shirt he wore against the bleak cold of the San Francisco morning. His partner hadn't moved in twenty minutes.

Joey leaned back in the driver's seat, eyes closed behind dark glasses. His mouth was open slightly and he breathed deeply, but he was aware of Kevin fidgeting. Motionless, he mumbled, "You rattled Sherry's cage. What did you expect, roses?"

"At least I had the balls to complain. You just bitched behind his back."

"Yeah, but you and Sherry are both Irish, probably grew up in the same bar. I'm an underprivileged Italian."

"Next thing, you'll be asking for protected class status."

"I deserve it, being stuck with you as a partner. By the way, in case you didn't notice, Sherry has been by twice."

Kevin had noticed Lieutenant Glen Sherry, all right. Joey was right. Sherry had assigned them to a useless stakeout just to show who was boss. He felt the acid churn in his stomach. Though he was the senior partner, Joey was an undercover star, and Kevin knew Sherry was wasting him on a stakeout of a small-time coke dealer who wasn't going to show. Joey's pale skin, large, anxious eyes, and heavy beard often fooled people into thinking he was a strung-out coke fiend. Dealers fought to be first to sell to him.

"Hey," Kevin said, "look who's coming down the street."

Simp Jiminez was an addict in his thirties, going on fifty. Kevin had busted him twice for possession. "I'm a simple addict," was his usual plea when a cop caught him dirty. The nickname "Simp" stuck so well that he even used it for his welfare application. Thin and small, his shabby clothing marked him as one of the legions of San Francisco's homeless. Jiminez's health had deteriorated as his habit grew. He hustled a buck where he could, occasionally acting as a mule for some small deliveries.

Now Jiminez and Kevin spotted each other simultaneously, and Jiminez panicked. He turned and fled into the park.

"Let's see what Simp is nervous about," Kevin said to his partner.

"What about Sherry and the stakeout?"

"Fuck him. This gives us an excuse to get out of here."

Joey gunned the car around the corner and pulled behind a van parked at the curb. Simp paused in the park entrance opposite the one he had fled into. He looked around and, not spotting Kevin and Joey behind the van, crossed the street.

"He's heading for Potrero," Joey said, easing the car out, following Simp down the street.

Half a block later, Simp casually glanced back, saw the undercover car creeping along behind him, and jumped, his eyes bulging. The detectives laughed. Kevin waved him over. Jiminez took two steps toward them, then suddenly bolted.

"Son of a bitch. He's dirty!" Joey said. He whipped the car around a double-parked cab and pulled in front of Simp, slamming to a halt with tires screeching.

Kevin banged his head against the windshield visor. "Goddamn you."

Joey laughed as Kevin groped for the door handle. "Go get him, tiger."

Simp turned and ran in the opposite direction. Kevin closed on him quickly, both men swerving around pedestrians. Realizing the detective was catching up, Simp darted into a hallway. Too late. Kevin was close enough to see him throw three small glassine envelopes into a corner.

Simp turned and faced Kevin, the two men five feet apart. In a quick motion the addict whipped a switchblade knife from his pocket, the razor-sharp blade springing open, dully reflecting the ceiling light.

Kevin shook his head. Shit. His nine-millimeter, uncomfortable on the stakeout, was under the seat in the car. His heart raced and sweat wet his forehead. It wasn't from the run.

Heroin addicts were normally harmless, but hysteria could make a difference. Kevin recalled Owen Connolly, who'd been in his class at the Police Academy. A couple of years later, Kevin had been among the first cops to respond to an "officer down" call. Owen, on foot patrol, had turned the corner of Market Street when a Mission District bum, for reasons they never discovered, plunged a butcher knife into the rookie's gut. Now, Kevin remembered how they frantically shoved the young cop's intestines back into his body and tried to stop the blood gushing through the holes in his blue-uniformed shirt, meanwhile ignoring the frozen eyes and gray pallor spreading over Owen Connolly's face. It had been his first cop funeral.

Simp kept eye contact as he edged backward, reaching for the doorknob. The door was locked. Simp's eyes widened and he started forward, the knife pointed at Kevin.

"Let's not do anything stupid, Simp." Incredible. His voice was calm. He held out his left hand. "Turn the blade around and give it to me, by the handle. Real slow, Simp."

For a moment their eyes locked. Kevin balanced on the balls of his feet. Joey, making a U-turn, was probably just catching up to them with the car. A long moment ticked by.

Finally, Simp shrugged and relinquished the knife, handle first. Kevin closed the blade and dropped the knife into his pocket. No way would he let the junkie know that his heart felt like it would thump right through his chest.

"Where's the spike, Simp?" Still cool. Macho cop stuff. We all piss ice water. Ha!

The addict nodded toward his waist. Kevin patted him down, handcuffed him, and very carefully removed a hypodermic needle hidden in the seam of his trouser waistline. Every cop's nightmare. A needle prick from an AIDS carrier. He picked up the glassine envelopes containing white powder. Heroin. Big deal. Three lousy fixes. He safeguarded the needle, dropped the evidence into his pocket, and led Simp out of the hallway.

Joey had driven right up onto the sidewalk and sprinted for the hallway. He stopped running when he saw them and bowed slightly. "Good morning, Simp," he said with a pleasant smile. "Inspector McKay and I were quite hurt when we realized you weren't going to say hello." He waved an invitation for the addict to get into the car.

When Simp was in the backseat, Joey made no move to start the car, the detectives letting the silence work on the addict. Finally, bargaining with practiced skill, Simp said, "Mr. McKay, this is a nothing bust. All I had was three bags for my own kit. I can't take a bust right now. My daughter is gonna be ten this week. I need to be at her birthday party."

Kevin winked at Joey.

"Come on, Simp," Joey said, "we're not paid to be nice guys. We're cops. You're our collar for the day. Now we can go home."

"Look, officer, I'm just a simple junkie. I can give you a pusher. Let me go."

"Oh, sure, Simp. What will you do? Come down to the Hall of Justice in a week or two?" Joey wore a sneer.

"No. I mean right now." Simp's voice trembled. "You know me, Mr. McKay," he said to Kevin. "You was always straight with me, and I was with you."

Kevin shrugged, and Joey kept up the conversation. "Very admirable of you, Simp. Just for speculation, does this dealer have a name?"

"Angel Vinnie."

"Never heard of him. What's his real name?"

"I don't know."

Joey laughed, and started the car.

"I think his name is Hallman. I can take you to him right now. He just got a delivery."

"And you just scored from him?" Joey turned off the motor. Simp nodded vigorously.

"Let me converse with Inspector McKay for a moment." Joey got out of the car, and Kevin joined him on the sidewalk. They stood just out of Simp's hearing, observing the man's anxiety in the backseat.

Joey stroked his chin. "Ordinarily, I'd say we throw the shit in the sewer and give him a kick in the ass," he said. "He's down to sleeping in doorways. How much can he really do for us? But it would give us an excuse to get off this bullshit surveillance. I can't take much more."

"Yeah, and I don't think we ought to be taking any risks of a beef," Kevin replied. "Sherry is really gunning for us. By the way, whatcha do, stop to mail a letter? Simp pulled a blade and thought about carving his initials on my chest."

"Hey, you're superjock," Joey replied. "You even left your piece under the seat. I'm just a simple lover. Besides, if you got cut, I'd get your permanent spot in the squad."

"I knew you were in a panic about my safety."

They returned to the car, Kevin getting into the backseat with Simp. He said, "We'll go along, but it's got to be a done deal. You don't just point out Hallman to us. You take Joey in and set him up with Hallman."

"Man, I can't do that. I'd be dead."

"Simp, we'll make a lot of buys, probably not even bust Hallman. We'll do his supplier. It will be months by the time we bust out. No one will connect you with Joey."

Honest. Persuasive. The same old con game.

Simp stubbornly shook his head and looked out the window. "No way I duke a cop in."

Joey caught Kevin's attention and raised his eyebrows. They sat silently for a while, Simp refusing to look at Kevin. Kevin took the switchblade from his pocket and sprang the blade. Simp blinked. Kevin began to clean his fingernails with the point, watching the wheels turn in Simp's head. The addict knew that if he was charged with assaulting a cop with a knife, or even charged with possession of a deadly weapon, he was facing big-time trouble, rather than a ninety-day jail term or diversion into drug rehab.

The doper said, "How about I just show you his apartment? You make up a name. He'll let you in. He wants to unload his delivery."

"Sorry, Simp," Kevin said, putting the knife in his pocket.

"All right, all right," Simp mumbled.

"Where does Hallman deal?" Kevin watched Simp's face for any sign of evasion.

"On Mission, nine hundred something. I know the building."

At a phone in the corner gas station, Kevin dialed Lieutenant Sherry's number and left a message that they'd taken a known narcotics offender into custody for questioning and had left the stakeout. Then he called Inspector Bill Carey and asked him to meet them on Mission Street to back up a buy.

Returning to the car, Kevin motioned to Joey. Once again they talked on the sidewalk without Simp hearing.

"We need to kill some time," Kevin said. "Sherry wasn't there, but Carey will meet us on Mission in ten minutes."

"Mr. Charisma?"

"You have a better suggestion?"

Joey shrugged. "We also better call Sherry on the radio to cover our ass."

They picked up Bill Carey on the corner of Mission and Sixth Street. Carey was tall and gaunt. Kevin had never seen him smile.

"How they hanging, Bill? Sorry to take you away from the doughnuts," Joey said, star narc and part-time comedian.

Carey ignored him. He looked at Simp in the backseat, then at Kevin.

"What's happening?" he said to Kevin.

"Simp Jiminez, here," Kevin gestured, "is going to introduce Joey to a dealer by the name of Hallman. SOP says three men. I thought maybe you'd stay with the car, and I'll take the hallway while Joey goes in."

"I'll take the hallway. I don't want to deal with the assholes on the street." Carey looked at Kevin's muscular frame. "They'll probably leave you alone."

Kevin's druthers were to be close to Joey during the buy, but Carey was doing them a favor. Kevin got behind the wheel and Carey walked toward the building Simp had pointed out. Carey would go in first and wait in the hall. Joey and Simp would follow a minute or two later.

Kevin parked across the street. Good visibility. Everything was going down nice and easy. Too easy. He watched Joey and Simp walk into 918A Mission Street.

Chapter Two

Kevin watched a wino start to boost a Honda parked two cars ahead. Just as the derelict got the coat hanger inside the window, he spotted Kevin. Without a second's hesitation he abandoned the hanger and shuffled toward the corner. Kevin grunted. Joey could be getting blown away right now because someone mistook him for a doper, he thought. But they made him as a cop right away.

So he was the one who waited. And thought. The street around him was crawling with catastrophes—alcoholics, heroin addicts, coke fiends, mentally ill, petty criminals, pimps, hookers, you name it. The human flotsam of a busy, indifferent world, spinning in a crescendo of failure that wouldn't be heard even a block away. And he was immersed in their misery, a captive observer confined to a car that should have been junked two years ago.

Joey, meanwhile, was turned on, fully engaged in a battle of wits. Joey had to be sharp to pull off the buy, to stay alive, while he sat, nervous, trying to push aside doubts about whether or not the minuscule intrusion they made on the flow of life in the streets made any difference. They risked their lives, and sometimes other people's lives, by intruding, and in the long run it didn't make much difference to the Simp Jiminezes. If people wanted to put that shit in their veins, no one could stop them.

But you had to try to at least protect kids, Kevin thought. Yeah, that was important. It made a difference. And they'd make a big difference for guys like Hallman, who could end up serving a significant portion of his life in the joint. Life on the installment plan.

It wasn't profitable to think too much. The law was the law. We're cops, Kevin told himself. We enforce it. Getting philosophical could be distracting. Dangerous. Next thing you knew, you got careless, missed something and got blown away. Or ended up on your boss's shit list.

He thought about Joey, building up trust with people over a period of time, then sending them down for some big ones. He'd seen Joey's ambivalence when they busted out. Elation over cases well made, but a little shame too, at the betrayal. Joey turning away from the look in the handcuffed prisoners' eyes when they realized their buddy was a narc.

On the other hand, Kevin knew that Joey had zinged him more than once on how suspects trusted him too, would unload, pour out explanations about what they'd done and why, asking for his understanding, only to realize later that their words were used to convict them. "Kevin, the good priest," Joey had said. "The sincere face you want to confess to. The understanding person who'll give you absolution. But instead of ten Hail Marys penance, you get ten big ones in the joint."

Simp was coming out of the building. Kevin grabbed the door handle in case the addict decided to renege on his instructions to come back to the car, but Simp slipped in next to him.

"I did it. They's talking right now."

Kevin watched him wipe sweat from his eyes, trying to control the tremors. "Is Hallman going along?" he asked.

"I think so. Man, I did my part. He's in. He buys or he doesn't."

"What about the other cop?"

"He's on the stairs outside the apartment. Everything's cool. Hallman's all alone."

"Okay, Simp. This one's on us."

"Mr. McKay?"

Kevin steeled himself, Simp's need was fierce and his eyes were on the glove compartment.

"You know I can't, Simp." Kevin took out a business card and wrote on the back. He handed it to Simp. "This person at the Methadone Clinic knows me. Go over. They'll help you out. You've been there before. This time try to stay with the program." Great advice. Just what Simp was looking for.

Kevin opened the glove compartment, trying not to see the hope come into Simp's eyes. Damn, he didn't want to do this to the man, but it was important that he see that they weren't palming the dope. Kevin got out of the car and dropped the needle to the street. He ground the syringe with his heel until it shattered, then opened an envelope and dumped the white powder into a pool of dirty water by the curb.

"No! Please?" Simp begged.

When the third bag was empty, Simp spun around and walked down the street. Kevin turned from the sight of his hunched shoulders and stumbling walk. Another victory in the drug war.

Five minutes later Joey and Carey came out of the hall-way. Without a glance at Kevin, they walked toward Market Street. Kevin started the car and followed for a couple of blocks. When he was sure no one was watching, he pulled up next to the two detectives and they got in.

"It was cool. A good solid first buy." Joey held up a handful of drugs. "Let's check the recording." He took a small recorder from his pocket and played it. "Right on!" he said when both his and Hallman's voices were clear. "Take me to our leader, James." He gestured at Kevin. "No doubt he'll lavish us with great praise."

Next to him, Bill Carey snorted.

Chapter Three

It was quitting time when they finished their reports. Kevin called his friend, Father William Riordan, before leaving headquarters. The priest agreed to meet Kevin in the schoolyard.

The junior varsity was in a full-court scrimmage. The boys were glad to see Kevin and Father Riordan, who had played high school basketball together at Sacred Heart High School. Both were in good shape, and they ran evenly with the teenagers. Kevin played opposite Ronnie Blue, a fourteen-year-old who was already as tall as Kevin. Ronnie was clearly the star of the team, and Kevin played hard against him.

The boy took a second too long setting up for an outside shot, and Kevin managed to get his fingers on the ball as it arched upward. The ball bounced to Riordan, and he and Kevin broke for the basket at the other end of the court, the boys racing with them. At the last minute Riordan made a fancy behind-the-back pass to Kevin under the bucket. Kevin faked, getting Ronnie in the air, then scored.

"Lucky, old man." Ronnie grinned at him.

A few seconds later, at the other end of the court, Ronnie caught Kevin leaning and flashed in the other direction, driving for an easy lay-up. Kevin passed up the chance to foul him.

After a while, when the men had had enough, Kevin realized that for the last half hour he hadn't thought about Lieutenant Sherry and the police department, and that the ache in his stomach had faded.

"Come on back to the rectory for a beer," Riordan said to

him after they'd showered and dressed. "There's someone I want you to meet, and you can tell me what's doing at work."

The rectory study was comfortable. Worn leather chairs and an unimposing couch suggested an earlier, easier time, when the parish had been white and affluent. An elderly Irish housekeeper brought them two iced mugs of beer.

"It's Harp, Father," she said with a twinkle in her eye, carefully putting the glasses on coasters.

Riordan smiled. "Thank you, Mary." The priest took a long swallow and wiped his lips with satisfaction. "Ah, there's nothing like that first sip after basketball. How have you been, Kevin?"

Kevin told him how Sherry had ordered them off a promising investigation of a ring supplying drugs to schools, and instead assigned them to useless stakeouts. The priest was a good listener, occasionally sipping his beer, not interrupting during the fifteen minute summary. Riordan looked relaxed in a sport shirt and slacks, but he wore a somber look.

"It doesn't sound good, Kevin. I hate to think a policeman would let personality problems interfere with keeping drugs from youngsters, but I know better than to question your judgment."

"I suppose I'm just griping, Bill. I've had tough bosses before. Joey and I seem to have rubbed him the wrong way. We'll have to find a way to stroke him."

The priest rubbed his chin. "I could speak to the cardinal," he said. "I know he's quite close to Chief Ferrante, who, I might add, goes to church in this parish, unlike someone else I know."

Kevin ignored the remark about missing church. Bill Riordan never stopped trying, even though it had been years since he'd responded to one of his friend's jibes.

"I don't think that would be good right now, Bill. The police department muddles along, but in the end it somehow manages."

"Not unlike the Church. What do you plan to do?"

"I'm thinking of going to friends in the FBI or DEA to let

them know what's going on. Maybe they can informally exert some pressure to get the squad back to where it should be."

"Um . . ." Riordan finished his beer. "That would be going outside the agency. Is there a stigma attached?"

"You bet—if they find out who whispered. I guess it's like the Church, huh?"

Riordan nodded. "It certainly is. Of course, it's often better for everyone if the organization can straighten out its problems from within. The outside world can be harsh in its judgments, and unrealistic in its expectations of human perfection."

"I don't know about the Church, but expecting the narcotics cops to arrest drug dealers selling to teenagers doesn't seem unrealistic to me."

"No. Of course not. I was thinking of what's best for you in the long run. Going outside may burn bridges, although a word to the cardinal wouldn't be like going to the FBI. And I can tell you, the cardinal does wonderful things behind the scenes all the time."

Kevin sat facing the open door. He'd stopped listening. Riordan turned to see what he was staring at.

"Ah." The priest stood. "This was the person I mentioned. Kevin, meet Dana Rogers, our brand-new volunteer art director for the school."

Chapter Four

Kevin got to his feet, smiling. Her eyes were a wonderfully, oversized warm brown, matching the color of her hair. After a moment she turned her glance from his, shyly looking at Father Riordan, who was beaming.

Dana Rogers was slender and appeared fragile, but Kevin

recognized it was deceptive. She was around five-eight, and though she moved like a model, he could sense she had good muscle tone under the white blouse and navy-blue slacks. Dance classes or aerobics, he thought, imagining his lips on her long, graceful neck, and Dana Rogers turning to meet his kiss. Jesus. This had never happened to him before. Was it a reaction to his depression over Sherry and the department? He tried to control himself, vaguely hearing Riordan complete the introduction.

She held out her hand. He took it, enjoying the softness. A blush came into her cheeks, and he realized he was still holding her hand. Embarrassed, he released it.

"Father Riordan," Dana said, "I'll be through in half an hour. I wonder if you could have your housekeeper arrange for a cab."

"I have a car," Kevin said. "I'll be happy to drop you off."

Riordan laughed. "Kevin, you don't even know where Miss Rogers lives."

Kevin grimaced at Riordan and turned to Dana. "Miss Rogers, as long as it's within a fifty-mile radius, I repeat my offer. If it's further, we can negotiate."

She laughed. "I guess Russian Hill is within the boundary. Is this guy trustworthy, Father?"

"Of course not."

"Well," she smiled, "then I accept your ride, Kevin. See you in a half hour. Don't stand me up."

"I don't think you need worry, Dana," Riordan said.

Both men watched her leave. Thirty, Kevin thought, but she looked about eighteen for a moment when she was flirting.

"You son of a gun," he said to Riordan. "You gave me no warning. Where did that gorgeous woman come from?"

"Adam's rib, of course."

"Seriously, Bill."

"The Lord moves in mysterious ways. She came in last week and offered to set up an art curriculum for us. She's an artist, and a fine one. Dana showed us some photos of her portfolio. She trained in Paris. She offered to teach an art class to seniors and to train other teachers for the rest of the students."

"Do you think it's safe to leave her alone in a classroom with the seniors?"

"Not if their reaction is anything like yours."

Dana looked around Kevin's car, taking in the radio and microphone. "What kind of equipment is that?"

He reached out and lowered the dispatcher's volume on the radio. "It's a police car. Didn't Bill tell you?"

Her eyes widened. "No. I had no idea he was telling the truth when he said you were untrustworthy. Are you a detective?"

He sighed. "When I left work. Who knows about tomorrow?"

"Hmm, that sounds like a mystery."

"Do you like whodunits?"

"As long as they're make-believe. But I guess you deal with the real ones."

"When it pleases the bureaucracy."

"I'm up the hill on Taylor." She pointed to a high rise.

"Aha, spectacular view?"

"Yes indeed."

"Then you must be on one of the very expensive top floors. Bill said you were a fine artist."

"Do I detect a bit of detecting?"

"Dana, do you realize if I hook a right, within two minutes we'll be at Mario's, where I can spill some of the most delicious marinara sauce in San Francisco on my shirt?"

"I'm sorry, I'm busy tonight."

"Whoever it is, I can cut him a deal. Two years instead of life in prison."

"I didn't realize cops had a sense of humor."

"You think I'm kidding?"

"Tell you what. It's still early enough for an iced tea."

They were in one of the small alley cafés in the financial district. The police car was parked a short distance away, its official plate displayed on the dashboard. Kevin tasted his coffee.

"What makes a successful artist suddenly decide that an impoverished Catholic school needs her help?"

"What makes a busy detective take time to play basketball with underprivileged kids? By the way, I watched you from the rectory window. You're very good, aren't you?"

Kevin reddened. "Against kids. I'm a native. Where are you from?"

"Nice evasion as to why you work with the kids. I grew up mostly here in the city."

"Everybody's favorite city."

"I always hated that slogan."

"Why?" he said.

"Why? I don't know. I guess because it's tacky. And 'everybody'... I don't like being 'everybody.' Does that sound snobbish?"

"Yes. But you're so elegant, you can get away with it."

She looked at him for a moment. "Do you always come on this strong?"

"What do you think?"

"I don't know. You're making me uneasy."

He smiled, and enjoyed it when she couldn't resist smiling back.

"You know," she said, "you should smile more often. You look so serious when you don't."

"Occupational hazard. You never answered, why Sacred Heart?"

"Talk about your occupational hazard for a minute. I never met a cop before. What made you join?"

He grinned. "You mean how did a nice guy like me get into a racket like this? Actually, I was determined to be a professional athlete. A cartilage in my knee double-crossed me."

"It must have healed."

"No. It's tolerable for short periods, but I'll have it on ice tonight."

"You said something about the bureaucracy giving you a hard time. Is it really as crooked as it seems?"

Kevin's smile dimmed. "I wouldn't say crooked. It's just

that at times it seems the last thing the department wants is for us to do what we were hired to do."

"Well, I suppose it's our fault," she said thoughtfully. "The public, I mean. People want their vices and are willing to pay. I don't blame a policeman for being confused. I'd be inclined to look the other way a lot in your job. And my guess is that many cops feel the same way. . . ."

Kevin leaned back in his seat. After a moment he said, "That doesn't sound like the lady who volunteered to teach art for nothing."

"Why? It gives me pleasure to be an occasional do-gooder. And no one gets hurt by it." When he frowned, she quickly said, "I'm sorry. I'm being pushy." She reached over and clasped her hands over his. "But I grew up here, you know. I don't recall the police department's reputation being as pure as newly fallen snow."

Kevin laughed. "It's true, San Francisco was once a rough, tough frontier town, and it still has easy-money morals. If you love San Francisco, you have to take it as it is. Sure, some cops take money, just like the politicians, lawyers, and everyone else in the right position. For exactly the rationalizations you mention. It just was never my thing."

"Why not?"

"Why yes? If your work means something to you, why sell out?"

"Yes, I can see that. Still, do you ever get tempted?"

"Only in daydreams. Then I go play basketball with the kids. In police work, if you're careful, you don't get yourself in the position to be tempted, or send out vibes that you're interested."

She looked at her watch. "I really have to get home, Kevin. I can take a cab if it's inconvenient for you."

"No way. I'll drop you."

Kevin left her in the circular drive of her building after an exchange of phone numbers. Driving home, he remembered her appearing in the doorway of the rectory lounge. The background light had framed her as she brushed her hair away. It was a habit. It emphasized her femininity, and each time she'd done it while they were together, it called his attention to her beautiful eyes.

She had watched them play from the window, and had suddenly appeared after they finished a beer to ask Bill about a cab. She would have had to pass the housekeeper to get into the lounge. But if Mrs. Burke had called a cab, then Dana wouldn't have had a chance to meet him. Maybe she anticipated that he would drive her home; she hadn't been coy about exchanging numbers.

When Kevin pulled into his parking space in the rear of the Victorian where he rented the top floor, he realized he hadn't thought about Sherry all the way home.

Dana's phone rang. It was Carlos. He said, "Well?" His voice had the same grim coldness that had troubled her for a long time now.

"It went well. He took me for an iced tea."

"And?"

"I don't know, Carlos. It was such a short meeting. He seems like such a straight arrow, yet talks like a jaded San Franciscan. I don't like this business, you know."

"How well I know. You made it plain that you'd do it only in return for my leaving your life."

Dana fought tears. They had been so close. His cruelty could still hurt her.

"Did you agree to meet again?"

"We exchanged numbers, but I don't really want to go on with this."

"Is he infatuated with you?"

"I don't know."

"Are you infatuated with him?"

She should have known Carlos would get an easy read on her emotions. He always did.

"I sense that you like him," Carlos said. "Nevertheless, the answer to the question we discussed yesterday is very important."

"Of course." She let the bitterness show. "Your all-important work."

"But lovely Dana . . ." Carlos paused for effect. ". . . the answer is even more important to the future of your new detective friend. I want you to call him tomorrow. No, wait. Let him call you, I'm sure he will. Have dinner and a few drinks. Sleep with him if you wish, but find out what I need to know, and soon. Sweet dreams, my love."

Dana slammed down the phone. She shivered. The threat to Kevin McKay had been unmistakable. My God! How naive she'd been to think this was merely a small good-bye favor to Carlos.

She remembered Kevin's boyish smile. It started so slowly, then grew over his whole face and lit his eyes.

Chapter Five

Kevin looked across the musty squad room, with its scratched-up institutional gray desks. The narcs at the other end of the room seemed to move in slow motion in the flickering illumination of fluorescent lights well beyond their peak. Depressing.

There was a small outer office with a secretary, but the inner area was closed to the public, and a number of portable partitions passed for offices. The narcs and special employees—or S.E.'s, as the department labeled the snitches—used the back entrance and huddled behind the portable partitions. The S.E.'s were delicate souls who required privacy while they gave up their friends and colleagues in return for money or reduced sentences for their own crimes. And some of his fellow dicks huddled behind the same partitions for their own inaudible conversations that seemed to end abruptly whenever he or Joey approached. There had always been rumors about the unit. Considering the work they did, it was to be expected. But since Sherry took over . . .

It had been four days since Joey's buy from Hallman. Bill Carey's derisive snort over Joey's joke that Sherry would praise them for the buy had, of course, been prophetic. But Sherry hadn't jumped on them for leaving the stakeout either. Weird. Sherry hadn't said anything. Their report had been forwarded, and their worksheet scheduling the second buy for today had routinely been approved. He wasn't about to check with Sherry to see if the lieutenant had actually read the schedule before signing off on it.

The man was a pain in the ass. On a number of cases he'd assigned to them, Joey made quick buys from people who were obviously low-level flunkies. As soon as he made the second buy, required before the D.A. would consider prosecution, Sherry wanted the dealer set up for a bigger buy and bust. Kevin had protested. It had been the beginning of a strained relationship. It got worse when he pointed out to Sherry that although the final buys were for surprisingly large quantities, considering the flunkies they popped, the subsequent lab analyses showed the dope to be of very low quality. For some reason the stuff had been cut well beyond the normal level dictated by the greed of street dealers. Sherry bluntly told Kevin to mind his own business.

The lieutenant had also been critical when two cases he and Joey had pursued for more than a year fizzled. They'd moved up to a fairly high level in a San Francisco–based distribution ring, but when they accompanied federal DEA agents with search and arrest warrants, they found empty apartments and the suspects gone. It smelled.

Had it happened once, it could have been bad luck. But two no-show raids within three months didn't figure. There were any number of possibilities for leaks, ranging from clerks working for the court or prosecutors' office, to cops themselves. Kevin asked Sherry to request a joint investigation with the DEA. Sherry had chewed him out, telling him that the long-term projects were over, that they didn't work. But he, Sherry, was going to make it so hot for low-level dealers that they would be out of business. The distributors would give up on San Francisco. Joey and Kevin had looked at him in silent disbelief. Did he really believe that fiction?

Now, Joey brought him back from daydreaming. "The last buy was a snap," he said. "This one will be just as easy. What's to go wrong?"

Wrong? Anything could go wrong during a buy. Blood could splatter, and life flee in sudden muzzle flashes and the tang of gunpowder. Kevin was the senior, so the details of the buy were his call, and anything going wrong would be on his shoulders.

Neil Brennan would be the third man this time. Brennan had joined the squad a year ago, but had never worked with them before. He had a rep for being lazy and moody. The grapevine had it that Brennan was an old friend of Sherry's, and that the lieutenant had personally talked the Chief of Detectives into making him a narc. The day after the buy from Hallman, Sherry had temporarily assigned Brennan to work with them. Kevin had wanted Carey, who, despite his lack of humor, was a good dick. But he wasn't about to argue and give Sherry the satisfaction of turning down his request. They were stuck with Brennan.

Kevin studied him. In contrast to dark-haired, high-strung Joey, Brennan was red-haired, and seemed indifferent to what was going on around him. He dwarfed slender Joey, and even made Kevin seem small. Brennan wore a garish, red-checkered sport jacket over an equally loud sport shirt. He slumped motionless, chair tilted back, hands behind his head. His eyes were closed.

"What do you think?" Kevin said to him. "Last time, Carey was with Joey. We don't want to spook Hallman with a new face."

Joey cut in. "No problem. Brennan can stay outside in the hall."

The front legs of Brennan's chair hit the floor as he shifted his weight, and his eyes flew open. "The mother of all buys," he said scornfully. "Hallman, big fucking deal."

"Hey, Brennan, I got a message for you." Joey's face colored and he flipped Brennan the finger.

Brennan smirked.

Joey's eyes shifted to Lieutenant Sherry swaggering across the room. "Here comes our führer," he muttered.

Sherry had broad shoulders and a growing paunch. He paused in front of them. Kevin realized his hands were clenched under the desk. He reached for a pencil and began to doodle on the cluttered calendar covering his desktop.

"Brennan," Sherry crooked his finger, "come with me. I'm borrowing you for a surveillance."

"But Lieutenant," Joey said, "our buy is scheduled for 1100 hours."

"Then consider it unscheduled," Sherry said.

"But it's been on all week. You approved it on the work schedule." Joey looked to Kevin for support.

Sherry's hairline was receding, and a Gorbachev-like birthmark flushed on his forehead. His voice rose. "Look, Demanto, the San Francisco Police Department ain't a democracy. My vote is the one that decides things around here."

Kevin cleared his throat and forced respect into his voice. "Lieutenant, your SOP says we need three men on a buy. Is there any way you could get someone else for the surveillance, or maybe let us have someone from another team for the buy?" He gestured toward the dozen detectives around the room shuffling papers and talking on phones.

Sherry stood with his hands on his hips. "McKay, if you wanted to give orders, you should have studied to be a lieutenant, not an inspector. Get the message, you guys. Your buy is off until I tell you it's on again. Catch up on your reports. Come on, Brennan, I don't have all goddamn day." He whirled and strode away.

Brennan rose. "Bye-bye, girls." He waved the fingers of his right hand and followed Sherry.

"Is this the same lieutenant that chewed our ass yesterday for being the lowest team in arrests?" Joey said. "He won't even assign us a permanent third man, and the bastard gives us long-term cases, and his pets get the hangers. Now, when we finally have an easy one that we set up ourselves, he pulls Brennan away. Let's do the fucking buy anyway. We'll say we were just doing surveillance on Hallman and the opportunity was too good to ignore. Whatcha say, Kevin?"

Kevin glanced across the desk-cluttered squad room toward Sherry's office. "What are we going to do for a body mike? We can't draw one after that speech."

"Old reliable." Joey pointed to a cardboard Marlboro box containing a small Sony tape recorder. "I used it last time with Hallman."

"Yeah, but last time you had Carey with you as backup and I was in the street. This time it will be only me, and if you're in the apartment without a body mike, I won't be able to hear you."

"Look, Kevin, Hallman's nothing, and I'll tell you what—if he's not alone, I'll turn around and walk out. Let's record the second buy, it puts us in the game. Nothing will go wrong. I guarantee it, just like your suit." He flashed a grin, mocking a tasteless clothing ad that ran constantly on local radio and TV.

Kevin backed the cobalt-blue, new Corvette into a metered space across from Hallman's building on Mission Street. The car had been seized only two weeks earlier from a dealer, and hadn't yet been burned on the street. Nevertheless, the homeless men who had started forward to hit them up stared through the car window at Kevin, then moved away. Kevin looked at 918A Mission Street. A shithole. Run-down, rat-infested. Home to a fifth-rate dealer like Hallman.

"I don't know about this, Joey."

"Kevin, Kevin," Joey said. "What's to worry about? Hallman's no Cali kingpin. He's a Mission Street mope. Last time, I didn't even see a piece in the place. This is the second buy—even if we can't take him higher, we can bust him, later. We'll have another stat for Sherry."

"I'll be your only backup. And I'm two stories down on the street."

"Well, I'll let you in on a little secret. Neil Brennan as a partner didn't exactly give me a warm fuzzy feeling inside."

"Maybe I should wait in the hall."

"That's all we need. The car will be stripped if it's here at all. Sherry'll cut our balls off."

"Yeah, Joey, but that message from Sherry was loud and clear. He just about ordered us not to do this buy."

"All the more reason to make sure nothing happens to the car. By tomorrow the stupid fuck won't even remember. And the next time he starts to give us a hard time about stats, we can tell him we have another bust."

"What about an exit plan if something goes down?"

"Nothing's going wrong."

Joey got out. Crossing the street, he dodged a cab. He gave the rear of the cab an Italian salute, right arm into his crooked left elbow.

Chapter Six

Joey was right, Kevin mused, watching the second floor window of Hallman's apartment and at the same time measuring the pace of the street. Everything was cool, nothing amiss, no sign of risk. This buy would go down, routine. Joey was in no danger. Hallman was just another loser looking at a long fall for drug dealing. But Joey was wrong about Sherry forgetting. It would be fun to watch Sherry try to ignore them making a solid case while disregarding his imperious order. All the more enjoyable because Sherry hadn't assigned it to them. They had made the case on their own.

Sometimes dealers flipped as easy as Simp Jiminez, and the buy process immediately started again with the new patsy they fingered. Not that it made much difference. There was an unlimited supply of Hallmans. A drug shootout or bust always seemed to provide more applicants than the vacancies called for.

A transvestite hooker spotted Kevin, abruptly changed direction and headed back toward Market Street, window-shopping furiously. Kevin smiled. The raggedly dressed men milling about moved at half speed. It was almost time to head for Glide Memorial Church or St. Anthony's for a noon meal. Kevin saw two who wouldn't be eating lunch. They had scored a tourist for meal money. Their fifth of burgundy lunch was almost gone and they were pushing each other, their drunken voices more belligerent than their wrecked bodies.

It had been fifteen minutes since Joey went in. The two winos were nose-to-nose. Kevin didn't have time for them now. Neither one was strong enough to hurt the other, but with his luck, one of them would pull a blade and he'd have to get between them. That was part of the trouble of trying to work without a backup.

It wasn't long enough to start to worry, but Joey should have been out. A bus stopped in traffic, blocking his view of Hall-man's building. Damn. His fingers tapped a rhythm on the seat. It was a small buy, and the stuff had been so stepped on by the time it got to Hallman, they had joked that the lab might refuse it. Sherry and the police department didn't care about purity. As long as the six ounces contained just a trace of any illegal substance, it was a felony bust, good enough for the drug war stats. Arrest stats were enemy body counts in the drug war. He held his breath as the bus roared off in a cloud of black vapor.

Joey emerged from the doorway and hurried back toward the car. Kevin sighed. Routine, of course, but . . . it was good to see his partner return.

"What is it, Joey?" Kevin felt a spurt of alarm when he saw Joey's face. His partner was a good cop. Knew how to antici-pate and take care of himself. But now, getting into the car, Joey was pale.

"Get us the fuck out of here, Kevin," Joey said.

Kevin turned the key and the car's powerful motor rumbled. "What's wrong? You're not hurt, are you?"

"Get us out of here."

Kevin shook his head and eased the Corvette away from the curb.

"Turn the other way. Don't take us back to the squad. We better head for my place." There was a tremor in Joey's voice.

Kevin pulled to the curb. He faced his slender partner.

"Okay, sport. Stop pulling my chain. We always go back to the squad and log the dope and the tape in. You know that."

"I'm not taking this tape into headquarters. And I mean it, let's put some distance between us and Hallman's place."

Kevin saw stubbornness in Joey's face. He rolled his eyes skyward and eased back into traffic. Occasionally, he had to humor Joey on these buys. Stars could be prima donnas. He prodded Joey a couple of times during the short drive but his partner wouldn't say a word. He stared out the window with an uncharacteristic frown.

Kevin took in the living room of Joey's apartment. "I'd suggest a maid, but you obviously need a work crew."

Joey grunted. He took a cassette player from the desk. "Listen," he said, punching the play button.

"Ten-thirty hours, April twenty-seven. This is Officer Joseph Demanto, badge number 2986, San Francisco Police Department, Narcotics Investigation Unit. Present with me is Inspector Kevin McKay. This is case number 1993-2874. The suspect is Vincent Hallman, aka, Angel Vinnie, aka Victor Hall. The buy is scheduled for 1100 hours at 918A Mission Street, apartment 2K, where the suspect resides and does business. Six ounces of cocaine is the amount agreed upon for this buy. This officer previously purchased three grams of powdered cocaine, ten ounces of heroin, two ounces of methamphetamine, and eleven ounces of cannabis from suspect Hallman. The next sound on this tape will occur when it is voice-activated in the suspect's home."

Joey stopped the tape and stood. "You ready for the action?" Kevin nodded and Joey started the recording.

"My God, Hallman, what the fuck happened to you?"

Joey's voice on the tape was agitated.

"You're in bad shape! I'm calling an ambulance."
"No. No way. No ambulance."
"Look, Hallman, I was a medic in the army. I got to stop the blood from your forehead. You got any bandages?"
"First aid crap, under kitchen sink."
"Hallman, I can stop the bleeding for now, but you've lost a lot of blood and you need stitches."

Hallman's voice had faded even more. Kevin interrupted the tape. "Why the hell didn't you insist on an ambulance, Joey?" he asked.

Joey held up his hands for silence as Hallman, his voice faint, said:

"The bastards came in right after the mule made my delivery, screaming they were cops. The first guy had a strawberry birthmark on his forehead. He hit me twice with his gun. The other one, a redheaded giant with a fire-engine sport jacket, kicked me in the stomach."
"Jesus . . ."
"They took everything. The goods and eight grand. I'm finished. Nobody can work in this town."
"I still think I should call an ambulance, Hallman."
"No way. I know a doc who will fix me. I don't want any part of hospitals and more cops."

"That's it." Joey rewound the tape and turned off the recorder.
"That's it? Are you crazy, Joey? Why the hell didn't you stay and do it right? This was an armed robbery."
"Robbery? It was almost a homicide. If I hadn't come along, Hallman would have bled to death."

Kevin stood and paced the drab room. "We have to go back. I don't know how we explain leaving in the first place, but I'll think of something."

"Kevin, maybe you were daydreaming when Hallman described the people who did him."

"It doesn't mean anything. You know dealers often accuse cops of ripping them off, and lots of guys who rip off dealers pretend to be cops."

"Sure. And they wear jackets like the one Brennan had on. And they have birthmarks on their foreheads."

Kevin's mouth tightened. "I don't like Sherry and Brennan any more than you do, but we could be set up the same way. It's not up to us to jump to conclusions."

"And I ain't about to jump off a cliff either. You want to turn in the head of the narcotics squad as a 211 man, go ahead."

Kevin frowned. Section 211 of the California Penal Code defined robbery. "Two eleven doesn't exempt cops."

"Kevin, get real. No one will believe Hallman, and we'll be rats. You know what will happen to us." He stared at Kevin. "Where are you going?"

Kevin slipped the tape into his pants. "I'm going back to take a statement from Hallman, like we should have done in the first place."

"Oh, God," Joey held his head in his hands.

Chapter Seven

Back in the car, Joey made a final plea.

"Kevin, why not leave well enough alone? Hallman's going to blow town. We were never there."

Kevin took a red light on Market. Two gray-headed women

tourists hurried back to the sidewalk. At the corner of Mission Street he leaned on the horn, but they were pinned in by cars stopped in front of them for a red light. Kevin drummed on the steering wheel.

"I don't get you, Joey. Whoever these guys were, it could easily have turned into a homicide. Sooner or later they're going to kill. Sure, maybe they only hit dealers, but what about other people? Like you and me if we walked into the middle of the rip-off."

"Let's talk sense," Joey replied. "These guys are never going to be caught for taking off Hallman, and if you and me turn in a crime report with those descriptions . . ."

They pulled onto Mission Street.

"You a medic? You were never in the service," Kevin said.

"What did you want me to say, 'I learned first aid in the Police Academy'? "

Kevin parked in front of Hallman's. "Come on." He patted Joey on the shoulder. "I need you to get in. Hallman's not likely to open the door if I announce myself."

Both detectives stood well to the side of apartment 2K. Kevin saw that the flimsy door had been sledgehammered— just the way they did it on police raids.

"Hallman, it's Joey D. I got some bread for you."

"Go away, Joey. I'm out of business. I told you," Hallman mumbled through the closed door.

"I know. I know," Joey said, "but I got an idea how we can get you some traveling money."

The door opened a crack and Joey looked into the barrel of a Colt .45.

Joey stared at the weapon. Pressed against the wall on the other side of the door, Kevin was out of Hallman's sight. Kevin tried not to breathe.

Joey found his voice. "Take it easy, Hallman. It's just me."

"How do I know you're not the rat that fingered me?" Hallman said.

"Come on, man. I was the one stopped the bleeding. You'd be history now if it wasn't for me."

"Thanks for nothing."

Hallman fumbled inside the apartment. Eventually he undid the makeshift arrangement that had replaced the shattered door chain. Once again the .45 was pointed at Joey's chest. The detective remained quite still. After a moment Hallman turned and shuffled into the apartment.

Kevin, jumping in front of Joey, was on Hallman before he had taken three steps.

"Hey," Hallman yelled, and tried to raise the gun.

"Cool it," Kevin said.

He had a firm grasp on Hallman's gun hand. Kevin applied pressure on the barrel of the gun and pushed hard on Hallman's wrist in the opposite direction. The dazed Hallman didn't put up much of a struggle. Kevin eased him into a chair in the kitchen and slipped the gun into his jacket pocket. Hallman was very pale under the bandage Joey had put on.

"Now, just tell me what happened with the two guys who broke in," Kevin said softly.

Panic left Hallman's face. "You're another fucking cop. Go ahead. There's nothing left." He waved his hand around the torn-up apartment then turned to Joey. "What's your game?"

Joey shrugged and walked to the other room.

"Which of the two guys hit you, Hallman?" Kevin said.

Hallman's battered face was incredulous. "I don't get this." He stared for a moment. "You one of the goody cops after the dirty cops?"

Kevin changed the subject. "Let me take you to the hospital, Hallman. I'll make sure no one will bother you."

"Oh, you will?" Hallman sneered. "Sure, I'll testify just like a citizen and everything will be A-okay. Dream on. I'm out of here ten minutes after you guys leave."

"Maybe you'll be leaving with us, Hallman."

Hallman looked thoughtfully in the direction Joey had disappeared. "No. I don't think so. Your partner's pretty good. He'd fool most. Does he use? Not that it matters. But he only got one buy. You guys can't bust me for selling. I know the rules too."

Kevin held up the gun. "How about this?"

"Legal, the papers are in the drawer over there." He pointed toward the other room.

Kevin thought back on Hallman's record. He was right. He had misdemeanors on his sheet but somehow had avoided a felony conviction. As crazy as it was, thanks to the National Rifle Association and their friends in the state legislature, the law allowed a creep like him to own a gun. "There's always material witness to a robbery," Kevin said.

With a laugh Hallman held out his skinny wrists. "Go ahead."

Kevin sat in a kitchen chair turned backward. "Look, Hallman, I know you're pissed, and I don't blame you. But just remember, after we report the rip-off, they'll know you're the only witness. You want a return visit from those guys?"

"What rip-off?" Hallman's smile was crafty.

Kevin sat silently.

After a couple of minutes Hallman got shakily to his feet. "Time's up, copper."

Kevin pulled out a business card. "Call me when you've had a chance to think about it."

"Sure." Hallman took the card and tore it in half. The pieces fluttered to the floor. He walked into the other room past Joey, who had sat listening to the conversation. Joey stood and followed Kevin out the front door.

"And now, Sherlock?" he said to Kevin on the way downstairs.

Chapter Eight

Kevin stirred his coffee. The day after Hallman's robbery, the partners sat across from each other in a small coffee shop on McAllister Street near the Federal Building.

"As I see it, we have three or four ways to go."

"This should be fascinating," Joey said, glaring at the waitress who had slopped coffee into his saucer.

Kevin waited until she was out of hearing. "The manual gives the choices of reporting to our commanding officer—"

"Lieutenant Sherry. That's great. I vote for that one. Do we wear suits and ties for the occasion and give him the Miranda warnings?" Joey blotted the coffee in his saucer with a napkin.

"That one's out. Next, we can go to Management Control, as our enlightened department now calls Internal Affairs. What do you think, Joey?"

"You're nuts."

"Or, the third possibility is we go to the police chief, either in person—"

"You're nuts."

"—or by direct memo."

"How about to the President of the United States?"

"That would be outside the department. But as long as you brought it up, we could go to the D.A.'s office or to the feds."

"Kevin, if I didn't know you to be a fanatical jock, I'd suspect you was knocking off some of the stuff we seized. I can't believe you still want to do something after you talked to Hallman. We've got nothing."

"Wrong, we've got res gestae on the tape."

"Jesus. First you're quoting the manual, next thing res . . . ? Whatever the hell you said."

"It's the law. Certain hearsay testimony is admissible if it's spontaneous—part of the act itself. So, Hallman's words to you on the tape are evidence. You'll never pass the test for inspector."

"A lot of good it would do me now. Anyway, Hallman's statement on tape washes out when he's interviewed and denies the rip-off."

"But you saw him all beat up, that plus the tape is reasonable grounds to believe a felony was committed. So, I don't think we have to worry about establishing the corpus delicti of a robbery. Besides, Hallman will come around and give a statement if we get him before a grand jury."

"You dazzle me with Latin. No doubt, the great Catholic schooling you got here in the city. But even if Hallman IDs them, they're cops, he's a junkie dealer. There's no case. Why can't you see it, Kevin?"

"I'm not saying there's a case now. It's a preliminary robbery investigation, but what choice do we really have, Joey? We can't sit on something this serious. We're not going to Management Control and accusing cops, we're just reporting what a victim said, the way the manual requires."

"You're going through with it no matter what I say."

"I just don't think it's the big deal you do. It's unbelievable that Sherry and Brennan would do something like that."

"You got a lot more faith in human nature than I do. Also, I saw Hallman bleeding to death. He wasn't pulling a con."

"Yeah, but it wasn't much of a description."

"Kevin, you've heard the same rumors I have about a cop rip-off gang. It's been whispered about for years."

"I'd hate to have you on my jury. But suppose for a moment it was Sherry and Brennan. Do you think they should get away with it?"

"I don't think people should get away with Whitewater or that Ted Kennedy should be in the U.S. Senate, but I ain't about to commit career suicide over it. How about we just sleep on it?"

"Tonight?"

"I was thinking about a month."

"I know. But if we sit on this and something else happens and we have to come forward then, we're in real trouble."

"You mean something like Hallman floating in the bay?"

"Yeah, and another thing, Joey. I forgot to mention I already logged the tape into the evidence room under the case number."

"So, eventually Management Control would come looking for us on the case anyway. I sure hope you know what you're doing, Kevin."

They returned to the squad room, but Kevin found it impossible to concentrate. His phone rang.

"McKay."

"Kev, Bill Riordan. I've given some thought to the problem we discussed. I have a suggestion. Can you drop by?"

Why not? He wasn't accomplishing anything at his desk. "Okay. I'll see you in about half an hour, Bill."

In the rectory, the priest was bubbling with enthusiasm. He could hardly wait until Mrs. Burke finished serving them tea.

"Kev, I kicked myself after you left. I should have remembered that the president of our Grand Knights club might be just the man for you to consult."

The Knights of Columbus. An organization of men who worked closely with the priests on church stuff. Kevin frowned. What was Bill talking about?

"Steve Bowles. Isn't he a detective captain?"

"Right." Kevin shook his head. "I don't know him. He's spent most of his time in patrol. Traffic duty."

"I've come to know him well, Kev. He's been enormously helpful to the parish—fund-raising, Catholic charities, youth work. The man has enormous energy and great character. I'm sure he would never approve of you being pulled from investigating a school drug ring."

"I don't know, Bill. The church is one thing. The police department another. Then too, it's a lot more serious now than a disagreement in management philosophy. Yesterday, my partner and I came across a dealer who had just been ripped off. The description he gave fit Lieutenant Sherry and another detective."

"Jesus, Mary, and Joseph!" The priest crossed himself. He looked anxiously at Kevin. "What are you going to do?"

"I'm not sure. The victim won't cooperate, so the whole thing is even more dicey."

"Robbery by policemen. You have to report it, Kevin. I'm sure Steve Bowles would give you good advice, but if you want, I'll go straight to the cardinal and he can arrange for you to see Chief Ferrante."

"I wish I knew Bowles." Kevin's tea was untouched.

"I have complete confidence in his honesty. Could you at least talk to him?"

"Well, he is next in the chain of command above Lieutenant Sherry, but we're not supposed to violate the chain."

"I'm sure that won't be a problem with Steve. Want me to give him a call?"

"No. Let me think about it. If we do talk to him, it should be on our own. The department gets funny about us going outside."

"Whatever. I hope this helps you."

And it did. Kevin actually slept well. Bill Riordan's steadiness provided a moral anchor. Despite the personal consequences, how could two cops fail to report the possibility of an armed robbery by other cops? The department would understand they weren't accusing anyone, they were just making a crime report.

The next morning, Kevin convinced a reluctant Joey to come with him to Captain Bowles's office.

"I think this is what the newspapers call a dual suicide," Joey said, nervous outside the captain's office, and Kevin understood, because he was too. Bowles's assignment to the Bureau of Investigations was a recent mystery, but maybe it was good that he didn't have a lot of old ties to the detective bureau.

Their knock brought a grunt to come in. The office was

windowless and sparsely furnished. A wall bookcase held the *Department Manual*, the *California Penal Code*, *Motor Vehicle Code*, and *Health Code*. One shelf contained a picture of Bowles in a police motorcycle uniform shaking hands with the mayor in front of City Hall. Next to it, a cheap vase contained a paper violet zinnia covered with dust. The rest of the shelves were empty.

Kevin noticed a framed certificate on the wall proclaiming that Lieutenant Steven Bowles had graduated from the FBI National Academy nine-week training class for police command officers. A good sign. Local departments were only allowed one candidate a year, and if they tried to send a known crook or an asshole, the FBI quietly turned down the application. There had been a number of years when no one from the SFPD had attended.

Kevin liked the way Bowles looked. Unlike a lot of brass, he was in shape, and there were no broken veins in his nose, like some of the old-timers who were too fond of the grape. Bowles motioned them to chairs and placed an unlit pipe in his ashtray. The pleasant aroma of the tobacco mix reached them. Bowles waited.

"Captain," Kevin began, "my partner and I were doing an undercover buy last week and came across something very unusual—"

Bowles held up his hand. "Why are you telling me about it instead of Lieutenant Sherry?"

"Er, Captain, I think it will be clear in just a second when you listen to the tape."

Bowles's eyes narrowed. "Was this an authorized buy?"

"Yes sir," Joey said before Kevin could explain the on-again, off-again drama with Sherry.

Bowles's nod was reluctant. "Go on."

"Sir," Kevin continued, "this was the second buy on a small-time dealer named Hallman. As I said, we have a tape—"

"I'd rather hear the summary from you first, then the tape," Bowles said.

Kevin felt perspiration on his forehead. "Actually, Captain, the tape—"

"Please, Inspector, summarize for me and make it brief. The Chief of Detective's staff meeting starts in fifteen minutes."

"Maybe we should come back later," Joey said.

Bowles noticed Kevin's glare at Joey. "Get on with it, McKay," the captain said.

"As I was saying, Captain, we had a previous buy on Hallman, and we wanted the second one because of the D.A.'s policy on—"

"You can assume I'm familiar with policy," Bowles said.

"Yes sir. Anyway, when Joey got to the apartment, he found Hallman bleeding badly. The man said he had just been robbed and . . . and that's the problem, Captain. He said they were cops."

Bowles frowned. "Does your commanding officer know about this?"

"We thought it best to tell you first, Captain."

"Why?"

"Well sir, when you hear the tape—"

"Look, Inspector, I understand English perfectly well, even if you don't. Tell me what you have to say."

Kevin took a deep breath. "Hallman gave a description that could easily have fit Lieutenant Sherry and Inspector Brennan."

There was a silence in the room. Bowles glanced sharply at Joey, who couldn't suppress a nervous grimace.

Bowles swiveled in his chair, facing Kevin. "Tell me," he said.

Kevin cleared his throat. "Hallman said one of the robbers was a heavyset man with a strawberry on his forehead. He was the one who pistol-whipped him. The other man was wearing a fire-engine jacket. That day Brennan was wearing a flashy red sport jacket."

Bowles frowned. "Where's the third member of your team?"

"Actually, Captain," Joey broke in, his voice a notch higher than usual, "we were working short-handed. Just before the buy, the lieutenant suddenly pulled Brennan away from us, said he wanted him for a surveillance."

"He authorized not following three-man SOP on buys?"

"Actually, sir," Joey said, "this was a routine buy. The three-man SOP is for officer safety. We knew there wouldn't be any danger."

Bowles just looked at him, and Joey shrank back into his chair.

"Why don't you play the tape for the captain, Joey?" Kevin said.

Bowles held up a hand. "Wait a minute. What did Hallman say to you?"

"He clammed up, sir, but I think you'll agree that the evidence on the tape and his physical condition confirm that a robbery took place. We're not accusing anyone. It's just that the sensitivity—"

"Enough," Bowles said. "Let's hear the tape."

Joey put the cassette player on the desk and fumbled with the evidence envelope. Bowles looked at his watch. Joey's fingers shook but he got the tape in and pushed the play button. The tape whirred but no sound came out.

"That's funny." Joey stopped the tape.

Kevin frowned at him. "You must have put it in backward, Joey. Reverse it."

"No. I'm sure it's right. I marked it."

He fast-forwarded the tape and stopped it. Again he hit the play button. The tape continued to whir. Both detectives stared at the cassette recorder.

Bowles's eyes were hard. "I want both of you to submit a signed memo to me by 1100 hours explaining all this. I'll be back from the chief's meeting by then. I warn you, if you're trying to excuse making an unapproved buy or to cover up something else you did by making these kind of charges, I'll have you prosecuted. Now get out."

Chapter Nine

Kevin stuck a piece of paper in the typewriter and began tapping at the keys. Joey looked over his shoulder.

"Kevin, you're not going to tell me you were in too big a hurry to copy the tape, are you?"

"No."

"What? Why the hell didn't you tell Bowles you had a backup tape?"

"Frankly, I didn't have time, I was stunned that the tape had been erased. By the time I started to tell Bowles, he was on his way out."

"Well, your performance has been consistent so far."

Kevin stopped typing and looked at Joey. His partner was beginning to lose it. "Joey, don't you see? That tape being tampered with means Sherry is guilty as hell. We have a new ball game, and we have to be damn careful."

"I guess I'm not supposed to say I told you so. It's a little late for being careful."

"We need to stay cool. I had hoped Bowles would have seen our side."

"See our side! He looked like he was trying to decide whether we got thirty years or life without parole."

"It's not that bad. We got off on the wrong foot, that's all. But now we have to hang tough and make our case. It's not the worst thing in the world that we have a copy of the tape up our sleeve."

"Gosh. Forgive me for being worried."

"Joey." Kevin reached out and touched his arm. "It's no time to start feeling sorry for ourselves. I'm concerned about

Hallman. One of us better run over to his place and get him out of there, by the scruff of the neck if necessary. The other one can do the memo."

"I'm not up to explaining this bullshit. Just try not to get us in any more trouble." He got up. "Kevin, suppose . . . I mean . . . suppose Hallman's . . ."

"Just call 911, like you should have the first time. Joey, make damn sure you look the building over before going in. If anything looks funny, call me, I'll be right there."

"Do me a favor. Stay here. I'm in enough trouble."

Both men stiffened as Lieutenant Sherry bustled from his office and headed for the elevators. They glanced at each other and, without a word, followed Sherry at a distance. An elevator door clanged open. The up arrow flashed and Sherry got on without seeing them.

"I guess you're going to tell me it's safe for me to check out Hallman now," Joey said.

"With you, one never knows what's safe. I remember how you knew the Hallman buy was routine."

Joey hadn't needed Kevin's advice to check out the scene carefully. He drove a badly dented old dope car around the block twice before parking near Hallman's. Inside the building, he listened to the silence for a minute, trying not to inhale the urine-saturated air. He took the creaking stairs slowly and froze when he heard a sound from above. Even in daytime the light was dim, almost total darkness. Crouched on the stairs, he eased his gun from its holster, slipped a flashlight into his left hand, and waited. When the sliding sound came again, he got down on one knee and aimed the light and gun in that direction.

Joey flashed on the light. A black shape hurtled at him.

"Ugh," he gasped, starting to shoot.

A huge black cat narrowly missed his head as Joey managed to get his finger unclenched from the trigger. The cat landed on the stairs below him with a thud and disappeared into the darkness.

"Jesus." He was shaking. He leaned back against the wall, breathing deeply. Slowly, he went up to Hallman's apartment.

Once more he stopped, concentrating all of his senses in the dark hallway. Finally, he flashed his light on Hallman's door. It was ajar, and Joey wondered why. He turned off the flashlight and strained to hear. Nothing. One step at a time, he moved forward. He turned sideways and slipped through the narrow opening, crouching and covering the apartment with his drawn gun.

The apartment was totally dark. He stood motionless, breathing as lightly as he could, but there was no sound. Using his flashlight, he found a wall switch. He flicked it and swung into a two-handed firing position. Nothing happened. The room stayed dark. Cursing silently, he turned on the flashlight and moved quickly through the rooms, gun in hand. No one was in the apartment.

Joey sat on a hard wooden kitchen chair and let his heartbeat return to normal. He tried other light switches. The electricity was off. Using his flashlight, he searched the small apartment as best he could, ignoring the sour smell of dirty laundry and the odor of rotting food on the unwashed plates in the kitchen. He found no indication of where Hallman might have gone. But he'd known he wouldn't. This wasn't TV. Carefully, he examined the kitchen floor. Kevin's torn-up business card was gone.

Joey had been gone about thirty minutes when Lieutenant Sherry returned. Kevin, halfway through the memo, paused, watching Sherry. Just as he was about to enter his office, Sherry turned and their eyes met. Kevin kept his glance steady, but a cold chill ran through his stomach. Sherry hadn't tried to disguise his hatred before closing the office door. So, Bowles had told him.

It violated every principle of investigation. The advantage of surprise was gone. He'd been mentally sketching out a couple of possibilities, like recorded phone calls to Sherry pretending to be Brennan, or the opposite, from Brennan to

Sherry. Now there would be no possibility of an incriminating statement being surreptitiously recorded in a sting.

The coldness in his stomach deepened as he realized that Bowles would never have made the decision on his own. He must have taken their story to the staff meeting. The decision to warn Sherry, instead of investigating him, had to have come from the Chief of Detectives himself, Vincent Ferrante.

Kevin took the paper from the typewriter and began retyping. This time he didn't address it to Captain Bowles. They would send it directly to the police chief. And the subject would no longer be "narcotics investigation." Now, under the subject heading, Kevin typed: "Allegations of Criminal Conduct by Members of the Bureau of Investigations."

At the far end of the room Neil Brennan's phone rang. He picked it up and after a short conversation sauntered over to Sherry's office. He entered without knocking. Kevin watched him emerge fifteen minutes later. Only when Brennan slipped back into his desk chair did he look at Kevin across the room. It could have been Sherry all over again. Kevin felt the hair rise on his neck. Their looks had held no apprehension. It had been pure hate. What had he gotten poor Joey into?

Chapter Ten

They knew, Kevin realized. The beat of the squad room had subtly changed. The invisible communication system that somehow ensured that every rumor worked its way into all police units had conveyed to the narcs that he and Joey were pariahs. There hadn't been overt group whisperings, or unusual gatherings in the men's room, but Joey and he were being eyeballed. Somehow, within the last hour, some version—no doubt highly distorted—of their sin had made its way to the people in this room.

Joey, with his sensitive narc antennae, which picked up potentially dangerous changes of rhythm among street people, had probably been aware of it before him. But Joey had said nothing. He had reported Hallman's absence and the ominous dangling chain on the apartment door without the slightest emphasis. It was the first time Kevin had seen him without his distinctive vitality.

He sat gazing at the wall with a copy of the memo Kevin had written on the desk in front of him. He'd read it an hour ago, and had yet to comment. Not that Kevin blamed him. "A strawberry on the forehead," and "a fire-engine jacket," were pretty unpersuasive on the flat white page. It all seemed shallow, and the explanation—"The recording tape of the buy had apparently been tampered with"—came across as the petulant whining of people trying to cover their asses. Joey, like Kevin, was waiting for the call to Captain Bowles's office. Kevin realized he was exhausted. They should probably grab some coffee and a sandwich. Bowles hadn't called at eleven o'clock, or twelve, or one. It was now almost three.

Kevin stirred himself. "Joey?"

Joey didn't move. He'd heard, but didn't seem to have the energy to speak.

Kevin continued low enough so the others couldn't hear. "Bowles must have called Sherry to his office and told him. He came back about a half hour after you left. In case I don't get a chance to say it later, watch your ass. Both he and Brennan would do anything to hurt us."

Kevin's phone rang. Joey jumped.

Kevin let it ring. He could guess who it was. "I still can't believe the bureau warned Sherry and Brennan instead of doing an investigation. We would have come out okay if they had."

"You better answer the phone, Kevin," Joey said.

Kevin picked it up. "McKay."

"McKay, this is Captain Bowles. You and Demanto come to my office."

* * *

Bowles's dead pipe still sat in the ashtray, but the aroma of the mix was stale and sour in the late afternoon. He held out his hand for Kevin's memo. When Kevin gave it to him, Bowles handed each of them a sheet of paper, then put on glasses to read the memo.

Kevin looked at the paper Bowles had given him. It read General Order Number 215:

Effective April 29, 0800 hours

Transfers:	Rank—Name		From Unit:	To Unit:
	Insp.	McKay, Kev.	Narcotics Unit	Sexual Assaults Unit
	Off.	Demanto, Jos.	Narcotics Unit	Fugitives Unit

by Authority of Chief of Police

Kevin gaped at Bowles, whose eyes bore into him.

"Why is this memo to the Chief of Police instead of to me as I directed?" Bowles said.

"Captain, I don't understand. How come we're being transferred?" Kevin couldn't keep the anger out of his voice.

"The transfer is routine. If you have any questions, you can direct them to the Chief of Detectives—" He paused. "—in writing. Now how about answering my question?"

"The manual gives us the option of bringing allegations of misconduct directly to the attention of the Chief of Police. Are you ordering me not to send the memo to the chief?" Kevin felt his face flushing.

Bowles opened his mouth to reply then thought better of it. His eyes locked into Kevin's.

Kevin forced himself to be calm. "Captain, as senior member of the team, I made the decision to report this incident. It was my decision to address the memo directly to the chief. Officer Demanto is one of the best undercover officers the department has. He shouldn't be transferred like this."

"I told you, McKay, the transfer is routine." Bowles picked

up his pipe and looked smugly at Kevin. "Clear out your desks and report to your new commanding officers at 0800 tomorrow."

On the way back to the squad room Kevin caught himself daydreaming about playing on the department sports teams. During his thirteen years on the force he had consistently participated in basketball, softball, and football. His mind filled with memories of the beer and pizza parties after the games. The inevitable roasting, boasting, and exaggerating among the cops had grown louder and funnier as the beer drinking progressed. A lump formed in his throat.

In the corridor ahead of him, Joey's dejected shoulders were a silent rebuke. He had gotten his partner flopped. Sexual Assaults Investigation was a dumping grounds—a hot spot where they waited for you to fuck up, but the Fugitives Unit was even worse. They were supposed to pick up the dangerous psychopaths who skipped bail—people charged with or convicted of violent felonies. And Fugitives Unit cops were supposed to collar them without SWAT backup.

Joey and Kevin had each carried a cardboard box of their desk contents to their cars. They hadn't been delayed by well-wishers from the unit. No one had acknowledged their departure, although every eye had watched them clear their desks. They stood awkwardly in the parking lot.

"I'm going over to Sacred Heart to shoot some hoops with the kids," Kevin said. "Come with me, Joey. It'll make you feel better."

Joey shook his head. "Take care, Kevin." He offered his hand.

Kevin shook it. "Where are you headed now?"

"You heard Bowles—the Fugitives Unit at 0800. I'm going to the equipment desk and drawing a protective vest."

Kevin tried to think of something to say.

"You ought to get one too," Joey said.

Kevin shrugged. "Sexual Assaults doesn't make that many arrests."

"I know," Joey said.

Chapter Eleven

At ten minutes to eight the next day, Kevin entered the Sexual Assaults Unit squad room. He hesitated a moment in the doorway before locating the lieutenant's office. Two detectives sat drinking coffee from plastic cups. They watched him approach. He recognized the fat red-faced detective as the Bureau of Investigation's representative on the Police Officers Association board of directors, the cops' collective bargaining organization.

The chubby detective looked around the room, then nodded guardedly. "Hello, Kevin," he said, and stretched out a hand. "I don't know if you remember me. I played ball at Sacred Heart, long before your time, of course."

The other detective was younger and had dark black skin. Powerful shoulders hid under his sport jacket. Some softness had invaded his waistline.

"You played ball?" he said. "What was it, spitball?"

"Barney Brady," the heavier detective said, releasing Kevin's hand. "Pay no attention to our local Mau Mau leader. The only good thing about him is that he took an Irish name, Flip O'Neil." He pointed at the other detective, who remained sprawled in his chair studying Kevin. Barney Brady continued, "He's actually not a bad guy when you get to know him."

"And you, B&B," Flip O'Neil said, "aren't a bad guy either because you're out in the open about your opinions, and don't hide behind a white sheet, like your brethren racists. So," he inclined his head toward Kevin, "this is the famous Kevin McKay, sentenced to join our illustrious unit. No doubt you're

48

here to report to our valiant commander, Lieutenant Affirmative Action."

"Ha, that's rich," Barney Brady said. "It was your lawsuit that started all the affirmative action bullshit."

"Kevin," Flip O'Neil said, "don't let us delay you. Being on time is one of our leader's many eccentricities. If he gets too hyper, just mention that he looks pale, and you'll soon be released while he tends to his delicate health."

Barney Brady winked at Kevin, who turned and walked to the unit commander's door. LT. RICHARD GARZA was stenciled on the frosted glass of the partially open door. Kevin knocked.

"Come in."

Kevin went in, shutting the door behind him. A slender brown-skinned man sat behind the desk. He wore a striped, long-sleeve yellow shirt with a brownish tie. His suit jacket was also brown and hung neatly on a hanger on a coatrack in the corner.

"Lieutenant, I'm Kevin McKay. I was ordered to report this morning."

"Yeah." The lieutenant stayed behind the desk, examining him.

Suddenly, he was out of the chair and around the desk. He stopped just a few inches from Kevin's face.

"Did those jerks out there call me 'Lieutenant Affirmative Action' yet?"

Kevin blinked.

"Of course." Garza smiled. Whirling around, he paused to straighten a framed document from the Marine Corps stating that Corporal Richard Garza had been honorably discharged. The discharge hadn't needed straightening.

Garza spun back to Kevin. "You come with a jacket. You wrote a memo outside the chain of command."

When it was apparent that Garza was waiting for a comment, Kevin said, "Do you know what the memo was about, Lieutenant?"

"You bet your ass I do, and I'm not about to discuss it with you. Just remember one thing about this unit, McKay—no matter what those guys call me, I'm the boss. I run this place. If you got a beef, come to me. I don't want anyone going over my head. Understand?"

Kevin nodded.

"I'm not obligated to tell you this, but I've been told where to assign you. Our Chief of Detectives believes in hands-on management." Garza made a face. "You're going to work with Flip O'Neil on the ski mask rapist." Garza never stopped moving as he spoke, fiddling with things on his desk. "It's a series and it's red hot. If Ferrante would leave us alone for a month, we might solve it, but . . . Never mind. I'll be watching you, McKay, but I'm a straight shooter. Do your job and keep your nose clean. Another thing, I don't want your former partner, Demanto, hanging around here. Got it?"

Kevin stared at him.

"Well, what are you looking at?"

"Your face is kind of red, lieutenant. You don't have a fever or anything?"

Garza bounded to the wall mirror. "Kids." He pointed to a lone framed photo on his desk. He and his wife sternly looked out over the heads of two serious-looking boys who appeared to be about ten years old. "They bring everything home from school. That's all, McKay." He fumbled in his desk.

Kevin, closing the door, saw the lieutenant putting a thermometer in his mouth. He returned to where Barney Brady and Flip O'Neil were still talking. Flip O'Neil looked up.

Barney Brady said, "You weren't in there long. Did you use the pale gimmick?"

"Flushed," Kevin said, and sat at the desk next to Flip O'Neil. He began to inspect the desk drawers.

The black detective watched. "Uh-oh," he said. "I feel bad news coming."

"I've been assigned to work with you on the ski mask case," Kevin said.

"Ah, yes. The San Francisco Police Department is a wonderful organization," Flip said. "Did our leader explain his decision?"

"It came from upstairs."

"That figures. I'm not in enough shit; I have to get saddled with the number-one target in the department. I won't be able to take a leak without someone looking over my shoulder. I don't suppose I could appeal to the POA?" He glanced at B&B.

"Well, if you was to consider a little leeway on your affirmative action lawsuit . . ."

"B&B, you'll go down in history as one of the great labor leaders. By the way, McKay, you might as well know he's called B&B because he slops down Benedictine and brandy, not because of his initials. In fact, his fondness for booze is the reason he was assigned here."

"And you?" Kevin asked.

"Him?" B&B laughed. "As if his radical shit isn't enough, he can't keep his fly zipped. His wife showed up with a double-barreled Winchester. Blew the door off, but Flip was fast on his feet."

Kevin turned toward Flip, who gazed serenely at B&B.

"Flip," B&B said, "never mind the rumors about Kevin. I saw him play at Sacred Heart. He was a star, but a team player. He's good people, no matter what management is saying."

"Yeah, until you end up in one of his memos to the police chief," the black detective responded.

B&B looked worried. He waited to see if Kevin would reply.

A slight smile played on Kevin's face. "You don't think I'm good people, Flip?"

The black detective put his hands behind his head and smiled at Kevin. "You're a motherfucker."

No one said anything.

Flip's smile got broader. "A real motherfucker. Just like everyone else around here."

Chapter Twelve

Carlos Castellano waited on Harrison Street in a rented Mustang. He'd been watching the Harriet Street exit of police headquarters. Lieutenant Glen Sherry drove from the underground garage and turned left on Harrison, heading toward the Seventh Street ramp to Highway 101. Carlos started the Ford's motor. He waited a full two minutes to be sure Lieutenant Sherry wasn't being followed. He'd tailed Sherry before, and knew the man to be dangerously unobservant. Sherry's cockiness was one of many characteristics Carlos found annoying.

Carlos also checked his own rearview mirror. He couldn't think of any possible way someone could have shadowed him, but he'd stayed out of jail by being careful. Except for the one unlucky occasion that had led to his business arrangement with Lieutenant Sherry.

He had just started in the organization. The Mentor was still in California and in charge of operations. In July of that year, Carlos was assigned to deliver a kilo of pure cocaine to an apartment in the Mission District and to bring back the cash. It was routine until the door suddenly shattered and three men rushed in with guns drawn, screaming, "Police! Freeze or we'll blow your fucking heads off!"

They didn't resist, but one of the buyers didn't move quickly enough. The heavyset man who had yelled smashed him twice in the face with his gun. Blood spattered onto Carlos's white Armani shirt. Carlos and the two buyers were handcuffed and shoved into a closet. Hearing the closet being locked, he felt a flash of relief, realizing they were being robbed and not arrested. But he hadn't anticipated the Mentor's fury. Sixty thousand dollars in buy money and a kilo of unstepped-on cocaine were gone.

Rumor had it that the Mentor was a former soldier from the Gambino family in Brooklyn. No one ever called him by any name other than Mentor. But some believed he was still a power in the Mafia. Others said he had been allowed to go out on his own, yet had all the mob contacts he needed. Different sources held that the Mentor had been sent to rejuvenate San Francisco's anemic Cosa Nostra. All of the speculation was guarded and no one in the organization ever dared check any of these tales.

He was thought to be in his late sixties. He was small, and wore shaded eyeglasses that failed to cover the hardness of his eyes. His receding hair showed only traces of gray. He wore a silk brown shirt open at the collar, Italian slacks, and Gucci loafers.

"That was very careless of you, Carlos. I will be forgiving this time since you are so new, but you owe the organization sixty thousand dollars." The Mentor's voice was soft, but the intensity of his words and unwavering glance were unnerving.

Carlos was stunned. At the time, he was making four thousand a month.

They were in a suite at the St. Francis Hotel, on Union Square. The Mentor didn't use the same location twice. The Mentor turned in his chair. "Alphonse," he said to the bodyguard who never left his side, "tell Moe to dock Carlos half his pay until we're even. Have the buyers, Tyrone and Phil, hit. They were careless. They let the location of the meet become known. We must instill discipline."

A week later an early morning jogger cut through the parking lot at the Shoreline Wetland Preserve along San Francisco Bay. Thinking the lone car in the lot might provide a glimpse of lovers still at it, he glanced into the vehicle. The sight of Tyrone and Phil sent him on a sprint to the nearest phone booth, and 911. The two drug buyers had been shot through the back of the head. People were careful about offending the Mentor.

Business was good, and Carlos was rewarded with a larger

share as his responsibilities increased. He paid back the sixty thousand within five months. Then he was set up.

He was sent to sell to a new customer in San Mateo. The organization had already checked out Paul Ballesteri and made one kilo sales to him, twice. He was a longtime dealer in southern California but new to the San Francisco area. He had done four years in Leavenworth for dealing. But the organization didn't know that Ballesteri had recently sold to an undercover DEA agent five times before being given the choice of cooperating or doing fifteen big ones in the federal pen. Ballesteri wore a wire for the government when he bought three kilos from Carlos.

A week later he asked if Carlos would meet another contact, who wanted to set up a middle-level operation supplying Redwood City, Menlo Park, and East Palo Alto. He wanted to discuss an initial buy of five kilos—big enough to overcome the organization's caution. The Mentor decided that Carlos should attend but not say anything incriminating. The Mentor didn't like Ballesteri's sudden introduction of a new friend. The organization would do some checking.

So Carlos went to the meeting. The new contact was garrulous, coarse, greedy. Everything an up-and-coming drug dealer should be. He wanted to set up a first buy of five kilos and hardly bothered to haggle on price and purity.

"What do you think?" the Mentor asked Carlos.

"I think he smells."

The Mentor nodded. "So do I. Don't go near him again. Ballesteri wants another kilo, which seems reasonable. Just be careful."

Since he had no instructions on what being careful meant, Carlos stashed the dope in the trunk of a car rented under a false name and parked it two blocks from the meet. He walked toward the apartment on Geary where Ballesteri waited. Carlos looked over the street very carefully. He didn't see anything suspicious. But in the apartment, Ballesteri was on edge.

"Where's the dope?" Ballesteri said.

Carlos noted beads of perspiration on the man's forehead.

Dope? No one ever used that word. Shipment, goods, perhaps. But dope, never.

Carlos shrugged and didn't say anything.

"Hey, here's the money. You want to count it?" Ballesteri got up and opened the suitcase filled with cash. "Here, count it. What's wrong with you today?" he asked when Carlos remained seated. "The last time you talked to me, we agreed the money was good, right?"

There was way too much conversation, Carlos thought, trying to catch Ballesteri's restless eyes.

"What's the problem, Carlos? You agreed to this meet, remember?"

Carlos still hadn't said a word. He got up and started for the door.

"Hey, where you going?" Ballesteri yelled.

The bedroom door swung open and two men in suits and ties came forward with drawn guns.

"Federal agents, Carlos. You're under arrest for violating Section 21 of the United States Code. Turn around and put your hands against the wall."

Ballesteri walked into the bedroom. Carlos didn't look at him. While one of the agents frisked him, the other read him his rights. A third man, casually dressed, came into the room.

The federal agent who had told Carlos he was under arrest said, "We have you cold. If you cooperate and tell us the truth now, I can promise you that information will be given to the court. I'm Agent Thomas Saunders." He pointed to the third man. "This is Detective Neil Brennan, San Francisco P.D."

Carlos gave no sign of recognizing Neil Brennan, one of the three men who'd broken into the apartment and robbed him a year earlier.

Following organization instructions, he provided only his name and address. He told the agents he was a wholesale art dealer. Failure to identify yourself only led to the magistrate denying bail.

Carlos called the organization's attorney from the federal detention pen. Three hours later the attorney posted a security bond for the $100,000 bail without exchanging a word with

Carlos. Both the attorney and Carlos knew what the Mentor's instructions were in these cases. The next day, however, Carlos, the attorney, the Mentor, and ever-present Alphonse gathered in a suite on the thirty-second floor of the Hyatt Embarcadero Hotel. The panoramic view of San Francisco Bay was dramatic, but none of the men even glanced out the window.

Carlos briefed the attorney, who then gave his analysis. "We can assume that the first three-kilo buy by Ballesteri is solid evidence for the government. On the other hand, there may be some problems with the wire he was wearing. The government's thriftiness in buying equipment is often helpful to us. But even if the buy evidence is good, the U.S. Attorney's policy is not to prosecute without two solid buys. Two or more buys prevents the defense of entrapment, which could be a problem for them since Carlos has no prior record. Carlos deserves credit for remaining silent in the latest incident, and he had no drugs in his possession. On the other hand, they may want to play hardball trying to find out who he is."

"Are you sure he is in no jeopardy?"

"I'm confident, Mentor"—even the attorney called him Mentor—"that unless they should bring in some evidence which wasn't produced at the hearing, they will not file an indictment."

"Good. And where is Mr. Ballesteri these days?" the Mentor asked.

"Federal witness protection. We can bet we won't see him around here again."

Carlos didn't mention Neil Brennan. Phil and Tyrone had been killed because of the cop robbers, and Carlos saw no reason to remind the Mentor of the incident. He was encouraged by the lawyer's expectation that he would not be charged.

However, the DEA was more interested than the attorney had anticipated. Carlos had made a three-kilo sale and met for a five-kilo sale without blinking. The government was interested in his contacts, especially since he was a Peruvian citizen. Before someone from the organization had a chance to recover the rented car with a kilo of dope in the trunk, it was towed for overtime parking. When the trunk was opened, the San Francisco police were called to take custody of the bags of white powder. The car pound was quite experienced in what to do in such cases.

The DEA was routinely notified in seizures of that size. An agent noted the proximity to the apartment on Geary where the meeting with Ballesteri took place. DEA cops obtained a search warrant for the rental car and went over it for fingerprints, but Carlos had worn gloves. They then talked to the young girl who had rented the car to him. Looking at his picture, she remembered the handsome young man with good manners and very sexy eyes. The United States Attorney brought her and the other witnesses before a federal grand jury. Carlos was indicted on three counts, with a maximum penalty of forty-five years in federal prison.

Sitting in court with his attorney, Carlos thought about his thirtieth birthday, coming up in the next week. He was uneasy. He had no intention of making a deal with the government, but he knew the Mentor was considering that possibility. Carlos was one of the few people who met personally with the Mentor. He remembered the demise of the two dealers who had been no threat to the Mentor and whose offense, at the time, had seemed innocent to him.

Waiting to be called before the judge, he noticed a flurry of activity. Another case was being arraigned and people were approaching the front of the courtroom. Federal agents displayed their identification cards on their jackets. Carlos's eye caught a police badge. He stared. It was the man who had done the pistol whipping. He was wearing a San Francisco police lieutenant's badge. He was the one who'd led the others in the robbery. The lieutenant testified briefly and then sat in the front row, waiting to be dismissed.

Carlos's case was next, and although the bail had been increased to $250,000, the United States Attorney wanted more. He lost the argument, and the organization attorney signed the securities pledged to guarantee Carlos's appearance for trial.

Carlos left the attorney on the courthouse steps. He hurried to a nearby branch of the Bank of America where he had a safe deposit box. In a stationery store next to the bank, he purchased a large manila envelope and a piece of white paper.

Handling the paper by the edges, he printed:

Lieutenant, the enclosed is yours without strings. I believe you may be able to do me a favor with little effort to yourself. This is only a token of how much happiness may come your way. You will receive an equal amount within two days as another token of goodwill.

Carlos put the note and five thousand dollars in hundred-dollar bills into the envelope and sealed it. He returned to court. He was pleased to see that the lieutenant still sat in the front row. About ten minutes later the man rose and swaggered down the aisle, his eyes roaming the courtroom, lingering a moment on Carlos, whom he had just seen make bail.

Carlos got up and followed the policeman into the hallway. He watched him enter the men's room. No one was with him. Carlos followed him in. Lieutenant Sherry stood at a urinal. Carlos took the one next to him. The room was momentarily empty. Carlos waited until Sherry glanced at him. Then, without a word, he placed the envelope on top of the urinal in front of Sherry and walked out. He hurried down the stairs and into a lobby phone booth from which the stairs and entrance were visible.

Ten minutes later Lieutenant Sherry left the building alone. Carlos was pretty sure that the cash rested in the cop's pocket. If the lieutenant had reported the money, there probably would have been some police activity. Carlos stayed well behind Sherry for four blocks before the man turned into a bar. Another sign that no official action was being taken.

The next day, Carlos staked out police headquarters on Eighth and Bryant. Several months before, a flunky in the organization, trying to impress him, had pointed out the entrance on Harriet Street the narcs used. He now hoped the man had been right.

Carlos was pleased when, two hours later, Lieutenant Sherry emerged from the underground garage in an unmarked police car. He drove to Golden Gate Avenue and pulled into the basement of the Federal Building, where the United States Attorney, the FBI, and the DEA had offices. Carlos waited across the street. An hour and a half later Sherry drove out of the garage. He worked his way through heavy traffic to Washington Square Park. Sherry parked illegally on a hydrant, tossing a police identification plate onto the dashboard. The lieutenant crossed the street and walked into the Washington Square Bar and Grill. It was lunchtime.

Carlos touched the envelope on the seat next to him. A week earlier the Mentor had been complaining about an upstart drug operation working out of the second floor of a flophouse on Third Street off Folsom. He had sneered that they were so dumb, they received "goods" at the same time Tuesday and Thursday mornings. Carlos had been curious. He checked and the Mentor had been right.

This time, Carlos's note to Lieutenant Sherry contained information on the Mission Street location and delivery times. There was also another five thousand dollars in cash. Carlos walked past Sherry's car. No one was watching. Casually, he took a Slim Jim burglar's tool for opening cars from under his coat and forced it through the driver's window. Within thirty seconds he opened the door, tossed the envelope onto the driver's seat, and relocked the car. He walked to a bench at the far end of the park and read the *New York Times*.

Sherry came out of the restaurant an hour later. Carlos saw him pick up the envelope and get behind the wheel. Sherry looked around, then opened the envelope. Carlos moved behind a bush. Through the shrubbery he saw Sherry get out and look in a full circle. The policeman got back in the car. It was two-thirty on Wednesday afternoon.

The next morning Carlos circled the location on Mission Street that he had tipped Sherry to. The dope was delivered precisely on time. Five minutes after the courier had gone into the building, Sherry and the two other men who'd robbed Carlos went in. Ten minutes later the three policemen walked quickly from the building. Around the corner a driver waited for them with the motor running. They got in quickly and the car pulled into traffic. Carlos didn't wait for any of the dope dealers to come out.

The following day Lieutenant Sherry again had lunch by himself. This time he parked legally on Union Street and went into Perry's. When he returned to his car, Carlos was sitting in the passenger seat.

Carlos smelled alcohol on the policeman's breath. "Good afternoon, Lieutenant. That bundle is merely for your time." He nodded toward the five thousand dollars he had put on the seat.

Sherry stuck the money into his pocket. "What's the game?"

"I won't waste your time or mine, Lieutenant. I can supply you information like yesterday's from time to time, and I am also willing to match what I have already given you for a slight favor."

"I'll bet it's slight. Make your pitch."

"You saw me arraigned in federal court. It's a circumstantial case. A kilo of cocaine was found in the trunk of a rented car. My lawyer doesn't think they can put me in the car, but I'm not a gambler."

"If it's a federal case, I don't know what I can do about it."

"One of your men, Neil Brennan, was there. He booked the drug evidence into the San Francisco police evidence room. My lawyer saw it on the papers. We need that evidence to be missing."

"It's been done before," Sherry said, "but it's tough and it involves other people."

"The case number is written on the first bill in your packet, and the name of your detective on the second. I'll check back with you next week. I'm willing to give you any expense money necessary for others. If you're not interested, I'll have to try something else."

"I'll have an answer by Wednesday," Sherry said. "Where do you want to meet?"

"What time will you have lunch?"

"Probably the same time. I'll come back here."

On Wednesday, Sherry told Carlos that the evidence package in his case had somehow gotten lost. He handed the empty evidence envelope with the case number to Carlos and winked. It had been the start of a profitable relationship.

Carlos had the organization attorney verify that the evidence had disappeared before paying Lieutenant Sherry the rest of the money and disclosing the whole scheme to the Mentor. Carlos knew he was taking a risk telling the Mentor that he had engaged in unauthorized action. But he'd used his own money and the action had been successful. The attorney said the charges had been dismissed. More important, the risk that Carlos could be prosecuted and was in any way a threat to the Mentor had been eliminated.

As Carlos had hoped, the Mentor was happy and began to use Sherry to destroy competition and obtain crucial intelligence about police and DEA operations. Sherry was not only delighted with the money he got, but with the improved arrest statistics, which kept him happily in command of the Narcotics Unit. But now, following Sherry, Carlos was apprehensive for different reasons.

Chapter Thirteen

The lieutenant was increasingly nervous, Carlos thought, driving well behind Sherry, and his calling for an emergency meeting was a bad sign. Sherry always drove at an even sixty miles an hour on the freeway, so Carlos was confident he could catch up. He stayed far enough behind to observe any tail. The gray police department Dodge cruised in the middle lane of Highway 101. Carlos hung back for a while, carefully observing the other vehicles behind the police car. Just to be on the safe side, he edged behind a red Porsche in the left lane and maintained seventy miles an hour until he passed Sherry, who never noticed him. Carlos knew tail cars often stayed in front of the vehicle they were interested in, but he saw nothing suspicious in any of the cars ahead of them. He decided to stay in front of Sherry and arrive first.

Carlos left the freeway at the Embarcadero Street exit in Palo Alto. Sherry was prone to grumble about meeting so far away, but it was safer, especially now. Carlos crossed the Camino Real and entered Stanford University. Embarcadero became Galvez Street, and Carlos stayed on it until it dead-ended in front of Stanford's landmark, the Hoover Tower, which he had heard students refer to as the late president's last erection.

Carlos pulled into a metered parking space and put two quarters in the meter. One would be more than enough, but he didn't want some citation-happy parking enforcer lingering about because there were only a few minutes left on the meter. He walked to a bench facing the direction Sherry would come from.

Carlos wore a tan sport jacket and brown slacks that enhanced his slender, dark good looks. He opened the *Wall Street Journal* and checked the variety of mutual funds he owned. Believing individual stocks were too risky, he'd put laundered money into California real estate and other investments, accumulating several million dollars over the five years that he had served the Mentor. He never carried less than eight thousand dollars in cash. He also kept $200,000 in a numbered Swiss account and a similar amount in a Cayman bank. Drug dealing was a business that could require immediate liquidity.

Ten minutes later Sherry pulled into a metered parking space and turned off the motor. He saw Carlos on the bench but gave no sign. Carlos stared down Galvez Street until he was certain no one had followed Sherry. He walked to his car and drove several blocks to University Avenue, Palo Alto's main street. He turned right on Cowper, parked in a public lot, and walked around the corner to Il Fornaio restaurant. He'd timed their arrival so the lunch hour was just about over. By two-thirty the bustling restaurant had emptied somewhat. Carlos selected a table in the rear and waited for Glen Sherry.

Carlos found Sherry unusually tense. "I'm telling you, Carlos," the lieutenant said, "that damn memo is going to cause real trouble. I think somehow the DEA people got a copy, and what's bad is they didn't even mention it to me. If they thought it was bullshit, they would have joked with me about it."

"It was unfortunate that you let two narcs you couldn't trust deal with Hallman."

Sherry's face colored, and the birthmark on his forehead got red. "I told them not to make that buy. McKay and Demanto violated a direct order from their commanding officer. McKay's so damn righteous, but he plays basketball during duty hours."

How strange, Carlos thought. This man who had been involved in many armed robberies and taken countless bribes was truly indignant at others for disobeying an order. And for playing basketball? Carlos had known about McKay for several weeks now, long before Hallman became an issue. Sherry had alerted him to the possibility that McKay might be trouble, as indeed he turned out to be. He'd personally followed McKay before sending Dana Rogers to meet him.

Sherry continued, barely acknowledging Carlos's hand signal to lower his voice. "Hallman—that scummy junkie. I should have blown him away when I first had the chance."

Both men remained silent while their food was served. The bulky lieutenant wore a light-colored sport jacket that was too small. Carlos thought he looked like a racetrack tout, out of place in the elegant restaurant. The policeman had a pizza special from the wood-fired oven. The pizza overflowed with mushrooms, peppers, and sausage. Carlos had soup and salad.

"How the hell could anyone predict that McKay would put something like that on paper? And it was him. His partner, the wop, just went along," Sherry said. "That's ironic. McKay is part of the tribe. We all went to the same schools. I even played basketball against him once. Outside of a couple of dikes, no one rats on another cop. Even the queers keep their mouths shut."

Carlos looked away as a strip of cheese from the pizza rolled down Sherry's chin. The lieutenant wiped at it with the back of his hand.

"You were confident that the memo was buried," Carlos said.

"I pulled some strings. The memo *was* buried. My man in the evidence room took care of the tape they did on Hallman, and McKay and the wop got the treatment. They were both flopped from Narcotics and labeled rat. And I've taken some steps to see that McKay gets in trouble with his basketball."

"Really? It doesn't seem like much, playing basketball during his lunch hour."

"Every little thing that makes McKay look bad helps me. I also sent Brennan to make sure that McKay's basketball players get all the grass they want."

"At the school?" Carlos was alarmed.

"Nah. Too hot there. At the housing project where the kids live, around the corner."

Carlos was dubious. He had little faith in Sherry's judgment. And he well remembered Brennan's flamboyant appearance. If the cop got caught supplying drugs, it could blow up. But he knew there was no use trying to influence Sherry. It would be ideal if Dana Rogers was able to bring McKay onto the payroll. If not, Carlos knew he couldn't rely on Sherry. His latest actions had the touch of panic.

"The trouble is, the damned Attorney General is looking for headlines," Sherry continued. "The A.G. wants to be governor. And if the State Investigation Commission schedules a hearing, so will the gutless Police Commission. Neither the mayor nor the chief have the balls to tell the commission to sit it out and let it blow over. And, of course, the idiot D.A. will think he's got to do something. Also, I have a feeling that DEA internal investigations may be snooping right now."

"Will Hallman testify?"

"No."

"How can you be sure?"

"For the best of all reasons. I took care of him personally, but if they get the wop or McKay on the stand, this thing could get out of hand. I'm solid in the P.D. right now. The chief, and the chief of the bureau, don't want waves. They're pissed at McKay for blowing the whistle. If other cops get the same idea and start yakking about stuff, the media will have a field day. The whole department will blow up. The mayor will have to clean out all the brass. A lot of contracts will get broken, and some of the people getting forced out can give the media plenty of shit on the mayor. Believe me, McKay is persona non grata with everyone, including the Police Officers Association. They were going to censure him, but I killed it. Too much publicity. I'm telling you, Carlos, this damn commission—"

"When is it scheduled?"

"Sixty days from today."

"That gives us some time," Carlos said. "Do you think McKay might suffer a memory loss for the right price?"

"Forget it. He thinks he's Eliot Ness."

Carlos frowned. "I don't understand."

"That's right. I keep forgetting you're a foreigner. It was a TV series about a Treasury agent, supposedly untouchable, sent Al Capone up. Total bullshit, of course. No one made more than the Treasury people during Prohibition. We need two accidents and no witnesses." Sherry glanced around the restaurant.

Carlos smoothed his linen jacket and gazed vacantly into the courtyard. Sherry might well be right, he thought, but taking out two cops was heavy. He would have to be sure it was necessary before recommending it to the Mentor.

"Anything to do with cops, I need to go higher," Carlos said. "You know that."

"Yeah. Well listen, buddy, you better realize this ain't just my problem. I won't go alone." He stared at Carlos, who remained silent, hiding his contempt.

Carlos paid the check and asked, "Do you have any other suggestions?"

"Yeah. You need to make me a hero with DEA and the department to get this off my back. I'll need a big seizure and a couple of patsies. They can be flunkies, as usual, but if you give them to me in time, we'll do the same deal. Bid them up to big level kilo deals."

Carlos nodded. They had done it before. It wasn't even that expensive. The law treated kilo dealers with the same severity whether the kilo was of high quality or had been stepped on so much that it was practically worthless. And the DEA and Sherry found it convenient not to mention the low quality of the seizure at the obligatory press conference they held celebrating the "breaking of another dope ring." Everyone, including the media, was happy. That is, everyone except the patsy who unexpectedly found himself going to the federal pen for fifteen years. The organization made sure the unfortunate one had no information to trade for a lighter sentence. American prisons were full of such people, while key players like he, the Mentor, and Sherry got rich.

"What about Petris, the florist? The last time we met, you were going to arrange something," Carlos said.

"Yeah. Our do-gooder businessman." Sherry laughed. "You sent one of your guys to try to persuade him to stop writing letters about the drop, and I sent Brennan to tell him there was nothing the police could do." He chuckled. "There was no hard evidence and we were too busy. The guy is unreal. He wrote another letter on Brennan and mentioned your guy threatened him. Luckily, all his letters so far have been to the department, and I decide which get logged in."

"As I mentioned, it would be very inconvenient to move the drop right now," Carlos said. "Since Petris is the only one who ever complained, I was thinking he might have an unfortunate accident."

"Petris isn't the only one who knows how to write letters. Look at this."

Sherry handed Carlos a copy of an anonymous letter. It was stamped as having been received two days earlier and had been given a control number.

"I don't understand." Carlos looked up from the letter. "This alleges that Petris is receiving and shipping drugs from his flower shop."

"Yeah." Sherry was smug. "There's another one coming in

today that will say he receives a carton from Liberty Shippers in Miami every Tuesday morning filled with coke and heroin. You just make sure that such a carton arrives next Tuesday, and we won't have any more trouble with Petris."

Carlos frowned. "I'm not sure about this. The man has no record. Arresting him won't do much. The trial wouldn't take place for months, and the District Attorney probably won't prosecute on just one shipment."

"We ain't talking trial. We're going to take his business. These anonymous letters will get us a search warrant. When we recover the dope, I'll get the feds to seize the business under the seizure laws. It will take years for Petris to try to prove he's innocent. Even if he does, his business stays shut. Mr. Busybody won't be in a position to be upset by your operation across the street."

"Is it that easy?"

"Absolutely. It's a civil action. No bullshit about proving guilt beyond a reasonable doubt. All we need is probable cause to believe the florist shop is being used for drug business. You just make sure the shipment arrives Tuesday. Me and Brennan will be waiting for the Parcel Post truck. Petris gets a dozen packages a day. He won't notice the extra one. As soon as he signs the receipt, we'll nail him. He'll make my day. I'll get a nice addition to my activity report at the same time we take care of an asshole."

"All right. We'll send the package. And another just like it the next day."

"Good idea. It's not necessary, but it will add a little frosting on the cake."

They left the restaurant, and on the sidewalk Sherry asked: "By the way, what does your girlfriend, Dana, say about McKay? I hear McKay flipped for her. Calls her three or four times a day from his desk." Sherry's smile was self-important. He knew he'd surprised Carlos.

Sherry looked toward his car and failed to notice Carlos freezing at his mention of Dana's name. Carlos was furious that Sherry had even learned of Dana's existence. One of his rare mistakes had been letting Sherry spot them a year earlier outside the Fairmont Hotel on Nob Hill, where they'd just dined in the rooftop restaurant with its spectacular view of the city. They'd been using Dana's car. No doubt Sherry had followed them and saw that he stayed at her apartment, then obtained her name from the Department of Motor Vehicles. Later, he'd casually dropped her name. Carlos knew that Sherry expected he'd be impressed, and perhaps intimidated. Sherry had not known how close he came to dying that day.

Carlos had actually followed him home, looking for an opportunity to kill him, but after an hour his rage cooled enough for him to realize that the Mentor might suspect him if Sherry was killed. Taking unauthorized action was very dangerous in itself. And the loss of Sherry, who had enabled the Mentor to eliminate competition and control northern California's cocaine distribution, would have caused the Mentor considerable unhappiness. Carlos didn't want to be the source of the Mentor's unhappiness.

But now Carlos's rage returned. With an effort, he contained himself. How had Sherry known? It was probably as simple as his bugging McKay's desk phone. Dana had been strange recently, but she was frequently moody, and he hadn't paid attention. During the past year, she'd become more and more depressed. Finally, she asked him to get out of her life. He decided to humor her for a while, knowing that eventually she would come back to him. They would enjoy life, spending the money he had accumulated as soon as he had more time. In the meanwhile, he knew she could be very helpful checking out McKay. By then Carlos knew about McKay's basketball activity at Sacred Heart. Sending Dana as a volunteer had been brilliant. Sherry had assured him that McKay was unreachable, but there was too much riding on the outcome not to be sure.

"I just hope you haven't been foolish," Sherry said. "I hope her apartment is clean. McKay is probably shacking with her by now."

"You needn't worry. It's clean." Carlos savored the idea that someday it was going to be a pleasure to get rid of this fool.

"I still think an accident for McKay might be the best idea," Sherry said.

Carlos nodded.

As soon as Sherry left, he called Dana, but got her answering machine. The Mentor wouldn't want him to sit on Sherry's call for emergency action. He would give Dana another week or so to test McKay, but in the meantime he would inform the Mentor of the danger.

Chapter Fourteen

Carlos took only a carry-on bag on the flight to New York with continuing service to Orly. He knew that since his arrest, the Federal Drug Enforcement Agency had entered his name into its airline computer file. He'd been stopped twice when returning from France, once in New York's Kennedy Airport, the other time in San Francisco. On each occasion he'd been subjected to humiliating baggage and body searches. But he hadn't been stopped in years, and attributed it to the fact that he had never been convicted, while so many other more viable suspects had been put into the computer files. He also felt that carrying only one light bag on an overseas trip allayed suspicion.

During his two-hour wait at Kennedy, Carlos sent a coded cable to Alphonse, the Mentor's assistant in Saint-Tropez, requesting an immediate meeting. Within thirty minutes he had a coded reply. The Mentor, out of caution or reasons of his own, set the meeting for two days later.

Once in France, Carlos took a cab from Orly to the Crillon on La Place de la Concorde, where he'd booked a room for one night—knowing federal agents couldn't afford to loiter around such places. It amused him that the elegant hotel was across from the American embassy, which was filled with bumbling bureaucrats who thought themselves so clever as they waged a futile war on drugs that created such extraordinary profits for the organization.

The Mentor kept subordinate travel to a minimum, but provided credit cards from a French corporation when travel was necessary. He approved of expensive lodging for security purposes. Ordinarily, Carlos would have enjoyed a layover in Paris, where he'd met Dana and spent the three happiest years of his life, but he was uneasy about what was happening with Lieutenant Sherry. The man was untrustworthy, and Carlos hadn't liked Sherry's near panic during their last meeting.

Despite the long trip, Carlos was wide-awake and it was only three P.M. He wanted his wits about him when he met with the Mentor, with whom a slip of the tongue could be fatal. He decided to take a cab to the Louvre and return to the hotel for a suitably late dinner in the ornate dining room. His connecting flight to Nice wasn't until eleven A.M. the next day.

Summer was tourist season. He drifted with the crowds, and once again frowned with disapproval at the hideous new triangle glass underground entrance to the museum. The crowds and the noise intruded on his thoughts. The Louvre was a magnet for him. It was near here that he had met Dana.

Carlos's father had been only a middle-level customs official in Lima, Peru, but his position and closeness to the country's president had made him rich. Carlos had been enrolled in the Louvre. His undergraduate major was in art, which was quite convenient since the president of Peru was discreetly investing an illegally obtained fortune in art work. With his father as the intermediary, Carlos was acquiring a good part of the treasure in Paris.

Carlos became known as a buyer and, despite his youth, was on the invitation list for exhibits. One night, he attended an art reception for three Left Bank artists. The paintings didn't appeal to him but then art rarely did. To him it was business, and he looked at art works as investments that would be likely to appreciate.

About to leave the gallery, he declined a glass of champagne. As he walked toward the exit, he saw Dana at the far end of the room and stopped. She turned back to the woman next to her and talked animatedly, but he knew she'd been watching him. He signaled the waiter and took a glass of champagne. Strolling slowly back to look at Dana's work, he tried hard not to stare at her. She was breathtaking. Her hair was in a ponytail, emphasizing her lovely, slender neck. It was an expensive gallery, and the crowd was dressy. Dana wore a simple but elegant black gown cut low enough to show a full bosom. A string of pearls and a minimum of makeup made her resemble a painting of a young princess hanging in the Louvre.

Dana found herself looking at the slim, dark man in the expensive Italian suit. He seemed young enough to be a student, but his poise and clothing cast him in a different light. There was a touch of sophistication, even mystery, about him. Her artist's mind imagined the smooth, firm skin under the expensive clothing. She laughed to herself. It wasn't just the artist. It was the woman.

Dana had been studying in Paris for almost four years. She'd had a number of affairs, but the head-over-heels romance that the city cried out for eluded her. She didn't brood over it. Her work required an intensity that left her drained.

But now her pulse quickened. From the corner of her eye she saw him approaching. He floated almost like a panther stalking prey. She felt a tightness in her chest that she had never felt before. Ridiculous. She was twenty-six. What could he be? At the most, twenty-four.

Actually, Carlos was just twenty-five, but it didn't make any difference. They left the gallery together that night and suppered at L'Elephant on Rue du Trésor, where she gazed into Carlos's eyes until she was dizzy. At one A.M. they kissed hungrily on the kissing bridge overlooking the Seine, just as millions of lovers had before them. She spent the night at his tiny apartment on the Isle de la Cité. And for the next three years they couldn't get enough of each other.

Carlos purchased three of her paintings for his father's

patron at prices triple what they listed for at the gallery. They never discussed his source of wealth, but the mystery only made him more alluring to Dana. Both her femininity and her artistic instinct sensed another side to this handsome, suave young man's character, and it fascinated her and led to a passion she had never felt before. There were times in the soft Paris evenings when a mere glance from his brown eyes made her shiver and set her heart racing.

Dana knew she was so enveloped by Carlos that her painting had become secondary, but aside from this, she was totally happy. This sometimes somber man turned her on as no one else. And she knew it was the same with him. She delighted in her ability to lift him out of his usual dark seriousness and turn him into a laughing, loving boy. Then she received a midnight telephone call from her father in New York that ended their euphoria.

Her parents had been divorced for ten years, and Dana had been brought up by her mother in New York, but usually spent summers with her father in San Francisco, where he held a high position in banking. Her parents were civil toward each other, but she knew it was forced. They tried to spare her the pain of their animosity. During the phone call, her father was as gentle as could be, but his news was devastating to Dana. Her mother had been killed in an auto accident returning from a weekend in Westhampton. There would be a family burial, and her father had booked her onto a flight to New York the following day. He would meet her at the airport.

Carlos was caring. He comforted her, but said it was impossible for him to go with her. He didn't give reasons, and Dana was too hurt to ask why. He took her to Orly Airport and wrapped his arms around her, telling her to return when she was ready. But her mind was already trying to cope with the grief and the ordeal of attending services with family members who met only at funerals and weddings.

Oddly enough, her anticipated heartache at being separated from Carlos didn't develop. Instead she felt a curious sense of relief. Her father was close to her during the services in New York, and when he asked her to return to live with him in San

Francisco, she accepted. She loved Carlos but knew that if she were ever to paint again, she must recover some of the inner self she'd surrendered. She wrote a love letter to him from San Francisco explaining as best she could that she wouldn't be returning to Paris. Carlos never answered.

Dana got along surprisingly well with her father's second wife, although she was only five years older than her. The couple lived in a mansion near the Presidio and generously provided her with a roomy bedroom, and converted another room into a bright studio overlooking the bay. Some afternoons she would drive through the Presidio to the Palace of the Legion of Honor and spend an hour with the works of the old French masters. Afterward she would take her topcoat from the car and walk to her favorite spot to watch the late fog gradually sweep over the Golden Gate Bridge, feeling her mind drift away from the past classics to her own work. When she got home, she painted feverishly until the light filtering through her spacious window faded.

A year went by and Dana finished three paintings. Her father offered to sell them at high prices through a friend who acquired art for large corporations, but she held off. She wanted a San Francisco exhibit first. Something that would launch her. Once a month she traveled downtown to Union Square to purchase art supplies. One day, leaving the store with her purchases, she glanced across the street. Carlos was standing in a doorway watching her.

She stood frozen in shock. Then she rushed across the street and embraced him, laughing and crying as he smothered her with kisses and whispered his love. Only later did she wonder how long he had followed her, and why so stealthily? And why had he remained motionless until she ran to him?

Carlos's position in life had changed dramatically after Dana left Paris. His mother had died when he was ten, and his father had never remarried. Carlos had been brought up by a governess, and he and his father observed a formal politeness with each other.

Ten months after Carlos received Dana's letter telling him

that she would not return to Paris, his father called and, in his elegant language, conveyed the impression that something was wrong at home. Carlos said he would immediately return. His father's elaborate courtesy deserted him and he said sharply, "Under no conditions are you to return to Peru."

Carlos was stung, but quickly realized that his father's urgency was for his benefit. When his father then sent him to Colombia to visit Ricardo Martinez, an old family friend, he didn't protest. Martinez was a high-level drug dealer who welcomed Carlos warmly. Carlos enjoyed horseback riding throughout the extensive plantation and tennis at the luxurious club which Martinez owned in partnership. Martinez and his wife took Carlos to sumptuous dinner parties in the area and made him feel welcome. He spoke each week to his father, who always called at eight P.M. on Thursday evenings.

On his third Thursday in Colombia there was no call. Carlos wasn't immediately concerned, but when ten days elapsed without word from his father, he went to Ricardo Martinez. Martinez put his arm around his shoulder, not noticing Carlos flinch at the unexpected familiarity.

"Carlos, the president fled Peru two weeks ago. Your father hoped that the new regime would appreciate his services, but unfortunately, they only considered his loyalty to, and work for, the president. He was arrested and charged with stealing government funds. We are trying to find him and get him out, but . . ." Martinez shrugged.

Carlos felt his eyes water. He understood the meaning of Martinez's words. His father was gone. He was alone in life with only the few thousand dollars he had managed to stash away during the years in Paris.

A week later Martinez asked him if he would like to travel to America with him on business. Carlos knew there was only one acceptable answer. It was on that trip that Martinez introduced him to the Mentor and he began his apprenticeship in the organization. He had remained impassive when they offered to let him work in Los Angeles or San Francisco. San Francisco. Dana. He had meekly chosen San Francisco, never mentioning Dana to Martinez and the Mentor.

After six months in San Francisco, he began to follow Dana. He had to be very sure she was safe and didn't have contacts that would alarm the organization. It took him weeks of surveillance to feel confident that he could resume their relationship.

Their passion blazed anew, and when Carlos brought her to the apartment on Russian Hill and asked that she live there, Dana was more than willing. It took her a while to understand that Carlos would only stay with her occasionally. She had already sensed a change in him, a wariness that had not been there in Paris. Of course, she had known in Paris that the money Carlos spent was funny, but she was nonjudgmental. And she continued to feel that true artists accepted and recorded the human condition. They weren't reformers. Historically, artists had often been supported by all sorts of patrons. That didn't bother her. It was Carlos. The new hardness. At times an aura of cruelty surrounded him.

Once, he asked her to take a package to the airport for him. When she refused, they had a heated argument. Another time, Carlos brought three tough-looking men to the apartment and coldly told her to leave the living room. Dana was tempted to stand her ground, but realized they might call her bluff and have their discussion in her presence. There were things she didn't want to hear, so she went into her studio. But when the men left, she threatened to move out if Carlos ever used the apartment again for a meeting. He had ignored her protest, but had never attempted another conference.

Their only other serious disagreement involved his refusal to tell her where he would be. He left for days at a time without warning, not even a phone call. When she complained, Carlos coldly told her that his whereabouts were none of her business. That argument had been shattering, and Dana began to think about leaving him. It was hard to admit that the spell of Paris was gone forever, but she realized that Carlos had changed in ways that killed her love for him.

He disturbed her as a woman but fascinated her as an artist. She found a new dimension in her paintings. Men appeared in them differently, sometimes with a sinister mien as her relationship with Carlos grew stormy. She found him demanding, exploitative, sometimes tense, and increasingly disrespectful to her. She began to feel repressed and, for the first time, slightly afraid of him and what he was into. Inevitably, the magic of their lovemaking was affected, and her passion for him, so enveloping in Paris, cooled.

Chapter Fifteen

Carlos flew from Orly to Nice and rented a car to drive to Saint-Tropez. The Mentor's yacht, *California Angel*, was one of the largest in the harbor. Carlos thought it ugly and ostentatious. It would not have done in his father's circle.

Alphonse met him at the dock and greeted him as if they saw each other every day, even though it had been almost two years since their last meeting. He took Carlos to a cabin where he carefully went through Carlos's lone bag while Carlos stripped. Carlos knew the routine and had no objection, remembering his previous encounters with government agents wearing wires.

The Mentor greeted him warmly. Carlos hid his surprise at the difference a couple of years had brought to the Mentor. He had always been small and slender. Now he was gaunt. Deep sockets under his eyes underscored the wrinkles and veins in his skull. Carlos realized he was well into his seventies. He was unsteady on his feet, and Carlos wondered about the man's health.

But the Mentor's eyes were sharp and his voice steady. He said, "I know there must be good cause for you to travel all this way, Carlos." Carlos wondered if there was a hint of a reprimand in the comment.

"Yes, Mentor. I am afraid we have an emergency surrounding Lieutenant Sherry. It was at his urgent request that I called for a meeting."

"I see," the Mentor said.

Alphonse sat impassively next to the Mentor while Carlos told of his meeting with Sherry and the man's near panic. The Mentor never took his eyes off Carlos and didn't interrupt. He had made a lot of money because of Lieutenant Sherry.

"Is it your opinion that the lieutenant is accurate about the danger that Hallman and the two policemen pose?" the Mentor asked when Carlos stopped speaking.

"Yes. And Lieutenant Sherry is an equal danger." Carlos picked his words carefully. People had died for making careless comments in this man's company. He didn't want the Mentor to detect that he wanted Sherry eliminated.

The Mentor frowned. "True, but unlike the two cops, he is valuable to the organization."

"If he survives."

The Mentor moved restlessly. "Is there any question about his surviving if we do what he asks about McKay and Demanto?"

"I suppose not."

"What is it, Carlos?" The Mentor reacted to Carlos's hesitancy.

"Sherry did make an overt threat to talk about us if he gets in trouble."

The Mentor waved his hand. "Overt or not doesn't matter. We know what the risks are even when people swear their undying loyalty. The question is, can Sherry continue to help us?" The old man's watery blue eyes studied Carlos, and blue veins stood out in his skull. Nevertheless, the Mentor always conveyed an air of menace. Carlos stayed alert to subtleties in the man's comments.

"If the jobs are done well and made to look like accidents . . . because if it appears two cops were murdered, the heat will blow us out of the water." Carlos knew when to back off.

"Fine. I need to think about this." He turned in his chair. "Alphonse, Carlos will stay with us for a few days. Take him ashore to the right stores so he can dress appropriately. And tell the captain we sail in an hour. We will anchor in the usual spot off the public beaches and a catered lunch will be brought aboard."

Carlos was discouraged. "Excuse me, Mentor, but don't you think I should return immediately to keep an eye on things?"

"But if I thought that, I would have told you to return, wouldn't I?" the Mentor said. "Is there any other reason for you to return that I am unaware of?"

"No sir. None at all. I didn't mean to imply that I doubted your understanding."

"Of course you didn't." The Mentor smiled, and Carlos felt a chill, looking at the skull-like grimace.

With Alphonse's help, Carlos was back on board within forty-five minutes carrying a new swimsuit, shorts, deck shoes, and tropical shirts. They sailed for about twenty minutes and anchored off the topless and nude beaches. A motor launch brought a lunch of fruit, fish, and salad out from one of the hotel restaurants.

The Mentor barely touched his food but enjoyed watching every forkful Carlos and Alphonse ate. Carlos allowed himself a glass of a very fine Bordeaux. He would need a relaxer. He had been here before with the Mentor, and he knew what was coming next.

The Mentor sat on a boatman's chair in the bow while Alphonse set up a powerful telescope on a tripod.

The Mentor chuckled. "It looks like a fine day at the beach. They're packed in."

Carlos could see in the distance that there were many bathers and the sand was crowded with walkers and sun worshipers.

"Ah, Alphonse, this is a real beauty." The Mentor's eye was glued to the telescope. "Carlos, my young friend, come and tell me what you think of this one."

Carlos looked through the lens at the naked body of a twelve- or thirteen-year-old undeveloped female. If it hadn't been for the frontal view, he couldn't have told whether he was looking at a boy or a girl. "Lovely, Mentor," he said.

"Yes indeed." The Mentor snatched the telescope back.

Carlos knew better than to try to excuse himself. This appraisal would go on for hours, and his participation was required.

"Now, here's a specimen of a different nature, just as attractive in its own way." The Mentor again beckoned Carlos.

"Unique, Mentor." Carlos hid his disgust, gazing at the magnified image of a woman weighing at least three hundred pounds, wondering what possessed her to frequent the nude beach, or any beach. Her breasts hung like huge melons. She had shaved her pubic hair and her sex showed bright red.

"Alphonse, tell the boy to bring me lemonade and a grapefruit mineral water for Carlos."

Carlos started. It had been three years since he had just once expressed a preference for grapefruit-flavored mineral water aboard the yacht. The Mentor had a way of surprising you with his memory for details. And scaring you. It was always a reminder to be cautious around him. He realized that Alphonse was being given an afternoon off from sharing the Mentor's voyeurism. The duty would fall to him. Later, women and children would come aboard to cavort on deck or in the Mentor's cabin.

Taking the telescope once more, on the Mentor's command, he viewed an even younger nude female. As he watched, mouthing an admiring comment, a truly beautiful nude woman around twenty walked in front of the youngster and Carlos was reminded that it had been six months since he and Dana had made love. He felt a stirring but put it out of his mind. His first time on the yacht, he had accepted the Mentor's offer of a teenage beauty, not realizing that the Mentor sat as a spectator.

Carlos let his mind shift. What decision would this old man make about Sherry? And why the delay? It occurred to him that Alphonse's accompanying him to the store had been more than a simple courtesy. He had not been alone for an instant, and the way he had been shown to his cabin indicated he was expected to sleep on the yacht. Once again he felt a chill despite the hot French sun. Were they blaming him for Sherry's blunders?

The *California Angel* attracted a number of nubile young females who swam from the nude beach. The Mentor delighted in welcoming the giggling youngsters on board. He served them fruit and champagne, and if they were anxious enough, he took them below for a tour. Carlos knew that on occasion he also offered the more adventurous ones a line of coke in his cabin. Carlos was careful to keep his disapproval from showing. He knew that the gendarmes in the Saint-Tropez harbor police station were on the Mentor's payroll, but it still seemed foolhardy. On the other hand, what was left in life for a man the Mentor's age, with more money than he could ever spend?

After several hours of peering through the telescope, the Mentor sent his first mate ashore in the launch, and a short time later the obese woman and the young girl, who was her niece, came on board. They were initially overwhelmed and shy, keeping themselves well covered in shorts and blouses. But the Mentor was patient and sly. He plied them with compliments and wine and encouraged their interest in Carlos sitting in the shade. Within an hour they were nude again and easily lured down to the stateroom. Carlos went to the stern, stretched out on a mat in the shade, and dozed, half listening to the high-pitched laughter and mock screams coming from below.

After the guests were put ashore with a suitable cash present, the yacht sailed back to the harbor berth. At eight P.M. the steward served an excellent baked fish dinner on the bridge. They dined looking out at the hordes of tourists crowding the promenade. Some lovely and not-so-lovely ladies of different ages made overtures to come aboard. The Mentor was titillated but did not comply.

They followed the same routine the next day. This time three different females came aboard in the afternoon. And at eleven that evening, after another superb dinner in the harbor, the Mentor allowed a Gypsy woman and her extremely young daughter with baby fat into his cabin.

By the following evening Carlos's self-control was strained. He wondered how much longer he would be kept on board. But when they anchored in the harbor after returning from the beach mooring, the Mentor told him to dress. They were going ashore for dinner. At eight-fifteen P.M. Alphonse pulled up on the promenade in front of the yacht in a silver Rolls. He stayed behind the wheel, and Carlos opened the rear door for the Mentor and joined Alphonse in front after a gesture from the old man.

It was beginning to get dark as they drove out of Saint-Tropez and began to climb into the sparsely settled mountains. Carlos felt the hair on the back of his neck rise and another chill shoot through him. Was this the way it ended? He had no choice. He had been directed to sit in the front seat. He didn't dare turn to watch the Mentor, who was silent. The only sound in the smoothly floating machine was the soft playing of "La Mer" on the car's tape deck. The countryside was rough and there were few houses. By the time they stopped in front of the Ramatouelle restaurant overlooking the Baie des Camarines, Carlos was not in a mood to appreciate the beauty of the quaint mountain town or the view of the valley. Alphonse stayed with the car.

Inside the restaurant the owner made a fuss over the Mentor, who was charming. The food was excellent and Carlos began to unwind. Nothing would happen during dinner, at least.

The Mentor sipped a red wine that was listed on the menu for five hundred francs. "You know, Carlos," he said, "I have no children. I never thought about it much or regretted it, given the business of my life, but I'm going to be eighty next month."

"You don't look more than sixty-five, Mentor," Carlos said, covering his confusion. This was a strange twist for a man who had been determinedly, even viciously, aloof. What was going on? He felt another chill. Was he a condemned man having his last dinner while his executioner got sentimental over it?

"You have done well. I'm free to tell you that the organization will let you take control of northern California depending on how you handle the present troubles. I am moving on to other things." The Mentor reached his skeleton hand across the table and patted Carlos on the shoulder.

Carlos was stunned. He would take the Mentor's place. The money! *Mon Dieu!* It wouldn't be garish yachts for him. And he wouldn't be in until he was eighty. Just a few years. Dana would be over her foolishness. They would travel. Villas in Italy. An apartment in New York. They would invest in art. She could paint to her heart's content.

"I am gratified by your trust, Mentor," he said.

"Remember, Carlos, it is a trial. As to the other matter, the organization has hired F. Bly. As you know, he is very expensive but the very best. He will take care of your two detectives if necessary. You have two weeks after you return to see if they will cooperate. If not, signal Alphonse by telephone. You will say, 'The clients are ready to be entertained.' " The Mentor chuckled over his choice of words, which would trigger the killing of Kevin McKay and Joey Demanto.

Carlos had heard of the legendary assassin. "How will he contact me in San Francisco so I can point out the targets?"

"Ah, Carlos. To know Bly is to die. Even I only know of him. You need not worry. Bly is already in San Francisco and is studying each of the subjects. By the time you return, he will be ready to take them out."

Carlos felt that the Rolls floated back to Saint-Tropez rather than drove. What an unexpected reward. He had come with bad news, but had nevertheless been promoted. And he had come close to dismissing the Mentor as senile, but the man, under cover of his play, must somehow have held an international conference for days from the ship's phones or radios.

Carlos now realized that the Mentor hadn't known whether he'd be ordered to kill or promote him. The old gangster would have killed him. But Carlos knew the Mentor was pleased it turned out the other way. And the assassin was already at work in San Francisco. Inspectors McKay and Demanto would soon either be history or on the payroll, and it wouldn't be long before he had Sherry making even more money for them than he had under the Mentor's direction.

PART TWO

The Ski Mask Rapist

Chapter Sixteen

The glistening black and white San Francisco police car moved slowly in the normal bumper-to-bumper traffic on Columbus Avenue in North Beach. Terry Fisher had run the vehicle through the car wash. Now, as the end of her tour approached, the unit's sparkle still pleased her. Her partner, George "Piggy" Waldron, was behind the wheel now. Normally, she didn't care for his driving, but coasting into the final hour's letdown, she was glad to daydream about her evening date while routinely keeping an eye on the crowded street scene.

Two Chinese girls in their blue-and-white elementary school uniforms giggled, pretending to be oblivious of a fat man taking their picture to show the folks back in Dayton. His thin, tense-faced wife nervously beckoned him. The cable car was coming a block away and there was already a crowd waiting to get on. A small blind man who wasn't blind stood motionless behind his dark glasses, the pot at his feet half filled with folding money. Not a bad day, unless he'd stacked it all himself, Terry thought, feeling the beat of the street and liking it. Everything was cool.

A minute later she frowned at the man in a not very clean raincoat. He'd been watching the schoolgirls. She searched her memory. She'd never seen him before. Still, she would check him out if he lingered.

A young Hispanic woman in late pregnancy moved awkwardly in the crosswalk in front of them. Piggy Waldron pointed at the woman's stomach.

"It took a real prick to do that."

His voice was harsh and his laugh grated on Terry's ears. Her eyes narrowed, but she gave no sign of hearing him. She'd learned early on that her criticism only encouraged him.

The radio crackled.

"Three twelve Adam,"

The female dispatcher's voice was calm, which Terry knew didn't mean a damn thing one way or the other. She sighed. It was ten minutes to four, and she had a seven o'clock date with Craig Lewis, the newest agent in San Francisco's FBI office and the hottest male she'd met in years. She resisted the temptation to chill the call and let the oncoming watch handle it, knowing that Piggy wouldn't go along. Of course, if it were near lunch hour, she would've had to fight to get him to take the call. But this could be overtime, and Piggy always needed the money for his gambling habit. She pushed thoughts of Craig Lewis out of her head.

She picked up the microphone. "Three twelve Adam." Terry fumbled with the clipboard on her lap and clicked a ballpoint pen as she spoke.

The dispatcher was coldly impersonal. "Three twelve Adam, female complainant, possible assault 261, 19½ California, apartment 68. Time of occurrence unknown. Victim incoherent. Advise if ambulance needed."

"Damn!" Terry muttered. Section 261 of California's Penal Code was rape. Terry got even more annoyed as she saw Piggy Waldron's smug smile. Inevitably, bits of his lunch found their way onto his uniform shirt, earning him his nickname among fellow cops. He slowly eased the car into the right lane, pausing for a crowd of tourists heading for Fisherman's Wharf.

Terry fretted at her partner's slow response. She would have moved the unit. Sometimes the victim really needed help, or the suspect was still there, but Piggy belonged to the "due speed gang," the growing number of cops who sneeringly quoted the duty manual's instruction to respond to emergencies with "due speed, consistent with pedestrian and vehicular safety."

Piggy and the others took their sweet time. If you were slow enough, it was all over when you got there. You didn't end up in the hospital, or in front of the citizen review board, and no one ever criticized you for responding with "due speed."

Terry shook her head at the tourists freezing in their shorts in the fog. California was the land of sun. Right? So it made sense to wear light clothing. The visitors never noticed the natives wearing overcoats and winter jackets in the summer. And no one ever seemed to warn them about the cold, damp July fog sweeping in from the Golden Gate Bridge. They would stand oohing at the beautiful formations of rapidly advancing grayness until suddenly they were shivering with goose pimples, looking vainly for the disappearing sun. Still, the policewoman acknowledged, the money they left behind paid police salaries, inadequate as they were.

Terry guessed that Piggy was probably hoping it was a torture rape or even a homicide so he could rack up max overtime. Ordinarily, she would have welcomed a late call herself. In the month she'd been dating Craig Lewis, she visited Victoria's Secret and Nordstrom on Market Street three times—normally, places that were off limits for her. Her lingerie purchases alone had totaled more than her week's take-home pay.

Also, Terry, like most San Francisco cops, lived in the suburbs, and getting out of the city in rush hour traffic would be hell. Even worse since the earthquake. She wanted to be stunning in her new black dress when Craig rang the bell. Otherwise he'd be in the shower with her again, and after three hours of nonstop sex, it would be send out for pizza or Chinese once more instead of the nice dinner and dancing he'd promised. The rat knew his tongue in her ear and thumb brushing her nipple silenced her halfhearted protests. The only defense was to be dressed and waiting to go out.

Terry liked men looking at her trim figure and dark good looks, and the new dress was well worth the four hundred dollars she had paid for it. She wanted Craig to notice the heads turning and the envious male glances when they crossed the dining room or cuddled on the dance floor. And she wanted to enjoy the women wishfully eyeing her handsome escort with the fabulous bod. She hoped the call would be unfounded.

Piggy Waldron parked the black and white on a hydrant, sucked in his huge belly to ease past the steering wheel, and got out of the car, elaborately hitching up his gun belt. He put his uniform hat on his bald head. He'd worn it the first two weeks they were partners, until even his ego had to concede Terry wasn't turned on by his presence. She'd often wondered if he knew how much she despised him. She constantly fought claustrophobia, the feeling of being trapped in the police cruiser with the smell of cigars and beer farts that clung to his gross body. She tried unsuccessfully to get another partner, but there wasn't much hope. The only appeal was to her lieutenant, who could have been Piggy's twin. They shared the view that there was no room in police work for "cunts and queers," and that the department was selling out to "niggers, spics, and slopes." Of course, they had gotten a little more careful about saying such things in mixed company, but Terry didn't have any doubts about their beliefs.

She surveyed the apartment house entrance while Piggy walked nonchalantly forward. The dispatcher had said the victim was incoherent and the time of occurrence unknown. Caution signals to a cop, except to a not-too-bright veteran like Piggy, who had been lucky for twenty years and sneered at Terry's "rookie bullshit."

The security guard who was sitting behind a desk in the lobby let them in, then tastefully retreated after indicating he knew nothing about their summons. Terry's eyes roamed the lobby, and it hit her: this was it. The sense of anticipation most cops got. The feeling something was about to happen, mingled with challenge and the slightest tinge of danger. People intrigues. Adventure. Usually it was boring crap, gritty sludge, or pure gore, but, she conceded, coping with the unknown lures us to police work and keeps us hooked.

She let her senses go, carefully recording the spacious lobby, marble flooring, and the mirrored glass reflecting the beautiful vase filled with birds of paradise on an ornate wrought-iron table. She touched the flowers. They were real. She was always amazed that the lush blooms had no fragrance. Her eyes caught her own image. She liked the neat, blue-figured reflection, with the no-nonsense brunette hair tucked under the uniformed cap and her right hand hovering near the fifteen-round Colt in its crisp leather holster.

There were two elevators. She pressed the button, and almost immediately one of the doors opened.

When they reached the sixth floor, Terry stood in the dimness of the hallway and took a deep breath. She noted that the three ceiling lights down the corridor were lit, but the one above the apartment door was out, and she wondered if it was a coincidence.

Standing in the semidarkness of the landing with her partner, Terry could empathize with the kind of terror the woman inside the apartment must have felt. This was a nice building in a good neighborhood. A woman should have been safe. Hold on girl, she cautioned herself, not every one of these calls turns out to be legit by a long shot. Let's see what it looks like before cussing out the lousy system created by the male world.

The brass nameplate centered on the door read J. REMICK. Terry, not sure what might be inside, kept her hand lightly on her gun. She touched the bell. Chimes sounded and Piggy let out a loud belch. Terry jumped. Damn him. She was as angry at her own tension as at his grossness.

"Who is it?"

Terry barely made out the faint broken sound from behind the door. "Police officers, Miss Remick. Did you call?" Terry's voice was firm, professional, and she hoped reassuring to the woman inside.

The door opened as far as the chain allowed. Terry stepped forward so the woman could clearly see her police uniform. The door closed and she heard the chain being slipped loose.

"Come in."

The woman's face was badly bruised and her eyes red from crying. She was taking deep breaths, trying to stop sobbing. Her off-white bathrobe was belted tightly and made her appear small, although Terry saw that she actually was slightly taller than her own five-foot-seven. The woman retreated into the apartment and headed down a hallway.

"Hold on, Miss Remick." Terry's voice stopped the victim.

It was important that she control this. "Is anyone else in this apartment right now?"

The woman shook her head and blanched as the movement caused pain.

"Did you say yes or no?" Terry stood still. If this was a domestic dispute, there could be some drunk inside with a gun or knife and looking for a fight.

"No." It was a hoarse whisper.

"Why don't you take the victim inside? I'll wait out here. She'll feel more at ease talking to you," Piggy said.

"Okay," Terry said, surprised at Piggy's sudden sensitivity.

The woman did seem relieved. Her left eye was swollen. Both eyes would be deep black by morning. Terry wanted to go into the kitchen to get ice for her, but it would have to wait. Questions needed to be asked. She would have to be a cop first, woman second.

Terry saw that the woman's ring finger was bare. "Miss Remick," she said, "before you tell me what happened, do you need an ambulance?" The policewoman noticed that the victim was pressing her right hand into her left side. It could be a fractured rib.

"No. Please. No hospital." She spoke softly. The woman started and her eyes went to the open door to the living room as the television blared the sounds of a baseball game.

Terry walked over and shut the door. That son of a bitch, Piggy. He probably had a bet on the Giants. She should have known he couldn't care less about how the victim felt.

"I'm Jane." The bruised woman stretched out her hand, and Terry immediately liked her.

Terry Fisher saw that under the bruises Jane Remick was a beautiful woman. And she moved with an understated femininity that gave Terry a moment of envy. The policewoman wondered. A model? She was graceful. And the apartment was beautifully furnished and located in a high-rent area. Better than even a cop and FBI guy could do on two salaries. Not that Craig Lewis was the marrying kind, but . . .

"I don't know how he got in, officer. He was just there. And the gun. He said he'd shoot me if I didn't do what he wanted. And he laughed. My God, that laugh." Jane shuddered.

"He's gone and we're here now." Terry lightly touched her shoulder. "Go on."

"I was in my robe, about to take a bath. He made me turn around and handcuffed me from behind. And he punched me in the face. That was the first time. I was screaming and he slapped real hard. He said he'd really hurt me if I didn't stop."

Terry glanced into the bathroom, noting an oversized bathtub and large soft towels matching the pastel wallpaper, not like her dump with its stall shower. Looking again at Jane's bruises, she felt a twinge of guilt for comparing bathrooms.

"Jane, I'm going to ask you to try to remember his exact language before your memory begins to fade. It could be important in catching him."

"Catching him?"

Terry tried to identify the expression fleeting across Jane's face. "Do you think you could identify him?" she said.

"I . . . I don't know." Terry saw naked fear in her face before Jane broke eye contact, turning toward the bed. She walked to it and sat still, holding her side. "No. I didn't get a good look at him." She looked down and put her hands over her face. "Oh God, I'm so embarrassed, so depressed. I don't know what to do."

Terry lightly touched her shoulder again. "I know it's bad now, but it will be okay. Remember, you didn't do anything wrong. He did."

"Oh sure." The victim began to sob.

"Look, Jane, I appreciate it's tough, but I've got to ask you these questions."

"I'm sorry. I know it's your job." She wiped her red eyes with a tissue. "I'm glad that . . . that there are women on the police force. It's just that I feel so . . . so rotten, humiliated. Can I take a shower? Would you stay?"

"Jane, it's important that you don't shower just now. We need to take you to the clinic where a doctor will examine you. They're sensitive. It may even be a woman doctor."

"Examine me? I don't understand."

"They'll comb your pubic area. They'll probably find hair, perhaps some semen." Terry didn't want to tell Jane that they would also take a blood sample to test for AIDS and syphilis.

Restless, the woman got up from the bed and walked slowly away from Terry. "They don't have to test me. He didn't rape me. He just beat me up. And he had . . . he wore a mask. I didn't see his face."

Studying her, Terry reflected that sexual assault victims often lied. And who could blame them? Some animal violated them, and then the cops, doctors, lawyers, and courts did it all over again. This woman was sexually assaulted, yet she took hours to report it. And she broke eye contact and turned away. But it wasn't because the victim was embarrassed with her. And the mask? That didn't sound right. Was she lying about that too? And why?

If it was true that she was only punched during a robbery, Terry wasn't required to do more than file the crime report. But she was sure that it was a sexual assault, and it called for an immediate response by the Sexual Assaults Unit. They would determine if the crime-scene people should respond for an evidence search. Terry wrestled with her conscience. Jane Remick was a decent woman. Deep down she was strong. Terry believed she would eventually tell the truth. Right now, Terry didn't have enough to justify calling Sexual Assaults. No one could blame her if she just filled out the forms and went to dinner with Craig.

Oh, hell, she said silently, knowing her dinner date with Craig Lewis was history.

"Excuse me, Jane. I've got to call in. Did he touch the phone at all?"

"No."

Nevertheless, Terry used her handkerchief and handled the phone delicately.

"McKay, please," she said when it was answered. Terry hoped Kevin McKay would be there. She didn't feel like trying to convince some other inspector, which is what the SFPD called detectives, to respond. But Kevin would come. She had worked with him on another case when he was a narc. Unlike so many of the assholes in the department, he was thorough, and he cared about people. McKay had actually talked her into studying and passing the test for inspector. The rest of those guys . . . their balls shriveled when they had to compete with a woman. Terry couldn't wait to see Piggy's face when she got promoted. Kevin was a sweet guy. Maybe that's why they were on him all the time.

Chapter Seventeen

A mile away from the affluent building from which Terry Fisher was calling headquarters, Joey Demanto pranced about his tiny kitchen. His apartment in the Mission District was reasonably cheap and unreasonably small and seedy. But Joey, moving rhythmically in his red Jockey bikini shorts, was momentarily happy. The smell of the sweet grass Amanda had started on wafted in from the bedroom, and he felt himself getting hard as he set out the cheese, sourdough baguette, and red wine. The weed she brought with her was the latest "Magic Humboldt," a product of the federal government's one success in drug interdiction.

The feds had gotten the Congress to sic the military as well as the Customs Service on dope coming into the country. It had zero impact on the big money drugs, cocaine and heroin. But cannabis had bulk, and Mexican Gold and other delicacies were vulnerable. The net impact was that California's number-one cash crop became cannabis, and Humboldt County, where the cops looked the other way, produced stuff ten times more mellow than what had been coming over the border.

Smoking a joint never did much for him. Maybe it was

being a cop, he thought, although plenty of his colleagues seemed to get off on the stuff. He'd smoked some joints in the army before becoming a cop, and it just wasn't his thing. But a few puffs and twenty minutes of pulsating Lisa Stansfield sent Amanda into way-out sex. Last week he'd taken a few hits to keep her mellow, and she had blasted into an all-night orgy. And tonight he had a couple of new bed toys from Good Vibrations. It's lucky he hadn't taken Amanda shopping with him. The customers and clerks would have devoured her on the spot.

Good Vibrations was on Valencia Street half a block from the Mission District police station, Joey Demanto's first assignment as a San Francisco cop. It was an upscale lesbian sex shop, and thoughts of the dizzying array of vibrators and body oils, along with the fragrance and music coming from the bedroom, were creating a bulge in Joey's shorts.

He stopped bouncing to the music and frowned as the doorbell rang repeatedly. What the hell? No one knew where he lived. Except . . . No way. Goddamn! The department had treated him and Kevin like felons. They had no fucking right to bother him at home, especially now.

Joey moved quickly to the front door, picking up his Smith & Wesson on the way. He clicked a round into the chamber. You never knew who might be outside in this part of San Francisco. He closed the bedroom door. He didn't want Amanda losing the mood.

"Who is it?" Being a cop for seven years had taught him to automatically stand to the side of the door.

"Bruno . . ." Joey hadn't caught the last name. Once again he cursed the landlord for being too cheap to put a peephole in the door.

"I don't want any, go away," Joey kept his voice low enough so it didn't penetrate into the bedroom.

Whoever it was outside the door said something unintelligible.

Shit! He had to get rid of this guy before Amanda came out and started bitching. It was probably an asshole with leaflets or something. But Joey kept his gun down by his thigh just in case. He opened the door a crack.

It slammed into him, knocking him back into the room. Instinctively, he crouched into a firing position. The nine-millimeter flashed up and pointed at the middle of his visitor's chest.

Sergeant Bruno Iannello, the Chief of Detectives' driver, looked down from his six-foot-three, 220-pound stature at Joey Demanto's five-foot-eight, 160-pound body, naked save for his red bikini. Iannello stared incredulously at the gun.

"What the fuck?" he said, his fat neck bulging and face reddening with anger. Then his head jerked up as he sniffed the air like a champion golden retriever. "Dope. You're out of your fucking head on dope." A massive frown covered his brows. "You little shit. I should lock your ass up."

"Who are you? Freeze, motherfucker, or I'll blow your head off." Joey, weaving back and forth, rolled his eyes and waved the gun.

"What?" Iannello hesitated, his eyes fixing on the gun. "Take it easy, Demanto. It's me, Bruno, you know, Chief Ferrante's driver. You know me," he pleaded, suddenly nervous.

Joey Demanto waved his head and blinked his eyes, motioning Iannello backward. The sergeant paled. He moved slowly, putting both hands palm forward, placating.

"It's okay, Joey. We're all in this together. Right?" he mumbled, slipping slightly as he crossed the threshold.

Joey jumped forward and slammed the door in Iannello's face, pushing the dead bolt into place.

Iannello pounded on the door. "You dirty little fag bastard, open that door or I'll break it down. You didn't fool me. I'll shove that gun up your ass and pull the trigger."

"All right, Bruno, go back to the car. I'll talk to Officer Demanto."

Joey, leaning against the wall, his heart racing, recognized the smooth voice of Chief of Detectives Vincent Ferrante.

"But Chief, he's out of his skull on dope and he pulled a gun on me."

"Nonsense, Bruno. I saw it all. It was simply a misunderstanding. Now go back to the car and call my wife on the car phone. Tell her I'm coming home for dinner with her and the kids in about an hour."

Joey's knees were still shaking as he heard Bruno retreat, muttering curses. Amanda had a pretty good stash of grass in the bedroom, and the ramifications of Iannello barging in and seizing it wouldn't have been pretty.

"You can open the door, Joey," Ferrante said. "I assure you, you're not under investigation in any way. I simply need to talk to you."

Ferrante wasn't Iannello by a long shot. He spoke softly but was no one to screw with. Joey Demanto thought about not opening the door and decided against it. The Chief of Detectives, unlike his dumb sergeant, wasn't going to get involved with a member of the department smoking a little grass.

"Okay, Chief. Hold on while I open the door."

Joey opened the dead-bolt lock and suddenly realized he was in red bikini shorts. He snatched open the closet door and slipped into his trench coat before letting the Chief of Detectives in. Reluctantly, Joey backed into the room as the other man moved forward.

Ferrante was tall, dark, and slender. He wore an expensive camel's hair topcoat against the damp San Francisco fog. It was belted casually in a knot showing his handsome pinstripe, light wool, double-breasted Italian suit with a discreet red paisley tie. His face was slender, and he wore his sideburns deep to accentuate his long delicate Roman nose.

Joey put his head down to hide a giggling impulse to call him Don Vincent. Ferrante's nose twitched just once, and Joey remembered stories that he had been the sergeant in charge of Mayor Moscone's security. He was used to ignoring the smell of marijuana.

Unfortunately for Moscone, Sergeant Ferrante had been on vacation when ex-cop Dan White had decided to regain his honor by offing His Honor Moscone. The media had cried for Ferrante's scalp, but the new mayor and new police chief hadn't been at all angry at Ferrante's alleged breakdown in security. His career had prospered.

The chief's eyes swept the bachelor poverty and disorder of

the room and turned to focus on Joey, taking in the red bikini as Joey hastily belted the trench coat.

There was a noise in the bedroom.

"You're entertaining?" Ferrante said.

"A woman," Joey said too quickly, not knowing what Ferrante might think about the red bikini.

The Chief of Detectives waved his hand. "Aha! But we no longer worry about such things as gender."

Sure you don't, Joey thought, watching Ferrante brush the fabric before he sat on the lopsided leather couch. Joey slumped into a battered canvas director's chair.

"You're probably wondering about the house call. I regret any inconvenience, but I came to see you about a delicate matter, and too many tongues wag around headquarters even in my own office. You once—"

Both men turned as Amanda slammed open the bedroom door.

"Where the hell are you, Joey? I want you. Now."

She was nude, and both men stared at her statuesque beauty. As tall as Joey, she had the firm, full breasts and hourglass figure of a nineteen-year-old, her tawny red hair long, matching the color of her full bush. It contrasted nicely with the milky whiteness of her skin. Her eyes narrowed and fixed on Ferrante. She liked what she saw.

"Are you joining us, handsome?" she said, moving forward. "Take a hit." She held out the joint.

Joey Demanto winced, but no one noticed. Ferrante shook his head and showed a lot of teeth. Joey noticed the warm smile wasn't at all fatherly, and Ferrante's eyes lingered on Amanda's breasts.

"Unfortunately, I must go. If you give us just a couple of minutes, I'll send Joey right back to you," Ferrante said.

Amanda shrugged and shook her fine head of hair. Both men watched intently as she swished away. Just before she got to the bedroom, she leaned an arm on the doorjamb and looked over her shoulder with a big smile.

She closed the door behind her, and Ferrante sighed. "Magnifico! I commend you on your good taste and good luck,

Joseph. But now as to why I am here. I have an assignment for you. A good opportunity to get out of the Fugitives Unit and to rebuild your career."

After a one-sided, ten-minute conversation and a couple of halfhearted questions from Joey, Chief of Detectives Vincent Ferrante breezed out of the apartment without ever mentioning that the highly confidential information he assigned Joey to investigate had just come from his former boss, Lieutenant Glen Sherry.

Chapter Eighteen

Kevin McKay prowled Jane Remick's apartment while he waited for Terry Fisher to bring her home from the clinic. Terry was a good cop. She had a way with victims. Her instincts were probably right—another woman had been raped. And it could well be the ski mask rapist. Terry would get Jane Remick to cooperate at the clinic. They'd have physical evidence of the assault and one more confirmation of hair and semen. But it cost four thousand bucks for DNA analysis. Unless he could produce a suspect, Lieutenant Richard Garza wouldn't even discuss it.

Kevin was thirty-six and had been a cop for fourteen years. He didn't get to see many apartments like this. Most of the victims came from poor or lower-middle-class backgrounds, but this apartment cost dough. There were six rooms, and each of them contained expensive, unostentatious furniture. Some of the paintings and sculptures looked like originals. He was no expert but had taken an art course in college. The art work, like the furniture, was interesting and in good taste. Definitely classy. The apartment had a quiet, yet determinedly feminine personality. It was a place lived-in and enjoyed. The absence of dust and the impeccable order suggested daily maid service. He liked it. He took a deep breath, trying to identify the subtle scent of a perfume that lingered throughout the rooms, surrendering only to a cigar smell in the vicinity of the uniformed cop watching the baseball game on television.

The ski mask rapist's M.O. had always been to attack his victim in her bedroom. Kevin had asked Terry not to bag evidence from the apartment, in case he wanted the crime-scene technicians to respond. Now he sat at a small dressing table, facing away from the mirror and toward the bed, and let it flow through his mind, envisioning the attack the way other victims had described it.

Somehow the predator had gotten in. His M.O. was usually forcible entry through a window. But Kevin hadn't seen any sign of a break at the windows. On the phone Terry Fisher had mentioned the front door. But he'd looked closely, and there were no tool marks.

In any event, once inside, the rapist terrified the victims with the gun and mask, threatening to kill them. He followed the shouted threats with savage punching and slapping, intimidating the women into being handcuffed from behind. Twice he found women nude coming from the shower. Others were either partially or fully dressed. He ripped their clothes off and shoved their faces into the bedding, alternately fondling their breasts, pubic areas, and buttocks. He screamed obscenities and punched and slapped them. The terrified victims tried to stifle their screams and moans lest it subject them to even more violence. Often he left them trembling, handcuffed and tied to the bed for over an hour, while he ransacked the apartment, stealing credit cards, cash, and jewelry.

And, Kevin mused, he kept returning to his victims helplessly lying on their stomachs, unable to see him. Sometimes he just stood close, letting them sense his presence. Sometimes he struck them without warning. Other times he whispered softly in their ears and caressed them as a lover. Finally, he forced them to suck him. Then he would rape the women, choking them until they almost lost consciousness. His final attack was to sodomize them. By that time the poor women were exhausted and submissive. If they were still able to talk, they begged for their lives. No one had seen Ski Mask's face, and Kevin knew he would continue his campaign of terror until eventually he'd go all the way and kill.

Kevin studied the luxurious quilt on the king-sized four-poster bed. It was torn in a couple of places. He put on infrared glasses and bent over the pastel sheets. There appeared to be a couple of small bloodstains. He hoped they belonged to the rapist. Other stains looked like semen. Putting the glasses back in his jacket, he saw an expensive alarm clock on the floor, its glass shattered. And one of the bed lamps had been tossed to the corner of the room. Jane Remick had put up a fight.

He looked again at the king-sized bed. It was out of sync in this delicately feminine room. Abruptly, he strode to the walk-in closet, quickly going past the woman's clothing. Finally, he came to a man's slacks and sport jackets. The jacket labels were Christian Dior and Nino Cerruti. The sport shirts were a hundred percent silk. Two suits and four dress shirts indicated they had been fitted to order in Hong Kong along with six flowering silk ties.

He moved along the clothes rack, perusing the woman's clothing. There was a lot of it, and he guessed it was equally expensive: Saks Fifth Avenue, Armani, Wilkes Bashford, Henri Bendel. And none of the shoe racks stretched across the floor under the clothing were empty. Kevin stopped and touched a cream-colored suit. He dropped the sleeve and strode back into the bedroom, gazing again at the signs of how Jane Remick's life had been violated.

He went into the bathroom and found a man's razor, shaving cream, and cologne in the smaller of two medicine cabinets. But clearly it was a woman's place, with cosmetics, soaps, lotions, and perfumes filling the shelves. There were two flowering, hanging begonias gracing the high window which looked out at a panorama including Alcatraz and the Golden Gate Bridge. He saw the same view from the living room window next to the fireplace. This was Jane Remick's apartment all right, but a man visited often enough to keep a set of clothes in the closet and shaving gear in the bathroom. And it was a cinch that bucks were no problem. Kevin went back into the bedroom wondering who paid the rent.

"Hello, Kevin." Terry Fisher paused and turned toward the woman with her. "Jane, this is Inspector McKay from the Sexual Assaults Investigation Unit."

Jane Remick's face was drawn and bruised, but Kevin saw that she was beautiful. He felt a flash of anger at the rapist. He wanted to hold the woman's hand and tell her he was sorry, that they were trying. But it would be a lie. The department wasn't trying. There should have been ten detectives assigned to a guy this dangerous, but Ferrante had put it all on him and Flip. When Ski Mask finally killed, they would be the scapegoats. He tried to control his emotion. Stalling, he turned and shut off the television set, to the chagrin of Officer Piggy Waldron. Kevin walked to the picture window. The fog had unexpectedly blown out and a deep blue sky heightened the color tones of the orange-red sun sinking behind the Golden Gate Bridge.

He took a deep breath, trying to collect himself, wondering if Jane Remick had seen the rage and frustration in his eyes. Of course she had. What the hell was wrong with him lately? He was beginning to lose it. He motioned Terry Fisher into the vestibule and asked for her report.

"She's ready to collapse, Kevin. I'd like to stay with her. . . ." Terry paused, hearing the baseball game turned on again. "At least Piggy lowered the volume," she said. "As I was saying, we're already two hours into overtime, and the captain just buzzed me, saying in no uncertain terms to bring ourselves and the car into the station. He said to turn the case over to you, although I won't repeat how he referred to the Bureau of Investigations."

Kevin asked, "Did the doc at the clinic confirm the attack?"

"After a little medical double talk he did. Traces of apparent semen in the vagina and anus, scratches around the vagina and anus. Also, lacerations on her wrists consistent with being handcuffed. And good samples of flesh from under her fingernails. Her ribs are badly bruised. She fought the bastard. The doctor also indicated that he had combed foreign hairs from her pubic area. If we come up with the guy, the physical evidence will nail him."

"If. That's the problem. We have great physical evidence from the victims, and their credit cards have been used. We have a sure-fire conviction except for the little technicality that we don't have a suspect. But with the mask . . . we don't even get to do a lineup of the registered sex offenders."

"Umm, Kevin . . ." The policewoman hesitated.

"What is it, Terry?"

"She's real fragile right now so I didn't pursue it. You know, she's never copped to being raped, even though the medical evidence is pretty conclusive. I didn't push her, just chatted nice and easy on the way back. But she did slip and say something, then clammed up."

Kevin nodded, listening closely.

"She said the scar along his jaw was almost incandescent when he was choking her. It terrified her."

"Jesus!"

"Right. If he'd been wearing a mask, she wouldn't have seen the scar."

"I've been praying for this. If she can ID him, we have enough evidence so he'll never walk the streets again." Kevin had been looking at the unlit lightbulb above them. He took out a handkerchief and screwed the bulb in. It lit.

"That's interesting," he said. "I'll have the tech crew dust the bulb and area. That's one more thing to ask the victim about."

"Yes. But go slow, Kevin. Jane Remick is close to breaking. I think you better bring her along slowly."

"Yeah. You're right. I sure don't want to schedule a photo lineup before she's ready to cooperate. We'd end up in court with a shaky identification. But this animal is getting more vicious. It's just a matter of time before someone resists and he kills her, or kills her even if she doesn't resist."

"I know. I wish I could stay with her and help you more."

"You've been great, Terry. In the first place by calling me, and now in handling the victim the way it should be done."

Terry glowed with pleasure and joked, "Then you won't mind my using you as a reference if Chief Ferrante interviews me for the bureau?"

"No. Don't put me down as a reference," Kevin said, thinking about the hot water he was in after the Sherry memo. Anxious to talk to Jane Remick, he didn't notice the look on Terry's face. "I'll send your partner out."

Terry was stung. How stupid could she be? She ground her teeth. He had a nice smile and gentle manner, so she made the mistake of thinking he was different about women than the rest of the guys. The hell with all of them! She would stay on patrol.

Jane Remick sprawled on the chaise lounge and cried for twenty minutes after the police left. The policewoman had comforted her. And Inspector McKay. She hated lying, but she just couldn't tell them about Henry. She started sobbing again. It was just too much. Henry would be furious. And, of course, it would be her fault. Everything that went wrong was always her fault.

Chapter Nineteen

Kevin picked up the phone in the squad room and listened to the cheery voice of Lisa Roberts. She was a rape crisis center counselor that he had worked with on his first case with the Sexual Assaults Unit.

"Kevin," Lisa said, "I may have a lead for you on the ski mask case. A woman named Beth Miller came in today and swears the ski mask rapist tried to break into her house in Industrial City. The local cops busted him, but don't seem very interested in her information."

Kevin sighed. There were so many false leads. "Is she playing with a full deck, Lisa? We never got a notification from Industrial City on our Teletype alarm."

"Definitely. She may have something. The way she describes the cops there . . . well, it may be nothing, but I think you should know he had a gun and mask in his car trunk when he was busted."

"Okay, I'll check it out. Thanks for the tip. I owe you."

Joey Demanto slouched down behind the wheel of his rented Toyota Corolla, scowling while he watched police officer Samuel Robbins being smothered by a pack of affectionate and raucous kids. This job sucks, he thought, reflecting on yesterday's visit from the Chief of Detectives. Here he was, lurking around a schoolyard, and he didn't like the way the nun was looking over the car. He'd be lucky not to get reported and rousted by a couple of baton-happy cops. And who was he watching? Just the policeman of the year, according to the *Chronicle* and the media.

Robbins looked good in his crisp blue uniform. He was inside the fenced schoolyard behind the sixty-year-old red-brick building. Within the fence, the yard was as clean and neat as the black and white uniforms the nuns wore. Outside the sanctuary, discarded paper and dirt from never-swept streets swirled in capricious San Francisco winds. It was gray and chilly. Joey rolled up the window.

He conceded Robbins was a natural for media canonization. He was black, and came from a welfare background. He'd been raised by aunts and other relatives. Robbins starred as an athlete, won a scholarship to Berkeley, and joined the San Francisco Police Department after graduating. He'd even served as president of the local chapter of the NAACP for one year. Tall, slim, and good-looking, Robbins soon got assigned to head up the department's Police Activities League, where he became the favorite of every school and children's group in town.

And the fucking Chief of Detectives had him shadowing Robbins. It was nuts. Look how much the kids loved him. Why did I let myself get talked into this? Joey asked himself, feeling slimy. That slick bastard Ferrante had shafted him and Kevin for reporting what they were supposed to report. And now Ferrante had him surveilling a cop! He should have known better than to listen to him. But what the hell choice did he have? Ferrante was—like the Godfather. He'd made him an offer that he couldn't afford to refuse, dangling a transfer from the Fugitives Unit.

His career was probably finished anyway, Joey thought. He and Kevin McKay had the bad luck to have been around Lieutenant Glen Sherry at the wrong moment. But McKay was San Francisco, Irish. Star jock of the right Catholic school, while he, a wop from Kansas City, was an airplane ticket away from going back to the family deli with his tail between his legs. He'd be slicing provolone and have to listen to a million, "We told you so, nothing but fags and foreigners in San Francisco."

They should know! Joey laughed. The high of being an undercover cop in a fabulous city where you could satisfy any dream. And the women! All his high school jerk-off fantasies and more. That is, until you fuck up. But they didn't even fuck up. He and Kevin got fucked up by Sherry and the system. And McKay . . . He'd assumed Kevin knew what he was doing. Ha!

Still, he was a guy who wouldn't think twice about putting his life on the line for you. Balls of steel. But that had been the problem. On the other hand, neither of them deserved the treatment. They got the shaft, and the department lined up behind a dirt-bag like Sherry.

Joey Demanto was a master at surveillance. He had a build and personality that allowed him to move unnoticed through any kind of crowd. He carried several changes of clothes in his car trunk, and just slipping on a workman's cap or a black leather jacket kept people from realizing that he was hanging around them. Given five minutes, he could change from being a truck driver in a working-class neighborhood, to blend in as a sharp young attorney or businessman in the financial district, swinging a leather briefcase and walking down the street among a mass of commuters from Marin County.

But this was a neighborhood where blacks, Latinos, and white kids fought it out in alleys and the park. And gays frequenting park benches and public men's rooms had been bashed by teen rat packs. Three weeks earlier two gays rendezvousing in the dusk on a park bench across from the school had been shot. One was DOA from a head wound, the other suffered a punctured lung. He had fled the hospital and San Francisco. The case was unsolved.

A black and white slowly cruised past, and Joey noticed out of the corner of his eye that he was being looked over. Wearing blue jeans, tennis shoes, and a nondescript gray windbreaker, he left the car and walked up the street. Sitting on a bench across from Sacred Heart's elementary school, he felt queasy. Behind him were gracious Victorians, their bay windows perfect for little old ladies to peek from and report creepy-looking people like him. The neighborhood had held its value. Held! Hell, the old Victorians were going for three fifty. A hell of a lot more than he would ever be able to afford unless he joined the scum like Glen Sherry.

There were No Loitering signs all over the place. How in the world could he explain his presence here? The only people who hung out were parents and . . .

He felt, rather than saw, the black and white radio car slide up behind him. Using all his willpower to ignore it, he glanced down at the *Chronicle* he carried and pretended to be reading, noticing that it was a week old. Great!

"Hey you."

Joey turned and felt a flash of relief. A young policewoman approached, her baton still in its holder. He was glad to see her bald, fat-bellied partner stay behind the wheel. He didn't trust old-timers.

"Get on your feet and move toward the wall. Keep your hands at your sides."

Joey stood up, slowly unleashing his Al Pacino smile. He'd

been strictly forbidden by the Chief of Detectives to identify himself as a cop. Despite all his time in the department, he was pretty much unknown. Unlike other narcs, who were constantly booking suspects in district stations, Joey had rarely surfaced. When they did make an arrest, it was Kevin who booked the prisoner. San Francisco was only fifty-five square miles and didn't have that many cops out of uniform, but Joey had served three years in the police department in Kansas City. San Francisco had taken advantage of his experience and anonymity, putting him into deep cover for long-term drug investigations.

So, he would have to charm his way out of this. Joey didn't go for policewomen as a class, but he had to admit this chick was cool. She had dark hair and a nice face. He studied the firm body under her uniform shirt and liked the way her trousers climbed her ass as she bent over to look at the newspaper he'd been reading.

"Anything wrong, officer?" He kept his smile steady and slowly reached toward his pants pocket to produce the phony ID Chief Ferrante had provided him with.

She moved so fast he was flat-footed. There hadn't been any motion toward her baton. She simply kneed him viciously in the balls. He sank to his knees and lost the coffee and greasy doughnut that had been breakfast. He was dizzy with pain. Both of his hands went down to surround his aching groin. He sank to the ground.

Jesus! Somebody ought to stop this police brutality! he thought. The bitch never gave him the slightest warning. He was only going for his ID.

She relieved him of the identification and spoke into her radio requesting a name check. Joey wondered what kind of cover Ferrante had provided him and prayed it hadn't been as a registered sex offender. She stood over him waiting for a reply. Gradually, the pain eased and his breath came back, but he stayed quite still.

"Ten-four." She spoke into her shoulder mike.

Joey watched wide-eyed as she bent over, her brown eyes hard.

"Now listen to me, dirt-bag. Never reach in your pockets when you're being questioned by a police officer. Understand?"

"Yeah."

"I'm not going to bust you on a bullshit loitering charge and have you walk in ten minutes. But if I ever see you around kids again, I'm going to charge you with child molestation and attempted assault on an officer. I'll get you registered as a sex offender." She glanced at his groin, and Joey clamped his hands tighter around his balls. "And next time I'm not going to leave you with a second chance to fuck anybody. Do you understand?"

Joey nodded, keeping his eyes on her.

"I asked you a question, mister."

"Yes, ma'am, I understand," Joey said.

"Then get on your feet and get out of here before I change my mind." She tossed his ID at him.

Joey got up gingerly. A wave of pain sent him to his knees. He saw her smile. He stood and walked slowly away. Her partner, who had not moved from the radio car, leered and gave him the finger.

Chapter Twenty

After an hour in Industrial City, Kevin acknowledged he was having a bad day. This interview was failing because his partner, Flip, had deserted him. It had been happening all week. Kevin knew it was either a woman or booze, and wondered which one he should worry about more. They were logged in as doing the investigation together, and if Flip got shot by a jealous husband or fell asleep behind the wheel and killed himself, the head hunters in Management Control would be all over him.

Besides, he could use Flip O'Neil, who had a way of conning assholes, like this guy he'd been arguing with for the past half hour. Sitting in the small detective squad room of the Industrial City Police Department, Kevin felt himself losing it. He knew his face was getting red and he heard his voice rising.

"Look, Detective Clark, this could well be the same guy we're after in San Francisco. There's a mask, a gun, and an attempted assault. It fits the M.O.," he said to the sallow-faced, suspicious-eyed man facing him with folded arms.

"I don't think so. He wasn't wearing a mask or carrying a gun. That's what you guys had on your Teletype. Besides, he didn't rape her. It was a burglary, pure and simple. She just happened to be home."

Kevin tried to stay cool. "We've had a lot of experience with this kind of case in the city. It's true, the victim didn't see a gun or mask, but your patrol guys nailed the suspect two blocks from the scene, and there was a mask and a starter's pistol in the trunk of his car. That's damn close to the M.O. And the M.O. is never exactly the same. The victim's memory is always off a little. All I want to do is look at your files and evidence on the case. What's the problem?"

"Yeah, sure. The city. Big-city dicks. You know everything. It was a ski mask in the trunk. People do ski, you know." Clark's face darkened with anger. "And how did you get that information about the car trunk? It's supposed to be confidential."

Kevin shifted in his chair, realizing he had lost it. Flip would have stroked this guy and made him feel like Sherlock Holmes. Instead, he had him pissing on the San Francisco P.D. Clark was "a crimes against property" dick. If he admitted it was an attempted sexual assault, the case went to "crimes against persons," and Clark lost a slam-dunk conviction for attempted burglary. He probably only got a couple a year. This was his big case. Trouble was, Kevin thought, they might lose an important lead to a series rapist good for at least sixteen jobs within the last eighteen months, and God knew how many more in the future. And he couldn't tell Clark he got the information indirectly from the victim, who thought Clark was an asshole who didn't listen to her.

"Well, believe it or not, we know how to investigate too," Clark continued. "We know our town and citizens and our own people. We haven't had to bust a cop here in twenty years. So even though we're just a hick town, we know something about policing. And I'm not going to have some glory-hungry San Francisco cop screw up my victim's memory so she can't testify just so you guys can hold a press conference."

Kevin McKay ignored the insult. California cops often made cracks about the San Francisco P.D. being an "eastern style" department, a thinly veiled allegation of police corruption. "When's the trial?" Kevin asked, giving up.

"In a couple of months," Detective Clark said, tight-lipped.

When Kevin returned to his desk in San Francisco's Hall of Justice, B&B said, "The boss wants to see you, pronto," nodding toward Lieutenant Richard Garza's office.

Kevin raised his eyebrows. "Did he say what for?"

The fat detective grinned. "It wasn't to see if you won the Elvis look-alike contest."

"Give me a break, B&B. I've been getting shit on all day, and I don't have any idea where Flip is," Kevin said, watching Brady's jowls bouncing. B&B was a couple of inches taller than Kevin, and his 240 pounds were evidence of his deep appreciation of San Francisco's good food and liquor. He was known for his skill in finding expensive restaurants willing to comp him on dining, and jealousy guarded his methods from colleagues. Kevin, uneasy because he still hadn't heard from Flip O'Neil, frowned at B&B.

"You can relax about that," Barney said. "Our leader is concerned about overtime. That's my deduction of what he wants to *'dialogue'* with you about." B&B smiled, mimicking the lieutenant's constant use of the word. "Come with me for a morale-building feed at Post Trio, after you get your balls slapped."

"Overtime is one thing he can't get me on. I usually don't even put in for it."

B&B smirked. "Never underestimate the bureaucracy."

Lieutenant Garza wore a polyester plaid suit off the rack from Sears. Frowning ferociously at the papers on his desk, he looked up as Kevin entered the office. His expression didn't change.

"You wanted to see me, Lieutenant?"

"If you have the time, McKay." Garza's mouth twisted downward and his hard brown eyes fixed on Kevin. "We got to dialogue this out. You're working overtime against department policy."

"Hold on, Lieutenant." Kevin held up his hand. "I put in a lot of time on this ski mask rapist, but I know there's a freeze on overtime so I didn't put in for any overtime pay."

Garza's fingers drummed on the desk. "That's what I mean. You're violating the chief's order, and the law."

"What?"

"Look." Garza waved a copy of a general order at McKay. "We can't let you work unless you're getting paid. See." He pointed to the bottom of the sheet. "That's the police chief's signature. Only patrol people get overtime under the contract agreement. No overtime for detectives unless it's an emergency. So don't give me any bullshit. I'm trying to dialogue this out with you so you don't get me or you in trouble."

"I don't get it. We have a series rapist. I'm trying to catch him. I'm not even asking to get paid for overtime."

Garza had a short fuse. "It's FLSA, don't blame me!" he shouted. "Why don't you ask your fucking cousin on the fire department what it's all about?"

"My brother's on the fire department."

"Yeah. Well, whoever. The point is, you can't work unless we pay you. And there's an order freezing overtime. So don't work. And I know I can't dialogue with you. Not after the famous Sherry memo you submitted, so look in your mailbox. Unlike the rest of the guys, you got it in writing."

Kevin's fists were clenched. It infuriated him that the Sherry memo would be used against him, even for something as ludicrous as this.

Garza didn't notice Kevin's fury. "And another thing, where's your partner? Is it too much fucking trouble for him to drop into the office once in a while?"

Kevin felt his anger fading. He didn't want to have to "dialogue" with Garza about Flip's absences right now.

"Okay, Lieutenant. Whatever you say. How are you feeling?"

Garza calmed down. "Me?" He looked at Kevin suspiciously. "I feel fine. Why?"

"Just that the flu seems to be sweeping the bureau."

"Yeah?" Garza reached for his drawer containing the thermometer. He caught himself. "Okay. We had our dialogue. You can go now," he said.

Kevin left as Garza was examining his tongue in the wall mirror.

"Am I crazy or is he?" Kevin asked B&B. "What's the fire department have to do with this?"

Brady glanced at the lieutenant's closed door before speaking. "For once old Affirmative Action Garza is correct. Years ago, the national firefighter's union got Congress to pass the Fair Labor Standards Act, also known as FLSA, so management can't knowingly let people work more than their basic week without pay."

B&B was the Bureau of Investigation's rep on the Police Officers Association board of directors, the cops' collective bargaining agency, so Kevin assumed he knew what he was talking about.

"Don't mean shit whether the sucker volunteers or not. No offense to your own generous spirit, of course." B&B smiled. He slapped Kevin on the shoulder. "Come on, kid. All work and no food makes Jack a dull boy. Let's go have a couple of horns and something light and delicious like clams casino, a bowl of cioppino, sourdough bread, and a plate of home fries, my treat."

Kevin's phone rang, saving him the trouble of telling B&B his stomach was so tense that he couldn't think of food.

"McKay," he said into the receiver, waving the other man away.

Chapter Twenty-one

Inspector Flip O'Neil laughed so hard that he had to put down his binoculars. His white teeth contrasted with his deep black skin. He bet the dude who had been eyeballing the children would be pissing blood tonight. Terry Fisher was quite a lady, he thought. She'd caught the sucker with a shit-eating grin on his face reaching into his pocket. The jerk hadn't been able to make a move. Good thing too, with her asshole partner too lazy to even get out of the car to back her up—although he'd seen Terry in action on another occasion, and she didn't seem all that much in need of a backup.

Flip had been responsible for the radio car responding. He'd found good cover on the roof of the school, sitting comfortably on a stool and peering down at the yard through a slit in a brick wall surrounding the heating unit, which was unused at this time of year. People on the ground couldn't spot him, but with his glasses he had a fine view. He'd been swinging his glasses between the dude and Sammy Robbins for about twenty minutes before Sister Mary Phillipe had gently coughed behind him.

"Inspector O'Neil?"

Flip was concentrating so intensely he jumped.

"I'm sorry," the middle-age nun said. "I didn't mean to startle you, but that young man has been there for an hour in his car. I wanted to know if you think I should ask Officer Robbins to check him out. Do you think he's registered?"

Flip hid his amusement at this nice religious lady doing cop rap. Under California law, convicted sex offenders had to register with the local police each time they established a new residence. Investigators referred to sex cons as "registered."

"I don't know, Sister Mary," Flip said. "But you're right. He is suspicious. I've been watching him too."

He thought for a moment. He wanted some more time to observe Sammy Robbins. "Maybe it's better to let a patrol unit do the check." He scribbled on a piece of paper. "Just call this number. It's police communications. Tell them who you are and about that dude, er, that man. It's best that you don't mention me. They'll send someone right away."

"Fine." Sister Mary Phillipe took the paper. She turned at the stairway. "By the way, Inspector O'Neil, you needn't have worried. I won't blow your cover."

Indirectly, Lieutenant Glen Sherry had been responsible for Flip's rooftop surveillance. Weeks before Kevin had submitted the memo to the police chief, Sherry had mentioned that McKay and Demanto were "untrustworthy" to Carlos Castellano, who took nothing for granted, least of all Sherry's judgment. Carlos had followed Kevin for a couple of days, and it had given him the idea of having Dana Rogers volunteer as art director at Sacred Heart.

The day of the memo, Sherry had been summoned by Chief of Detectives Ferrante.

"It's fantasy bullshit, Chief." Sherry had hid his unease.

"I assume that or I wouldn't be sharing it with you. However, it does indicate that you don't have control of your personnel."

Sherry realized then that Ferrante's anger was directed at the people making waves, not at him. "Chief, you've got to understand, McKay spends his time playing basketball with black kids at Sacred Heart. He's a frustrated priest. This memo comes from my getting on him and his partner about low productivity. You know I've delivered the best stats of any narco commander. It ain't easy with two deadbeats like McKay and Demanto. I'm a churchgoer too, but I still have to maintain discipline." Sherry hadn't mentioned that the basketball playing was during lunch hour.

Ferrante rubbed his chin, thinking aloud. "We give our inspectors latitude due to professionals, but playing basketball on duty with the caseload we have . . ." Ferrante rose and looked out his window. "We don't assign people to spy on members of the bureau." He paused, his back was to Sherry. The lieutenant listened intently. He knew Ferrante. Something was coming. "On the other hand, if there was some sort of allegation, even anonymous, that another cop—"

Sherry coughed. Ferrante turned toward him, and Sherry nodded to show he was following the conversation.

"Let's see. Sammy Robbins hangs around there a lot too. As far as I know, he's clean, but if there was some suspicion of him, we'd have to investigate, and . . . the report naturally would have to include information on the school. If it showed McKay AWOL, playing basketball . . ."

The following day, Ferrante received an anonymous letter alleging that a black uniformed officer had been molesting children at Sacred Heart. The letter also indicated that a copy had gone to the mayor's office. Ferrante had thought it his crowning touch to assign McKay's former partner to investigate. Who would dare accuse them of trying to set up McKay if the report of his rule breaking came from Demanto?

Ferrante made sure that George, his administrative captain, logged the letter in their confidential file. George handed it to patrol officer Nate Lincoln, who was assigned on temporary disability. Nate was a member of the Officers for Justice, an association of black officers in the San Francisco P.D. Nate was bored stiff. He loved patrol, but his police car had been rear-ended two weeks ago and his knee badly wrenched. Before sticking the letter in the file, he casually read it. Suddenly alert, he went to the copy machine and ran off a copy before sticking it in the file.

Then Nate called Flip O'Neil, who was the founder of

Officers for Justice, and during the next coffee break, Flip sat across from him in the cafeteria.

"What's happening, Nate?" Flip asked.

"Something weird. Look at this." Nate slipped him the letter.

"Man, this is bullshit. Mind if I keep it?"

"Be my guest."

Flip folded it and put it in his pocket.

"That has to be about Sammy. What do you figure, someone angling to take his job?"

"You never know in this department. But I'll look into it. Let me know if anything else comes in."

On the roof of Sacred Heart, Flip noticed Terry Fisher's radio car continuing to circle the school area for twenty minutes after the suspect limped away. He was glad she'd done a record check on the guy. He'd review her field interview report later to see if the character needed a follow-up.

A priest with dark curly hair graying at the temples joined Sammy Robbins with the children. Flip wasn't sure, but it seemed that both the priest and Robbins gave more attention to the little boys, especially the black ones. Flip thought he must be Father William Riordan, the athletic director, according to Sister Mary, principal of the elementary school. She had cooperated with him all week, after he'd told her he was working on a possible child molestation. Of course, he hadn't mentioned the letter.

Nothing wrong with either the priest or Sammy giving special care to the little ones, right? Flip asked himself. These were the kids at highest risk of dope and violence. Or was there?

Below in the schoolyard a bell rang and the children slowly began to file inside. Sammy Robbins shook the priest's hand and left. Once again wondering what this could be about, Flip stashed his binoculars, collapsed the little folding chair the nun had provided for him, and started to go. The metal gate to the schoolyard clanged and sounds of kids razzing each other made him pause.

One mystery solved, he thought. This was how his partner

spent his Wednesday lunch hours. Flip reopened the folding chair, sat down, and took out his tiny pair of binoculars. He watched Kevin McKay lead a dozen kids toward Father Riordan, on the basketball court. Kevin and the priest shook hands, and the priest put his arm around Kevin's shoulder and gave him a little hug. Father Riordan wasn't going to shoot hoops with them today, but he went to each boy in turn with a greeting. Six of the boys were black, and all of them were as tall or taller than Kevin.

Flip guessed this was the Sacred Heart prep basketball team. The kids appeared too young to be varsity. For another half hour he watched Kevin work patiently with the boys.

Kevin had stripped down to an old pair of basketball shorts, and Flip shook his head. In clothes his partner didn't look like much. But damn, he thought, look at those legs and arms. He looked like a brute. But he was lightning fast, not at all clumsy. Flip had seen him give that little-boy smile, like the nice kid down the street who checks you out at the supermarket and wouldn't hurt a fly. But he wouldn't want to go up against Kevin McKay, and he had three inches and twenty-five pounds on him. Live and learn.

Finally, Kevin blew a whistle, and the group, joking and horsing around, headed up the street toward the prep school gym, which apparently was in use by the varsity team.

Flip folded his chair, picked up his empty plastic coffee cup, and went down to say good-bye to Sister Mary Phillipe, promising her he'd be back the next morning. Then he went to a deli and had a corned beef sandwich and black coffee, lingering over the sports section of the newspaper to give Kevin plenty of time to shower and get back to the office.

Walking to his car, he passed a liquor store. He turned back and went in. The store was empty. The young woman behind the counter watched the big good-looking black man search the shelves. She took in the cashmere sport jacket, white shirt and tie, and sharply pressed slacks. It was a nooner, she guessed. He was going to pick a bottle of champagne or a good zinfandel, and she wondered which hotel they'd use. Or maybe it would be the lady's apartment.

Flip picked a pint of bourbon. "Is this the cheapest you have?" he said.

"It's only six-seventeen. How much cheaper can it be?" she asked.

"Just asking, sweet one. Can't be too careful with a buck nowadays, right?"

"Sure," she said, giving him change from a ten. She went back to the *People* magazine she was reading.

In the police garage, Flip looked around to make sure he was unobserved, then unscrewed the cap off the bottle of bourbon. He took a full mouthful and swished it around his mouth for fifteen seconds before making a face and spitting it onto the concrete. He did this twice again, then locked the bottle in the glove compartment. There was no way he could explain spending time staking out a cop, but knocking down a few bourbons wouldn't upset anyone.

Upstairs in the squad room B&B was holding court. Kevin and two other dicks stood there as B&B leaned back in his swivel chair enjoying the attention that a good storyteller gets.

"So this guy goes to the brothel in Nevada, where it's legal, you know. He asks the madam, 'How much for a woman?' 'Fifty bucks,' she tells him. 'That's okay,' the guy says, 'but I'm a very strong union man. Is this a union house?' Well, the madam shakes her head looking at him like he's crazy. So he goes down the road."

Kevin stood relaxed with a half smile, enjoying B&B's performance. Still smiling, he nodded at Flip, who walked closer, opening his mouth in a huge yawn. Kevin, picking up the bourbon on his partner's breath, frowned slightly and looked closely at Flip, who gave his full attention to B&B.

"So, in the second house," the rotund inspector continued, "the madam tells the guy that a girl costs seventy-five bucks. Once again he goes through the union stuff, and the madam tells him no, but he asks if she can recommend a union house. She thinks for a moment and then gives him an address down the road. Of course, as soon as he's out the door she calls the other madam and warns her about the union guy who's on the way. So, the guy gets to the third house and asks the price.

Two hundred fifty bucks, the madam tells him. The guy screams, saying the other houses only asked fifty and seventy-five dollars. 'Yes sir,' the madam says, 'but you understand this is a union house. Our girls get health, dental, and retirement plans.' Anyway, the guy grumbles. But what can he do? He forks over two hundred fifty clams and then looks at this juicy little seventeen-year-old and says, 'I'll take her.' 'Oh, no sir,' says the madam, 'that's your girl over there.' She points to the corner where this five-foot, two-hundred-pound butterball with warts is sitting. The guy yells, 'What are you talking about? I gave you two hundred fifty bucks. I want the young girl.' The madam says, 'But sir, this is a union house. We go by seniority.' "

Kevin, who had heard the joke before, smiled while the other two detectives guffawed.

"Outrageous," Flip bellowed, slipping into his street black dialogue and slurring his voice. "No wonder our raises stink. Our own labor delegates are anti-union."

"Ah, beware of the dark Irish. They've a fierce temper," B&B solemnly warned Kevin.

Flip gave B&B a playful punch in the shoulder, but it was powerful enough to jolt him.

"Police brutality by a minority against the senior inspector," B&B complained.

"Complain to your union delegate," Flip said. "Although everyone knows the lazy fucker won't do anything."

Lieutenant Garza opened his door and peered out to see what all the noise was about.

B&B caught Flip's bourbon breath. "Have one," he said, raising his eyebrows toward the lieutenant. "Very good for a sore throat." Flip took a mint. Lieutenant Garza vanished back into his office, wearing his usual frown.

"What's happening, man?" Flip said to Kevin.

"Maybe you should tell me, Flip. I could have used you yesterday. That jerk of a dick in Industrial City told me to flip off, no pun intended. You remember that case. I think it may be our man with the mask. You probably could have conned Detective Clark into letting us talk to the victim."

"Hey, I told you, I'm out doing invaluable work developing informants. Why don't we just wander out and talk to her?"

"I'm getting my ass chewed on an hourly basis here." Kevin nodded toward the lieutenant's closed door. "I can't afford to get beefed from Industrial City, or by the D.A. out there. By the way, the boss did sort of suggest that you drop around once in a while."

"Racism!" Flip yelled. "B&B, what are you going to do to protect me?"

"The usual," B&B said.

"You're in big trouble then, Flip," Kevin said, smiling at his partner's mock glare at B&B.

Chapter Twenty-two

Bernie Ray had been an inspector in the Juvenile Unit forever. Kevin guessed that he had only spent a few years on patrol, but he knew the streets from the kids he handled. Raul Santiago, the man arrested for the Industrial City break-in, had been one of his clients.

"Trouble." Ray sighed. "Like if you were going to make the perfect bad kid, he was the way you'd go."

Ray was fit enough for fifty. Kevin wondered if he'd be as burned out at Ray's age. He scratched his head and asked, "How old for his first bust?"

Ray opened a manila folder and ran his index finger down the lines. "Twelve. Grabbed by the CHP. He was with four other kids in a car stolen in Monterey. Can you imagine? A twelve-year-old living in San Jose, all the way in Monterey ripping off a car. Anyway, I picked him up when he was fourteen. Unfortunately, they had moved here. He beat the shit out of a fourteen-year-old girl in his class. Year before in San Jose, he threatened a teacher with a knife. I checked his background. Like I said, classic. His father, Felipe Garcia, a Mexican national, picked artichokes on a farm outside Watsonville. His mother, Rose Santiago, was a high school dropout. She stayed with cousins and worked on the same farm one summer. Felipe Garcia had a wife and six children in Jalisco, Mexico. Worked the season in Watsonville. He was able to return home with twelve hundred dollars for his family.

"You know the deal, laborer in the open fields with the hot sun. Papa around thirty, strong. He hit on Rose. You know how they are at fifteen. Gorgeous and flirts. Probably shared a bottle of wine one night after work, or some grass. Hot summer romance. But come September, when Rose reports for her final paycheck, Felipe's long gone. She never saw him again. She moves in with her aunt on the east side of San Jose. Seven months later Raul's born, four months before Rose turns sixteen.

"You know the game, single mom, monthly welfare check which her aunt grabs. According to the aunt, at first Rose liked playing mom. But when she sees the partying she's missing, she starts staying out overnight. During Raul's first ten years of life, Mom is busted three times. First, for drinking under age, then being under the influence of drugs, and finally for possession."

Ray shrugged elaborately. "Auntie complained a lot. Rose beat the kid and neglected him. But, you know, juvenile court bullshit—keep the family together. Some family. Anyway, Rose was always diverted to a family child-abuse clinic."

The Juvenile inspector flipped a page in the file. "Raul got three months probation on the hot car. Turns thirteen, he threatens another kid in junior high with a knife. He also threatens the female teacher who stopped him. By this time Rose is in treatment for heroin addiction. His aunt's on a social security pension, sixty-seven years old. Fucking judge asks me what I think. I tell him deportation. No sense of humor. He actually threatened to drop a letter on me. Anyway, the poor aunt gets appointed guardian. The judge gives Raul a stern lecture and more probation.

"Six months later he's apprehended for breaking into a liquor store and stealing a case of wine. Judge doesn't ask me this time, sends him to juvenile ranch for two months. Great rehabilitation. Week before he turns fourteen, he really beats a thirteen-year-old girl in high school. Now he gets Youth Authority—Vacaville. Vacationville I call it." Ray looked up. "Get this. His counselor there reports concern over Raul's frequent sullenness and refusal to participate in group activities, but praises him for not joining any of the various gangs in the institution. Released after a year. When he's seventeen, he drops out of high school, where he was still ranked as a sophomore.

"Cited twice during the next year for smoking pot. If you ask me we ought to give him all the pot he wants. Next, he's busted for suspicion of being under the influence of PCP. Ordered to report to a drug treatment program but never does. They got a six-month waiting period for admission, so who cares?" Again Ray shrugged.

Kevin was tired of the monotone, but the Juvenile detective read on. "A day after his eighteenth birthday he's busted for burglarizing a senior citizens' home and stealing cash and a VCR. Raul woke up an old lady. Poor gal can't even walk. She screams. He punches her, but a security guard grabs him in the parking lot. Back he goes to Vacationville, and this time stays until his twentieth birthday.

"He got a high school GED at Vacaville and gets hired by the city of San Francisco as part of a program for rehabilitating juvenile offenders. Then he marries. Got kids now.

"While his wife is knocked up with the second kid, he's busted as a Peeping Tom outside the public housing project. Case dismissed. Complainant failed to appear. Next arrested by a security officer at Macy's department store who observed him shoplifting a gold bracelet from a jewelry case." Ray closed the file. "Now, he's over twenty-one and you're welcome to him."

* * *

Back at his desk, Kevin shook his head over Raul's adult probation report. There was no disposition. Raul's first adult arrest was for groping a woman in Union Square. Despite all the law enforcement computers, it happened frequently and no one could ever explain why.

There were no further arrests until Raul Santiago was twenty-four. He had broken into a woman's apartment and stolen money, jewelry, dresses, and lingerie. A neighbor had called 911. Uniformed cops caught him on the stairway. This was only his second adult conviction, but the judge looked at his long juvenile record. Raul was sent to the state correctional facility at Soledad for two years. He was released after a year for good behavior, which was standard operating procedure for inmates who didn't annoy the guards too much or get caught stabbing another inmate.

San Francisco gave him his job back. He was now twenty-six and worked in the transportation department for the city and county of San Francisco as a mechanic responding to broken-down buses.

Kevin put a check mark next to Raul's name on the list. He could be Ski Mask. Peeping Tom, assaulting women, bad relationship with mother, elderly aunt too weak to be a positive influence. On the other hand, he had been married five years and had two children. Turning the pages, he overheard his partner on the phone.

"Mrs. Miller, I'm Inspector Flip O'Neil of the San Francisco Police Department's Sexual Assaults Unit. I'd like to talk to you about the recent case you were involved in."

Flip drummed his fingers on the desk. "Well, it's quite similar to a number of cases we have here, and Lisa Roberts, whom I believe you know from the rape crisis unit, called us. Yes, ma'am. I do understand that you were not raped, but I really would appreciate it if you could give me a half hour of your time."

Flip was silent, then said, "I could be at your place in around forty-five minutes, depending on traffic. . . . Umm, you're right. It is terrible now in the city since the earthquake closed some of the freeways. You will talk to me? That's great,

Mrs. Miller. One thing, Mrs. Miller, I want you to call 723-1475. It's police communications. Ask for extension 971. My partner, Inspector McKay, will verify my identity. I don't want you to be frightened when I ring your bell. I'm a black man about six-foot-two, and I'll show you my identification card, okay? What? No, ma'am, I didn't think anything about you being prejudiced. It's just standard procedure for us to say this to witnesses."

It wasn't at all standard, but Kevin knew Flip always did it. He had been reported too many times to 911 when he appeared without letting witnesses know he was black.

"Flip," Kevin said as his partner was leaving, "sorry I sounded off. Do you want me to go out there with you?"

"No way, honky. I just calmed the lady down. If she saw your Irish mug, she'd report us right away and Detective Clark would put both of us in the can. Take it easy." He grinned. "I'll see you tomorrow."

Kevin returned to the register for sexual offenders, brooding over the list, as he did almost daily. The list was as essential as a badge, gun, and handcuffs to the squad. If the victim didn't know the attacker and there were no other hot leads, like a license plate or fingerprints, the register was the first place to look. Most of the time it was possible to quickly match the M.O. with a new parolee. But Ski Mask made it tough. It was the mask, of course. Routine called for a photo lineup of the most likely suspects from the register. Ski Mask had made that impossible. By not letting any victims see his face, he had increased the tendency of frightened victims to give a range of descriptions as to height, build, and possible ethnic background.

There were 2,200 people currently registered in the area as sex offenders. He had eliminated five hundred on his first run-through. They were either back in jail or had moved to another state, or their physical description was so different that he drew a line through their names. But it still left so many possibilities that he looked for shortcuts. Like his trip to Industrial City. A lucky break could save months of frustrating unproductive investigation.

Ski Mask had to be stopped.

Chapter Twenty-three

Kevin picked up Dana at Sacred Heart. They had been seeing each other every day.

"Why don't we walk to dinner tonight?" he said.

"I'd like that."

Dana had been set to challenge Carlos. She was determined not to be used to spy on Kevin. She would confront Carlos, tell him she was going to stop seeing Kevin, but if there was the slightest hint of a threat to him from Carlos, she would warn him. But Carlos had disappeared. There hadn't even been a phone call from him.

Kevin. She rolled his name on her tongue. She realized with a mixture of excitement and dismay that something had developed between them. It was difficult to think of not seeing him again.

It was Kevin's night not to be on call. He left his pager in the police car's glove compartment. Someone else could carry the weight tonight, when he had a date with his girl. Dana looked great in cream-colored slacks and a cranberry-tinted blouse, and wore sensible walking shoes that left her two inches shorter than him. They walked toward Chinatown in the glow of a mild San Francisco dusk.

A homeless man approached them. Dana stiffened, but Kevin casually gave the man a dollar. "You should never give them money," he said.

Dana looked for a trace of humor, but his face was serious. "Excuse me, but didn't I just see you give him a dollar?"

He laughed suddenly. "Unless you can tell," he said, "which

125

ones will spend it on booze or drugs. Whatever that guy's problem is, he's not using."

She felt a sense of calm that flowed from Kevin's gentleness. She realized without surprise that they had been holding hands for the last two blocks.

She said, "You don't seem like the kind of man to become a cop."

He smiled. "Back to that again? Lots of different people end up as cops."

"Was it your boyhood ambition?"

"Not especially. I wanted to be a professional athlete, but, like I told you, I hurt my knee. So I went to the University of San Francisco, just drifting. I had late classes one night. Afterward, I was walking to my car. It was pretty dark. A girl screamed. I couldn't see clearly, but she was struggling with this guy. He was dragging her off the path into the shrubs. I ran up and pulled him away. I didn't really know what to do. But he had torn her blouse right off. She was hysterical. It didn't seem right to let him go, but I was more concerned about her. Then he attacked me. He had a knife. I had no choice. I defended myself. Finally, the police responded and took him to the hospital. I gave them my name and address and forgot about it."

"Why the hospital? Why not jail?"

He frowned. She could see he didn't like talking about it. "I was afraid of the knife. I hurt him so he wouldn't have a chance to cut me."

"And the girl?" Dana asked.

"She was pretty shook up, but the guy hadn't had a chance to . . ." He grew silent.

"And that's why you became a policeman? You felt good about saving the girl?"

"No. I mean, yes. I felt good about that, but I didn't really think too much about it then. But a week later this inspector contacted me. It turned out the attacker was real bad news. They had been after him for a year. He'd hurt a lot of people. The investigator was interesting, a real professional. He began to tell me about the work he did catching these rapists. I had a lot of contact with him before and during the trial. The inspector pushed me to take the police test that was coming up. I did. It wasn't exactly like I had the choice between becoming a cop or a business tycoon. It was a steady job."

"And a chance to do good?"

His eyes twinkled. "What? Cops doing something good?"

"I forgot. You're such a tough guy."

They had walked a mile. Dana felt a kind of soft mist enveloping them. She brushed against Kevin and felt the hardness of his biceps and shoulder. They crossed to Jackson Street. On the corner of Montgomery, Kevin stopped and pointed.

"That's the Sherman Bank. The general was a banker before he wasted Georgia during the Civil War. A strange combination of careers."

"How do you know so much about San Francisco?"

"Oh, the McKays have been here forever." He gave a boyish grin. "Ex-convicts from Australia. In fact, one of my forebears was hung a few blocks from here by the Committee of Vigilance. They had their headquarters on Sacramento. Called it Fort Gunnybags."

Dana shook her head. "The vigilantes. How terrible. Was he guilty?"

"Aren't we all? In fact, he was one of the Sydney Ducks, a gang of crooks originally from Sydney. The family here disowned him. Reportedly, before he was hanged. Still, it's better to do justice in a courtroom. Although sometimes . . ."

She came very close then to telling him about Carlos, but Kevin was leading her through the doorway of Ciao's restaurant. The delicious smell of cooking garlic and the bright, cheerful ambiance of the place pleased her. Luciano, the waiter, came over.

"Kevin! Come, my corner table. It's yours."

The people waiting glared at them. Kevin's face colored, but he turned to Luciano and grinned. "Let me introduce Dana."

"A movie star." Luciano bowed.

"You should smile more often," she said when they were seated. "Your whole face lights up. I can see into your soul."

"We should all smile more often. What do you see?"

"A good soul." She touched his hand.

Luciano took her order for a glass of pinot noir. He was back in a minute with her wine and a glass of milk for Kevin.

Dana laughed. "Milk? Are you an alcoholic or a coke fiend?"

"No. It's just an old habit from when I was training. Tell me about your painting. You're talented, according to Bill."

"Thank you. I was lucky. When I was in school here, one of my professors was French, trained in Paris. He urged me to apply for a scholarship to the Louvre Academy. I was accepted and studied there for three years. I'm just beginning to exhibit now."

Luciano was back with antipasto that hadn't been ordered. Dana tasted the eggplant. "Delicious. They make a fuss over you here!"

"It was my beat for a while when I was in uniform."

"And?" she said.

"One of the cooks went nuts one day, running around with a knife. They thought it was great that I didn't shoot him."

"What did you do?"

"I sang Irish ballads. He gave up right away."

"Come on. What did you do?"

"Actually, we just talked to the guy. Gave him a chance to calm down without losing face. Ever since, they treat me like I'm the mayor."

"What was it like walking a beat?"

"It took some getting used to. Everytime there's some police scandal in the news, you can feel people staring at you. No matter that it was some other department, even as far away as the LAPD, and those guys make lots of nasty headlines. Other times you're invisible. People don't even see you. Except the crooks."

"Did you work in any other neighborhoods?"

"Oh, I worked almost everywhere. The most interesting was

the red light district, the Tenderloin. I don't remember many slow tours there."

"I've always been fascinated by that name. Where does it come from?"

"The best story I heard was that it was copied from New York. There's a section in Manhattan where the same kind of stuff goes on." Kevin grinned. "Well, it seems that years ago, a New York police captain was put in command of that district and was gleefully anticipating the graft he was about to collect. He rubbed his hands and said, 'After all those years of being stuck in the Bronx, now I've got myself a piece of the tenderloin.' The name stuck."

"Of course, the part about graft doesn't apply to the San Francisco police." Dana raised her eyebrows.

Kevin shrugged his shoulders. "I'm beginning to think you're a buff. All you want to talk about is police work."

"Buff?"

"A name we have for cop wannabes."

She laughed. "I'm sorry, but you're the first policeman I've known. And not only a policeman but a narc."

"Well, there's a story to that too. I annoyed one of my fellow cops, not knowing he was going to be a captain in the Bureau of Investigations by the time I got promoted to inspector. He thought it was funny to get me assigned to Narcotics Investigation."

"It was. You have the map of Ireland all over your face. How could you do undercover work?"

Kevin grinned. "I never did the buys. I was the case coordinator. The backup guy on the recording unit. But you'd be surprised, I'm a good listener. The suspects often spilled stuff to me that amazed us."

"That I can see. There is something about you."

"Except I'm not doing so well with you. Why don't you spill something?"

"Me? You want me to confess?" She giggled. "Okay. There was this caper, or do I say heist?"

"You could simply tell me why you wanted to meet me."

Dana stared at him.

"Eventually you will," he said quietly. "It's okay. I'll be patient."

She recovered. "I guess it was obvious that I found you attractive . . ."

"And?"

She shrugged. "Well, as I was saying, I committed this huge bank robbery a few years ago and I thought you were already on to me."

"You've never been arrested."

"Gosh, you can tell just by talking to me?"

"No. I ran a computer check on you."

"You're joking. No. I can see you're serious. I don't think I like that, Kevin."

"Maybe not, but I *am* a detective. You showed up suddenly at Sacred Heart and you just happened to ask Father Bill to get you a cab right when you knew I was sitting with him."

"Don't flatter yourself."

"I don't, that's why I checked. You mentioned you watched us play, so you knew we were in the lounge. And you could easily have called a cab yourself or had Mrs. Burke do it. And every time we meet, you interrogate me on police work. Sooner or later you'll tell me what it's all about." He smiled.

"I think I'm insulted. I thought all this attention was for me, and all you're really doing is working on a mystery."

"Look, Dana. You aren't the best actress in the world. We both know why I call you. Anyway, I'm willing to humor you to keep you from disappearing."

The antipasto dishes were taken away and the entrées were served. For a while they ate without talking.

Then Dana asked, "Was the narc stuff fun?"

"No. I'm glad to be out of there. I just didn't like the way it was done."

"Who did you annoy this time?"

"Um, that's a subject I can't share with you."

"What's your new assignment like?"

"I'm working on the ski mask rapes."

"I've read about him. Terrible."

"He scares the hell out of a lot of women. The safest thing to do is to sleep with a cop." He gave her a slow smile.

She laughed. "You have this innocent little boy expression, then every once in a while you turn lecherous."

"My Catholic upbringing. It's better for us."

"Sinful?"

"Absolutely delicious."

"Shouldn't you be directing all of your energies to catching the ski mask guy?"

"Right. But nobody's perfect."

"Why can't you catch him?"

"The mask. We have a few hot suspects, but none of the victims saw his face except the last one, and she won't admit it."

"Really?"

"Well, you know how it is with sugar daddies who pay the rent."

Dana flushed. Did he know? But he was looking over his shoulder for Luciano. His comment had nothing to do with her. He turned back.

"What's wrong?" he said.

She shrugged.

"I guess that sounded cold, but it's just cop talk. Actually, she put up a hell of a fight. She's quite a gal, but I think she's afraid if she cooperates she'll lose her patron."

"And?"

"I have to find a way. He's attacked a lot of women, and sooner or later he'll really hurt someone. What's your advice?"

"It's hard for me to answer. I think I'd kill a man who tried to rape me."

"And if he had a gun?"

"He'd have to kill me."

His face was grim. "We don't preach that fate-worse-than-death crap anymore."

"I didn't mean it that way. I'm just saying how I feel."

At that moment Luciano put a plate of biscotti and two espressos on the table. "A treat, on me." Dana glanced at her watch, surprised. They had been in the restaurant almost two hours. Kevin chatted with Luciano for a moment and gave his credit card for the bill.

"Do you think another woman could help get the victim to talk?" Dana asked.

Kevin sipped the espresso. "A good female officer handled the initial investigation and didn't get very far. Are you suggesting a noncop?"

"Well, if she didn't talk to the policewoman . . ."

"I have to talk to Jane Remick tomorrow. Would you like to come along? It's strictly against regulations."

"Me? Oh, I don't think so, Kevin. I never did anything like that. I wouldn't know how."

Kevin sat looking at her.

"You're making me feel guilty," she said.

"I'm sorry. I didn't want our dinner to be a downer."

"It wasn't, Kevin. It really wasn't. I tell you what. I'll go along only if you tell her in advance and she agrees."

"It's a deal," he said.

Kevin didn't want to say good night. He tried to keep the small talk going, but she was far away, her eyes absently fixed on a man's fingers resting on top of a partition that hid the people on the other side. A heavily jeweled ring glistened on the man's middle finger. Kevin picked up a slice of lemon from a saucer on their table. Slowly, he raised it above the man's fingers. Dana came back to earth.

"Kevin." She shook her head in disapproval.

He kept the lemon in place and smiled into her eyes. Dana shrugged at his childish threat, then blinked as Kevin actually squeezed the lemon, splashing juice liberally over the fingers, which quickly disappeared. Still smiling, he placed the spent lemon slice next to her, enjoying her shock. He picked up the wine menu and pretended not to notice the heavily built man who had moved around the partition. The man looked down at the squeezed lemon slice next to Dana, then at her. Red-faced, she could only manage a silly smile.

Kevin stayed engrossed in the menu. After a moment the man moved back to his seat.

Outside the restaurant Dana turned to him. "You're one crazy policeman."

They were standing close to each other. Kevin slipped his arm around her waist. Her left hand reached up behind his head. She pulled him to her, pressing her body against his, and kissed him with a craving that ignited Kevin. He moaned and leaned into her, both of them oblivious to the tittering passersby.

Early the next morning, Kevin sprawled naked across her bed, looking out the picture window at the early sailboats racing toward the last wisps of fog clinging to Angel Island.

"What is there about lemons that turns you on?" he asked.

Dana had been running her fingers across his back. She slapped his rump hard. "It showed a dimension to your character that tipped the scale."

Kevin grunted.

Her hand inched downward. "Will you pose for me, my beautiful one?" she said.

He took her other hand and touched it to his lips. "No."

"No?" Her fingers moved past his buttocks and inside his legs. Kevin shivered. "Don't be so brave," she said. "Tell me you surrender." She drew her nails firmly along the inside of his thigh.

He rolled over. His arm pinned her and his mouth closed on hers. She trembled and tried to put her arms around him but couldn't move. She pressed her mouth against him and her teeth sank into his lips as she alternately bit him and ran her tongue frantically inside his mouth.

"Okay," he said a moment later, reaching inside her robe and finally allowing her hands to race across his body. "I surrender, but all I'll give up is my name and badge number."

"I doubt very much that's all you'll give, Kevin."

Chapter Twenty-four

Industrial City was aptly named—ten square miles of small factories and assorted shipping businesses bisected by the freeway. Four hundred thousand or so cars zipped through each day on U.S. 101, depending, of course, on the time of day—actual zipping was only possible from ten A.M. to two-thirty P.M., between morning and evening rush hours. Industrial City's fifteen thousand residents absorbed the carbon monoxide fumes of those working in San Francisco and abiding in the more lush environs of Atherton, Menlo Park, and Palo Alto. Fumes of a surprising number of fanatics who commuted all the way to San Jose helped overload the atmosphere. Most days, the ubiquitous yellow air permeated the fifty mile peninsula, flowing south past the San Jose foothills to farmlands where it descended upon the artichokes and brussels sprout crops marketed throughout the United States as healthful California produce.

Flip O'Neil drove his unmarked police department Ford through the haze, cruising one of the small residential enclaves tucked among the tire businesses, machine shops, and garment factories. Sagging trees sheltered small green lawns and two-bedroom cottages that were now termed "starter housing within a twenty-minute commute of San Francisco" by real estate agents. The modest structures were priced at $200,000. But Mrs. Beth Miller lived in a rental on the bottom floor of one of a dozen two-story duplexes painted hospital off-white. Flip noticed a street sign warning that it was a neighborhood crime watch area. The sign said, IF I DON'T CALL THE POLICE, MY NEIGHBOR WILL.

134

He tossed the police mike over the steering wheel in the hope that the neighbors would see it and omit their civic-duty police notification. A squat, bald man halted his yard work to glare at the detective crossing the street to Mrs. Miller's apartment. The guy looked like he was about to challenge Flip, but taking in the detective's size, he settled for standing with his hands on his hips. Ordinarily, Flip would have flashed his teeth, said, "Hi, bro," and offered a high five, but he didn't need Detective Clark and the Industrial City cops interrupting his talk with the victim, so he conspicuously took out his police identification and rang Mrs. Miller's bell. It was answered almost immediately. Flip held his ID up to the peephole and announced himself.

When they were in the living room, the woman, somewhat nervous, asked, "Will you have a cup of tea, Inspector O'Neil?"

"That would be very nice, Mrs. Miller," Flip said, though he didn't want tea. He was looking forward to getting home for a cold beer with Trish, but knew it helped to let witnesses do something with their hands.

The phone rang and she picked it up in the kitchen. "Yes, Mr. Blanda, I'm fine."

She lowered her voice, but Flip was able to hear. "Oh, no. He's a policeman. Yes, I'm quite sure. Thank you. I appreciate your concern but I'm just fine."

Flip smiled to himself. No doubt that was his friend from outside. He was probably the first black they'd seen in this neighborhood since it was born. He couldn't blame them, since every day there was some new story on TV of black dope pushers blowing each other away.

While Mrs. Miller was in the kitchen, Flip surveyed the small, immaculately kept apartment. A dog whined and scratched behind a closed bedroom door. The living room was modestly furnished. He sat on the sofa facing a dining area off the kitchen. A collection of eggs and spoons filled the shelves along the opposite wall. The dining room table seated four, and a dark wood cabinet held a flowered set of china. A rocking chair faced a twenty-one-inch television console to the side of the coffee table where he placed his notebook. The TV had stereo speakers, and he guessed the usual CD and tape deck were behind the paneling. The room had cheap blue wall-to-wall landlord carpeting. It would have been dismal, but Mrs. Miller had flooded it with plants and flowers and made maximum use of the light from the windows and a sliding glass door to the tiny, green-shrubbed patio. He noticed the bar on the patio door was engaged.

Flip declined cream but dumped a lump of sugar into what was surprisingly good tea. "Excellent," he murmured. "What kind of tea is this, Mrs. Miller?"

"Peking orange." She smiled. "Have one of these macadamia nut cookies. I baked them myself."

Flip, who had gained fifteen pounds in the last month, sighed. All in the line of duty, he thought. He had her nice and relaxed. If he turned down the cookie, he'd have to start all over again. And if he didn't get off these school surveillances soon and get back into the gym, he'd be the first black sumo wrestler in San Francisco history.

"Mrs. Miller, I won't take much of your time and this may be a false alarm. As I understand it, a man broke in here around ten days ago."

"It was exactly twelve days ago, Inspector, and it is not a false alarm."

Flip blinked. Mrs. Miller was small, around fifty years old, wore eyeglasses and had auburn-colored hair fixed in what looked like a home permanent. He hadn't expected her to be assertive.

"But first I apologize if people stared at you," she said. "I know it's wrong, but they're actually nice people. They're just frightened and haven't had the experience I had. I'm a librarian and have worked with all kinds of children."

"I didn't even notice, ma'am."

"I'm sure you did. I guess you have to go through it all the time. But let me tell you why I think it was the ski mask rapist. I moved from San Francisco because of him. I read in the papers about him, and I'm sure it's the same person. Look." She stood and motioned Flip to come with her. "This is the window he came in. I noticed the screen was loose and called the landlord the day before Santiago, the man they arrested, broke in."

She moves from San Francisco, so this must be the guy, he thought. Sure! Except who knows? This was a sharp lady. And, Ski Mask's M.O. most of the time was to case the place, unscrew the screen, and come back to attack later. Maybe the old gal was right. There was a mask and starter's pistol in Santiago's car trunk.

"I tried to tell Detective Clark, but he wouldn't listen. I read that the rapist studied the victim's home for days, and now I'm sure he was doing that to me."

"What makes you think so, ma'am?"

"I'm allergic to cigarette smoke. For two days I kept smelling smoke. Finally, I went out and looked. Sure enough, there were a dozen butts under the window. And the screws had been taken from the screen, and the screen put back in place. As you can see, the window latch is simple. He probably opened it with a knife."

Flip knew that Mrs. Miller's description of the M.O. was right on. Smoking had been part of it.

"I told Phyllis, she's my next-door neighbor." Mrs. Miller pointed to the left. "We set up a signal. If either of us knocked like this—" The woman gave three sharp raps on the wall followed by three faster knocks. "—then the other one would immediately call 911."

"Is that what happened?" Flip said.

"Actually, no. I smelled cigarette smoke and heard some scratching at the window. I didn't wait. I went into Phyllis's apartment and called 911."

"That was quick work, Mrs. Miller."

"Yes, but I can't say the police were terribly interested. I had to talk five minutes to get them to believe me. And then they took forever to respond. He was actually in my apartment by the time they got here."

Flip scratched his head. The report said Santiago had been caught a block away.

Mrs. Miller saw his puzzlement. "He ran when the police

car came by with their lights blinking. They actually sped right past us and had to turn around. Are they supposed to use their lights on this kind of a call?"

"It's different everywhere." Flip wasn't about to get into a discussion of Keystone Kops.

"Anyway, Phyllis and I went out to show the police where he was hiding behind the shrubs." She handed Flip a little cellophane bag full of cigarette butts.

"Thank you, Mrs. Miller," Flip said.

"I used tweezers to pick them up." She smiled. "From watching TV. It's probably the wrong way."

"No. You did right, Mrs. Miller."

"One other thing. Did I read correctly that on one case the rapist cut himself so that you have his blood sample?"

"Yes, that was in the newspaper."

"And that the blood sample showed the rapist had Rh, AB negative, a relatively rare blood type?"

"That wasn't supposed to be released, but you're right, it was in the paper."

"I'm glad it was. It's another reason why I think Raul Santiago, the man they arrested, is really the ski mask rapist."

"What?" Flip was startled. "Did he cut himself here?"

"No. But I'm a librarian. I did some research. Mr. Santiago's mother has Rh, AB negative. So it's quite likely that her son has that type as well. I don't know if that was what you found in the other cases, but if it is, he must be your man."

Flip frowned. "Mrs. Miller, could you tell me how you found out about his mother's blood?"

"Simple. I went to court when Santiago was charged. By the way, it's disgraceful that they let him out."

Flip nodded. "Please, go on about the blood."

"Well, his aunt appeared in court to vouch for him. She mentioned that his mother was a drug addict and had been arrested. She's now in a treatment center in Santa Clara County where one of my oldest and dearest friends is a nurse. I won't tell you her name, but I assure you she didn't make a mistake on the blood type."

Flip grunted. Jesus. They bumbled around, and this little lady probably solved the case. Wait until he told Kevin.

"Mrs. Miller, you wouldn't consider giving up the library and joining our squad, would you?" Flip smiled.

"You're very kind, Inspector." She matched his smile. "I just hope someone locks up the terrible man doing this for the rest of his life."

"I can promise you it will happen when we get him. And it may well be that you helped. There is a reward, and you deserve it if Santiago is the man."

"Thank you. Putting him away is reward enough, but . . ." Her eyes trailed the apartment. "It would be nice to get some new drapes."

Flip paused at the door. "Mrs. Miller, I don't want to frighten you, but as you know, Santiago is out. The ski mask rapist did go back to the victims in a couple of other cases."

"Just let him try. I purchased some security since he was last here." She opened the bedroom door and a huge German shepherd bared his teeth and growled at Flip.

The detective opened the front door. "That's great, Mrs.—"

The animal lunged, easily brushing aside the frail woman. Flip jumped through the doorway and slammed the door, wincing at the huge thud as the dog hit the door full-force. Shaken, the detective walked toward his car. The bald, squat man leaned on a rake and grinned at his sudden departure.

"Take care, Archie," Flip said, passing the man, who did resemble Archie Bunker.

"You helping a nun," Trish Jordan said. "It's too much, but you're a good guy underneath all the cop posturing, Flip. Do you think there's anything to the letter Nate gave you?"

"Would it be too bad a pun to say God only knows? After I talked to Nate I checked, but the department has no record of child molestation in the area."

"Flip, the letter said it was a cop. You know there wouldn't be a report."

"Don't be so sure. The letter said a black cop. Plenty of

people in the SFPD love to screw up black cops, and Sammy Robbins is so classy he makes a lot of people jealous."

Trish stroked his hair. "I still don't understand why you haven't told Kevin. Doesn't he ask where you are all morning?"

"Checking up on your partner? It's just not done. Besides, I conned him into thinking I'm boozing it up so he doesn't ask too many questions. Kevin's too hung up on this Catholic stuff. He even gets all emotional about the rape cases we handle, let alone something involving the kids he coaches. He'd make a big deal, and all we've got is an anonymous letter."

"Still, the thought that kids at a Catholic school—"

"See, that's what I mean about you Catholics. Why you, and not a swinging, singing Baptist like me?"

"Your accent isn't funny and you better not be swinging anymore, lover man. But the rest of your day. God. It's wonderful! The German shepherd, and you fleeing for your life." Trish's laughter rolled over Flip like a calming mountain stream, and the tension flowed from his powerful shoulders.

"It wouldn't be so funny if Rin Tin Tin had taken a nip out of your pleasure stick, though. Would it?" he said.

Trish reached down between Flip's legs. "I'm going to have to do a close inspection just to make sure." She took off her turquoise glasses and bent over him. "Umm, what is this big black pipe doing all soft and squishy?" Her tongue flickered quickly and Flip gasped. "Now that's more like it," she said.

He reached down and stroked her hair. Suddenly, she was upright, laughing full in his face. "Little Miss Marple solved the whole fucking ski mask case and you big dicks can't even catch a cold."

"Speaking of big dicks, angel . . ." Flip pulled her close. He felt himself soaring toward the familiar ecstasy that Trish alone could take him to. Who would believe she'd been the only woman in his life for more than seven years? He laughed. Certainly not his ex-wife.

Chapter Twenty-five

Flip had decided to skip his last morning stakeout of the school so he could tell Kevin about his interview of Mrs. Miller. At his desk adjacent to Flip's, Kevin took notes. He chuckled at Flip's vivid description of the German shepherd.

"I'm going to have to buy you a box of dog biscuits before this case is over," Kevin said. "Do you think we should check with the D.A. about a warrant?"

"I don't think we have enough yet. Santiago's a parolee. We could get his parole agent to check his apartment, but I'd like to size him up first. He sounds almost too good to be true after talking to Mrs. Miller."

"If it turns out to be Santiago, let's make sure she gets the award. She actually did a hell of a job."

"Absolutely. If it is Santiago, Industrial City will probably give Detective Clark a commendation."

"I wouldn't be surprised. I was thinking we might give Santiago a little jolt if we were waiting for him when he finishes work."

"Sounds good. In the meantime let's go over the other winners." Flip picked up the sex offenders register.

The two detectives sifted possibles, hot possibles, and unlikelies. They had agreed to try to identify the four most likely suspects. They worked through the morning, pausing only for phone calls.

"Kevin," Flip rubbed his eyes, "let's take a break and grab a sandwich before they shut down the cafeteria."

Over coffee Kevin said, "Let's face it, none of these guys looks as good as Santiago."

"True. But you know the game. Zero in on a single suspect too soon and you're sure to be sorry."

They went back to their desks and continued to go through the sex register.

"It's almost time for our talk with Santiago, and we've only agreed on these four." Flip pointed to files on Richard Jackson, Tony Santucci, Douglas Rupe, and Julius Butler. All four were registered sex offenders.

"Trouble with Jackson is he was in the can on at least one of the cases we credited to Ski Mask," Flip said.

"Yeah, and the problem with Rupe is he has a tight alibi for two other cases."

"And Butler was supposedly living in Oregon for the last year. I suppose he could have come back without anyone knowing about it, but we know Ski Mask really cases the victims. It's hard to see an out-of-town rapist pulling it off. Then we have Santucci. But his parole officer is pretty strong on him being shaped up."

"Not many of these guys ever rehabilitate."

"You got that right. If they kept eighty percent of these assholes locked up, we wouldn't have anything to do around here. Still, it could be any one of these four, or a dozen others in the register." Flip tossed the files on the desk.

"Or someone not in the register at all."

Flip glanced at his watch. "Hell, we're not getting anywhere. Let's go and see if we got lucky with Santiago."

Raul Santiago walked from the garage with a blue windbreaker slung over his shoulder.

"Police officers, Santiago, we want to talk to you." Flip flashed his badge.

Raul Santiago flushed, and a thin scar running from his chin to his ear glowed. Kevin and Flip made eye contact, remembering. Terry Fisher had reported that the victim, Jane Remick, said it turned incandescent during the assault.

"Wh-Why y-you come to wh-wh-where I work. Y-You ain't supposed to."

"That so, Santiago?" Flip stuck his thumbs inside his belt

and rocked back and forth. "You're up on your rights, huh? What about the last woman you attacked? Did you read her rights to her?"

Santiago was angry and nervous. "I-I-I'm gonna, com-com . . ."

"Sure, you do that, Santiago." Flip glared at him.

"It's just for a few minutes, Raul." Kevin spoke softly.

"I-I d-don't . . ." Santiago took a deep breath, trying to control his breathing.

"We can do it the hard way or the easy way," Flip said. "We'll book you at the station for refusing a parole check—"

"Flip," Kevin said, "why don't we just walk over to the park." He gestured to Santiago, pointing out a bench in the small park across the street. "We only have a couple of questions, Raul."

Raul Santiago walked stiff-legged between the two detectives. When they got to the bench, Kevin sat and indicated that Santiago should sit next to him. Flip stood a couple of feet away.

Kevin faced him on the bench. "Tell us what's happening, Raul."

"N-N-Nothing, I'm c-clean."

Flip laughed. "Sure, Santiago."

Kevin held up a hand. "Flip, why don't you get us a couple of coffees? Want one, Raul?"

Raul shook his head. His eyes burned with anger watching Flip walk away.

"Now we can talk," Kevin said. "How you making it, Raul? Any problems?"

"J-Just the ones y-you c-c-cops make. P-People I w-work with . . ."

"I'm sorry, Raul. We have to do this once in a while. How's the wife?"

Kevin kept Raul talking for about ten minutes. As casually as he could, he asked Raul if he remembered where he was the night of the attack on Jane Remick. Raul said he wasn't sure. Maybe he took his wife to the movies or to see her mother.

Kevin saw Flip looking a question at him from the edge of the park.

"Raul, my partner's coming back in a few minutes. Is there anything you want to tell me before he comes back?"

"I-I p-p-paid. I-I did my time. I'm c-clean."

Kevin nodded and patted Raul on the shoulder. "Here's my card, Raul. Anytime you want to talk, give me a call."

Raul stuffed the card in his pocket and walked away without a backward glance.

Flip joined Kevin. They watched Raul walk to the parking lot.

"Goddamn, when I saw that scar . . ." Flip paused.

"Me too, but as you said, whenever you zero in on a suspect too soon, you're in for a disappointment."

"At first I thought the stutter was just because he was nervous."

"It wasn't. I talked to him for ten minutes when you went for the coffee. He relaxed. But he never got a sentence out without a stutter."

"A stutter that bad, and not one victim out of thirty-nine cases ever mentioned it. Shit." Flip handed Kevin a container of coffee. "You owe me two bucks."

"No way. I just wanted you to take a hike. You didn't need to buy anything." Kevin sipped at his coffee.

"I had to maintain your reputation as Mutt, didn't I?"

"Jeff, Mutt is the short one."

"Mutt, that's what I meant." Flip stretched his two-inch advantage over Kevin to four inches.

Kevin drove back to the squad room. "You want the front or the back of the list of victims?" he said.

"Which one you want?"

"I don't know. I'll take the front, I guess."

"I was thinking I'd like the front. That part of the alphabet should be easier."

"Anyone ever tell you you're paranoid, Flip?"

"I know I am. Doesn't mean people aren't out to get me."

Kevin pondered for a moment. "I have to remember that one."

"Better still, remember just a couple of victims who heard Ski Mask stutter. Then we don't have to waste all day calling them."

Kevin grunted. "One of us would have recalled the crime reports or M.O. file mentioning a stutter. It wasn't there. We'll check the victims again but it's a waste of time."

"I know," Flip said, "but we have to be sure."

"How many did you get to talk to?" Flip asked Kevin. They had spent hours on the phones calling one ski mask victim after another. Each detective asked the victims to recall the rapist's words, carefully avoiding any mention of a stutter. After listening again to the victims' accounts, they finally asked if the women had recalled anything unusual about Ski Mask's speech. None had.

"I called nineteen, spoke to eight."

"I called twenty, ten answered. I thought you picked the easy end of the alphabet?"

"That's why I don't bet on sports."

"I came up with zero." Kevin shook his head. "No one remembers a stutter. You too?"

Flip nodded. "I also called Santiago's parole agent and asked why the hell his report doesn't mention Santiago's stutter."

"What did he say?"

"The usual. He isn't a detective so he doesn't care about stutters. He has a caseload of two hundred fifty, etcetera."

"Did he say that the stutter is permanent?"

"Sure did. Says it's the most noticeable thing about Santiago. I'm afraid it's back to the drawing board for us. I guess we just tough it out and go over the four guys we picked out of the register."

"Maybe we should go to the lieutenant and see if he'll ask Ferrante for more people," Kevin said. "We should have a task force of at least ten, given the number of assaults."

"Why don't you go directly to Ferrante? I hear you're buddies."

"Or you could. At the same time, you could ask him to file

an amicus brief in your discrimination lawsuit against the department."

"As I was saying, it's back to our top four unless you have a better suggestion."

"We do have a pretty strong hint that Jane Remick, the last victim, saw his face."

"You said she won't admit it."

"Well, to tell you the truth, I've been afraid to ask her."

"You, who jump over tall buildings, piss on Chiefs of Detectives, police chiefs, and commanders of narcotics squads, afraid?"

"The thing is, we're nowhere. Especially since we discovered Santiago's stutter. If I ask Jane Remick if she saw his face and she denies it, we're in trouble. Even if we get her to tell the truth later and she picks him out in a photo lineup, her ID won't stand up because of her previous denial."

"That's true, but do I see a suggestion lurking?"

"Well, I'm going over to say hello to her this afternoon. I was thinking of taking another woman, a civilian, with me."

"Your squeeze?"

Kevin smiled. "This lady volunteered to teach art to the kids at Sacred Heart. But she's very feminine and smart. What if I should leave the room and she asks Jane if she saw the rapist's face?"

"It's an outrageous ploy to circumvent the courts. Also, it's strictly prohibited by department rules. Did your lady friend agree to do it?"

"Do what? You don't know a thing."

"Quite correct. Good luck."

Chapter Twenty-six

"Please come in." Jane Remick opened the apartment door. She attempted casualness, but couldn't resist staring at Dana.

"Miss Remick, as I mentioned on the telephone," Kevin said, "this is Dana Rogers. We're on our way to Sacred Heart school, where we both do some volunteer work. Are you sure you don't mind? This is just a routine follow-up visit I'm required to do."

"No. Of course not," Jane Remick said. She led them into the living room and gestured toward the couch. When they were seated, she asked, "Would you like some coffee?"

"That would be great." Kevin spoke before Dana could decline.

Dana stood up. "Let me help you."

Kevin watched the women walk to the kitchen. Jane had a few pounds on Dana and she lacked Dana's athletic muscle tone, but both women were unusually attractive. Kevin forced his mind away from the thought that Ski Mask could have handcuffed, taunted, and raped Dana. It was just the luck of the draw which victim he chose. He listened to them chatting in the kitchen. Jane apparently used an Italian coffee maker, and Dana mentioned that she also had one. She's doing pretty well, he thought, hearing Dana compliment Jane on the chocolate-flavored French roast blend of coffee. Anything tasted good after the Hall of Justice poison.

"Good," he said, complimenting Jane on the coffee. Her face was drawn, and occasionally a hint of panic showed in her eyes. It had only been a few days. "How's it going for you, Jane?"

"I'm going to move. I don't think I'll ever feel safe here."

"How terrible," Dana said. "I'm sorry."

"Thank you. Look . . ." Jane paused, embarrassed. "I know you mean well, but I was in therapy before it happened. My therapist is really helping. I just don't want to get into this rape counseling."

Dana blushed. "I'm sorry. I knew I shouldn't have intruded. I'll wait downstairs."

Jane touched her hand. "No. Please finish your coffee. I didn't mean that you should go."

Kevin took out his notebook. "It was my fault. Dana isn't a counselor. I didn't think—"

"Please, both of you, stop apologizing." Jane Remick managed a smile. "Really, it is nice to have someone visit. I'm from Los Angeles and don't know many people here."

Kevin scuttled his plan to ask Jane if he could use her phone in the other room so that Dana could be alone with her. It would be too obvious.

"Jane, I only have one question, and we'll be on our way." Kevin flipped through his notebook, pretending to look for something. "As I recall, when we interviewed you, you said the man with the mask did talk to you. Do you recall anything about his voice? Anything different?"

"It was different—bizarre. I hated his voice."

Kevin nodded encouragement.

"Soft and mean. Very mean, trying to scare me, and God knows he did." She gazed toward the window and her eyes watered.

"Jane, I hate to keep opening old memories, but what was different about his voice?"

"Just that it was so mean, so smooth, it made him more scary."

Kevin sighed and put his notebook away. "Well, thanks for your time and the coffee. I can tell you, it's not what we're accustomed to at—" Kevin's beeper went off. He glanced at the telephone number. It was Flip's extension.

"You can use the phone in the other room," Jane said.

"Are you sure? We were just leaving."

"No. Go ahead. I'll pour us some more coffee."

After Jane had returned to the living room and poured coffee in Dana's cup, she asked, "Are you his girlfriend?"

"Well . . . I really do teach an art course at the school. Honestly," she said, seeing Jane's look of disbelief.

Jane smiled. "If you're not, he certainly wishes you were. He can't keep his eyes off you. He's cute. So polite. It seemed like only he and the policewoman who came really gave a damn about me."

"I can tell you he really does care. The man who did this to you is evil. He's hit on a lot of women."

"I know. I feel so guilty about not . . ." She paused and looked at Dana. "It's hard to explain."

"I'm sure."

"You see it all the time in the newspapers and on television, but I never believed anything like this could happen to me. Then Henry's reaction . . ."

"Is he your boyfriend?"

"He's no boy, but yes. I wonder if all men, husbands and all, act like him."

Dana shook her head. "It must be very difficult for you."

In the other room, Kevin waited patiently. B&B had answered and told him to hold on. Flip had gone to the elevators. He would try to catch him. Kevin heard Dana and Jane in the living room but was unable to distinguish their words.

"Kevin," Flip was puffing, "B&B got me downstairs. The old fart can still move." Kevin heard B&B say something in the background. "Anyway," Flip continued, "we may have a break. Remember the other day when I talked to Santiago's parole agent about the stutter? Well, I also told him about the scar and that we had checked the records without finding any. I asked him if the other four possibles we picked out had recently developed any scars on their faces. He didn't remember any but said he would check it out. He just called. Turns out on his recent bust, Richard Jackson, got into a fight in the holding cell. Barone, the parole agent, said the report indicated he needed some stitches on his face."

"Did Barone remember the location of the scar?"

"No. As luck would have it, Barone was on a day off when Jackson made his last visit to the parole office. Another agent saw him. Naturally, that agent is water rafting some goddamn place where there are no phones. I'm going over to the emergency room where they treated Jackson to see if I can get a look at the records. How are you doing with Jane Remick?"

"I'm not sure, but your page came through at just the right time. Gave my friend a chance to chat. I should be in the office before you get back from the hospital. I'll wait for you."

"Don't stay past five. You'll violate the chief's FSLA order on overtime."

"Yeah. Take care, Flip. I think Dana and I better get out of here. We're wearing out our welcome."

But when Kevin returned to the living room, he found the two women chatting about art. He sat and sipped coffee.

After a couple of minutes Dana said, "Kevin, I think we took enough of Jane's time."

"Not at all," Jane said.

Kevin stood. "Jane, do you still have my card?"

"Yes." She rose.

He moved toward the entrance hall and Dana joined him. "Well, don't hesitate to call anytime. I did put my home number down too."

"I know. That was nice of you." Dana joined Kevin at the door. Jane took her hand. "You've been very kind. I'll call about tomorrow."

Going down in the elevator Dana asked, "Did you arrange for the beeper to go off?"

"No. I'm not that smart. Did it help?"

"I'm not sure, but I'm glad that it wasn't a trick. We may have lunch tomorrow. She's going to call in the morning. She did hint she felt badly about not telling you something."

"Hmm, and she's going to lunch with you. I may have to put you on the payroll."

"It's strange, but I feel guilty, like we're manipulating her. Do you ever get the feeling?"

"All the time. But it's part of my job."

"The end justifies the means?"

"I hope so. Taking someone like Ski Mask out of circulation is necessary, and it's never easy."

Dana nodded. "Still . . ."

"By the way, the call from Flip could be important. Jane Remick mentioned that the rapist had a scar on his chin."

"But the mask?"

"Exactly. I think she pulled it off. That's why she's so vital to us. She's the only one who's seen Ski Mask's face. Anyway, one of the suspects we think is a possibility recently got into a fight and needed stitches. We may have a red hot suspect to put in a photo lineup for Jane."

"I can see how fascinating this is. Pieces of a jigsaw puzzle. Did the question about his voice mean anything or were you just trying to put her at ease?"

"Well, since you're almost a partner I guess I can tell you. We had a red hot possibility. For a number of reasons, he looked like our man. Then Flip and I interviewed him and he had a heavy stutter. Beyond control."

"I see. Why didn't you just ask her if he stuttered?"

"You really have to be careful in this business. Without meaning to, you can plant something in the witness's memory."

Kevin and Dana stood in front of the building. He took her hand. Impulsively, he leaned forward and kissed her. Dana put her arms around him and buried her head on his shoulder.

"This is crazy, Kevin," she murmured.

Neither of them noticed a car parked at the curb down the street. The ski mask rapist slid lower behind the steering wheel. He often revisited his victims, especially one as delicious as Jane Remick. Then too, no one before had ever seen him without his mask. He had made his usual threat that if she cooperated with the police he would return and kill her.

Kevin placed his arms on Dana's shoulders. He was stunned to see a tiny tear in her eye.

"What is it, Dana?"

She shook her head. Damn, he thought. I should stay with

her. Get to the bottom of whatever's bothering her, but Flip might have something important.

"I have to get back to the squad. Can I drop you some-place?"

"No. I'll walk. It's only a few minutes, and it's a beautiful day."

She squeezed his hand and abruptly strode away. He watched her for a moment before going to his car and driving off.

The man in the parked car sneered. A cop! But the bitch wasn't. She was even more delicious than Jane Remick. She must be his girlfriend. Ski Mask watched Dana walking up the street, then started the motor and slowly followed her.

Chapter Twenty-seven

"McKay." Kevin answered the phone at his desk.

"Kevin, this is Dana."

Kevin had spent the night at her place and only left her a couple of hours earlier, but he was happy to hear her voice.

"I'm afraid I have some bad news for you," she said. "Jane Remick just called and canceled our lunch date."

"Damn! What did she say?"

"Her boyfriend, Dr. Henry Winter, apparently convinced her not to get involved."

"Did she tell you why?"

"Yes. Kevin, she started crying on the phone. I felt terrible for her. It seems he's married, and prominent in San Francisco. The apartment is in his name. He's afraid it might come out if she gets involved in the case."

Kevin glanced at his watch. "Do you have any more information on him? What kind of doctor is he?"

"A chiropodist. He has an office on Taylor, off Clay."

"Dana, it's a quarter to ten. My partner and I are going to visit Dr. Winter and try to get him to call Jane so that you can still go to lunch. Is that okay with you if we can pull it off?"

"I guess so, although from the way she spoke, it doesn't seem likely. Also, I guess I should mention that Jane said Dr. Winter does something for the mayor. They're friendly."

"Will you stay by your phone?"

"Yes. I'm sketching this morning."

While driving to Dr. Winter's office, Flip said, "So, good citizen Dr. Winter is tight with the mayor. Maybe his honor has bunions." Kevin had filled him in on his conversation with Dana.

"He's a chiropodist. After seeing Jane's apartment, I expected at least a brain surgeon or a lawyer."

"Don't underestimate the power of Uncle Sam's health insurance." Flip parked in a bus stop right next to a sign that said NO STOPPING—BUSES ONLY. They got out under the glare of a bus driver who pointed animatedly at the sign. Flip gave him a friendly wave and smile. The bus driver gave them the finger.

"The world is not becoming a kinder and gentler place, Kevin." The black detective heaved an exaggerated sigh.

"Yeah. Thanks to arrogant government employees like you who flaunt the law in the face of outraged citizens."

"Me? What about you? Yesterday you parked on the sidewalk in front of a whole bunch of tourists."

"That was different. You said you were hungry, and I know how vicious you get when you're not fed. Here it is." He pointed to the entrance to Dr. Winter's office.

The office was crowded with a dozen women, none of whom appeared to be under sixty. They approached a young, gum-chewing receptionist.

Flip produced his identification. "Police officers, miss. We need to see Dr. Winter for a moment."

"Do you have an appointment?" The girl's eyes were dull.

"No. It's a police matter." Flip pocketed the badge.

"The doctor doesn't see anyone without an appointment. Perhaps one of the assistants could see you for a diagnosis."

Flip leaned his big shoulders into the counter window. The dullness left the receptionist's eyes. She backed away, watchful.

"Now, let's try again, sweetheart." He handed her his and Kevin's business cards. "You can get off your beautiful posterior and give these cards to the doctor and tell him we want to chat with him for a minute. And don't be too long or I'll be unhappy. Do you understand?" He looked at her bug-eyed.

She arose with a sullen look and slouched away. Kevin and Flip took seats next to a lady with purple hair who had listened in fascination.

"Such young men to have foot trouble," she said. "Is it from walking a beat?"

Flip gave her a friendly smile and nodded. "But how does a pretty young lady like you come to be here?"

"Young lady, go on." She smiled. "I could be your grandmother, except for the color, of course."

"I have it on good authority that my grandmother was white. Not as pretty as you, unfortunately."

She giggled. "He's a charmer," she said to Kevin, then turned toward Flip. "I've been coming to Dr. Winter for twenty years. I'm one of the few patients he still sees personally. My girlfriend," she gestured toward the woman sitting next to her, "only gets to see one of the assistants."

"There's nothing like loyalty," Flip said. "You must have bad feet to come for twenty years."

"She has a corn. All he does is trim it for her once a week," the other woman said.

"Can't he take the corn out?" Flip asked.

"Would you, if the government paid you forty-five dollars just to sweet-talk Gertrude for ten minutes a week? Me, I've got a weak arch. I see one of the young doctors only a couple of years out of school. Winter doesn't keep up like Dr. Evans."

"And how long have you been coming, darling?" Flip asked.

"Almost as long as Gertrude, but Dr. Evans knows I really need to see him every week."

"Of course," Gertrude said. "How else is he going to put his son and daughter through Stanford?"

Two patients left and two other women went inside the doctor's chambers. Almost immediately the front door opened and two more women entered. The detectives began to calculate Dr. Winter's income from the assembly line operation. They could hear the receptionist answer the busy phone. She made two appointments after telling the callers that the first available appointments were in two weeks. The next call was from Dr. Winter's stockbroker. The doctor took the call.

"A very wealthy man." Gertrude smiled.

Five minutes later the receptionist buzzed the doctor and told him his real estate broker was on the line.

"He owns half of San Francisco," the woman next to Gertrude explained.

"How many assistants does Dr. Winter have?" Flip asked.

"The first few years, none. Then he got so many new patients," she gazed at her friend, "he took on an assistant. He keeps three, more or less, but he turns them over every three years. Too shrewd to keep them on long enough to have to make them partners."

"Mr. Gates from the mayor's office," the receptionist said into the phone, after buzzing the doctor.

Flip and Kevin exchanged glances.

"Henry, Dr. Winter," Gertrude said, with undisguised pride, "knows everybody. He's a big shot in politics."

Flip continued to pump the ladies about the doctor's practice. About five minutes later Kevin's beeper sounded. He glanced down at the number paging him. "It's the boss," he whispered to Flip.

"Who is your boss?" Gertrude asked.

"The Chief of Detectives," Flip said. "Luckily, my partner and I are personal friends with him."

"That's nice," Gertrude's friend answered. "My son Eddie is an attorney. In Los Angeles, one of the top firms."

"Of course, he's older than my Bobby," Gertrude said. "Bobby finished his internship at Johns Hopkins, going to specialize in radiology, you know, cancer," she informed them.

"I'm sure he'll do well," Flip said.

Kevin decided not to call from the receptionist's desk with the two ladies hanging on every word. He found a public phone on the corner. He waved away a Vietnam vet with a sign, holding out a hat full of singles. His call was answered on the first ring.

"Garza."

"Kevin McKay, Lieutenant."

"Yeah. Listen, McKay, I just got a call from George, Ferrante's administrative captain. Someone from the mayor's office called with a beef that you guys are harassing a Dr. Winter. What's going on?"

Kevin laughed. "That's hot shit. We're sitting in the doctor's office right now cooling it while he's calling City Hall. He told Jane Remick not to cooperate with us. We need her to do a photo lineup."

"Yeah. I remember. The uniform cop, what's her name, Terry Fisher, mentioned that the victim may have seen Ski Mask's face. What's the doctor's problem?"

"Jane Remick is his squeeze. He doesn't want any publicity."

"Okay, Kevin, you guys know what's up on this end. Officially, you didn't hear my page. You were in a high rise or something."

"Right."

Kevin motioned Flip into the hallway and related his conversation with Lieutenant Garza. "Flip, I'm going to rattle Winter's cage. I'm in so much shit it doesn't matter. Why don't you go to lunch or something?"

"Ha, and give you a chance to drop a memo on me to the chief? No way. Come on, let's have some fun."

They returned to the receptionist, who was on a fresh wad of gum. Her eyes reluctantly left the *Hollywood* magazine on her desk to focus on Flip filling the narrow reception window.

Flip bellowed at the top of his voice, "I want to know why the doctor is keeping me waiting!"

The girl's eyes widened. The room grew still and all the patients sat stiffly in their seats watching Flip. Except Gertrude, and her companion. Flip was their friend. They tried to reassure their fellow patients with smiles.

The receptionist sat mesmerized. Flip continued at the same volume. "It's because I'm black, isn't it?"

The patient nearest the door stood and edged out. Three other women gained courage and followed.

Kevin began to wonder what Flip would do next. The receptionist seemed pinned to her chair.

"I'm not going to stand for it, hear?" he bellowed.

The remaining women rushed toward the door. Only their buddies, Gertrude and her friend, stayed, and their faces reflected concern.

An inner door opened and a man in a white coat surveyed the almost empty waiting room. Bald and pale, mid-sixties, he wore thick eyeglasses. He was thin and appeared positively anemic. He looked up to meet the detectives' eyes.

"I'm Dr. Winter. What can I do for you gentlemen?" He spoke with quiet confidence.

"Do for us?" Flip's voice edged even higher. "Do for us? We've been waiting here for thirty minutes to talk to you about a police matter." He pulled out his notebook and continued just as loud. "Do you know a Miss—"

Dr. Winter's confidence was gone. "Please." He held up his hand. "Come into my office."

They sat in his office. On the wall behind him was his framed diploma from some school of chiropody in New York that Kevin had never heard of. Next to it was his license to practice in California. Both frames were ornate.

Flip glared at the doctor, but behind his desk, away from the waiting room, Winter's confidence was coming back.

"I think you should talk to my attorney."

"Look, Winter, you can talk to anyone the fuck you want, but I'm talking to you. What's this bullshit about you telling your squeeze, Jane Remick, not to cooperate in my investigation?"

Winter again moved his hand in an effort to get Flip to lower his voice. "I can assure you, I never—"

Flip rose and put his hands flat down on the doctor's desk.

He leaned forward, and Winter pushed his expensive leather chair as far back as it would go. Flip lowered his voice, this time to a dramatic whisper. "This is my case, Winter, and I don't give a fuck who you know. You get on the phone and tell Jane Remick that she better cooperate starting now, or I'm going to slap the cuffs on you." He reached to his belt and dangled a pair of handcuffs in front of Winter. "I'll drag you through the waiting room. The charge is felony obstruction of justice, and I'll make sure the *Chronicle* has a photographer there when I take you handcuffed into the Hall of Justice. Now get on the phone. I'm tired of waiting."

"Are you saying you won't even let me call my lawyer?" Winter's voice shook.

Kevin put his arm on Flip's shoulder. "Cool down a minute, buddy. Go take a leak or something. Let me talk to Dr. Winter."

Flip turned his glare at Kevin. "Five minutes. I'd like nothing better than to drag this little rich prick out of here. And I'm going to take all his fucking records with me. We'll see how the feds feel about him cutting toenails every week for forty-five bucks a throw and charging the government for foot surgery. Those old broads told us what a rip-off he's got going. Doesn't even see most of them, the motherfucker." With a last look at Winter, he stormed out of the room.

The doctor turned to Kevin. "It's legal. It's got nothing to do with who pays the insurance."

"I'm sure it is, Doctor. My partner's been under a lot of stress lately."

"I have a good lawyer. He can't do that, I mean arrest me and take my records. I'll have him fired."

Kevin shrugged. "The department has been trying to fire him for some time." Kevin put his index finger to his head and made a circle. "You know, disability."

"My God. And they allow him to carry a gun?"

"A Glock. It's nerve-wracking, but what can they do? You know, civil service, affirmative action and all. Look, Doctor, I think I can get him out of here at no cost to you. I can understand that a man in your position might not want any publicity.

I can promise you that your name won't surface if Jane Remick cooperates with us. I'll see to it that it will never come out."

Winter stroked his chin. "And you and your partner will leave?"

"Right."

Winter smiled. "Okay. It's a deal." He stood and extended his hand to Kevin.

Kevin sat and smiled at him.

"I agreed it was a deal." The doctor frowned.

"I know how busy you are, Doctor. We need that call to Jane now. I'll just sit here while you talk to her. You know, in case there are any questions."

Winter swiveled in his seat, anger evident in his face. He dialed a number.

"Hello, darling." A nauseating sweetness replaced the anger in the doctor's manner. "I've been thinking it over. The best thing would be for you to fully cooperate with the police." He paused for a moment, listening. "Yes, tell them. I'm sure they will keep it confidential." He raised his eyebrows at Kevin, who nodded.

"Your lunch, today?" Again the doctor looked at Kevin, who nodded affirmatively. "Yes, go ahead. Have lunch, I'm sure it will be fine." He hung up. "Well? Will you leave now so I can get back to my practice?"

Kevin stood. "Oh, one more thing, Doctor. I hope you won't make any more calls after I leave. If my partner gets the feeling that you double-crossed him, he'll be back. And I won't be with him."

"No?" Winter couldn't resist curiosity.

"He's getting wilder and wilder, and I don't want to be around when he goes over the edge. I don't need that kind of trouble. Have a good day, and thanks for your help."

"Did he give you a free foot job? You were in there long enough." Flip pulled the unmarked cruiser into the headquarters parking lot.

"No. I wouldn't leave until I heard him call Jane Remick and tell her to cooperate."

"He's slick, though. How do we know he's not calling her right now?"

"I told him a certain demented policeman would return without my calming presence if he double-crossed us."

"You getting to be the best little Mutt I worked with."

"Jeff. Mutt was the short one."

"That what I said, Mutt." Flip, laying on the street accent, stretched himself and looked down at Kevin.

Chapter Twenty-eight

"What? I don't understand." Dana had answered Kevin's call on the second ring.

"Jane will go to lunch with you."

"Are you sure? She was adamant about not going."

"I was there when Dr. Winter called her. She'll go."

"I can't wait to hear how you did it. Did you beat him up?"

"Just verbally. Dana, use your instincts on how far you can go with Jane Remick, but we're anxious for her sake as well."

"Really?"

"Yes. Think about it for a minute. Ski Mask has struck thirty-nine times we know of, and there are usually two for every one reported. He's fanatical about keeping his face covered. If he knows she saw him, she's in real danger."

"God. I never thought of that. I'm going to encourage her to move."

"That might help, but her only real safety is if we lock him up for life."

"She wanted to talk yesterday. If she still does, what exactly are you asking her to do?"

"It's simple and easy. Sometime during lunch find out if she can identify him. If she says yes, call me as soon as possible, and Flip and I will bring a photo album to her place. A dozen or so pictures. She won't even have to come to headquarters. We're going out to interview a suspect now, but you can leave a message. If Jane is willing, we don't want her to have time to change her mind. We'll come out this evening."

"I'll try."

"Great. Talk to you later."

Ski Mask was patient. He considered that his great strength. He was again parked across from Jane Remick's building. If she didn't come out, he'd decided to go in when the security man went to lunch. Jane Remick would pay for her arrogance, he vowed to himself, and for her carelessness in leaving keys around. While she was handcuffed and helpless in the bedroom, he'd discovered a junk box on the bottom of her closet, and a number of keys strewn among the screws and washers. He'd experimented and now had a key to the entrance door and one to her apartment. The important one was to the building door. She would probably have the chain lock on, but he was prepared to use a different technique to gain entry this time. That was his genius: he was flexible.

He'd first seen Jane Remick when he had taken his wife and her foolish old mother to have her feet fixed. She'd spent a lot of time inside with the doctor. When she left the office, he'd followed. She'd walked fast and looked in store windows. At first he had been afraid she would notice his old car in the window reflections, but when he'd seen how absorbed she was in her own image and the crap on display, he'd grown bold with excitement, actually parking behind her once instead of creeping along in traffic.

He'd seen her go into the expensive high rise. A fat old white man in a uniform smiled and buzzed her through the door. He had wondered about a back entrance. Then the security man looked at his watch and got up; a smoker, he guessed. His heart had begun to beat faster. Sure enough, the old man left.

He'd gone to the outer lobby and looked at the directory.

J. Remick, apartment 68. He'd been about to return to his car when he'd noticed the light above one of the elevators. It was coming down. Out of the corner of his eye he'd seen an elderly lady with glasses emerge. He'd pretended to be ringing the bell to one of the apartments.

When the old woman opened the front door, he'd said loudly, "Thank you, I'll be right up." He moved smoothly and held the door open for the woman. "Good morning." He'd gotten out as she peered at him. He'd strode confidently into the lobby and pressed the up button, noticing in the reflection from the shiny elevator door that the old woman had continued on her way. On the sixth floor he'd found apartment 68 and pressed the bell. Chimes sounded within the apartment. This had been the tricky part. Usually he cased his love affairs, but he could also take advantage of an opportunity.

"Yes, who is it?" Jane Remick said through the door.

Ski Mask heard his own voice, smooth, powerful, and in control. "Flowers from Dr. Winter, Miss Remick."

Hearing her fumble with the inside locks, he'd pulled the ski mask over his face. Jane Remick opened the door with a wide smile, which vanished when she saw the mask. She gasped.

He'd laughed, and swung the gun up into her face.

She screamed, and he pushed her roughly inside, slamming the door shut. He remembered how she had pulled his mask off and fought. When he'd finally pinned her down and slugged her, she'd gone limp.

But this time would be easier, he thought. Now she knew there was no escape from him.

In his car he frowned at a person briskly approaching the building. It was the woman. The conceited-looking bitch who had been with the cop. Was she going to Jane Remick's apartment? Where else? Two of them at once. He had often dreamed of this. He began to fantasize. He would force them to have sex with each other while he watched. Then force them to fight over him. They would understand that the one who pleased him most would live. The other would die. Of course, they would both die, but he would not let them know that for a long time.

Frank Sealy, a retired San Francisco cop who worked thirty hours a week to supplement his pension and social security check, looked again at his watch. Damn. It was ten after twelve. Since the rape, security had been tightened. Sealy had to wait for Bobby Smith, the maintenance man, to relieve him at the front desk. It used to be a good job, Sealy thought. He'd been allowed to roam around. Now he was stuck. The Giants were playing the Mets in New York. Because of the three-hour time difference, he would catch the game on television in the employees' lounge. He knew that's where Bobby was—watching the game, the SOB.

Frank walked out onto the sidewalk. He didn't see any tenants coming. He stepped inside and closed the entrance door so that it would open only with a key. He'd go back to the employees' room and kick Bobby's ass out to the front desk.

Ski Mask watched with interest. The moment he saw the uniformed man leave his post, he got out and locked the car. He walked to the entrance and glanced in. Nobody. He slipped the key in the lock. It didn't turn. He pulled it out and tried the other key. It clearly didn't fit. He ran his finger along the ridges of the first key. They were rough. It was an extra key that hadn't been used.

"Come on, Bobby, damn it. You should have been out to relieve me fifteen minutes ago." Sealy watched the television screen while he spoke.

"Hold on, man. It's two out and two men on. I want to watch Barry Bonds. There's two men on."

"Yeah, and if one of the residents comes in and no one is on the desk after what happened to Miss Remick last week?"

"Okay, okay, Frank. I'm going." Bobby hung in the doorway.

Ski Mask rubbed the rough edges of the key with his thumb. He slipped it into the lock. Once again it refused to turn. He wiggled it back and forth. Finally! On the third try it clicked into place and the lock turned. He went to the elevators and hit the up button. He looked down the hallway where the security guard had vanished. In the distance he heard the baseball game on television and could see a man in a work uniform standing in the hall looking into the room.

An elevator door opened. He stepped in and pressed six, Jane Remick's floor. The door closed, cutting off the roar of the baseball crowd coming from the television set.

Walking to the front desk, Bobby Smith smiled. Barry Bonds was superman. The home run he just hit must have been 440 feet. The Giants were going all the way this year. Coming even with the elevator, Bobby heard the cables. He glanced at the indicator and saw that one car was in the lobby and the other was rising. Someone on one of the floors must have pressed a button to come down. The light stopped on six. He continued to the front desk. It was too bad that he and Frank couldn't watch the game together, but the boss had threatened to fire them if he found the front desk unmanned. Damn criminals, he thought. They ought to gas all of them.

He sat at the desk, picked up the newspaper and turned to the sports section. After a look at the headlines, he put the paper down. He would wait for the tenant coming down to leave so that they wouldn't see him reading the paper. He frowned. The elevator hadn't moved, it was still on six. It didn't figure. Unless . . . no, Frank had only been away from the front desk for a minute. Not long enough for anyone to have come in and gotten on the elevator. More likely someone on six had hit the button then remembered they had forgotten something and gone back to their apartment. The car would probably come down as soon as they got back in the elevator.

But it didn't.

Six was Miss Remick's floor, Bobby realized. He and Frank would be in big trouble if anyone had gone up to see her unannounced. He walked back to the employees' lounge.

Ski Mask stood still on the sixth floor. It was quiet. He walked the floor, pausing at the door of 68. He pressed his ear to the crack. A smile crossed his face. He heard soft voices inside. Two beauties waiting for him. He reached for the door key but paused when he heard a siren in the street. The siren stopped. Probably nothing, an ambulance or fire truck, a heart attack a block away, but he walked to the end of the corridor to look out the window onto the street.

"Bobby. First you're late. Now you're back here again." Frank was pissed.

"I didn't come to watch the game, Frank," Bobby said, staring at the TV screen. "Something funny happened, is all."

"I'll bet." Frank watched the new Met pitcher warming up. He wouldn't do any better than the others. The Giants were hot. "You better go back to the desk, Bobby. I'll let you know if they score again."

"No. I'm not kidding, Frank. When I went out a minute ago, one of the elevators was going up. Did anyone get on just when you was coming down here?"

"No. It's been real slow. Only one lady a few minutes ago to see Miss Remick. It's probably one of the tenants coming down."

"That's what I figured, but the car is still sitting on the sixth floor."

Six. Damn! That was Remick's floor. Frank got up and put on his uniform jacket. "All right, I'll go up and have a look. But you're not staying in here to watch the game while I'm gone."

"Frank," Bobby protested, "it wasn't that at all. It's just funny. The elevator stopping like that, like someone was going up while you and I were changing."

Ski Mask checked the street and found that he was right. The siren had been an ambulance, double-parked on the corner now with its emergency lights flashing. Going back to apartment 68, he took the key and fitted it into the door. This time the lock turned smoothly and he quietly opened the door a crack until he saw that the chain was engaged. He braced the door open with his foot, listening to the conversation to make sure neither woman had noticed the door being opened. With his right hand he adjusted the ski mask over his face. He used his other hand to reach into his pants for the small but powerful chain cutter. He would snap the chain and burst in, gun drawn and covering them before they knew what happened.

He grew still, straining to hear. The elevator was in motion. Silently, he closed the apartment door and watched the elevator. It had stopped on this floor. The doors started to open. Ski Mask spun the other way and walked quickly toward the fire exit stairwell. He was a few feet from the exit.

"Hey, mister, just a minute." Frank Sealy's voice was gruff. "Stop right where you are."

Ski Mask moved into the stairwell. Without hesitation he took the stairs up two at a time. He crouched at the top of the landing out of sight and watched as the sixth floor fire door opened slowly.

Son of a bitch, Sealy thought. He was puffing from his run down the hallway. He hadn't given much credence to Bobby's report, but felt he had to make a show of responding. Now he knew who he was chasing—Ski Mask. He'd read of the series rapes.

His job was to be an unarmed watchman, but he'd been a cop for twenty-seven years. Management didn't know. In fact, not even Bobby knew that he carried a .38 caliber Chief's Special in his pocket. It was only a snub-nosed five-rounder, but it fit nicely in his pocket and was accurate enough in this kind of a situation.

Frank knew he could call 911 from Jane Remick's apartment, but this guy was right in his hands. And he had his gun to hold him. He had confidence in the gun. He wouldn't hesitate to use it if he had to. He saw himself giving the television interview. Modest, of course, but he could imagine the fuss when he stopped after work for a couple of beers at Morty's Tavern and the guys there, and some in the P.D. who remembered him, realized that Frank Sealy had collared Ski Mask. He imagined Molly's pride when he got home, and the reaction of their son, Frank Junior, when Molly called him in New York. He eased the gun from his pocket and slowly opened the fire door. Then he jumped through the door, swinging his weapon around in a circle.

Unaware of the drama in the stairwell, Dana and Jane left

the apartment and went to the elevator. The car rested where Frank Sealy had left it. They got on. Jane pressed the button for the lobby.

At the front reception desk, Bobby was sweating. Frank had only been gone a couple of minutes, but he was wondering if he should call 911. Now two elevators were on the sixth floor, but one of them was beginning its descent. He sighed with relief. Frank was coming down.

Bobby was confused when he saw Dana Rogers and Jane Remick emerge from the elevator. He started to ask Miss Remick if she'd seen Frank, then thought he shouldn't alarm her after what had happened to her last week.

"Hello, Bobby," Jane Remick said.

"Miss Remick," he replied with a shy smile.

The women left, and Bobby stared again at the elevator indicators.

On the seventh-floor fire stairwell landing, Ski Mask moved back out of Frank Sealy's sight. The fat old man had a gun. It didn't scare him, but he had to plan around it. It wasn't good strategy to allow someone with a gun to be behind you leaving a building. He would kill the man and take his gun. At the moment, Ski Mask had only the starter's pistol that looked like a .45 semiautomatic. He would leave with a real gun. He listened and realized that the old man was slowly going down the stairs. That wouldn't do. Ski Mask rapped his metal cutting shears against the metal door. He took a construction knife from its sheaf and ran his finger carefully along the sharp blade. He eased into the hallway and waited.

Frank heard the noise. So, Mr. Mask. You're up there, are you? he said to himself. Trying to slink away. Frank Sealy knew he was taking the stairs a little too fast, but this guy wasn't going to get away from him. And, if Ski Mask didn't stop next time he yelled, he'd get a bullet in the ass.

Frank eased the door open onto the seventh floor and repeated his maneuver of swinging around, gun extended. It was just what Ski Mask had anticipated. He grabbed the gun with his left hand and plunged the knife into Sealy's throat. Sealy's eyes bulged. He dropped the gun and staggered backward.

With both hands he pulled the knife from his throat. Ski Mask jumped away from the spurting blood and smiled as he saw life fade from the man's eyes.

In the lobby, Bobby tried to decide whether to call the police or the manager. Finally he dialed the manager, whose office was a mile away. "Mr. Phillips is out," the girl said. "May I help?"

Bobby hung up without answering. He called 911. The phone was answered on the fifth ring, but it seemed like half an hour to Bobby.

"Police emergency."

"The security man went to check something and he hasn't come back."

"Do you have an emergency to report?" the call taker said.

"I don't know. It's the poor guy's lunch hour. But he went to the sixth floor and didn't come back."

The woman's voice was a trifle annoyed. "Sir, this is an emergency line. Is this an emergency?"

"I think something must have happened to him."

"What do you think happened, sir?" This time the sir was extended and the sarcasm wasn't lost on Bobby.

"Look, I'm going up to look, but if I don't call back, you better send someone."

He hung up. Bobby looked at the stairwell. After a moment of indecision, he took the elevator in the lobby to the sixth floor.

The dispatcher shook her head. "You won't believe this one," she said to her friend in the next station. "Guy called because his buddy is late coming back from lunch."

Her friend smiled. "Send the Tactical Unit."

Ski Mask liked the feel of the security man's gun. If anyone tried to stop him from leaving the lobby, he would shoot them. But the lobby was empty when he emerged from the stairwell.

Bobby was just getting off the elevator on the sixth floor.

Ski Mask took his handkerchief and opened the front door.

On the sidewalk he took a deep breath of crisp air and walked slowly to his car parked across the street.

Chapter Twenty-nine

Flip handed Kevin the brief emergency-room description of Richard Jackson's injury—an incised wound an eighth-inch deep, cleanly cut, lower mandible (jaw). The report concluded that the wound was likely to heal with minimal scarring, since the edges had been sutured with twenty-four stitches.

"The doctor was a wordy SOB, wasn't he?" Kevin said.

"If you scwed as much flesh as he does in a day, you'd be the same way," Flip said. "Come on, I'll drive."

Richard Jackson lived in a welfare trap on Folsom Street just a few blocks from a gentrified area with expensive town houses boasting sparkling views of the bay. The earthquake had made developers rich by so damaging the Embarcadero Freeway that it had to come down. Rumor had it that some politicians and other insiders had also done quite well by having advance knowledge of the zoning changes that would allow condominiums to sell for high prices.

The detectives, however, parked in front of a faded wooden structure untouched by urban progress. They walked to the third floor trying hard not to inhale the odor coming from the overabundance of unwashed bodies.

"They live better in the joint." Flip wrinkled his nose and knocked on the door of Jackson's third-floor room.

"Yeah?" came the answer.

"Police officers, Jackson. Open up. We want to talk to you for a few minutes." Flip's voice was calm enough, but at the same time conveyed the idea that opening the door wasn't optional.

Jackson's small, threadbare room smelled of dirty socks and cigarette butts. An eleven-inch black-and-white television set flickered through a game show. The room was dim. Jackson walked away from the detectives before either one of them got a good look at his jaw.

"You must be working nights," Flip deadpanned. He nodded at the TV. "I'm glad we didn't wake you up."

"My parole agent didn't get me a job yet." Jackson was sullen but wary. He stood in the dark part of the room.

"Don't be so antisocial, Richard," Flip said. "Come on over here in the light where we can see each other."

Jackson shuffled forward. Both detectives stared at the distinctive scar running down the left side of his jaw.

Kevin spoke softly. "Richard, you know we come around for routine checks. Nothing to get uptight about. How you been making it?"

"Okay."

"Getting laid much?" Flip said.

"Man, I don't even look at women. I mean, the way I got set up. I never touched them bitches. I was innocent. It was some other guy."

"Yeah, sure, Jackson. Hell of a coincidence, though, the way all seven of those ladies identified the wrong guy."

"Man, that's history. I been out over a year. I'm clean."

"Have you ever been over to California Street, Richard?" Kevin said.

"No. I don't know that street."

Flip grabbed Jackson by the shirt. "Do we look like fucking morons? You lived in this city ten years. You know every one of those streets. And you were over there at 19½ California Street last week, weren't you?"

"Hold on, Flip." Kevin took Flip's hand off Jackson's shirt. "Come on over here. Sit next to me, Richard."

Jackson moved quickly away from Flip. "Man," he implored Kevin, "I was with my mom. She lives in Castro."

"Stop the bullshit, Jackson. We haven't even mentioned

what day or what time of day we're talking about. You know she saw you without your mask. Save all of us a lot of trouble. Give us the scoop." Flip glared at him.

"Mask?" Jackson stood. "Someone's flaking me. I never had no masks." He turned to Kevin, pleading, "You know that. Those jobs they sent me to the joint for. I didn't have no mask."

"You mean those rapes you never did?" Flip said. "The ones where all the ladies mistook you for someone else?"

"Man, you can't do this to me. It ain't right," Jackson screamed at Kevin.

"Assume the position, please, Mr. Jackson." Flip took out his handcuffs.

Jackson leaped past him and was almost to the door when Kevin cut him down with a body block.

"Now, Mr. Jackson, that was not very nice. We will have to tell the judge about your attempt to flee the jurisdiction of the court. Unless, of course, you would like to tell us what happened over at 19½ California, then I think we could forget to mention it. Right, partner?" Flip asked Kevin.

"Right. Now, Richard, you've heard them before, but I'm going to read your rights." Kevin took a card from his pocket. "You have the right to remain silent. You have a right to an attorney . . ."

Jackson said nothing while Kevin continued reading his rights to him. Tears ran down his face.

"Do you want to tell us about it, Richard?" Kevin said softly.

"I never was there. I never had any mask. You shouldn't do this to me!" he screamed.

Kevin and Flip went back to their desks after booking Jackson on suspicion of violating Section 241 of the Penal Code. Both men smiled at each other.

"I don't want to get too optimistic, but if your girlfriend convinces Jane Remick to cooperate in a photo ID, I think we just wrapped up Mr. Ski Mask. He was lying like a rug."

Kevin agreed. "Yeah, he's dirty about something. Then too, he tried to run." He stretched. "But I should have had a message by now from Dana, if Jane Remick was willing to do the lineup."

He dialed Jane Remick's apartment. After ten rings he hung up and called Dana Rogers.

"Hello."

"Dana?" Kevin said. "Is everything okay? I thought you were going to call me after lunch?"

"I was, but something terrible happened. Jane agreed to do your lineup, but when we went to her apartment to call you, there were police all over."

Kevin frowned. "What happened?"

"They told us one of the men who worked there had been killed. Jane was upset so we came here."

"Hold on." Kevin turned to Flip, who was listening. "See what you can find out about a homicide at 19½ California."

"Okay, but ask her if we can do the photo lineup, where they are now, Kevin. Don't take a chance on her changing her mind."

Kevin nodded and spoke into the phone.

"Dana, we'll try to find out what happened at Jane's building. We'll be over to your place in about half an hour, if it's okay with you. We can do the lineup there. It shouldn't take more than a few minutes."

"It's fine with me. We'll be here."

When Flip didn't come back from Homicide immediately, Kevin went through the mug file and picked out ten pictures for the photo lineup. Two were men over six feet, weighing more than two hundred pounds. None of the victims had described their attacker as being even close to that size. In addition, Kevin put the photos of two police officers who roughly fitted the descriptions and had volunteered to let their pictures be used. It was a routine procedure to test the victim. Four out of the ten photos were easily eliminated, and if the victim picked one of them, her credibility was nil. Kevin threw in the photos of Jackson and the three other top suspects they had focused on after eliminating Raul Santiago. He needed two more to make up ten. He took the top two on the stack. One was of

Santiago. Shrugging, he included it even though they knew Santiago was out of it.

"Did you know a retired cop named Frank Sealy?" Flip asked when he returned.

"No." Kevin shook his head.

"Seemed he was part-time security at 19½ California. Was on his day off when Jane was attacked. But today someone stabbed him."

Kevin frowned. "What was it about?"

"A whodunit right now."

"What floor?"

"Great minds run in the same channel. I asked that myself. It wasn't Jane's. One up, in the stairwell."

"When the Homicide guys canvassed the building, didn't anyone mention that we had a ski mask attack there last week?" Kevin asked.

"Yup."

"They knew and didn't notify us?"

Flip nodded.

"How come?"

"Well, unofficially one of the dicks kind of led me to believe that the Homicide commander said something to the effect that he would tell Garza, but under no condition was anyone to talk to an inspector by the name of McKay."

Kevin stared at Flip.

"Come on, Kev." Flip touched him on the shoulder. "Let's do the lineup before something else weird happens around here."

Kevin didn't say a word on the way to Dana's apartment. Homicide dicks had withheld information that could have been important just because he was on the department shit list. They would probably have been happy to pass information on to Sherry if drugs had been involved, he thought.

Dana opened the door, and the men said hello to her and Jane. Flip looked around the spacious apartment, which took up half a floor. San Francisco Bay stretched before them from the Golden Gate Bridge to Alcatraz and the Embarcadero.

"Beautiful." Flip whistled and looked at Dana, who colored slightly and gave a small smile.

"Jane, this is simple and straightforward," Kevin said. "We have pictures of ten men for you to look at. We want you to see if you can identify the man who attacked you. Some of the men look like each other, but you must only pick one, and only if you're sure. Take all the time you need. Go through all the pictures before you decide, and remember, it's important that you be sure before you pick one. Dana, you can stay if you like, but you must not say anything. This is a legal procedure, and there are rules that we have to follow." He placed the photo album on the coffee table, and he and Flip sat opposite Jane Remick.

She took a deep breath and looked at Dana with a small smile. Dana smiled back. Jane turned to the first photo and studied it for a moment. She turned the page and looked at the second picture. Looking up, she shook her head from side to side. She turned the page and looked at the third picture closely. "This is him!"

Kevin shook his head. "Jane, we asked that you look at all of the photos."

"I don't have to. This is the one."

Kevin and Flip stood and looked over her shoulder to see which mug shot she'd identified. It was a picture of Raul Santiago.

For just a moment Kevin's shoulders drooped and an expression of disgust crossed Flip's face. Dana couldn't see the photo. She wondered why the men had reacted that way. Jane, still looking down at the picture, hadn't noticed.

Kevin sat down. "Jane, just for the record, would you please go through the rest of them?"

She shrugged and turned the pages, studying each photo. She didn't hurry, but didn't pause either. Flip and Kevin watched closely when she came to the ninth photo, which was of Richard Jackson. Jane turned the page without hesitation and looked at the last photo.

"I looked at them all just to humor you." She smiled. "But I was sure as soon as I saw him. I'll never forget his face."

"Jane," Kevin said slowly, "I know we've been over this before, but was there anything besides that scar that was unusual about him?"

She leaned back and concentrated. "Unusual? No. I can't say there was."

"Did he talk to you much?" Flip asked.

"God, yes. He was there for hours. I'll never forget the cruelty in his voice."

"Did he have an accent or anything?" Flip asked.

"No. Not really." Jane looked at the two detectives. "Is there something wrong? You will arrest him, won't you?" She looked worried.

Kevin stood and smiled. "Jane, you've been terrific."

"We really appreciate it," Flip added. "We know this hasn't been easy for you."

Jane frowned. "I don't understand. Why didn't you answer my question about arresting him?"

Kevin said, "That decision will be up to the District Attorney. We'll meet with him first thing tomorrow, and we'll let you know."

Dana had a puzzled look on her face, and Kevin turned away from her inquiring glance.

Driving back to headquarters, Flip said, "Goddamn. Back to square one. You can be the one to tell Jane Remick that the D.A. won't touch Santiago with that stutter of his."

Kevin slumped back in his seat.

"Your girlfriend's place, fabulous." Flip turned from the steering wheel and started to ask if artists made that kind of a living. When he saw the expression on Kevin's face he stayed quiet. Great minds run in the same channel. Nuff said, he thought.

Chapter Thirty

Joey Demanto sat next to his phone holding an ice bag to his groin. He'd dialed Chief of Detectives Vincent Ferrante's beeper number, as he'd been directed to do when he had something to report. Well, he had something to report, all right. He shifted the ice bag to a new position. He'd told Ferrante that staking out a school was a dumb idea, and then that lousy policewoman—

He picked up the phone on the first ring.

"Demanto."

"Joseph, I thought we agreed that you would not contact me from this number." Ferrante's annoyance was evident underneath the smooth, formal politeness he cultivated.

We agreed! You mean you ordered. Well, his balls felt like they were falling off, and he wasn't about to hang around some public phone until the great Chief of Detectives decided to answer his call.

"Yes, sir," Joey said, "but something happened—"

"Twenty minutes in It's Tops Diner. You know where it is? South Market and Van Ness."

The phone clicked and Joey looked at the receiver in his hand, then slammed it down. That son of a bitch. He could hardly walk, and now had to play Russian spy games. And Ferrante was pissed at him for using his own phone after he almost got him Rodney Kinged at Sacred Heart by a couple of uniform goons.

Twenty minutes later Joey sat in a booth nursing a cup of coffee. It's Tops was a fifties-type diner off the beaten track. He'd eaten there a number of times, and the food was great, especially if you were in a mood to bulk up or raise your cholesterol level. Joey loved the old jukeboxes and records, the pictures and memorabilia of a different time. But it wasn't the kind of place where he'd expect Vincent Ferrante to dine.

Joey watched Ferrante get out of his black Lincoln. Bruno Iannello glared in at Joey, then pulled a discreet half block away to park at a fire hydrant. Ferrante casually glanced around before walking into the diner. He wore a form-fitting gray trench coat with the belt tied in a nonchalant knot around his slender waist. Once inside, he unbelted, and Joey saw another expensive Italian suit that hadn't come off the rack. The detective wondered where the clothes came from, knowing Ferrante sure as hell hadn't paid retail for them.

"Yes, sir. Where would you like to sit?" If he hadn't been in such pain, Joey would have smiled. The young, obviously gay waiter had one side of his head shaved and the other dyed in a vibrant chartreuse. He wore dangling gold earrings. His blatant come-on had strained Ferrante's cultivated style of old world impassiveness. He brushed past the waiter without a word and slipped into the booth opposite Joey.

"Well, my young friend, what is it you have to report that caused you to forget security?"

"Chief, I'm hurting. I told you sitting on a school wouldn't work. A couple of patrol cops almost killed me."

"You look remarkably alive. Tell me what happened and what you observed about Robbins."

"The kids love Robbins and he seems to enjoy what he's doing. I couldn't see anything suspicious. But this old nun must have reported me. A radio car came by. Before I could show the ID you gave me, this young bitch of a policewoman just about kicked my balls over my shoulder. I can hardly walk. That's why I called from home."

"How long did you observe before your little run-in with the law?" Ferrante asked.

"I watched Robbins for about an hour. And it wasn't a little run-in."

"So?"

"I moved from my car after the nun started staring at me. I was just sitting on a bench when the cop braced me."

"Cop? I thought you said there were two?"

"There were. Thank God the old-timer just sat in the car."

"You mean one little policewoman caused you all this misery. You couldn't protect yourself?"

"Chief, she never gave me a chance. She told me to get up and I did. Then she looked at the *Chronicle* I had. Unfortunately, it was a week old. I reached for the ID you gave me. Wham! Before I knew what happened I was on the ground holding my balls. And you know what she said to me? If she saw me around again she'd flake me on a child molesting charge and register me as a sex offender. And she looked down at my balls and said she'd make sure I never fucked anyone again. Those were her exact words. I'd never fuck anyone again."

Ferrante swallowed his slight smile after seeing Joey's reaction to it.

"Chief, I'm not kidding. The department ought to do something about brutality. I didn't resist at all."

"You might have been more careful about using a week-old newspaper. And you haven't been on the street for a while. The uniform cops are understandably a little uptight when people they're questioning reach into their pockets."

"Goddamn, Chief, I just smiled at her. She didn't even take her baton out of its holder. There was no warning. I would have put my hands in the air."

Joey had raised his voice. Ferrante soothed him. "I'll speak to the chief of patrol. Did you get her name?"

"Her name tag said Fisher. She's young, dark-haired, in her twenties. I can pick her out of a photo lineup."

"That won't be necessary. I'll take care of it. Did you observe anything else? Any other cops around?"

"No. I wasn't there very long."

Ferrante's beeper sounded. He looked down at the phone number. "It's the chief. Excuse me a moment, Joey. I need to call." He nodded toward the public phone in the corner.

The waiter rushed over and poured coffee Joey didn't want. "Your patron is gorgeous. Where does one meet his type?"

"In the police station," Joey said tartly.

The waiter giggled. "How romantic. You were both naughty in public on the same day. What a wonderful coincidence. The times I got busted I was never so lucky. They always put me in with street winos. If you should ever tire of him, I'd love the number."

"I'll be sure to tell him," Joey said, watching Ferrante return.

The waiter flitted away, beaming over his shoulder at Ferrante, who didn't notice. "I'm going to have to leave, Joseph. But I suggest you find another way."

"Thanks, Chief."

Ferrante showed no sign of noticing Joey's sarcasm. He patted him on the shoulder. "Feel better. And remember, no more calls from home. Your number is on record in the department. And this investigation is dynamite, as I told you. If a policeman is involved in molesting children, it will destroy the department's reputation. We won't get any public cooperation. We won't be able to do our job. There's a lot of responsibility riding on your shoulders, but I have confidence that if anyone can get to the bottom of these allegations, you can."

Yeah, and if bullshit was cash, I'd be rich, Joey thought, watching the debonair Chief of Detectives signal for his limousine.

Ferrante regretted that it hadn't gone according to plan. When Glen Sherry had come to him with the story that McKay apparently spent a lot of on-duty time at the school playing basketball, it seemed to have potential. If McKay's own partner investigating a child molestation case did the surveillance and had to report McKay being there on duty, it would have been possible to discredit McKay and dump him back to uniform. Now, with what had happened to Demanto—before he'd observed McKay playing basketball even once, let alone the frequent observations they would need for discipline—he would have to rethink his plan.

* * *

Ferrante walked briskly into his office in the Hall of Justice. At his large desk he pressed a button.

"Yes, sir," his administrative captain answered.

"George, bring me those files of the top six candidates for appointment to inspector. The ones I looked at yesterday."

A moment later Captain George Anthony stood before Ferrante's desk and waited for him to look up from the report he was reading.

"What is this about, George?" Ferrante pointed at the memo on his desk.

"It just came in, Chief. Homicide called. An ex-cop named Frank Sealy was killed this afternoon. He was a security guard in a high-rise. It's just preliminary stuff. Homicide doesn't have anything else yet."

"How surprising. Was the chief's office notified?"

"No sir. As I mentioned, it just came in. Do you want me to send it to them?"

Ferrante looked at the captain until he began to fidget.

"Are you suggesting that we send the police chief a message saying we don't know what the fuck we're doing in BOI?"

George reddened. "No sir. I mean, I thought you wanted—"

"George, I've told you before, I do the thinking. You do what I tell you. Now, give me the folders."

Ferrante flipped through the files until he came to Terry Fisher's. The captain stood waiting for instructions. He knew better than to sit uninvited.

"Bring her in for an interview in a couple of days. I want to appoint her next week."

"Er, Chief," the captain said, "we don't have any openings in any of the sections right now."

"We'll put her in the Sexual Assaults Investigations Unit. They had a big increase in workload."

"Chief, the civil service regulations require interviews for all six of the top candidates before you can make a selection."

"You take care of the red tape. Interview the others if you have to. I want her. We'll be expected to have more women in the bureau, and we might as well get those who are going to do some work. Also, tell Lieutenant Garza to get his useless ass up here. I want to discuss where Terry Fisher will work. Then get on the phone and tell Ralph Benedetti in Homicide that if he wants to continue in command, he better give us information immediately. It doesn't do a damn thing for me to know an ex-cop was killed."

In the outer office, George threw the files on the patrolman's desk. "File those," he said.

"Where, Captain?" the fat patrolman asked.

"Where do we usually put personnel files, Riley? Under homicides? Put them in the personnel files."

God, what a mood the boss is in, George thought. Ferrante was supposed to see his squeeze tonight, and instead of getting a good blow job, he had to do a little police work. Like it was his fault or something. The captain dialed Lieutenant Garza's number.

Chapter Thirty-one

There were monthly training meetings for sex crimes investigators in the Bay Area. Usually Kevin found them dull. The other cops seemed to like the chance to get to San Francisco for the three P.M. sessions, but little valuable information was exchanged during the formal meetings. He had thought about skipping the meeting, but since Flip was off on his own someplace and Terry was busy settling in, Kevin got B&B to drop him at the FBI office on Golden Gate Avenue.

He was pleasantly surprised to find the lecture interesting. Brenda Phillips was an FBI agent who had worked for two years out of the FBI Academy in Quantico, Virginia, in the criminal profile unit. She'd been assigned to the San Francisco office and was today's speaker. Her presentation was on the psychology of recidivist sex criminals.

She was a petite five-four, and wore a dark blue pinstripe suit with a white blouse. Her neat blond hair was bobbed, her minimal makeup emphasizing attractive hazel eyes. A lot of what she said made sense, and he related it to Ski Mask. Twenty-four male and only two female investigators made up the group. There was a bit of macho asshole stuff, but she was cool under some questioning. A couple of times it had been openly sexist. Some of the guys didn't like being lectured by a woman. Kevin was a little surprised that Craig Lewis, who had been introduced as a new agent in the San Francisco FBI office, had led the pack of harassers. Bureau people usually stuck together in public.

At one point Agent Phillips was talking about an M.O. quite similar to that of Ski Mask. She was explaining that this type of rapist was usually compulsive about continuing his attacks but nevertheless adept at avoiding capture.

Craig Lewis interrupted. "Look, Brenda, a lot of us have years of street experience as cops. I did five years as a detective in Cleveland before joining the Bureau, and like these guys here, we know that it takes basic police work and not a lot of theory to bag these assholes."

A couple of cops sitting next to Lewis nodded.

"I don't argue with that," Agent Phillips answered. "But sometimes a good psychological profile can be of help to investigators if you don't have a hot suspect. For example, after studying a large sample of convicted rapists, we found that the majority of them were sexually immature and had a record of not being able to relate to women. Most of them could achieve sexual gratification only by terrifying or hurting their victims. In those situations it's almost as if they become a different personality. That could be useful background stuff to look for if you've got a case fitting that profile."

"Now you're on a subject we find interesting, Brenda. Give us the lowdown on female sexual gratification," Craig Lewis said. There were two or three male chuckles.

Brenda Phillips flushed and turned to the class. She started to speak, but nodded at Kevin when he put up his hand.

"Agent Phillips, I'm working on a series rape case that I'd like your opinion on. Would it be possible to get some advice from you after the class?"

"I'd be happy to talk about it," she said, obviously pleased. "I'm afraid my time is up. If there are any more questions, I'll be around for a while."

It was traditional that most of the class adjourned to nearby Charley's Bar and Grill for a couple of drinks, and in some cases dinner. Kevin sat at a table with Brenda Phillips, comparing the ski mask M.O. to the one she'd described in her lecture.

"Look, honey." Craig Lewis slid into the booth and put his arm around her shoulder. "I was just trying to lighten up your lecture a little. Hope you didn't mind a bit of humor. I didn't embarrass you, did I?" He smiled.

She forced a smile and removed his arm. "Actually, it's always a little embarrassing to see someone in the Bureau make an asshole of himself in public."

"God, if I wasn't happily married with three kids, I'd pursue you to the ends of the earth."

"You've already tried hard enough, Craig." Brenda Phillips looked him in the eye. "And the answer was no! Even before I found out you were married."

"She's tough, isn't she?" Craig stuck his hand out to Kevin. "You're San Francisco P.D. I didn't know you guys were that chivalrous. I mean, the way you came to her rescue just when I had her wiggling up there. By the way," he laughed, "she's very married, so you're wasting your time."

Kevin ignored the hand. "She didn't need any rescuing. I wanted some information. I still do, and you're wasting my time."

"Hmm, an unfriendly local. Okay, you two. I get the message. You want to be alone." Craig winked and went up to the bar.

"I apologize. Supposedly he's a good investigator," Agent Phillips said. "His wife is back in Chicago with the kids until they finish school next month. Some of these guys are what we in the Bureau call transfer bachelors. It lasts until Mama and the kids arrive. You know, it's one of the big advantages you guys have in local law enforcement. They can't ship you all over the country."

"True. On the other hand, you guys have all the dough. And the news media prints your press releases and leaves you alone. With us it's duck hunting. And we're sitting ducks. Then, if we start comparing training, and labs and buy money, and equipment—"

"Enough already." Brenda Phillips shook her head. "All I wanted to say was don't pay attention to Craig Lewis."

Kevin smiled. "No problem. He doesn't bother me. It's just that I hate to see guys act like that. It gives men a bad name."

"By the way, sexy one, how is it that we never go to your place?" Terry Fisher ran her hand through Craig Lewis's thick dark hair. He had come from Charley's Bar and was now spread across her bed fully clothed, claiming exhaustion after a twelve-hour day. She was on top of him and brushed his lips with a light kiss. Smelling alcohol, she probed with her tongue. It wasn't beer. His tongue actively responded and his hands moved under her skirt. She tried to get up but his powerful arms locked around her and his tongue deftly pursued her ear. He thrust upward, and she thought, My God, he gets hard so quick. He was as crazy about her as she was about him. She usually liked to begin slow, but with Craig, she was as impatient as he. Terry fumbled at his zipper and forgot her curiosity about where he'd been drinking and why she had yet to visit his place.

Later, warming up some frozen ravioli, she heard Craig singing in the shower. Actually, his voice wasn't bad. She laughed. He was also talented in bed. He made her feel so complete. So wanted. Like a movie star being pursued by a fanatical fan.

Feeling her nipples harden again and the warmth spreading upward from between her legs, she hummed. People would be shocked to see the upright FBI man sucking her toes and running his tongue up and down her thighs while she gasped in anticipation of how he was about to drive her crazy. She put the ravioli back in the oven and turned the heat low. Dropping her robe on the floor, she joined Craig in the shower, and his singing gave way to other activities.

Finally, at eleven o'clock they had ravioli by candlelight and sipped the Chianti he'd brought with him. She noticed the price label indicating it cost $5.98. So Craig wasn't the biggest spender, but looking across the table at his handsome face, she was content.

"One other thing you'll appreciate my doing today, gorgeous, is putting in a good word for you with one of your bosses. I was at a meeting with Chief of Detectives Ferrante and mentioned your name."

"I wish you hadn't done that, Craig. The department is very funny about outside influence."

"Have no fear, my sweet. He ate it up."

Actually, Craig hadn't gotten within six feet of Vincent Ferrante, who had put in an appearance at the conference and left. But Craig had stayed too long in Charley's. He knew he'd once again stood Terry up for dinner, and thought it wouldn't hurt to tell a white lie. After all, he would have given her a boost if Ferrante had given him a chance.

Men! Terry swore to herself. They had to control everything. She deserved to be appointed based upon her test scores and record. But no. It had to be the good old boy network. On the other hand, Craig was sweet to try. Look what had happened when she joked with Kevin McKay about using him as a reference.

Chapter Thirty-two

Lieutenant Richard Garza sat in the fourth floor office of the Chief of Detectives. Garza ignored the sign on the wall, which read: OLD AGE AND CUNNING WILL WIN OUT EVERY TIME OVER YOUTH AND IDEALISM.

"Richard," Chief of Detectives Vincent Ferrante said softly, "the police chief just burned my ear because the mayor burned his ear. And the reason the mayor got upset was five women's groups crashed his City Hall press conference on the budget crisis and demanded to know why women are being attacked and terrorized by the ski mask rapist. And, of course, the women's groups were thoughtful enough to let the media know in advance that they would disrupt the mayor's speech. Which means, tonight every television station will show the mayor being embarrassed, and tomorrow the *Chronicle* will have a front page story and a picture of a woman grabbing the microphone from His Honor. Which means that tomorrow the Chamber of Commerce will jump on the mayor's ass saying crime is killing business. Tourists stay away. Hotels and restaurants are empty. Then the mayor will call the chief and jump on his ass. Then the chief will call me and—"

"Jump on your ass," Lieutenant Garza finished for him.

"Correct." The Chief of Detectives gave a small, tight smile stolen from *The Godfather*. "Therefore, I would like to know what you suggest I tell the police chief when he calls me."

"Why don't you tell him the women are fucking right." Garza's voice rose. "And so is the Chamber. The mayor reduced the number of cops and froze overtime. What the hell does he expect?"

"I presume you do not wish me to quote you to the chief?" Ferrante said with a sinister lisp taken from *Godfather II.*

Lieutenant Garza shrugged.

"One thing I will tell him is that I assigned a female officer to work on the case," the Chief of Detectives said.

"Another woman? The last one didn't last two months. This affirmative action bullshit may look good to the media, but it doesn't catch rapists."

"Nor do your valiant male detectives, Lieutenant. Do you by chance have any leads that I can tell the chief about?"

Lieutenant Garza sat tight-lipped.

"Do I need to produce my secret clearance so you can tell me?"

"Chief Ferrante, my two best investigators are on the case. I talked to McKay last night. I think we're close, but it would be a disaster if the mayor shoots off his mouth right now."

"I asked what could I tell the Chief of Police, not the mayor," Ferrante said.

"Yeah." Lieutenant Garza scowled.

"While I'm quoting you on the mayor's budget, should I also tell the chief you don't trust him not to reveal to the mayor confidential information about the investigation?"

Lieutenant Garza shifted in his chair.

"Who else is on the case with McKay?" Ferrante asked.

"Inspector O'Neil."

"That's wonderful. You have a black activist who probably scares the shit out of every white woman he interviews. In fact, George tells me we got a call from the mayor's office that he hassled a doctor. What was that all about?"

"The doctor's girlfriend was a ski mask victim. The doctor told her not to cooperate with us."

"Well, it happens that the doctor was cochair of the mayor's election finance committee. Do you know what that means?"

"No. Does it mean that the mayor's money men are allowed to obstruct justice when their squeeze is involved?"

Ferrante put up his hand. "There's nothing wrong with my hearing, Richard. I'm just saying that it's one thing to ruffle feathers if you're solving cases, but Ski Mask is still unidentified. And McKay, who . . . Do you think McKay is stable?"

"He and O'Neil do more work than the rest of the squad combined, including the useless POA delegate you saddled me with."

"You trust McKay?"

"He's a good cop."

"Really? And what about his famous memo accusing Lieutenant Sherry of taking bribes from dope dealers, robbing them of money, and selling dope he steals from them?"

"I don't know about all that. Remember, you flopped McKay from Narcotics to me after the memo. All I'm saying is he cares about victims and makes good cases. The D.A.'s office asks for him on the tough rapes."

"And dropping a memo like that outside the chain of command? Is that the way they trained you in the Marine Corps, Richard?"

Garza stared out the window. A red fireboat steaming toward Pier 39 showed off. Its powerful water cannons sent funnels of white water into the blue sky.

"Let me remind you," the Chief of Detectives continued, "the Sherry memo is far from dead. The State Investigation Commission has it on the agenda for discussion next month. Which means our own illustrious Police Commissioner will also put it on the agenda. It's a time bomb ticking. The department's reputation is at stake, and if you're called to testify about McKay's stability, you'll give him a testimonial as a great cop?"

"All I can say is he does his job."

"Well, Richard, I wish I could say the same for you. But the ski mask case has not been solved, has it? And you have a very angry policewoman saying she was harassed out of your unit. So, let me tell you what is going to happen. A policewoman by the name of Terry Fisher is going to be assigned to your unit, and you are going to assign her to work with McKay and O'Neil on the ski mask case. And, since her predecessor complained that she was driven out of the unit, you will personally debrief her every day to see if she is happy. At the same time you will be able to find out from her how the ski mask investigation is proceeding and just how stable Kevin McKay really is."

"You're putting a rat in my unit?"

"Not at all, Lieutenant. But at six P.M. each day you will call me and report what Inspector Terry Fisher reports to you. Is that clear?"

"Suppose she says McKay is a good cop?"

"You're not to worry about that, Lieutenant. Just run along now." The Chief of Detectives waved his hand. "Make believe you're back in the Marine Corps and obeying orders like you're supposed to."

Two hours later Terry Fisher was ushered into Chief of Detectives Ferrante's office. She'd been notified the day before to appear for an interview regarding an appointment to the Bureau of Investigations. She spent a nervous twenty minutes in the anteroom pretending to read a magazine. Her mental state hadn't been helped any by the obese cop at the reception desk trying to look up the black skirt she'd worn for her interview. The cop wore a shoulder holster which, along with his white shirt and pink tie, called attention to the fat spilling over his waistline. He picked at a typewriter in between unembarrassed glances at her legs.

When Terry was finally ushered into Chief Ferrante's office, she was pleasantly surprised that he rose to greet her and actually moved from behind his ornate desk to shake her hand and wave her to a chair.

He smiled. "Let me be the first to congratulate you, Inspector Fisher." He shook her hand firmly and returned to his chair.

Terry flushed and murmured, "Thank you." She had expected him to make her sweat out an interview. It was nice that he wasn't playing games with her.

"Thank yourself. You excelled on the written test, in the oral exam, and people speak well of your work in the field," he said, suppressing a chuckle to think of how Joey Demanto would have reacted to his characterization of Joey's remarks about her work.

Terry was embarrassed. She glanced at Ferrante's famous wall sign on the dangers of youth and idealism without seeing it. She guessed Craig Lewis had really laid it on Ferrante, but she would never have gotten such a nice plug from someone inside the department.

"Terry . . . I hope you don't mind my calling you by your first name?" Ferrante said, sitting down. "While it's my pleasure to welcome you to the Bureau of Investigations, I also want to warn you that it won't be easy. Unfortunately, we still have some old-fashioned attitudes in the department, and that includes the B of I. Another female officer quit the Sexual Assaults Unit recently, complaining she'd been harassed. I want you to know that I informed the lieutenant in command that I expected him to personally guarantee that it will not happen to you."

Great, she brooded, they're a bunch of pricks, and this pompous ass thinks his giving an order is going to make it easier for me. Well, I suppose at least he means well.

"I want you to understand that you should come to me directly anytime you wish on any matter. Frankly, there are real problems with the unit, and I'm personally relieving you from following the chain of command. This is my direct number here, and this is my beeper number. You can call me twenty-four hours a day." Ferrante scribbled on a piece of paper, came around the desk and handed it to her.

Terry took the phone numbers. She was stunned. She didn't get it. What the hell was going on?

"Do you have any questions, Inspector?" Ferrante asked.

Terry hesitated. It would be perfectly normal to ask for an explanation of Ferrante's mysterious instructions, but she was now an inspector assigned to the Sexual Assaults Unit. She better leave well enough alone.

"No, sir," she said.

Ferrante shook her hand. "Then I suggest you go downstairs and report to Lieutenant Garza."

On the way out, Terry paused in the doorway, realizing she

might appear ungrateful. She turned and saw that Ferrante had been studying her legs. "Chief," she said, "thanks for your support. I appreciate it, and I'll keep your advice in mind."

He smiled broadly as she went out.

Terry paused in the entrance of the squad room. The place was gray. Institutional desks and chairs. A dozen white men sat shuffling papers, talking on telephones, or just shooting the breeze. It wasn't the kind of place featured in magazine stories about pleasant work environments. Conversation slowed as they became aware of her. She took a deep breath as she looked around, finally spotting a door labeled "Commanding Officer." The door was open a crack. Terry knocked.

"Yeah, yeah, come in." The voice wasn't friendly.

"I'm Terry Fisher."

He was scowling and yelling into the phone. "Well, I don't give a fuck. And you can tell him that in spades. The whole goddamn prosecutor's office isn't worth the powder to blow it to hell." He slammed the phone down. "They're all bastards," he said as if she knew who he was denouncing. His frown now found Terry.

Despite Ferrante's warning, Terry was unprepared for Lieutenant Garza's open hostility. "This is a tough unit to work in, Fisher. If you're a good cop, these guys will respect you. If they don't, it's not because you're a woman. They call me Lieutenant Affirmative Action, so don't take it personally if some of them aren't as socially pure in their manners as our Chief of Detectives. The point is, I'm the boss and they do what I say no matter what they say behind my back. And if they don't do the work, I kick ass. Did our great Chief of Detectives give you the form for your new ID card and badge and the information pamphlet on the bureau?"

"No."

"Of course not. The geniuses he surrounds himself with up there are so busy they can't be expected to do what they're supposed to." Garza rummaged in his drawer. He pulled out a form and the pamphlet. "Here. They're self-explanatory. Not that it means anything to the kind of people Ferrante sends me.

I'll have your new badge tomorrow. Look, I didn't pick you and I didn't pick your assignment, but I'm the guy you will dialogue with on a daily basis. You'll work with McKay and O'Neil on the ski mask rapist. We're getting a lot of heat from City Hall, and I have to report every day, which means you will tell me about the day's progress. Do you have any questions?"

Terry felt anger building up. "Yes. I'm a rookie here. I don't know anything about the ski mask investigation. It doesn't make sense that I'm the one who should brief you."

Garza jumped to his feet. His face was red. "Do you see that?" He pointed to his Marine Corps discharge on the wall. "We obeyed orders whether we understood them or not," he yelled.

Terry fought tears of rage. So this is the way it was. She wondered if she had done the right thing applying to be a detective.

Suddenly, Garza's face softened. He sat down and loosened his collar. "Look, I'm sorry I yelled. Sometimes I have a short fuse, but—"

She turned and started out.

"Hold on, Inspector," Garza said, getting up, "I'll introduce you to the squad."

Terry saw the men turn as they came out of the lieutenant's office. She realized they had probably heard Garza yelling at her.

"Gentlemen, I want to introduce our newest colleague." Garza was self-conscious but determined. "This is Terry Fisher. She came out tops on the promotion list and has an excellent record. I know all of you will give her every professional courtesy. She'll be working with McKay and O'Neil on the ski mask case. I'll appreciate any help that you can give her breaking in."

Terry saw Kevin McKay smile and wave at her. She was confused again. McKay didn't seem afraid to show friendliness to her. And Garza wasn't articulate, but he'd tried.

"Lieutenant, can I ask a question?" B&B said. "The section is at full strength. No overtime is being allowed for us. So how come we're getting another investigator if the department is so broke?"

"You and the Association can take your questions to the bureau chief," Garza said, spinning around and heading back to his office.

"Yeah, B&B." Kevin laughed. "What's the matter? You afraid the lady is going to find your restaurants?"

Barney Brady frowned at him and started to answer, but the rest of the squad was already laughing at Kevin's jibe so B&B just smiled. He lumbered from his desk and held out his hand to Terry. "Welcome aboard, Inspector," he said.

Terry knew he was the POA delegate and the organization had fought women every step of the way. She was tempted to ignore his hand but caught an almost imperceptible nod from Kevin.

"Thanks," Terry said, shaking B&B's hand and those of men who came forward. Five of them stayed at their desks and ignored her.

Chapter Thirty-three

Lieutenant Garza had a desk for Terry Fisher put next to Kevin McKay's. Terry thoroughly cleaned it and purchased a new desk pad to cover the scratched gray metal top. She placed a large police department appointment calendar over the pad. She brought a vase from home, and filled it with a bouquet of fresh flowers from the Flower Mart on Fifth Street. They were the only flowers in the dusty room. Next to the vase she put a framed picture of herself and Craig Lewis that had been taken by a street vendor in Ghirardelli Square. Craig hadn't been too enthusiastic at the time, but it was a great picture of them smiling and hugging. Terry had it enlarged and put it in a gold frame.

Kevin McKay came in. "Settling in, Terry?" He smiled, but Terry thought he looked beat.

"Right. Another hour of housekeeping and I'll start putting guys in the slammer."

"Right on." Kevin sat at his desk, then did a double take at the picture on her desk.

"He's great, isn't he?" Terry's smile was wide.

"That's the guy from the FBI, right?" Kevin frowned.

Terry looked at him, puzzled. "Yeah. Craig Lewis. Do you know him?"

"How long have you known him?"

Terry was pissed. What was this? She remembered again how Kevin had refused to be a reference for her.

"That's my business. What do you say we do some police work? Is there anything new on Ski Mask?"

She hadn't kept the anger out of her voice. Kevin looked down at his desk. Goddamn. That dirt-bag, Lewis. Terry was a terrific gal. What would it be like when she found out he had a wife and kids?

"Hello, McKay. Do any more rat memos lately?"

Kevin glanced up at Neil Brennan. Brennan had spoken loudly, and a silence fell over the squad. Kevin looked him in the eye but said nothing. Brennan stood with his hands on his hips. He was bigger and heavier than Kevin. Terry didn't know what this was about, but she sensed that Kevin was thinking of taking on this guy who was bigger than he was. Brennan moved closer to Kevin's desk and drew up some spittle. When he pursed his lips, Kevin got to his feet and moved forward.

"Okay, what's going on?" Lieutenant Garza, with his door partially open, had picked up on the sudden silence in the room.

"Nothing, Lieutenant." Brennan gave a big grin. "We was just having a little discussion on rodent food."

Garza squared his shoulders and strode forward until he was in Brennan's face. "Well, have it in your own squad. What are you doing here, anyway?"

"The captain sent me down to talk to Inspector Tunny. One of the hypes we picked up claims he has some information on a nigger gang-bang in the Dolores Street project, and it's Tunny's case."

Garza got even closer to Brennan, who stood slouched and unconcerned.

"Listen to me, Brennan. If I hear you use another racial slur, I'm putting you on report. Give your information to Tunny and then get the hell out of here. Do you understand me?"

"Hey, Lieutenant, I'm only here because the captain sent me. If you got any problems, talk to him."

Brennan turned and sauntered to the rear of the room, where Inspector Tunny grinned at him.

The lieutenant returned to his office and slammed the door. Kevin McKay stood motionless, his eyes burning into Brennan across the room.

"Kevin?"

Terry sensed he was just waiting for one more nudge from Brennan to charge.

He turned and looked at her absently, and she saw she was right.

"What?" he said.

"Do you think given the information you and Flip developed, we have enough for a search warrant on this guy, Jackson?"

"I don't know." Kevin turned away from Brennan and sat down. "When Flip gets here, we'll ask the boss if he thinks we should get one."

"Gosh, a meeting with Lieutenant Garza. That should be jolly."

Kevin smiled slightly. But he was still tense. "He's not bad when you get to know him."

"So, your name's McQuaid. Or did you say McKay?" B&B made sure the whole room heard him.

A black street person sat in a chair in front of the detective's desk. The homeless man was dressed in a torn and dirty shirt and stained blue jeans. He smelled of cheap wine. The black man smiled at B&B, showing a gap where his top three front teeth should have been.

"No sir, ossifer. I be Reggie McQuaid."

Kevin turned to Terry, ignoring B&B.

"Are you sure?" Barney had the squad's attention. "You kind of look like a McKay. You're not from County Clare, are you? Half the McKays came from there, the other half from the penal colony in Australia. Hey, you're not by any chance an Aussie are you?"

Most of the detectives were now enjoying the show.

The black man said, "Sheet, I'm just Reggie from Mission. You knows me. I sip some wine but I don't cause troubles. I just trying to tell you. The ossifer in uniform sent me to you 'cause the meter was out of permission when the man got cut and the cause of death was unterminated."

"Well, sir, Mr. McQuaid, let me first commend you for following the *ossifer's* suggestion and joining our community policing, crime prevention program. It's the police chief's favorite program. He'll be proud of you, Mr. McQuaid. Let me look through my desk here to see if I have a medal for you from the chief."

Some of the detectives chuckled. B&B went on, "Now, sir, you say the parking meter was out of *permission*. How did you deduce that fact?" B&B was cutting a star from a sheet of yellow legal paper.

"I 'duced it 'cause it yellow. You know the little yellow thing instead of the red dilation."

"Yes, of course, red *dilations*. Your cousin, Inspector McKay, often mispronounces that as a violation. But let's get on with the cause of the slaying being *unterminated*. That's quite serious, you know. Almost as bad as if the cause was undetermined. And you think the killer parked at the meter that was out of commission, excuse me, I mean, *permission*?"

Terry saw the back of Kevin's neck getting redder. Sexual Assaults is a great place to work, she thought. One laugh after another. The thin blue line. We all stick together like glue. That is, when we're not knifing each other. Terry picked up a crime report, but she could see Kevin was listening to Barney ridicule the black man.

Finally, Kevin turned, red-faced, toward B&B. "Hey, Barney, why don't you leave the guy alone?" he said.

"Ah! Just as I thought. You are a McKay. Your relative is coming to your defense. Well, here's your medal from the chief." B&B held up the paper star to Reggie. "See, it's got your name on it. Stand up and I'll pin it on. Men, give Mr. McQuaid a round of applause."

Kevin slammed his desk drawer and got up as the detectives clapped and the homeless man grinned in confusion. "Come on, Terry. I'll buy coffee. Maybe the asshole mood around here will be gone when we get back."

They were walking out when Flip O'Neil came off the elevator. "I got here in time for the coffee break, right?"

"Right. Come on," Kevin said. "You're not missing a thing in the squad right now."

They were halfway through coffee when Lieutenant Garza burst into the cafeteria. "Let's go. A woman has been raped and killed on Mason. It may be Ski Mask."

Chapter Thirty-four

Dolores Summers had lived in a modest one-bedroom apartment on Mason Street. The cable car ran by, and it wasn't Nob Hill. On the other hand, it wasn't known as a high crime area either. The street was taped off in front of the apartment building. Uniformed cops kept the curious crowd outside the crime scene tape. A big red-faced patrolman had a wino by the collar and was telling him what was going to happen if he staggered past the tape one more time. Across the street a shabbily dressed black man with a pot of money in front of him played a not so bad trumpet. A few heads in the crowd turned with smirks as he reached some high notes of Taps. The tech crew van was present along with a number of unmarked detective cars. Kevin parked their car in the crowd of police vehicles.

Lieutenant Garza surveyed the scene for a moment.

"Homicide ain't going to appreciate a mob like us barging into their crime scene." Garza nodded at Flip and Terry. "Why don't you two talk to the uniformed people and see what you can pick up? If there are witnesses about to disappear, don't rely on protocol. Interview them and tell the Homicide dicks about it later. Me and Kevin will see what we can find out upstairs."

Garza approached a balding man in a blue summer suit. A San Francisco lieutenant's badge was displayed in his belt holder. "What does it look like, gringo?" he asked.

"Rape, sodomy, beating, and strangulation, in that order according to the coroner," Ralph Benedetti, Homicide commander, said. "Do me a favor, amigo, and don't get the tech-scene artists temperamental by putting your big dumb feet and paws all over the place. I have to listen to enough bullshit from them about my own people."

"Do we know means of entry yet, Lieutenant?" Kevin said.

Benedetti looked sourly at Kevin, then at Garza. "Why'd you bring him?"

Garza's face turned red. "Don't give me any of that crap, Ralph. He's a principal investigator on the ski mask series, and I don't give a shit about department politics. There's going to be an uproar over this homicide. The media's going to say it was Ski Mask, and we better know whether or not it is."

Benedetti didn't like the answer. On the other hand, he wasn't about to risk getting his ass chewed by Chief of Detectives Ferrante if it turned out that he'd excluded the ski mask investigator from a related killing. Benedetti told Garza, "Entry was through a rear screen window on the fire escape. It was unscrewed and the window latch jimmied. It looks like the victim forgot about locking the iron grate inside the window. Maybe she was worried about getting cited by the firemen. She doesn't have to worry about that now. We don't have shit on this yet, Richard. You guys can look around, but I mean it. Don't get the tech crew upset. They're a pain in the ass, and they think nothing of running to Ferrante to complain. The new breed, whistle-blowers." He looked at Kevin, who brushed past him and went into the apartment.

"Hello, Pete," Kevin said to one of the tech crew. "Do you see anything that might link this guy to my cases?"

"The window entry fits the M.O., but who knows?" The heavyset specialist in coveralls spoke slowly. "We didn't recover any cigarette butts . . . maybe we'll get some fiber or hair matchups, but hell, that won't be for weeks. We just won't know for a while. Your guess is as good as mine right now."

Back at the squad room, in the lieutenant's office, Flip said to Garza, "We got zilch from the uniform people, and I thought Terry was going to have to kick that Homicide sergeant in the balls when he saw us talking to tenants."

"Yeah, I already heard about that on the phone from Ralph Benedetti," Garza replied. "So we have a whodunit. What do you guys think? Flip? You've been on every ski mask case. Any vibes?"

"Well, we briefed you. We locked up Jackson for what we thought was a slam dunk. Then the victim goes and IDs Santiago, who's got a mega stutter. So we had to cut Jackson loose. Not one of the victims mentioned a stutter. I don't know. Maybe Ski Mask did the killing, maybe not. Maybe we should get the D.A. to authorize search warrants on both of these turkeys. If we get lucky, one of them has credit cards and other goodies to tie him to the victim."

Garza scribbled a few notes on a yellow pad. He looked up. "How about you, Kevin?"

Kevin leaned back in the chair and closed his eyes. "It's him. We don't have any evidence yet, but I can feel it. The window. The way the girl was beaten. The handcuff marks on her wrists . . ."

"Were the cuffs recovered?" Terry asked.

"No. And no one will say for certain that the marks were from cuffs, but it looks like it to me. And he went through the apartment cabinets and dresser drawers just like he always does. I've been worried for a while that he was going to get to killing." Kevin wore a deep frown.

"On the other hand, we still aren't sure it was him," Garza cut in. "It's possible it was a prowler, or even a case of true love gone wrong, and the boyfriend is attempting to be clever."

Kevin nodded. "Right. But regardless, Lieutenant, Jane Remick needs to be protected. If he did this, she's next. He doesn't dare let her talk to us."

Garza frowned. "You sure didn't set the world on fire getting her to a photo lineup, then she bets on the wrong horse."

"What about protection for her?"

Garza looked at Kevin's stubborn face and shook his head. "You know the answer to that. Even if she cooperated and gave us a good ID, there's no manpower for guarding her. Every day I get a new memo from Ferrante or the police chief's office warning us not to use overtime. They should tell the criminals to be more fiscally conscious. They're not following the mayor's policy."

"I think we should talk to Thatcher," Flip said. "We can get a search warrant for Santiago and Jackson. If either of them is Ski Mask, maybe we can recover the victims' credit cards and jewelry. The blood, hair, and fiber will match, and we can lock him up."

Garza nodded. "Good. I'll go with you to the D.A.'s. I don't want that weasel bullshitting us."

"That's great, Lieutenant," Flip said. "Should we wait until you're finished meeting with Chief Ferrante?"

"Ferrante? What meeting?" Garza frowned.

"Didn't someone say Ferrante wanted to meet with Lieutenant Benedetti and Lieutenant Garza?" Flip asked Kevin.

Terry watched Kevin try to keep a straight face. He must have been terrible as a narc, she thought, and what the hell was Flip up to?

Garza hadn't looked at Kevin. He stroked his chin. "I better hang around just in case. You guys go over and talk to Thatcher. Tell him what I want."

"What was that all about, Flip?" Terry said as they left for the D.A.'s office.

"It will be self-evident to a fine investigator like you within a few minutes, right, Kevin?" He smiled.

Kevin nodded. Terry saw he wasn't in a mood for by-play.

Terry drove to the District Attorney's office, ignoring Flip's clowning in the front seat. A couple of times when she took lights on yellow, he threw his hands up, protectively covering his head.

Upstairs, behind his huge desk, District Attorney Bertram Thatcher looked even smaller than five-three. He stood to greet Terry, who thought he looked just like Truman Capote, then sat back down.

"Well, I'm glad to see that the police department has finally added some brains to this team," Thatcher said, neither concealing nor emphasizing the fact that he was gay.

"Yes, Bertram," Flip replied. "Isn't it a shame that the District Attorney's office is unable to match the gesture and we still have to deal with you? By the way, Lieutenant Garza sends his regrets. He's in a meeting, but if you insist, we can wait for him." Flip slid into a chair.

"That won't be at all necessary, Inspector O'Neil." Thatcher smiled sweetly. Terry, now understanding Flip's ploy, laughed at the picture of ex-Marine Garza and Thatcher in the same office.

Thatcher listened intently as Kevin described new information about Flip's meeting with Mrs. Miller, the attack on Jane Remick, her positive identification of Raul Santiago as the rapist, and the murder of Dolores Summers. When the two detectives finished talking, he leaned back in his chair, made a bridge of his delicate fingers and stared at the ceiling.

"Kevin, your instinct may well be right about the recent homicide. You have surprised me in the past. My major problem is that none of Ski Mask's victims have ID'd him. An identification would give us probable cause for arrest and search warrants. The one mistake we must not make is to move against Ski Mask on a faulty warrant and recover credit cards, jewelry, and other evidence that can be subsequently challenged as fruit from a poisoned tree. It would be a true tragedy, because absent a reliable eyewitness, that evidence is essential for conviction. And, from what you tell me, Jane Remick is not reliable. Even if you nailed the suspect in possession of the evidence, it would be excluded if the court determined that the search warrants were issued for insufficient legal cause."

"What about the blood-type information Mrs. Miller provided to Flip?" Kevin said. "Doesn't that build up to reasonable suspicion justifying a warrant against Santiago? And Jackson's scar, and the fact that he tried to flee?"

"Interesting . . ." Thatcher began to wipe his eyeglasses with a scented lavender linen handkerchief until Flip made a face and clutched his nose. Thatcher allowed himself a slight smile at the detective's posturing. "However, it would certainly be challenged that Mrs. Miller was acting as an agent of the police. Then too, how do we ask for a warrant when none of the victims, including the one eyewitness, remember a stutter? And in the case of Jackson, despite his scar, it seems to me that Jane Remick's failure to identify him is relevant, especially since she is the only victim to mention a scar. If I may sum this up . . ." Thatcher stood and strode back and forth. "Your position is that you have two equally weak suspects and you're asking for a search warrant in the hope that you will get lucky. My question is, do you want to risk your case? Even if you do get lucky and recover evidence, if—or I should say when—the defense makes a motion to suppress, and we lose on a ruling that the warrant was issued without probable cause, the evidence would be forever inadmissible. Lieutenant Garza would make one of his speeches about the courts handcuffing the police, but without a reliable eyewitness identification, Santiago or Jackson would go free even if they were guilty."

"Suppose we follow them," Terry said. "Could our observations provide reasonable suspicion for a warrant?"

"Ah. I was correct. We finally have an intelligent detective. The answer is yes. Observations of criminal activity would justify an on-scene arrest. Body and proximity search is permitted and could yield other evidence justifying warrants. Just be very, very, very careful not to bust him on a charge not amounting to probable cause or we fall into the same 'fruit of the poisoned tree' trap."

Chapter Thirty-five

Carlos Castellano landed at San Francisco International after twenty hours of travel. He ignored the jet lag and took a cab to the apartment on Russian Hill. He opened the door and knew immediately that Dana wasn't home. The weather had cleared, but walking through the spacious rooms, he paid no attention to the bay vista. Slowly and painstakingly he searched the apartment for any sign that Kevin McKay had been there.

The closets revealed nothing. Nor did the bathroom. Carlos flipped through Dana's notepad next to the phone without finding anything. Frustrated, he sat on the soft bed, thinking. He opened the drawer of the night table. It was empty. He went to the living room. Without looking out the picture window, he pressed a button and the electrically controlled blinds drew the drapes. Carlos sat in the darkened room. He would have to wait for Dana to return.

Dana closed and locked the door behind her. Walking toward the kitchen, she was startled to see a shadow on the wall. She whirled and saw a man watching her. Light from a crack in the blinds had thrown his sinister shadow on the wall in front of her. Her hand went to her throat. It took a moment before she realized it was Carlos.

"Hello, Dana."

"Carlos!"

His face was in shadow and his eyes glowed like a cat's in a darkened yard. "How have you been, Dana?"

Her fear gave way to anger. "If you really cared, you would have called."

"I'm sorry. That would have been very difficult. However, I'm not here to make you angry. I can see that you wish me to be gone."

Stiffly, Dana walked back to a hall table and placed her purse on it. Her face was white. She was aware that her hands were beginning to shake. She knew Carlos had deliberately upset her. And she knew what he wanted.

"Have you made any progress on what we discussed?"

Dana took a deep breath, aware that Carlos was scrutinizing her. "I think Kevin McKay will eventually cooperate with you, Carlos."

"Eventually?"

"Yes. I didn't get specific. You never told me to. But he's disillusioned with narcotics work."

Carlos nodded encouragement. "Tell me more."

"Well . . . " Dana hesitated. He knew her so well, she thought. He must know she was lying. But Carlos didn't understand people like Kevin, who couldn't be bought. "I think you should give me another week. I'll know for sure."

"You've been seeing a lot of him?"

"At the Sacred Heart school, where you sent me to meet him."

Carlos smiled, and Dana suppressed a shiver. "Thank you for your efforts, Dana," he said. "I'll check back with you in a day or two."

He went to kiss her, and she turned her face, offering her cheek.

A flash of anger came and went before he smiled. "I need to make a phone call, then I'll be out of your way."

Dana went to the kitchen and put on a kettle for tea. She

heard Carlos in the living room dialing and returned to the doorway. Out of his sight, she listened.

"Alphonse?" Carlos was silent for a moment, then said, "The client is ready to be entertained."

Dana grew even more puzzled when he immediately hung up. It was obviously some kind of a code. She pondered. What could it mean? She braced herself for another confrontation, but the next sound she heard was the front door softly closing.

Dana opened the blinds and sank onto the sofa. The bay scene had never failed to thrill her in any of its many looks. The fog sweeping in, golden sunsets, or as it was at the moment, whitecaps dotting the deep blue water moving under the Golden Gate from the Pacific Ocean. But now the apartment chilled her, and she realized it was past time that she told Kevin about Carlos.

She called Kevin's number, but another detective answered and told her Kevin was out of the office. She realized it was almost twelve. Kevin might be on his way to Sacred Heart. She would call again after lunch. The whistling kettle drew her to the kitchen.

Back in the living room, she sipped tea, watching the ferry from Sausalito cut its way through the icy bay water to its berth between Pier 39 and crowded Fisherman's Wharf. Carlos had been weird, trying to hide his anger. She felt a chill. He had changed so much. She would have to move immediately. This was his apartment. She couldn't very well ask him to surrender his keys, but she certainly wasn't going to let herself in for any more grilling.

Dana couldn't say why exactly, but she wanted to hear Kevin's voice. She went to her bag and found his business card. It had his pager number. She had never called it before and it was foolish to do so now, but she dialed the number and punched in her own number when she received the signal.

Kevin was having words with Ronnie Blue. He'd pulled the boy off the schoolyard basketball court. For more than a week Ronnie had been downright rude to him. Bill Riordan had raised his eyebrows a couple of times, but both men ignored it.

Kevin had been embarrassed. Teenagers were funny with their moods. It was best to pay them no mind. But something else was up with Ronnie. His play had been off, lackadaisical. Kevin had noticed the boy's pupils dilated a couple of times. He'd hesitated to confront him. It was hard to know what approach to take with kids. Especially kids who grew up in Ronnie's environment. They were surrounded by dope, violence, and crime. Threatening them about getting involved was useless. You had to help them come up with their own self-discipline.

But today Ronnie had thrown him a shoulder under the basket. It was a cheap shot and had taken the wind out of Kevin. He was about to ignore it when Ronnie snarled:

"Watch it, motherfucker."

Kevin was stunned. The boy had never used that language with him before. The other kids stared. Kevin looked at Ronnie's cloudy eyes and didn't like what he saw. The boy had deliberately tried to hurt him. Maybe it was a cry for help. Kevin took him by the arm.

"Let's take a break, Ronnie. We need to talk."

Ronnie tried to pull away, but Kevin applied pressure, letting him feel a little pain. Ronnie started to protest but realized Kevin wasn't about to take no for an answer. Sullenly, he walked to the far side of the yard with Kevin while the other boys resumed play.

"What's happening, Ronnie?"

The boy's eyes were on the ground. Kevin groped for an approach, discarding accusations of drug use, or banalities like saying he hoped Ronnie wasn't being lured into drugs. He sighed. "Look, Ronnie, you don't have to get sore just because I'm outscoring you two to one."

Kevin hadn't taken a shot yet, but his attempt at humor didn't move Ronnie. "Look, I don't want you mad at me. Another four years when you're a starter, I want good seats for the NBA championships."

The boy's eyes came up to Kevin's, and Kevin was unprepared for the hate.

"Ronnie . . ." Kevin heard the hoarseness in his voice. "I'm just trying to help as a friend, not talk to you like a cop."

"You so pure. You and your cop friends. Why don't you do something about your motherfucking narc friends doing the robbing and pushing?"

The boy turned and walked away, anger showing in his exaggerated ghetto shuffle. Kevin started after him, but stopped when his beeper went off. Damn! It was Dana's number. She had never used it before. Maybe it was something important. But he was puzzled. He needed to let Ronnie vent out. Why the hell was he suddenly talking about cops that way? And narcs?

Kevin headed for the rectory. He'd call Dana, then talk to Bill about Ronnie. The priest was smart and a good counselor. Together they could figure out what was bothering the boy and how to help him. He was an outstanding kid.

"Hi, Dana. You beeped me?" Kevin said when she answered the phone.

"Yes. I wanted to speak to you, to hear your voice—"

"Hold on a sec, Dana," Kevin said as he saw Father Riordan going out the front door. "Bill," he called to the priest. "Do you have a moment before you leave?"

"Extreme unction, Kevin—Mr. Hernandez. Heart attack." The priest put a stole around his neck. "I'll catch you when I get back." He hurried out the door.

Kevin turned back to the phone. "Sorry, Dana."

"You sound like you're busy. I shouldn't have called. I didn't want to interrupt your game."

"No problem. It's just that one of the kids is having a problem, and I tried to catch Bill Riordan to talk about it, but he's off in a rush. How are you doing?"

"Actually, there's something we need to talk about, but I realized we can't do it on the phone."

"Okay. What time do you want to get together?"

She hesitated, thinking of Carlos coming back. "Why don't I make dinner at your place. I feel like maybe I should be paying you rent, I'm there so much."

"The place is empty without you, Dana."

She was silent for a moment. They had discussed her moving in, and at the moment, she realized, she'd like nothing better. "I'll see you tonight," she said. "I'll pick up some stuff at the store and do a salad and Dijon chicken."

After he hung up, Kevin walked slowly out to the basketball court. He got back into the game and went all-out. Exercise was therapeutic for stress.

Dana sat with the phone on her lap. She shouldn't have let this happen. Kevin had touched her. She didn't want to lose him. How would he react when she told him about Carlos?

Chapter Thirty-six

The early morning fog had burned off, and the warm rays of the sun felt good to Flip O'Neil on his rooftop perch looking down on the schoolyard. This would be his last time on the roof observing. From now on he would be with the team full-time, shadowing ski mask suspects. Flip hummed to himself. Last night with Trish had been fantastic. After their lovemaking he had once again proposed to her. They had joked about whether it was number thirteen or fourteen.

"If it's thirteen, turn me down. You know it's unlucky."

"Okay," Trish said. "I'm turning you down, O'Neil. Just like last time. I'm not going to marry a man who cats around as much as you do."

"For seven years it's been all you, and you know it." His big right hand lightly squeezed her breast while his left hand touched her cheek. "From now on, it's only you. For the fourteenth time, will you marry me?"

She put her hand over his and pressed it to her cheek.

"You're so corny, but I believe you." Trish was crying and laughing at the same time. "Yes. Yes. Yes. But no big wedding. And the honeymoon is in Paris."

"Extortion!" he said.

But he had come to the school happy this morning. And Paris. Trish had been there but he hadn't. It would be a blast. And casually mentioning to the guys at work that he was honeymooning in Paris, another blast.

Flip's mood was also improved because he'd faced up to some things he'd been ducking. Driving to Sacred Heart, he came to grips with the fact that he'd been playing mind games with himself. Whatever was behind the anonymous letter, Sammy Robbins was clean. Nothing was happening at the school. And anyone who tried to set up a brother would be sorry. The Officers for Justice had some resources to fight back now. Politician and media friends and a few good people in the department, like Kevin, who would stand up.

The school bell rang and the young children headed indoors. Then the boys Kevin played basketball with came out to the schoolyard to scrimmage, and Kevin joined them a few minutes later.

Flip watched them begin a game. They were really going at it today, and Kevin was playing just as hard as the kids. Kevin's protégé actually slammed into Kevin a couple of times. The boy was playing with a fury today. Father Riordan left after a few minutes, and Flip's mood become somber.

He felt sorry for Kevin, who had never outgrown his boyhood. He was still wrapped in his parochial school days, and reliving them with these boys. Maybe it was because the department's reaction to the Sherry memo destroyed Kevin's illusion that the police department was the same as the warm, closed, and safe world of parochial schools. Kevin was too intense. Like with the rapes. He would get himself hurt again; in a way, a replay of the whole Sherry memo fiasco. Trish couldn't understand why he hadn't told Kevin about these surveillances, but Trish didn't know Kevin like he did. Kevin couldn't handle it.

Flip noticed that the young black boy, Ronnie, was having

words with McKay. The boy was off in his shooting and had stopped hustling. Kevin tossed the ball to the other players and went to the side of the court, where he put his arm on the boy's shoulder, smiling and trying to get him back into the game. But the youngster shook Kevin's hand off, then turned and walked toward the gate, his body language giving away teenage anger. Kevin looked after him for a minute, then went to the rectory. Ronnie Blue went out into the street. A few minutes later Kevin came from the rectory, got back into the scrimmage, and played like a demon.

Flip wondered what it was all about, but after watching for another ten minutes he decided he better go for a bite to eat and get back to the office. He wanted to make sure their new partner, Terry Fisher, didn't start thinking he was a complete fuck-off.

"I don't know what there is to hum about," Kevin said. "We're nowhere on this case." He and Flip were in shirt-sleeves. Their desks were cluttered with case files.

Flip decided it wasn't the time to tell Kevin about his pending marriage. "I guess we might as well go and talk to Tony Santucci, even though he's the only one of the top four we didn't use in the photo lineup for Jane," Flip said.

"We didn't have his mug shot that day, but it's not him. He's over six feet and two hundred pounds. None of the victims thought the guy was more than five-eight or -nine, and nowhere near that heavy."

Flip sighed. "Yeah, but like, you know, when most people believe something is true, it's usually wrong."

"Philosophy by Flip O'Neil."

"Shit, Kevin, we turned out to be wrong on Santiago, and probably on Jackson. We had to cut him loose today. You got any better ideas than hitting on Santucci?"

"No. Come on, let's do it. I'll let the boss know where we're going."

Lieutenant Garza was on the phone when Kevin entered his office. "Hold on," he said into the phone. Covering the mouthpiece, he nodded as Kevin told him about their decision to visit Santucci. Terry was due back any minute and would cover the phone. "Okay. Let me know how it goes. Take care." He returned to his call.

Several minutes later Garza hung up and went to the rest room. Returning, his eyes routinely roamed the squad room before going back to his desk; no problems. He pulled the ski mask file from a pile and paged through it until he came to mention of Santucci. Spinning in his chair, he punched the man's name into the computer terminal and waited for Santucci's criminal history to come up.

Garza frowned. Santucci had been busted for armed robbery twice, once for assault with a deadly weapon, and last year on suspicion of murder. The murder charge hadn't gone anywhere, but Garza noted that Santucci had done hard time in Pelican Bay, five years on the last robbery, and had done two in Soledad for the assault beef. There was an active warrant for a parole violation, which could have been anything from missing a visit to being a suspect in another robbery.

"Shit," Garza mumbled, realizing that he was reading the history of Dominic Santucci, and not Anthony. He got the correct date of birth from the file and punched it in. The screen brought up Anthony Santucci's record. No robbery or weapons charges, but he'd been arrested three times for sexual assaults. The first arrest showed a nolo contendere plea—no contest—but he'd done two years at Atascadero Institute for mentally ill sexual offenders. He'd drawn ten years on the last rape conviction, indicating that it had been heavy. Of course, with half time off for good behavior, and with credit for time served before trial, he had done only four years and a month in the joint. Nevertheless, Garza was glad Flip and Kevin were going to question him and not Dominic. He wondered if they were related. He dialed Dominic's parole officer. When he got voice mail, he asked if the Santuccis were related and asked for a call back.

"His parole officer thinks the guy is making it, Kevin. He's been reporting in every week. Even had a job for a while," Flip said.

Kevin pulled the department Ford to the curb. "Right. If we don't nail him for the rapes, we can turn him in for one of the mayor's achievement awards."

Flip laughed. "Here's the place. It's a worse shithole than where Jackson lived."

"You want me to be the nice guy again?" Kevin said after they had climbed to the third floor of a decaying tenement building on Harrison Street.

"Whatever."

Kevin pounded on the apartment door. "Police officers. We need to visit with Tony Santucci."

They heard a muffled curse from inside, then, after a moment, an angry voice. "Come in. The fucking door doesn't lock anyway."

The detectives entered and stood on each side of the door, taking in the small, dimly lighted room. At the far end was an open window leading to the fire escape and a tiny lamp table with a warm-up plate. Next to it was a dish with some of yesterday's scrambled eggs. Kevin felt his stomach turn. Santucci sat in bed, smoking. Kevin remembered from his sheet that he was six feet, but he looked bigger. He was clad in a muscle T-shirt that showed he'd pumped a lot of iron in the joint, and a pair of soiled cotton slacks that showed he wasn't into doing laundry. His shoe markings added to the visible foulness of the sheets. He hadn't shaved in a couple of days. The sour aroma of unwashed clothing and heavy cigarette smoke was the same as what they had encountered at Jackson's. Reluctantly, Santucci took his eyes from a game show to look at them. The nineteen-inch color TV appeared to be new.

"I had a job for a month. My parole agent knows where I bought it," he said, reading their expressions.

"You get a gold star." Casually, Kevin walked to the end of the room and looked through the half-open bathroom door. Small and narrow. Toilet, tiny sink, and closed plastic shower stall.

"What'd you expect to find, cut-up bodies?" Santucci sneered.

Kevin walked back, stopping in front of a closed door. "We

do the jokes, you do the time, Santucci," he said. "Mind if I look in the closet?"

"Fuck you unless you got a warrant." Santucci sprang out of bed.

Flip took him by the arm. "Take it easy, fella. You know we can call your parole agent. It's a condition of your parole."

"Go ahead, look." Santucci tore himself free, grabbed for the closet door handle and yanked the door open. Kevin moved over to stand next to Flip as Santucci angrily stood in front of the closet. Both detectives were looking into the closet when Santucci suddenly sprang forward, making for the front door. Kevin jumped in front of him and was propelled backward until Flip grabbed Santucci in a neck hold. The pressure eased and Kevin regained his balance.

There was an explosion of gunfire then, and Kevin was thrown backward. Santucci, on top of him, savagely smashed Kevin's head against the wall. Kevin felt himself going under, wondering what the hell had happened. Santucci's hands had been in sight. No gun.

It all went down in a split second, but Kevin felt a surge of survival adrenaline push him up. His vision was blurred and the room was spinning, but he could see Flip down on his stomach, his face desperate as he tried to hang on to Santucci's ankle. Still on his knees, Kevin thought, I've got a concussion. He fought for his balance and groped for the gun in his hip holster. Santucci wrenched free from Flip and kicked Kevin in the head. The detective partially evaded the kick but was moving very slowly. Santucci's shoe caught him in the forehead and he saw red circles. He started to black out but instinctively threw his arms around Santucci and thrust forward in a knee tackle. Santucci cursed and struggled, finally pulling Kevin's head back by the hair. Kevin was very weak but his head was slowly clearing. He released Santucci and used the man's forward momentum to shove him sideways away from the front door.

"Get him, Kevin."

Coming from behind him, Flip's voice was distorted and weak, instantly filling Kevin with dread. Flip had been shot.

Kevin got unsteadily to his feet and drew his gun. He was seeing double and he was terribly dizzy. Santucci, just a couple of feet from him, was opening the front door. Somehow Kevin leveled his sights. Santucci looked over his shoulder into Kevin's face and froze. Slowly, he raised his hands.

"I want a lawyer. I didn't do anything," he said.

Kevin squatted into a firing position, bracing his gun hand. He stole a look at Flip behind him and saw blood seeping through holes in the back of his suit jacket.

Kevin turned back to Santucci. "You worthless dirt-bag." Kevin started to squeeze the trigger.

"Don't. Please. You can't. Look, my hands are up. I'll get on the floor." Santucci's lips were quivering.

In slow motion Santucci dropped to the floor and proned himself out. He folded his arms behind his head. "You can't shoot me in the back." He sobbed.

Kevin fell back against the wall and vomited. He sank to a sitting position, fighting to keep his gun leveled at Santucci. He was glad that Santucci had his face to the floor.

Kevin wasn't aware of how long it took before he knew he wasn't going to black out, seconds or minutes, but when he could move, he knelt and felt for Flip's pulse, already knowing from the motionless body that there wouldn't be any.

PART THREE

The Chase

Chapter Thirty-seven

Dana, filled with the mundane pleasure of shopping in the neighborhood butcher shop and vegetable store, hummed to herself. The clerks and customers knew each other and talked like real people. It was what she loved about San Francisco. It wasn't quite Paris or Rome, but it was a far cry from the mall supermarket suburbs. She laughed inwardly at her little-girl awareness and pleasure that Kevin's key rested in her purse. He had happily given it to her, and hadn't even asked why she'd just about abandoned the Russian Hill apartment and spent so much time at his place.

Carrying two bags of groceries, Dana let herself into the apartment occupying the top floor of the well-kept Victorian. There was only one other apartment in the building, on the ground floor, and the tenants were so quiet, it seemed she had the house to herself.

A day or two before, Kevin had told her about the murder of Dolores Summers. He downplayed it, saying it was only a hunch; there was no evidence to support the theory that it had been the same man. But Dana shivered. She felt evil enveloping her. Carlos, the ski mask rapist . . . her beloved San Francisco now seemed ominous at times. Kevin's apartment would be a sanctuary. The spell of their love affair had diverted part of her mind from what Jane had gone through and what every woman now seemed threatened with.

She began to unpack the food in the kitchen. She'd been putting off telling Kevin about Carlos for far too long. Kevin loved her. She would have to trust that his feeling for her wouldn't change, that he would understand about Carlos.

The Victorian was in the Panhandle area. She'd fallen in love with the evening light pouring through a skylight and had set up an easel with Kevin's smiling approval.

This morning she'd opened her eyes at seven-thirty and with a pang learned he was gone. The brief note was sweet, urging her to have a good day. He would call later, and he signed it, *Love, Kevin.*

It warmed her. She'd propped it against the sugar bowl on the dining table. While the coffee was brewing she found his stereo and a six-disc CD player stacked with a Brahms piano concerto, Beethoven's Fifth by the Vienna Symphony, Gershwin's *Rhapsody in Blue*, Charlie Parker's jazz saxophone, a Basia concert, and one by Sting. Her policeman lover was complex, and the music filling her ears made her think about him.

Now, with the groceries tucked away, she was back at the easel, set up by the bay window overlooking the street. A blue moment came when she remembered Kevin's warning to stay away from the window and to keep the shades half-drawn. His concern for her made her feel tender, but she was determined not to let his cop's fears overwhelm her. Dana stroked the canvas, not noticing the tall, powerful man in the doorway across the street.

But F. Bly noticed her. The book on McKay said he lived alone. This would make the challenge a little more delicious, he thought, and when he succeeded, his reputation and price would go up a notch.

Despite his years of training, F. Bly was so engrossed he didn't pay any attention to the car down the block, where a man sat behind the wheel, also eyeing the bay window on the second floor.

As her brush flickered across the canvas, Dana had no idea she was visible to the two men on the street below. She lost track of the time. Suddenly, her back ached, and she realized it must be getting late. She placed her brushes in water and went to the kitchen to make tea. Absently, she turned on the small television set perching above the breakfast nook. She sat waiting for the water to boil. Normally, she avoided television, especially the news programs, which seemed to her an unending peering into human tragedies that should have been private.

The TV had been set on a station featuring an early news report. She didn't bother to change the channel, knowing she would shut the set off as soon as she left the kitchen with her tea. The announcer's voice rose and his face assumed the false somberness that she associated with the disclosure of some disaster. She was about to turn it off when she heard, "A breaking story about the shooting of a policeman." It occurred to her that a month earlier she wouldn't have paused in turning the set off.

The television picture shifted to a street location, and she watched transfixed as the camera closed in on a group of people coming out of a building doorway. The camera closed for an instant on the face of a man being wheeled away on a gurney. It was Kevin, and his eyes were closed. *"My God!"* The blood faded from Dana's face. She watched Kevin disappear into an ambulance. At first she thought he'd been shot, but the reporter at the scene said there were unconfirmed reports that the man being taken from the scene was a police officer who had suffered a head injury in a struggle with a suspect after the other detective had been killed. The reporter said the police were refusing to confirm any information at this time, but the police chief and Chief of Detectives had been seen going up the stairway.

The picture shifted back to the same phony, somber face in the studio as the anchor pretended once again to be concerned over another death. "Although the police are not giving out information, this neighborhood, like many others in the city, has been a scene of recent violence." The picture flashed to an old man on the corner. With a microphone shoved in his face by a reporter, the man's low, whining voice complained how what had once been a safe neighborhood was now a jungle.

Dana sat motionless, her mind blank as the shadows grew and the street traffic outside slowed. Abruptly, she became aware of the darkness. Shivering, she left the kitchen and went through the apartment, turning on every light. She dialed Kevin's beeper and his work number, knowing that it was futile, but she desperately wanted to be with him during his pain, and not stranded alone in his apartment, which was suddenly a foreign, alien place. She had no idea which hospital he'd been taken to.

Close to panic, Dana turned the stereo on full-blast, and consequently didn't hear the slight sound F. Bly made coming up the staircase, or the barely audible rasp of metal as he turned the doorknob to see if it was locked.

Chapter Thirty-eight

Terry Fisher and Father Riordan were trying to comfort Kevin in his hospital room. Terry had called the priest knowing how close he was to Kevin. She liked the boyish, handsome priest with compassionate eyes. She could see his obvious respect and affection for Kevin. Father Riordan was patient. She supposed he was used to the kind of traumatic grief Kevin was going through, but she found it disturbing. Kevin was a cop. Cops didn't go to pieces the way this man was. He kept staring at the wall. He appeared conscious, but they couldn't get a word out of him.

They had X-rayed Kevin's head and were going to do a brain scan. The preliminary diagnosis was a concussion and shock, but they wanted to keep Kevin a couple of days for observation.

Finally, Terry heard Kevin mumbling. She could barely hear him as he asked what happened to Flip. She gently replied, "We don't know who shot him yet, Kevin, but you know we'll get whoever did it."

Kevin gave no sign of hearing her. Father Riordan squeezed her hand and whispered, "He's not hearing you, Terry. He's in shock. His mind can't deal with this."

She nodded, not really understanding. He had to come out of this. They had a cop killer to catch. She took Kevin's hand and kept trying. "Kevin, you need to pull yourself together. We have to find out who did this to Flip."

Kevin turned and looked at her. Terry put her arms around him and held him close. His body was trembling, and she realized it had been all the time. "It will be okay, Kevin. We'll handle this the way Flip would have wanted us to," she said, but the warmth of her body and words didn't get through.

She felt a gentle hand on her shoulder. "Terry . . ." Father Riordan separated them. "Kevin's going to need time."

They watched as the doctor gave Kevin a sedative.

"I think after he wakes up, he'll begin to cope with this," Riordan said. "He's a very loving person, and his mind is rejecting reality at the moment. But he's also very strong. With God's help, and support from friends in the department, he'll be all right."

Friends in the department? Terry thought, bemused. "What about family, Father Riordan?" she asked.

"His mother and father are gone, but he and his brother are quite close. Unfortunately, his brother isn't in top shape right now. He's a fireman, and he's recovering from an injury. But later he'll certainly be a help to Kevin in coping."

"And you, Father. You're close to him."

She realized his eyes were watering and he was on the verge of crying. Well, even us pros have feelings, she thought, feeling her own emotions well up. She dabbed at her eyes and excused herself to go to the rest room.

When she returned, Kevin was out of bed. The doctor and priest were quite agitated. Terry looked questioningly at Riordan, who was pale.

"He's insisting on going home," the priest said.

The white-coated doctor talked to Kevin as if he were a child. "You've had a serious head injury. It will take two days of observation before we can determine the damage. Further-more, that sedative I gave you will make you too sleepy to take care of yourself."

"I'm going home. Dana needs me." Kevin was weak but de-termined. He began to dress.

Father Riordan looked at Terry. "I've seen him when he's stubborn. Can you take him home?"

She nodded. "There's someone spending a lot of time with him who will take care of him."

The priest stroked his chin. "I know Dana," he said, "but I must admit, I don't know if she's strong enough . . . for this."

Terry thought for a moment. "I'll bring him home and see. I'll be standing by and . . ." She tried to think of someone else in the department Kevin could count on. ". . . and I'm sure Lieutenant Garza will help."

"I don't want him alone for at least twelve hours after this injection," the doctor said, handing Kevin the papers to sign out.

Kevin said nothing on the drive to his apartment, and silently followed Terry up the stairs. She heard the music blar-ing from within and had to shout twice before Dana would open the door.

Dana was pale, and Terry knew she must have heard the news. "Oh, my God!" she blurted when she saw Kevin, threw her arms around him, and began sobbing.

Terry wondered if she should leave the two of them alone. They were both out of it. "Dana, how about some tea?" she asked. "Maybe it will help. I know I need to sit down before I fall down."

Dana nodded and led Kevin into the kitchen. They sat at the small table. Kevin looked down into his cup and drank only when they urged him to.

"The doctor gave him a sedative, Dana," the policewoman said. "He'll need looking after for twelve hours." She turned to him. "Why don't you lie down, Kevin? Maybe you can get some sleep."

"No." His face was set and his eyes were wide open.

Dana motioned her out of the kitchen. "I have some sleeping pills that are quite effective," she said when they were alone. "What do you think, Terry?"

"I don't know. On top of that injection the doctor gave him?"

"But he seems so wide-awake. I'm not sure I could handle him if he wanted to go out or do something crazy."

"Yeah." Terry sighed. "I suppose one wouldn't be a problem. He's a big guy." Terry looked at Dana's red eyes and strained face. "Maybe you should take one yourself."

Dana got two of the powerful pills that Carlos had given her months earlier and put them on the table. She would take one to show Kevin it was okay. She turned her head to point out the bathroom to Terry, and when she turned back, she saw that Kevin had taken both pills. He could use the sleep, she thought.

Terry returned and helped her get Kevin to the bed. "Are you sure you'll be okay, Dana?" Terry asked.

"I think so, now that he's sleeping. You've been so kind. And when he wakes up, the healing begins."

"Right," Terry said, hoping to God it was true. "Look, I'd like to stay with you, but you can imagine what's going on at work. But it's great that Kevin has you. Everyone needs somebody at a time like this."

"And you, Terry? I can see the strain you're under. Do you have someone?"

Terry's face brightened. "I have a great new guy, Craig Lewis. He's an FBI agent and—" She stopped, self-conscious.

Dana smiled. "I'm glad you have someone you can trust."

"Trust?" Terry laughed. "Well, yeah. I guess as far as you can trust any man." Realizing that this might not be what Dana needed to hear then, she continued, "Look, after I'm gone, lock all the doors and windows. You should be perfectly safe. Let me give you my home number, work number, and my beeper. If you have any questions, call anytime."

"Thanks, Terry. I'm so glad you're Kevin's partner."

Kevin's partner, she thought. Yeah, now that Flip was gone, she was Kevin's partner. The trouble was, he needed a dozen partners. Terry smiled. "Dana, why don't you take one of those pills and go in and join Kevin?" She squeezed Dana's hand. "He can use some hugging right now. And so can you." Come to think of it, so could she.

When Terry left, Dana carefully checked to make sure all the locks were secure. She looked at the sleeping pill and wondered if she should take it. With Kevin so totally out, maybe she should stay awake. But Terry was right, she decided. They both needed rest. She swallowed the pill, and a few minutes later was curled around Kevin in bed, joining him in deep, drugged sleep, while outside F. Bly and the ski mask rapist separately pondered how to kill them.

Ski Mask decided the rear window would be the best entry. The woman who'd helped Kevin McKay inside was a puzzle, but she was gone now, and it seemed McKay had been hurt. He began to fantasize how he would make Dana Rogers suffer and beg for her life before he killed her. Just like Dolores Summers. His hand drifted down between his legs and he was almost dizzy as he felt his hardness.

In the doorway, F. Bly laughed. So, McKay was home and hurting. He laughed. His casing of the house confirmed what he knew. Cops were the easiest targets. They were so convinced of their own power and guns that they never bothered with alarms and sophisticated locks. The downstairs front door to the Victorian would be easy, and he'd tested the front door to the apartment. It was secured by a simple latch lock, not even a dead bolt. He had an array of keys. One of them would work. And there would be no trace of entry. It would be a leaky gas stove explosion. No one would question why two despondent people were so careless, and the SFPD would be glad to be rid of McKay. They wouldn't probe that hard.

Chapter Thirty-nine

Chief of Detectives Vincent Ferrante was on his way to a meeting with the Chamber of Commerce and leading businessmen. The mayor had dispatched him and the police chief to calm the bozos. They were to convince them that crime wasn't going to ruin their livelihoods. Ferrante grimaced at the thought of the meeting. The fact that business and tourism were down since the earthquake and that the recession had caused the same fiscal pressures across the country couldn't be mentioned. Instead he and the police chief would vainly try to convince the group that crime wasn't up that much and the police were doing the best they could, without giving the slightest hint that they could use more cops. The mayor would have a representative present, and any indication that either of the policemen had encouraged the businessmen to ask for an increase in police strength would bring immediate displeasure from City Hall.

Ferrante's beeper sounded. He frowned at the message to call his office. Ordinarily, George would reach him through the police radio or his car phone. He signaled Bruno to pull into a gas station where he'd spotted a phone booth.

"I assume you had a reason for getting me out of my car, George," he said when his assistant answered the phone.

George was nervous. "Chief, we just got a couple of messages I thought you should know about, and I was afraid to use the radio or phone right now. You know how the media monitors those frequencies."

Ferrante's scowl deepened. "What are the messages?"

George cleared his throat. "First, a call came into communications saying, 'A shooting went down on Harrison.' A few minutes later the radio car team called it in as a member of the department shot. Now we hear he may be DOA."

Ordinarily, Ferrante wouldn't have responded to immediate crime scenes. He felt it was better to look things over afterward. Then, if mistakes were made, someone else was responsible. Ferrante said, "Enlighten me, George."

"Well, Chief, someone just told me the cop who's DOA is O'Neil. Him and McKay went to question a rape suspect."

Ferrante was silent as he pondered whether this required his presence, knowing the police chief and mayor would be most unhappy if he didn't go through the drill with the businessmen. But this was McKay, the whistle-blower. He decided it might be wise for him to take a look. The businessmen would have to bitch to someone else.

"All right, George, I'll respond. Has the police chief been notified?"

"I'm pretty sure he has, Chief."

"Well, call his office and make sure. Tell them that I'm going to the scene and that you'll take my place at the meeting with the businessmen."

"Right, Chief."

"And George, take care not to make the businessmen think something unusual is up."

"Yes, sir," the captain said, knowing better than to ask Ferrante how to tell the business group that the Chief of Police and Chief of Detectives were canceling at the last minute without arousing curiosity.

"Chief?"

Harrison Street was a mob scene. Police cars and the crime scene search vehicles were everywhere, and grim-faced cops were going through the crowd for witnesses. Ferrante turned in response to Lieutenant Ralph Benedetti's greeting and felt a little better. He had handpicked Benedetti over more senior lieutenants to head the prestigious Homicide Unit. It was common knowledge that three captain promotions were coming up and one would go to the Bureau of Investigations. Despite pretenses that the police chief made all promotions, everyone knew that Ferrante would decide who the new BOI captain would be. Benedetti could be trusted to handle this case without embarrassing the bureau.

Ferrante saw Lieutenant Richard Garza standing behind Benedetti. A great crime scene, he thought. All they needed was the school band and a couple of reporters.

"We just got here, Chief," Benedetti said, again trying to get Ferrante's attention, but the tech-crew chief outshouted him.

"Damn it, Chief, we can't process the scene with all these people here." The man waved his hand excitedly toward the people surrounding the body.

"Okay," Ferrante said, acceding. This case was going to be a son of a bitch. He didn't need the tech crew leaking to the press that the scene had been botched by the brass. "We'll move over there." He pointed outside.

Ferrante moved away from a couple of citizen eavesdroppers along with Lieutenants Benedetti and Garza. "Now," Ferrante nodded to Benedetti, "tell me what you know, and don't leave anything out because you think it's unimportant."

"Well, Chief, as I said, we just got here. A radio car crew was dispatched. McKay had passed out when they arrived. He's at the hospital, last I heard. He'd been holding a gun on the suspect. O'Neil was DOA. Shot in the back. It looks like a .45 or large caliber." Benedetti swallowed. "We don't have information on the suspect yet, Chief. I sent my people to the hospital with McKay to get his statement. He doesn't appear to have been shot, looks like a head injury. We can't get anything from the suspect either."

"That's great," Ferrante said sarcastically, and turned to Garza. "Richard, what the hell were they doing here?"

Garza spoke with difficulty. Although he'd never shown it, Flip O'Neil had been one of his favorites. "The prisoner is Anthony Santucci. They were questioning him about the ski mask rapes. Shit. No one thought he was that hot a suspect."

"We haven't recovered the murder weapon yet, Chief."

"Jesus Christ!" the Chief of Detectives muttered. "What do you mean?"

"It looks like the shooter was in the bathroom hiding behind the shower curtain. There were shoe marks in the stall. Three cartridge shells were on the floor just outside the bathroom. It looks like he came out blasting. Must have caught O'Neil from behind." Benedetti shrugged. "The window to the fire escape was open. He may have taken off that way. Somehow, McKay managed to hold onto the other guy until the uniforms arrived."

Ferrante thought hard. "We'll keep an open mind, but it's hard to see how two experienced cops could get caught from behind."

"It's not hard for me to see." Garza was angry. "Santucci had no violence on his record. They weren't going to bust him. How the hell could they expect a second guy to come out of the bathroom blasting?"

"Well, if McKay was the hotshot he thinks he is—"

"Bullshit," Garza interrupted.

"All right, all right." Ferrante held out his hands in a calming gesture. "As I said, we'll keep an open mind. Apparently, McKay is in pretty bad shape. Make sure you give him some time off, Richard."

"Yeah." Garza was subdued. "But that doesn't explain who shot him. One guy we should check out is his brother Dominic. He's a shooter, and there's a murder alarm out for him. I talked to his parole officer. He's bad news. Maybe he's the guy who was hiding."

"That's Ralph's job, Richard, but it's a good lead."

"What about McKay, Chief? The department always lets a cop work on his partner's killing," Garza said.

"Richard, be gentle with McKay. He's a basket case, from what Ralph says. For McKay's sake, I want you to give him at least a week off when he clears the hospital."

Garza, knowing he'd just been given an order, inclined his head in reluctant agreement. He wondered how much of the chief's decision was based on his desire to label Kevin McKay unstable before the State Investigation Commission could meet. Word was out that they would be holding a hearing soon on Kevin's memo alleging possible dope corruption in the police department.

"Besides, my people won't go for working with a guy who drops memos to the police chief," Benedetti said.

Chapter Forty

Terry got into her car and hit the gas pedal. It was getting dark, and she wanted a warm shower to wash away some of the day's pain. "Shit," she exclaimed when she was a block away, realizing she'd given Dana her old pager number instead of the new one assigned to her when she joined the Bureau of Investigations.

She swung the unmarked police cruiser around. Taking the corner sharply, she spotted Craig Lewis in the crosswalk, grinned, and blasted the horn. He jumped, angrily started to give her the finger, then saw who it was.

"What the hell are you doing here?" both said simultaneously when she pulled over.

Terry hadn't realized how stressed-out she was until she began to laugh wildly. After a moment Craig joined in. Then he sobered.

He leaned on the door of her open window. "Terry, I heard the news. I'm sorry about Flip O'Neil. I heard he was a hell of a cop. What happened?"

"We don't know bean turd yet, Craig, but there's something weird about it. That's why I'm here. Kevin McKay, his partner, took it real hard. I brought him home."

"And you left the poor guy by himself?"

"No way. He's got a roommate." She nodded toward the passenger seat. "Get in. I'll tell you about it."

"Just for a second." He walked around the car and slid in.

"I'm supposed to be doing a security check on a guy down the street."

"I'll bet." She looked at him suspiciously. "You're in Criminal Section. You don't do security checks. Is she a blonde or redhead? You haven't called me in three days."

He laughed and put his arms around her. "Listen, gorgeous one, you've fucked and sucked me dry. I don't even have the energy to look anymore."

She put her lips to his ear. "Craig, I've got twelve hours off. Come home with me. It's been a horrible day. I need you to put your arms around me and love me a little."

He squeezed her. "Any other time, Terry. You're right, I don't ordinarily do security checks, but I'm covering for another guy. If I fuck it up, he gets burned."

"Okay. I'll go with you and wait. I know it will only take you fifteen minutes if you hurry." She reached between his legs and stroked him. He tried to take her hand away, but she said, "No way you're getting rid of me tonight, Craig. I don't know what god of good fortune sent you my way, but I'm going to be very grateful, and I promise you will too."

He thought for a moment. "I can see you're serious. Okay, let me go to my car and make a call. Someone else can do the check. I'll pull up here and meet you. I'll be glad to pitch in. Now, more than ever, we have to stick together in law enforcement. Why don't you stay here and I'll be right back?"

"Great." She squeezed his hand. "On the way to my place I need to stop on California, to see a victim. I need to make sure of what she did at a photo lineup. Kevin's out of it, and Flip . . . well, I'm going to have to take over this ski mask investigation, and I need to make sure whether or not Jane Remick— she's the victim—is up to doing a fresh lineup for me. Anyway, it will only take a sec."

"No problem. I'll get my car." Craig got out.

F. Bly had decided to postpone his lethal visit. There was too much going on in the vicinity of the Victorian house. But Ski Mask hadn't seen Terry and Craig together across the street from the house. He was in the rear alleyway. The gun he'd lifted from the dead security man rested in his right trouser pocket. The rear pocket contained a ski mask. He carried the mask out of habit. He wouldn't need it this time. He tested the pull-down fire escape ladder while Kevin and Dana slumbered soundly above.

He would immediately kill the man with a shot through the head. The woman would be slower, more delicious. Killing the man like that would really scare her. He was pleased with himself for patiently waiting until the woman who brought the cop home had left the apartment.

Sitting in her car waiting for Craig, Terry wondered if she was getting a little batty. She was double-parked across the street from Kevin's place. Ordinarily, she wouldn't have worried that the wrought-iron gate into the rear alleyway was open, but it had been closed when she brought Kevin home. Oh, hell, she wouldn't sleep if she didn't check it out. She took a flashlight from the glove compartment and crossed the street. She played the flashlight over the gate latch but didn't see anything. Silly, she told herself. What did she expect to see? You didn't need a burglar's tool to open this gate, it simply swung open. Terry started down the stairs into the dark courtyard.

Ski Mask caught the movement of Terry's flashlight out of the corner of his eye. He wore tennis shoes and made no noise as he fled to the far end of the yard and started to unlatch the gate to the adjacent street. But the woman, who he now had no doubt was a cop, was coming, and her flashlight beam bounced over the yard. His heart was thumping. He hid behind a massive generating unit and took out his gun.

Terry spent a moment under the ladder Ski Mask had been planning to use, but nothing had been disturbed. Slowly, she walked through the dark courtyard, shining her light from place to place. Terry was just humoring herself. We're all a little jumpy right now after Flip, she thought, leaving her gun in the handbag slung over her shoulder.

Ski Mask could see her now. She appeared to be alone. If she looked behind the generator, he would shoot her and run from the courtyard to his car, which he'd moved two blocks away.

Terry played her light upward as she moved nearer to Ski

Mask, crouching behind the generator. Noticing that the lights were out in the rear of the house, she decided to leave. Kevin and Dana were probably asleep. There was no reason to wake them up. She would call in the morning and give Dana the correct number.

Ski Mask brought the gun up then, and sighted it on the back of Terry's head. She was only a few feet from him. He couldn't miss. He started to squeeze the trigger.

Terry lowered the flashlight. She'd seen nothing. Maybe it was normal to be paranoid after what happened to Flip. No. By definition, paranoid was abnormal, so . . .

His gun hand was steady. His sight never wavered from the back of her skull. Killing her would be so easy, but she wasn't the target. His pleasure was upstairs, waiting for the right time.

Craig would be looking for her, Terry thought. She was beat, and didn't want him to disappear into some cop bar somewhere. She walked through the alleyway toward her car. Dana had been right. Everyone needed someone to hold on to when shit happened.

Ski Mask lowered the gun and waited until the woman left the alleyway. Then he silently opened the gate behind him and walked away. The mood had been destroyed, but he would be patient. Strong, patient, and clever. He would be back.

At Jane Remick's building, Terry quickly got out of the car. "I'll run upstairs. It won't take long."

Craig Lewis unwound himself from the front seat. "I'll keep you company." His hand slid to the rear of her skirt.

"That kind of stuff will get you someplace," she said, thinking he was sweet to come with her.

Terry identified herself to the security guard in the lobby, and she and Craig moved toward the two elevators. The one to the left arrived first and they got in. When they were between the second and third floors, he reached out and abruptly hit buttons on the control panel. The lights went out and the elevator lurched to a stop.

"Craig, what the—" She realized he was on his knees, his

face nuzzling her crotch while his hands slipped under her skirt and deftly pulled down her panties.

"Hello there." His fingers were gently playing with her, and she caught her breath as a wave of pleasure overtook her. "God, you are crazy." She felt faint.

He lifted her leg, and before she realized it, had slipped her panties off. Excitement and fatigue were making her dizzy in the darkness as his lips and tongue floated over her thighs. I'm exhausted, stressed-out, she thought, trying to will her hands to stop him. Instead she was running her hands through his full hair.

"It must be stuck."

People were on the floor above pushing the elevator button. Craig showed no signs of stopping, but the passion left Terry immediately. She had canvassed this building. The people would recognize her as a San Francisco police officer when the door opened. She reached out, turned on the lights, hit the on switch, and moved away from Craig. She tried to get her panties back, but he just grinned and sniffed at them.

"Craig, the door is going to open."

His smile widened as he waved her panties in a circle above his head. But when the door opened, the corridor was empty. The people had gotten on the other elevator.

Terry was surprised that Craig had done something so crazy, and wondered if it was a mistake to bring him to Jane's apartment. But he quickly turned professional.

"This is where the attack occurred?"

"Right. The victim may be in real danger. We think Ski Mask did the rape murder over on Mason. This gal, Jane Remick, can probably ID him."

Craig was inspecting the front door locks. "Then she is in danger. Did he come in the front?"

"We don't know. For some reason, the victim is holding back." Terry rang the bell and identified herself.

Jane Remick hadn't heard what happened, and Terry didn't have the energy to discuss it. She introduced Craig as an FBI agent and steered them toward the living room. She wanted to set up an appointment with Jane Remick to see if another photo lineup might work. If she waited until Jane learned of Flip's death on television, it might be too late. She wouldn't be the first victim to run from violence. Craig didn't follow them. Terry noticed him drift into the bedroom. He was looking at the fire-escape window.

"Jane, something happened to one of our investigators today," Terry said. "I don't have time right now to fill you in, but I was wondering if we could meet at eleven tomorrow morning."

"That would be fine." Jane smiled absently at Craig coming into the room. "I was just leaving. Tomorrow would be much better." The phone rang and Jane went to answer it while Terry and Craig let themselves out.

"Don't try anything funny in the elevator. I'll be ready for you this time." Terry pressed the button for the lobby and faced him.

"Really." He swung her panties on his index finger.

She grabbed for them, but he was too quick. "You'll pay, Craig. And soon."

In the car, Craig quickly got his hand inside her blouse and bra and was stimulating her nipple. "Craig, cut it out. I'll have an accident." But again Terry found herself warming to his touch.

He moved closer and began to tongue her ear while continuing to fondle her breast. "Hmm, delicious," he said.

"Craig!" It came out half scream, half giggle. The car had sideswiped the curb as she pulled onto the freeway entrance ramp.

"Ah, but you have to pay the penalty for taking me away from duty tonight."

"I'll pay. I'll pay. Just let me get us home in one piece. Oh, Craig," she said. He'd moved his hand down to her thigh. She remembered her panties were on the seat next to him. "Please, Craig, you're driving me crazy. I haven't seen you in three days. You're making me so horny I'll pull onto the shoulder and rape you."

"Threatening an agent of the FBI. Ah, what do we have here that's so warm and wet?"

A tremor shot through her. "I mean it, Craig. If you don't take your hand out of there I'm pulling over."

"You don't have the guts." He ignored her plea.

She pulled to the side of the road and they bounced roughly along the dirt shoulder. Craig was thrown against the door. Before he could recover, she turned the motor off and climbed on top of him, covering his face with kisses. He responded, and a wild excitement flooded her. What was it with this guy? He turned her into a nympho. It wasn't just that he was a hunk. There was something intriguing under that smiling, wise-cracking exterior. Something of a rebel, outlaw personality that sent her off deeper than anyone else ever had.

"Craig, for God's sake we're right on the freeway," she protested as he lifted her from the car like she was a child.

"Okay, rape me," he said, pushing hard into her.

She felt dizzy again. "No, Craig. Someone will stop." He lifted her onto the hood. Her skirt was above her knees and she could feel the warmth from the motor on her bare ass. He was leaning on top of her, pinning her. She heard cars flying by and saw headlights, and then his hard throbbing sent her into an almost psychedelic dreamland. Her head was back and she looked at green and chartreuse stars flashing in the dark sky above. From a distance she heard herself crying, "Yes, fuck me, Craig, fuck me." She thrust furiously back at him feeling him get even bigger inside her. He treated her like a common whore, fucking her on the hood right here on 101. Craig moaned and a new level of pleasure hit her. She pulled him harder into her, sliding into a long rolling orgasm. She lay sprawled on the hood, only half listening to Craig, knowing there would never be another like it.

"Oh . . . oh, here come the *poo-lice.*" He laughed.

Craig slid off her, and Terry, still lost in bliss, pulled her skirt down and got into the car, vaguely aware that Craig was walking back toward a CHP car. They must have seen him zipping up, she thought, still submerged in a warm glow, feeling the stickiness of him oozing down her thighs.

"We just pulled over to change drivers, guys," Craig told the highway patrolman. "I'm FBI in San Francisco." He produced his credentials, which didn't seem to impress either the veteran male driver or his younger female partner. "The lady," he unleashed his best smile, "got a little drowsy, and I offered to take over."

The senior CHP cop nodded to his partner. "Fine. I'll just go up and say hello to the lady."

The younger officer picked up the signal. "Just for the record, I'd like to see your license. You can stand over there while you get it out." She pointed to a spot in front of the police car's headlights.

"You bet." Craig cackled. "You guys can't be too careful, the people you stop out here."

The CHP driver, forty-five, married, and with three kids, looked in the window at Terry. "You okay, lady?"

She was leaning back against the head rest, eyes half open. She turned her head and smiled happily at him. "No, officer, I'm not okay. I'm in heaven."

He looked at her disheveled clothes, then back at Craig, who had his young female partner smiling and chuckling at something he said. He turned back to Terry. "You're in heaven now, honey, but remember it's a long fall from the pearly gates back to earth." He walked back to the patrol car. His partner showed him a slip of paper. The registration of the car had come back as an SFPD vehicle from her radio check.

Driving away, his partner grinned. "Looks like some law enforcement fellowship was taking place tonight."

"Yeah," he grunted, pulling the cruiser into the left lane behind a red Porsche that must have been doing ninety.

Chapter Forty-one

The following day, Dana and Kevin awakened from twelve hours of sleep with the heavy feeling sedatives produced. Kevin was so down it was actually painful to be with him. But he was functioning. Twice he tried to call Trish, Flip's girlfriend.

"I don't know if anyone notified her," he said. "She's an account executive for a cosmetics company, travels a lot. It will be hell if she hears of this from a news story."

Dana said, "Horrible. Keep trying."

Kevin hung up without the phone being answered.

"Kevin," Dana said, "can we go out for a while? It might be good if we took a walk, got some fresh air."

He wasn't enthusiastic. "Okay," he said, "but first let me call B&B and see what's happening. I need to know when the funeral is scheduled."

Dana busied herself combing her hair while he talked on the phone, but she could overhear his frustration. "Damn it, B&B, tell me what's happening. What do you mean there's no information and a special team from Ferrante's office has clamped down on everything?"

After a few minutes he slammed the phone down, shaking his head. They walked to Golden Gate Park. Ordinarily, Dana would have enjoyed browsing through the De Young Museum, looking at paintings and art exhibits, but it was out of the question in Kevin's mood. They held hands and walked all the way to Ocean Beach, where his blue eyes focused unseeing on the breakers rolling in. It was warm and sunny and the wind-carried spray cooled them.

She moved in front of him, looking into his blue eyes, made even more incredible in this light. "Kevin," she said, putting her arms around him, "are you going to be okay? I've come to depend on you so much."

His eyes were vacant, and after a moment she realized she was holding her breath, waiting for his answer. She exhaled.

"Maybe you shouldn't depend so much on me," he finally said.

"But I have no one else. And you're so strong."

"But you haven't even trusted me enough to tell me why you sought me out." His voice was without emotion, but the harshness of the words hit her.

"I know, Kevin. It's not that I don't trust you, it's just so hard to talk about. I'll tell you everything soon. I promise. Right now you need grieving time."

He took her hands. "I'm not pressing you. I'm just trying to get you to understand that you can tell me. It won't affect us. If it wasn't for you, I don't think I'd have anything worth living for."

She burst into tears and hugged him. "Kevin, never say that. You don't really know me. I don't want the responsibility of your life."

"None of us want the responsibilities. We simply got them. I'd rather have my leg cut off than go through Flip's funeral tomorrow, but it's got to be done. Will you come?"

She thought for a moment. Suppose someone on the force recognized her and connected her to Carlos? Wouldn't it be bad for Kevin? He was watching her. She couldn't say no. "Yes, Kevin. I'll be there for you."

The day of the funeral was San Francisco gray. High winds swirled, and the bay was filled with whitecaps. Dana was dressed warmly but she shivered. She had never seen so many policemen. No. Not just policemen; she noticed a good number of women in uniform. And the cops' uniforms were all different. They must come from all around, she thought. The brief church ceremony had been sad but impressive. A clergyman had said a number of empty things, but two black policemen spoke with humor and warmth about Flip.

When Kevin stood in the pulpit to speak, she heard whispers sweep through the huge church. News of his memo to the police chief hadn't made him popular in the department. But Dana thought him absolutely beautiful in his blue uniform. He stood straight, and his broad shoulders and athlete's figure made him look like an advertising poster for police recruitment. The image vanished when he tried to speak. He started to tell an anecdote about Flip but choked up. People in the church shifted in their seats. Finally, with tears streaming down his face, Kevin said, "Flip was my friend, a good man, and a good cop."

He returned to his seat in the front of the church and the thousand or so cops present began to stream past the casket while the organ played. Some cops stopped and saluted. Dana felt her eyes water. Terry, sitting next to her, dried her eyes several times with a handkerchief.

When the church service ended, Dana rode with Terry to the cemetery, worried about Kevin. He'd been coming apart in church. She stood next to Terry and watched as Kevin and the other pallbearers carried the casket to the grave.

Why do we torture ourselves like this? Dana wondered. They were standing directly across from a small section reserved for the immediate family, but only Flip's sister and his two teenage sons were in the front seats.

"Normally," Terry told her, "the mayor and police chief would be behind the family. Politicians fight for those spots where the television cameras and newspaper photographers show them looking sad behind the grieving police families. But look at them. The mayor and chief are off to the side, out of photo range. It's weird."

Dana jumped as the first of the honor guard's shots resounded through the cemetery. When their military salute was finished, a bugler played Taps. The sad, wailing notes drifted into the gray clouds, and Dana saw movement in the ranks of cops standing at attention. Many of them were wiping away tears.

She realized that most of them had never known Flip. They were crying for themselves and their own families, for in those few seconds their mental defenses cracked a bit. Just for a moment they were forced to admit that they were as mortal as Flip O'Neil had been. All cops had the angel of violence sitting on their shoulders. Only good luck had kept the killers' gun sights from focusing on them. Dana realized that everyone without a badge was an outsider no matter how supportive. There was no way they could completely share the brotherhood cops felt for each other.

There was another brief prayer and then the minister's deep voice launched into the Twenty-third Psalm. "The Lord is my shepherd. I shall not want. He maketh me to lay down in green pastures. He leadeth me beside still waters . . ."

When he finished, the pallbearers ceremoniously folded the American flag covering the coffin, leaving its mahogany finish and brass handrails glistening obscenely above the open grave. One of the pallbearers presented the flag to the older of Flip's boys. The other boy got Flip's police badge.

Dana wondered if the red-eyed boys had been close to their father. How much would this ceremony and a flag and a badge make up for not having a father for the rest of their lives?

Terry whispered, "Normally, the chief would present the badge and flag to the family." She shook her head.

When the ceremony was over, she and Dana joined Kevin standing near the graveside. Dana thought he looked more peaceful with himself. A tearful B&B came and exchanged bear hugs with Kevin. Dana reached up and kissed Kevin on the cheek, and he slipped an arm around her waist. None of the group noticed Lieutenant Glen Sherry watching them from under an adjacent tree.

Kevin told them he was going to stop at Charley's for a beer with the pallbearers, then go into the squad to catch up on some reports. Terry and Dana decided to go to the Nordstrom cafeteria on Market Street for coffee, and who knew, maybe even a little retail therapy?

* * *

Kevin and the pallbearers had stripped off their jackets and sat at the bar in white shirts, black uniform ties, and blue trousers with gold stripes. You weren't supposed to drink wearing any part of a uniform, but no supervisor was going to say a word after a cop's funeral. In fact, half the people in Charley's were police sergeants and lieutenants in similar attire.

Kevin sat at the bar talking with Frank Clancy of the FBI. Clancy was heavyset and fighting a growing midsection. He had played second string football at Notre Dame before going to law school and joining the Bureau twenty-one years earlier. He was a sports fan, and had seen Kevin play basketball, base ball, and football on a number of occasions.

Clancy was liaison for the San Francisco FBI office with local law enforcement. That meant he often had the ticklish job of stroking egos on both sides when disagreements developed over jurisdiction or credit for newsworthy cases. He was also caught in the middle when the FBI investigated local cops for corruption or civil rights violations. Privately, he felt like telling the police chiefs and detectives who complained when the Bureau caught some of their colleagues dirty: *"Tough shit. If you can't wash your own laundry, don't complain when we have to do it for you."* But officially he took them to lunch and dinner and tried to placate them. He and Kevin were friends.

Clancy squeezed Kevin's shoulder and said, "Sorry, buddy. Flip was one of my favorite people."

"I know, Frank. Thanks." Kevin sipped at his beer.

"Are there any leads at all?" the FBI man asked.

"Damned if I know. For some reason, the brass has thrown a blanket over it. Flip was my partner, but today I hear Lieutenant Garza says he was working on child molestation."

"Hmm, interesting," the FBI man murmured, thinking this sounded like one of the familiar SFPD cover-ups. He wondered what was behind it, and knew he'd find out eventually. He usually did. Some cop, who was pissed at his boss, his wife, or the world in general, would pour out the secrets of the police world to his sympathetic ears over a late-night drink.

Hiding his distaste, Clancy watched Craig Lewis slapping

backs and laughing as he worked his way through the local
cops lining the bar. Why did he try so hard to be an asshole?
Clancy wondered. The San Francisco FBI brass weren't on to
him yet, but sooner or later they'd see what a phony he was.
The big tough guy, great lover, and super agent. But Lewis
didn't even carry his caseload, and thought he was clever in
sending in reports reflecting a lot more Bureau work than he
did. Of course, he wasn't the only one. Just the most obnox-
ious one.

Craig Lewis squeezed in next to them, and Clancy braced
for the overly hard back slap he knew was coming.

"Frank, you fat dog. I knew you'd have that big belly of
yours up to the bar." Lewis put his arm around Kevin, and
Clancy saw McKay's shoulders tense and his neck get red. He
likes him about as much as I do, Clancy thought, deciding
he should shoo Lewis out of there. Kevin was real down. He
couldn't handle a lot of bullshit today.

But before he could say anything, Lewis said to Kevin, "I'm
sorry as a nun's empty cunt about your partner. I hear he was
good people."

Clancy blinked. Even for Lewis this was too much.

Kevin shoved Craig's arm off and muttered, "Thanks,"
making it obvious he wanted Craig Lewis to go away.

But the big man grabbed Kevin again. "Hey, I hear he was
as big a swordsman as you, McKay. That makes him okay in
my book."

Kevin swung around on his stool. "Look, Lewis, I'm talking to a friend. Why don't you go home to your wife and children for a change? Or can't they stand you either?"

A few people at the bar had looked around at Kevin's raised
voice and red face. Frank Clancy glanced at the ceiling, but he
was chuckling inside. Lewis was an ex–physical education in-
structor at the Academy and all muscle. But Clancy had seen
Kevin McKay win gold medals boxing in the World Police
and Fire Games. Maybe something good was about to happen
to deflate an asshole.

"Hey, the unfriendly local." Craig Lewis turned to Clancy.
"You know what his problem is, Frankie? I'm fucking his cute

little partner, and he hasn't scored on her yet." He turned to Kevin. "Listen, buddy, she's hot enough to handle both of us. I don't mind sharing."

Kevin was on his feet. His right hand was quick. Before Lewis could stop it, Kevin's open palm was in his face and he shoved the FBI man backward.

"Get out of here, Lewis, before I forget where I just came from." Kevin's face was flushed.

Lewis's temper flared. He shifted his weight and swung a right that would have taken Kevin's head off if it had connected. But Kevin slipped inside the punch and deflected it with his left hand. He countered with a short, solid right that sent blood gushing from the bigger man's nose.

"Jesus. Stop those guys." An FBI supervisor next to them attempted to grab Kevin from behind, but missed when 250-pound Frank Clancy stumbled in his way.

Kevin's hands were a blur. Although Clancy was right next to him watching, he couldn't count the number of blows before Kevin put Lewis down with a right to the jaw, a solid knockout punch. It would have broken Lewis's jaw if Kevin hadn't slipped slightly in his shiny black uniform shoes.

The bar was bedlam. Clancy helped ease Kevin through the crowd and out a side door, saying, "Go home for a while and cool off, Kevin."

But he didn't. He headed straight for headquarters, where he changed out of uniform and washed the blood off his swollen knuckles. Craig Lewis's wild right had grazed his head, and the FBI ring the agent always wore had cut the skin on top of his left ear and along the side of his head. He washed the blood off and shrugged at the damage.

Leaving the rest room, he went to his desk. There was a note from Joey Demanto expressing sorrow over Flip and saying he needed to see Kevin, pronto. He had underlined "pronto." Kevin stuck the note in his pocket. He saw that Lieutenant Garza's door was partially open, and knocked.

Garza got up. "How are you, Kevin? You feeling better?" He paused, observing Kevin's head, ear, and swollen knuckles. "Is that anything I'm supposed to know about?"

"No, Lieutenant. I just wanted to talk about Flip."

"Yeah, sit down." Garza gestured at a chair.

Kevin sat.

"We really don't have anything yet, Kevin. And the case does belong to Homicide, you know."

"I know. But I hear strange rumors, like you gave Flip a confidential assignment and the Chief of Detectives put a lid on the case."

"You sure you're up to talking about this?" Garza's obvious concern for Kevin had given way to nervousness.

"I was his partner. I think I have a right to know."

"Yeah." Garza rubbed his chin and said nothing.

"Did you give Flip an assignment?"

Garza stood. He shifted his gaze from Kevin and looked out into the squad room, deserted now except for B&B, who was filing papers in his desk.

"Yes."

"Child molesters?"

"Look, Kevin, I can't really talk about this. Chief Ferrante put a lid on."

"I don't get it. A cop was killed. What is there to put a lid on? And how come no one told me about Flip's special assignment? I was carrying him all the time as being on the ski mask investigation."

"Yeah, I know you're upset. I don't blame you." Garza avoided his eyes. "But really you shouldn't tell people you were carrying Flip. You got enemies around here."

"He was my partner, Lieutenant. If you're not going to fill me in, I'll go to Ferrante."

Garza leaned forward in his chair, pleading. His dark eyes met Kevin's. "Please don't do that just now, Kevin. You know, Ferrante is no friend of yours. For your own sake, cool it for a while. Let things simmer down."

Kevin slumped in his chair. Suddenly, his concern over Dana, Flip's death and funeral, and the fight with Lewis, caught up with him.

Garza came around the desk. "You've been through a lot.

The Chief of Detectives personally suggested you take a few days off. I'm going to get B&B to drive you home."

On the way home, Kevin twice tried to get the normally vocal B&B to talk about the case, without success. But when they got to Kevin's place, the chubby inspector touched his shoulder. "Be careful, Kevin. This is a good organization, but if it turns on you, it can be vicious. Take Garza's advice and just cool it for a while."

Kevin sensed he was about to say more. "What else, B&B?" Kevin rested his hand on the door handle.

"Kevin," B&B said, "don't let people out to get the department use you. These phony people on commissions, and politicians, are all out for publicity. Out for themselves. Cops have to stick together and cover our asses. Remember, they're on top, and we're on the bottom. Take care, kid."

He slapped Kevin on the back. It was the first time Kevin could remember B&B telling him to take care without a smile on his plump face.

Chapter Forty-two

The day after Kevin had knocked Craig Lewis unconscious in Charley's, Frank Clancy was called to Ray Bloom's office on the eleventh floor of the Federal Building on Golden Gate Avenue. Bloom was Assistant Special Agent in charge of the FBI regional office. Clancy had been expecting the call.

Ray Bloom leaned back in his chair. "Morning Frank."

"Morning Ray."

Bloom studied Clancy. They had been in the same entrance class in the FBI Academy, and had both worked out of San Francisco for the past six years. Bloom liked and respected

Clancy. Agents like him were the backbone of the Bureau. Solid performers without ambition for promotion, totally loyal, never hotshots. He knew Clancy in his quiet way had done a good job in the delicate task of keeping the Bureau's working relationships with the locals in good order. He also knew that Frank Clancy's ability to get confidential information from local cops had helped the Bureau solve a number of big cases. More important, Frank's inside information had kept the San Francisco office from the kind of embarrassing publicity FBI offices suffered in other big cities when it came to light they hadn't uncovered or investigated blatant police brutality or corruption.

But Bloom's boss, the Supervising Agent in Charge of the FBI regional office, thought that maybe Frank Clancy was too low-key for the job. He'd asked Bloom to think about the new guy, Craig Lewis, for the position. Lewis was young, full of energy, and seemed to get along well with the local cops. The SAC mentioned that Craig Lewis had shown great courage in Chicago, where he'd taken on some organized crime people all by himself and killed one of them. Bloom had doubts. He viewed Lewis as unproven, but one didn't rise in the FBI by disagreeing with his boss. Bloom said he would think about it.

"How have you been, Frank?"

"Pretty good, except for the diet." Clancy patted his paunch.

"It's been a while since you stopped in." It was Bloom's job to run day-to-day operations, while the number-one guy handled Washington, the U.S. Attorney, local politicians, police chiefs, and big shots. Bloom relied on Frank Clancy to keep him up-to-date on local policing.

"Things have been very quiet. I haven't felt any need to take up your time."

"Right." Bloom sighed.

Clancy knew exactly what Bloom wanted to talk about, but he had to go through this ritual. Clancy would dole out the information bit by bit.

Bloom checked his desk clock and calendar. He had a luncheon engagement at Jack's with the president of one of the city's leading banks. The banker was going to request greater

FBI investigation of northern California's credit card frauds. Bloom had been looking forward to a couple of Bloody Mary's and a great piece of prime rib, but the boss had given him a hot assignment, for which he had to pick Clancy's brains. "What are you doing for lunch, Frank?"

"I was going to grab a sandwich in the cafeteria, boss." Clancy smiled.

"How about I buy you a small snack at Stars, instead?" The Bureau would pick up a reasonable lunch tag for them, but Bloom knew he would have to pay for drinks, and Frank Clancy always ordered two glasses of chardonnay at lunch. Bloom himself would have one Bloody Mary, and be out twenty bucks. Damn. Bloom pressed his secretary's call button.

"Mary, would you reschedule my lunch. See if you can set it up for next week. I'll be on my beeper and back for my two-fifteen appointment."

Twenty minutes later the FBI men were seated in the middle of the eye-pleasing dining room, enjoying drinks and the infinite variety of good-looking people frequenting the trendy restaurant. Both men recognized a number of local pols. It wasn't the kind of place either of them got to visit often, but Bloom wanted to loosen Clancy up.

"Ah, this is the way to live," Clancy said. "Maybe I should have gone for promotion, Ray."

Bloom, picking up the gambit, laughed. "I won't say anything about which one of us eats better, Frank." He glanced at Clancy's generous waist. "The boss asked me to give you a buzz on the rumor that one of our guys duked it out with a San Francisco inspector yesterday."

"It's no rumor. I was there."

"You *are* supposed to let me know about significant stuff, Frank."

"I didn't think it was that significant. We have our regularly scheduled meeting next Friday. I was going to mention it then."

"Well," Bloom blew on his soup, "I guess the boss thinks

it's significant when one of our guys is assaulted by a local cop in a bar."

Clancy smiled off the implicit criticism. "Our guy threw the first punch."

Bloom looked up, puzzled. "That's odd. The SFPD brass contacted the boss and sounded like they wanted to discipline the cop. Said he was drinking in uniform. Usually they're so defensive, they fight us all the way."

"That should tell you something." Clancy sniffed his wine and sipped some with obvious enjoyment.

Bloom remained silent while the waiter served the second half of his lunch, a small spinach and walnut salad. He looked enviously at Clancy's thick glazed pork chop garnished with rosemary and applesauce.

"What was it all about? The boss heard it started when the San Francisco cop made a crack about the agent's wife and kids. By the way, who are we talking about on both sides? We didn't get any names."

"The agent was Craig Lewis, and the guy who flattened him was Inspector Kevin McKay."

Bloom heard a little smugness and wondered if maybe the boss wasn't right. Sometimes guys stayed too long in Frank's job. Got a little too close to the locals. Forgot who they worked for.

"Tell me about it, Frank."

"McKay's partner was the cop buried yesterday. I was giving regrets from the Bureau. Lewis came over and made some dumb comments. One word led to another and he tried to sucker punch McKay."

"Did McKay say something about Lewis's wife and kids?"

"Yeah."

"Well, we don't condone brawling, Frank, but we don't castrate our guys either."

Clancy shrugged.

"Frank, the boss gave this to me. I need some more specifics. One version we heard was that you were actually helping McKay."

Clancy laughed. "Goddamn. All right, Ray. I don't want this

attributed to me. I've spent twenty-one years in the Bureau, and no agent's file has a critical comment from me."

"Go on." Bloom nodded his agreement.

Clancy then repeated verbatim the conversation between Craig Lewis and McKay, repeating Lewis's obscene comments about a nun and Terry Fisher without emphasis. The only slight inaccuracy in his account was that he was trying to break up the fight when he inadvertently bumped into another FBI supervisor who was also trying to stop the argument.

Bloom winced at Craig Lewis's language. He bet after he reported it to the SAC he wouldn't hear any more about Craig Lewis replacing Clancy as liaison.

"So what's going on with the SFPD?" Bloom asked. "Are they trying to use us to deball one of their own?"

"In my opinion, yes."

"But why?"

"Remember that confidential meeting we had with DEA a few months ago? McKay was the narc who dropped the memo on Lieutenant Sherry."

"Oh, boy," Bloom said. "You think they're trying to take care of a whistle-blower?"

"I know McKay. He's a straight arrow and a good cop. I never understood why we didn't follow up on his memo. There have been stories floating around for years about a team of cop dope robbers."

Bloom said, "Go slow, Frank. Remember, at the time, you were privy to some top Bureau strategy. You were told certain things only out of consideration of your loyalty to the organization and position of liaison. You know agents don't ordinarily get explanations of management decisions, and don't expect to. The long-term investigations we've been working on with the SFPD—that case on smuggling illegal immigrants, for example, and the one on Mexican and local crooks stealing cars for shipment to Mexico—we can't afford to jeopardize two years' work chasing a rumor of corruption within the SFPD. They gave us a lot of assistance. Don't let yourself get emotionally involved with McKay."

* * *

Chief of Detectives Ferrante was uneasy. Police Chief Sean O'Brien wasn't known for his balls. Sitting behind his big desk, he was clearly worried.

"I don't know, Vincent. Do you think it prudent to move against McKay now? The media might pick it up and accuse us of harassing a whistle-blower."

"That's just what I'm trying to avoid, Chief."

Ferrante and O'Brien had been on a first name basis all during their career competition. Now, Ferrante was always careful to address him as Chief, though the rumor among the troops was that O'Brien only had been appointed after he agreed to accept Ferrante as Chief of Detectives. O'Brien was almost invisible as police chief. Press conferences were held by subordinates, and the chief always declined invitations to civic functions where his presence might be recorded by the media. The other rumor in the department was that the mayor had required this to avoid any danger that the chief might use the publicity attached to his position to run against him. Ferrante was a North Beach native. He had been an altar boy for a young priest, Patrick Cody, who was now Cardinal Cody. The rank and file also believed Ferrante's political and religious clout had forced the mayor, and consequently the police chief, to give him a prestigious position. The mayor's rival in the last campaign was chairing the Board of Supervisors and had threatened to raise hell if an Italian wasn't given the Chief of Detectives' spot. It was obvious to all that if Chief O'Brien called it quits, or the mayor sacked him, Ferrante would move into the top spot.

It turned out all of the rumors were true. As a result, Police Chief O'Brien considered very carefully any suggestions made by the Chief of Detectives. He wanted to be sure Ferrante wasn't setting him up for early retirement.

O'Brien said, "I'm sure it's not news to you that the mayor is gearing up to run again, and he's as skittish as hell. He doesn't want any notoriety from the police department."

"Exactly, Chief. If we move against McKay before the State Investigation Commission calls him to testify on that memo he wrote to you, we defuse the whole thing."

"If it works." O'Brien doodled on a pad.

"I'm confident it will. And the department will look better if our own police commissioners schedule a hearing on McKay's memo before an outside agency does."

"And Sherry? I've never been that comfortable about him. There have been stories for years," the police chief said.

"He produces great stats. More arrests and seizures than any other narc commander in history."

O'Brien fiddled with a letter opener. "And our great friends, the feds? How will they react?"

"DEA loves Sherry. Good busts on TV and good arrest and seizure stats, as I said. And the FBI owes us. Those task forces we set up with them—in a few months there will be a bust-out. Great publicity for us and them. They won't rock the boat over McKay."

"You better be right, Vincent, or the mayor will drop both of us like hot potatoes."

Ferrante leaned forward with a gleam in his eyes. "Chief, let me explain why I'm confident that we can discredit McKay. I've learned something that will destroy him as a witness. Here's how I see the Police Commission hearing—"

O'Brien held up his hand. "I don't have time now, Vincent. I'm late for a luncheon."

Ferrante returned to his office. Twenty minutes later he called his captain. "George, I have a Bureau of Investigations memo for the chief's signature. Call his aide and see what time he'll be back from lunch."

A few minutes later Ferrante's phone buzzed. It was George. "Chief, Chief O'Brien is lunching in today. His aide said we can bring your memo in anytime."

Ferrante scowled. That bastard. If things went wrong during the Police Commission hearing on McKay, the chief didn't know a thing. He was on his own using the information Glen Sherry gave him about McKay's new girlfriend.

Chapter Forty-three

Terry Fisher got on the elevator and pressed the button for the fourth floor. As the doors closed she spotted two inspectors ambling toward the elevator with coffee containers. Terry pressed the door open button until they got on.

"Thanks." She got a perfunctory smile from the younger of the two men. After a casual examination of her figure, both detectives ignored her. She was a woman, therefore a secretary or clerk, not anyone important in the organization. She could have been invisible as the two men continued their conversation.

"Yeah, it happened in Charley's after the funeral."

"Sounds like McKay stepped on his balls again."

Terry turned toward the men but they never noticed.

"It sure does, but they say he cleaned the guy's clock, and he was a big sucker too."

"Well, McKay was always good with his hands. He won a gold medal boxing in the police Olympics, remember? Who was the fed? Anyone we know?"

"No. A new guy by the name of Craig Lewis."

Terry stared at them.

"What started it?"

"There are two versions. One, the FBI guy said something bad about McKay's partner. The other version is that McKay said something about the agent's wife and kids. He's supposed to be quite a stick man, and McKay threw his family status up to him."

"What's with McKay? Is he running for pope or something?"

"You got me. I always liked the guy. A little too gung-ho and a rule-book man, but now they say he's coming apart, blames himself for the way Flip O'Neil was killed."

Terry stood frozen. *His wife and kids.* She felt sick, like a piece of ice had formed in her stomach and was moving into her bowels. She thought of the intimacy she had shared with Craig. And all the time he was married with a family. She remembered now how Kevin had reacted to Craig's picture on her desk. He must have known Craig was married. *Oh, God, what a fool she'd been.*

B&B was waiting for the elevator when she got off.

"Terry, how are you?" He smiled, then looked at her red eyes. "What's wrong?"

"Nothing, B&B. New contacts, that's all."

"Well, take care. I'll see you later."

Despite Lieutenant Garza's direction to take time off, Kevin was at his desk. He started to say hello to Terry but swallowed it when he saw her face. She put her briefcase on the desk and headed for the rest room.

Fifteen minutes later she was back and outwardly composed. She ignored his bruised face and knuckles.

"Good morning, Kevin. What's up?"

"Morning, Terry." Kevin had guessed what was disturbing Terry, but he wasn't about to discuss Craig Lewis, any more than she was.

"Terry, remember before Flip was killed we were going to tail suspects? I still think we should."

"There are only two of us. It will be tough."

"Yeah, but I was thinking of asking my old partner in Narcotics to help if he has time. He's the best there is when it comes to tailing someone. He wanted to see me about something. I'm meeting him for lunch. Want to come along?"

"Sure." Terry buried herself in case files on past attacks by the ski mask rapist, but every few minutes her mind shifted to Craig Lewis, alternating between rage and regret for what could have been. She didn't get much accomplished by the time they left for lunch.

Joey Demanto was waiting for them in a coffee shop on

Howard Street. Kevin slipped into the booth across from him. Terry stood, immobile. Joey's jaw dropped open.

"This creep was your partner?" she said.

At the same time, Joey blurted, "This bitch is your partner?" That bastard Ferrante, he thought. After what I told him, he went and made her an inspector.

Kevin frowned. "You know each other?"

"Know her? She just about ruined my sex life. Permanently. It's what I wanted to talk to you about. Maybe I should have a word with you privately."

"Before you talk to this creep, Kevin, there's something you should know. You better talk to me, privately."

Terry refused to sit.

"Bullshit," Kevin said. "I can see there's some misunderstanding between you, but we don't have time for games. Let's clear it up. How do you know each other?"

"Are you sure you trust her, Kevin? What I need to tell you is very hush-hush."

"You can trust Terry. Now answer my question." Kevin turned to Terry and pointed to the seat next to him. "Sit down, Terry."

Joey gave Terry a dirty look.

"Okay. Once again, I'll assume you know what you're doing, Kevin, although last time I did, I ended up shit creek. But here's what I wanted to tell you. Ferrante put me on a confidential stakeout at the Sacred Heart schoolyard. Along comes Jane Wayne, here," he pointed a finger at Terry, "and without warning she kicks me in the nuts so hard I pissed blood for three days."

"You were on duty? Why the hell didn't you tell me? You acted just like a dicky waver, chicken hawk, or worse." Terry was embarrassed.

"In the first place, you didn't give me a chance to tell you anything. Secondly, Ferrante threatened my life if I identified myself as a cop."

The waitress came and Kevin ordered coffee for them and turned back to Joey.

"I don't get it. Why did Ferrante have you watching theschool?"

Joey glanced at Terry.

"Go on, Joey. Anything you say to me you can say to Terry."

Joey shrugged. "Ferrante told me the mayor's office had been receiving some dynamite anonymous letters alleging a cop had been molesting kids."

"Jesus! Was the cop named?"

"Not specifically, except that he was black." Joey watched Kevin's reaction.

"Black?"

"Yeah. And do you want to hear who Ferrante had me watching? Sammy Cop-of-the-Year Robbins, that's who."

"Sammy Robbins molesting kids? That's ridiculous. I know the guy for years. He loves kids."

Kevin stopped talking as the waitress deposited their coffee and took lunch orders. When she was gone, he said, "Did Ferrante have anything specific relating to Sammy?"

"No, Kevin. He showed me the anonymous letter. It wasn't specific except for the schoolyard."

Kevin brooded. "Ferrante's got more angles than a pool table. I can't believe the letter was on the level about Sammy."

Terry stole a glance at Joey and saw the same concern for Kevin in his face. Kevin wasn't hitting on all cylinders. She didn't think it was the concussion, but of course you couldn't be sure. He hadn't said anything, but she knew he was obsessed with not discovering the shooter hiding in the shower. He was taking Flip's death very personally. He had looked into the bathroom. No one could expect him to look in the shower too. It was a routine parole interview, but the more they told that to Kevin, the more he went silent.

Terry realized Joey was kind of cute in an ethnic way. God, she hoped she hadn't hurt him, but he should have known better than to put his hands in his pockets when a cop was questioning him. Still, he seemed to have forgiven her, for the moment.

"For now," Kevin said, "we have to let the Homicide guys

work the case, but eventually I'm going to find out who killed Flip."

"Kevin," Terry said, "Lieutenant Garza thinks maybe it was Santucci's brother."

"It's possible. If he was in the apartment when we knocked, he might have panicked, thinking we were after him on the murder warrant. I could get it out of Santucci in a minute, but the bastards in Homicide won't let me talk to him."

And just as well, Terry thought. "Maybe I should nose around Homicide a little," she said.

"Okay," Kevin agreed. "Later, we can all get into it. But Joey, Terry and I wanted to ask your help. We have a couple of hot suspects in the ski mask rapes. Flip was going to help us set up a surveillance. You're the best I know. Do you have time to help?"

"Sure, but I thought the way the shooting went down that Santucci was your man."

"No. I don't know what was going on in his room, but neither Flip nor I had much hope that he was Ski Mask. Will Ferrante let you work with us, Joey?"

"Right now, Ferrante seems to have forgotten about me. I'll help, provided this lady behaves herself." He gave Terry a grin.

Terry grinned back at him.

"Okay, we'll fill you in," Kevin said, and held up the case files. "I'm persona non grata around headquarters, so we'll brief you here and begin the tail right after lunch."

Chapter Forty-four

Ski Mask had a new target. Torturing and killing Dolores Summers had fulfilled him as never before. He lusted for the same experience. He could postpone killing Dana Rogers, the cop's girlfriend, until there were less cops around her. In the meantime, he'd followed a young blond woman to her dance studio. The sight of her trim figure in leotards excited him as much as seeing Dolores Summers dressed the same way. He remembered smelling her sweat after her workout, and the way it had increased after he tied her up and scared her. He began to follow the blonde.

Bonnie Taft was a stewardess. On her days off between flights, she took dance lessons at a studio on Broadway with twenty other women and two men. About half the group had aspirations for show business. The others, like Bonnie, enjoyed the exercise and dancing. The dance studio was simply a large room. Students had no place to change or wash up after dancing. Nor was the area upscale. It wasn't unusual for a group of seedy-looking characters to be sitting on the big stone staircase leading to the building entrance. And since there were no drapes or curtains on the windows, they could watch the dancers. Most of the men were more interested in drinking wine, but Ski Mask liked to sit among them and watch Bonnie while he envisioned his coming "date" with her.

There were several other locations he liked to visit when the dance class wasn't in session. He liked to park across the street from a high school where girls played basketball every day. It wasn't a great view, but he'd purchased powerful binoculars with one of his stolen credit cards, and after making sure he wasn't observed, he could get a close-up of some fine young girls in skimpy uniforms with the glasses. He also cased an apartment visible from Mission Dolores Park. A young woman who was careless about pulling down the shades lived on the second floor. He liked to spread a blanket in the park and watch. On occasion he would use his glasses, but had to be careful not to be seen pointing them at the house.

Joey Demanto and Terry began the surveillance of Raul Santiago on a Wednesday at 1500 hours. Learning that he was scheduled for a week of evening shifts, they followed him when he left home, having no way of knowing that Raul

Santiago had called in sick. Joey drove an old, well-dented black Volkswagen. When Raul parked his green Ford at a parking meter, Terry got out and window-shopped. Raul was a nervous type, glancing around, changing directions, popping in and out of stores, but the two detectives faded in with their surroundings and he never picked up on them.

After Raul settled on the steps of a building on Broadway with a group of other men, Joey parked at a meter up the street and Terry joined him. The men on the stoop passed a wine bottle around. The dance studio was high above the street and not visible to the detectives.

"Is there anything in his file indicating he's a wino?" Joey said.

"No, I don't get it. But one thing is sure as hell suspicious. The way he acts like he's trying to spot a tail. I'm going to jot down all the times and locations for the record. Do you have a pad?"

Joey, watching Raul, pointed at the glove compartment. He wondered if they had the wrong man. Rapists weren't known to be winos.

"Oh." Terry had opened the glove compartment and a pair of Amanda's bikini panties fell out.

Joey looked over. "My cousin borrowed the car." He smiled at Terry, who held up the garment with two fingers.

"Well, I wish I had her figure." Terry grinned, letting him know she didn't believe him for a minute. She placed the underwear back in the glove compartment and began to note Raul's actions on the yellow pad.

After a while Raul realized that Bonnie Taft wasn't in the class. He wondered if she was at home. He'd already removed half the screws from her rear window. It would only take a minute for him to get in. Then it would be a replay of Dolores Summers. But it was too early. It wouldn't be dark for a couple of hours. Slowly, he descended the steps, jostling an elderly man on the sidewalk. The man was about to protest, but seeing Raul's intense face, changed his mind.

Joey shot ahead, anticipating that Raul was headed back to

his car. By the time Raul turned the corner, the black Volkswagen was a half block away and Terry had her arms around Joey so Raul wouldn't see their faces. Over Terry's shoulder, Joey watched him pass his car and suddenly double back. Joey meanwhile described Raul's actions to Terry and tried not to be distracted by the smell of her perfume and her hand on his shoulder. This wasn't bad duty.

Terry tried to concentrate as well. This was just the kind of stuff the D.A. said would justify a search warrant. Joey was a pretty good cop, she decided, realizing that the impression he made at the schoolyard, when she'd rousted him, showed how good he was at undercover operations.

"Much as I hate to stop cuddling," Joey said, "he's back in his car." They moved apart and Joey eased the VW into traffic, staying well behind Raul's Ford.

"Son of a bitch," Terry exclaimed as Raul whipped his car into a U-turn in the middle of the busy street and sped away from them. "Oh, my God, you're crazy!" she yelled as Joey did the same and a transit bus bore down on them.

The bus driver slammed on the brakes and blasted the horn. Terry threw her hands up to protect her head. Joey accelerated and the bus missed them by inches.

She looked at him in disbelief. "You're out of your mind. If you decide to do that again, let me out first."

He had a wide-open smile. "I knew the bus had good brakes. Where the hell did he go?" They were stopped six cars back of a red light. Without slowing, Joey pulled onto the sidewalk and sent them crashing off the curb into a side street. In the distance, they saw the green Ford.

"You just missed that old lady on the sidewalk, Joey. How about you let me drive from now on?"

"Loosen up, babe, we still have him in sight, don't we?"

Raul turned into a one-way street the wrong way and accelerated.

Terry braced herself for another scare, but Joey exclaimed, "Shit, if I go after him, he'll spot us."

He raced to the intersection and sped in a circle, trying to spot the Ford, but it was nowhere to be seen. "Why do they

make it so goddamn hard to get a search warrant on these bastards, anyway? If he's clean, he walks. If the evidence is there
and he's dirty, what the hell difference does it make how we
got the warrant?"

Terry was hanging onto her seat with both hands as Joey got
more and more frantic tearing around corners. "Hold on," she
said. "Is that it?"

A green Ford was at the curb across the street from the park.
Joey slowed. "Yeah, that's the car. Now where the hell did
he go?"

"There he is."

Raul had spread his blanket on the park lawn. The two detectives parked at the other end of the street and watched him
for a while. "This looks more like it," Terry said as they observed him surreptitiously using binoculars to peep at a woman
in the apartment across the street.

"There he goes again," Joey said as Raul abruptly left the
park and got into his car. "He's sure jumpy."

Joey was able to hang back and still keep Raul in sight as he
drove back and forth through the streets, accelerating without warning and then hitting the brakes. Both detectives felt
reasonably certain they hadn't been spotted, despite Raul's
maneuvers.

His next stop was to watch the girls play basketball, and as
they sat observing him, Terry said, "This guy is weird, all
right, but we don't have anything that will specifically tie him
to the ski mask attacks."

"Yeah, but I'd love to open the trunk of his car."

"The Supremes wouldn't like that."

"They wouldn't like leaving their courtroom and running
around like we are either. Uh-oh, he's off and running again."
Joey eased the VW into traffic. Raul drove normally for a
while, and then pulled into a freeway exit ramp the wrong way.

"That dirty bastard! It's not fair. If I follow him, he spots us
for sure. If I don't follow him, we lose him. I hope the motherfucker runs into a truck coming out the exit. Whatcha think?"

"You're absolutely right. If we go up the ramp and live, he

knows he's being shadowed and he'll destroy the evidence. But Joey, if we don't, and tonight he kills someone . . ."

"Damn. I've lost people before, but this guy is something different. I don't think I could catch him now. He's probably swung around to drive with the traffic on the freeway, and he'll take the first exit. I guess all we can do is go back to headquarters and call the CHP. Maybe we got lucky and they bagged him for reckless driving."

Horns blared at him, but Raul got to the top of the exit ramp and whipped the car around so he moved with the traffic. He was happy. No one could possibly be following him. It was dark now. Time to go to Bonnie Taft's apartment.

Chapter Forty-five

The next morning, Kevin, Terry, and Joey sat in Bertram Thatcher's office. The prosecutor had formally expressed his sorrow over the killing of Flip O'Neil. He'd liked and respected Flip. Suddenly, his professional demeanor deserted him and he left the room.

The three detectives sat in silent confusion. Kevin reacted visibly, slumping in the chair, his head bowed. Thatcher was back in a couple of minutes. Without a word he settled behind his desk. He nodded at Kevin, who gestured at Terry, and she began to relate their experiences following Raul Santiago.

The three detectives had spent a worried night, but no sexual assault reports had been made. They had no idea that Bonnie Taft was lucky enough to be given an extra day off at her New York flight destination, and that Raul Santiago had found an empty apartment.

"I don't doubt for a moment that what you observed is highly suspicious," the D.A. said. "But to issue a search warrant, we have to link Raul Santiago's behavior to a specific crime or crimes. You're very close, but we need something more. And we do have the stutter problem."

Kevin handed Thatcher a sheet of paper. "That's a memo from the FBI database on series rapists," he said. "Brenda Phillips, their profile specialist, helped. They had a similar case in Alabama. Turns out the guy lost his stutter during attacks. Experts say the pathology is psychological. He was in control of the woman, resulting in self-confidence, which temporarily cured the stutter."

"Excellent. This will help if you recover credit cards and other evidence belonging to victims."

"How about we just stop his car and get his consent to search the trunk?" Joey asked.

Thatcher rolled his eyes. "As if an appellate court judge would believe that yarn. That's if it even got past a superior court judge without being thrown out as an unlawful search." Thatcher stood and began pacing behind his deck. "Look, I'm on your side. There's nothing I'd like more than to give you that warrant, but I have to lay out the law to you. We'll all be miserable if Santiago is the ski mask rapist and walks because the court excludes the evidence as illegally obtained."

"We understand, Bert," Kevin said. "We'll just have to keep trying." His beeper went off and he saw that he was to call Lieutenant Garza's number. "Bert, do you have a phone I can use?"

"Try the next office. It should be empty." When Kevin was out of the room, he asked, "How is he taking it? He looks terrible."

"He's hurting, but he's hanging in," Terry said. "It's probably a good thing he has this case to work on. Flip O'Neil's case—" She stopped.

"Yes. I've heard some strange rumors on how it's being handled." Thatcher shook his head. "Kevin blames himself?"

"Yeah," Joey said. "No way was it his fault. But that's Kevin."

Thatcher nodded. "I hope it works out for him."

In the adjacent room, Kevin dialed the lieutenant's number.

"Where are you?" Garza asked him.

"At the D.A.'s. We're still trying to get a search warrant on Santiago."

"And the lawyers still won't play ball?"

"No. But Thatcher says we're close. Some more surveillance should do it."

"Good. Kevin, I paged you because I just came from Ferrante's office. I got an order as your commanding officer to notify you to be present for a Police Commission hearing the day after tomorrow at two P.M. It's on that memo you submitted to the chief."

"Great. It's about time."

Garza was silent a moment, then said, "Listen, Kevin, off the record, I have bad vibes about this. There's something fishy about how fast this hearing was set up. Do you have a lawyer?"

"A lawyer? What the hell do I need a lawyer for? I didn't do anything wrong."

"Look, Kevin, I'm out of the loop on this one. Just a messenger. But watch your ass. These guys play hardball. By the way, I'll be there in case you need some support."

"Thanks, Richard." Kevin used Garza's first name to show appreciation for his concern.

When he returned to Thatcher's office, Terry read his face and asked, "What's wrong?"

"I'm not sure," Kevin replied. "Lieutenant Garza notified me to be present for a Police Commission hearing day after tomorrow at two P.M. He thinks something's fishy."

Thatcher leaned forward. "Kevin," he said, "I stay out of police department politics, but if for any reason they criticize your work or try to remove you from this case, I'll be more than willing to state publicly that you should remain as principal investigator."

"Thanks, Bert, but this is about a drug memo I sent to the police chief. It should be straightforward at the hearing."

An hour later the three detectives sat on a park bench near Thatcher's office and talked about the next step in investigating Raul Santiago.

"Tailing him ain't going to cut it," Joey said. "He's too slippery. We'll either lose him or alert him."

"I've got an idea." Kevin stroked his chin. "Last year I took a course on surveillance at the FBI Academy. We can stick a transmitter under Santiago's car. It comes with an electronic tracking device that tells you where he is all the time. We put it in a helicopter and maintain radio contact with the tail car. The surveillance team can follow him without ever having him in sight. That way it doesn't matter what Santiago does to shake us."

"That's great, Kevin," Joey said, "except the SFPD ain't likely to have that kind of equipment this century."

"That's why you're going to go visit our old pals in DEA. They have the best budget and equipment in law enforcement," he explained to Terry, "and we did them a few favors." Kevin wrote the name and number of the DEA supervisor on a card for Joey. "See this guy. He owes me one. And Joey, I'm not telling you to lie to him, but you don't have to tell him it has nothing to do with dope."

"Yeah," Terry said, "just imply that it's as important as dope. We know they won't allow this kind of electronic stuff to be used for anything as unimportant as keeping women from getting raped and murdered."

Joey opened his hands in appeal to her. "Give me a break, will ya? I'm just a grunt."

Kevin touched their shoulders. "Okay, let's get going. I need to check to see how Dana's doing, but we should plan on following Santiago again late this afternoon."

Chapter Forty-six

Kevin had returned to his apartment to pick up warmer clothes for the evening surveillance of Raul Santiago. "We're going to start following him in an hour," he told Dana.

"You're not going to leave me here alone?" she said.

"What's wrong?" he asked. "You seem scared."

"I don't know what it is," she said. "Sometimes it seems I'm so vulnerable here—that the two of us are."

Kevin was puzzled. "What makes you think that? Has something happened?"

"Please, Kevin." She hugged him. "Let someone else follow him. You've been with me every night. I can't stand the thought of being alone."

"There's no way he would know where I live," Kevin said reassuringly.

"But what if somehow he *does* know?"

"Terry and I will be on him all the time. There's nothing to fear."

"Suppose you lose him?"

"We have electronic equipment. We'll be tracking him even when we can't see him."

"Do you believe in intuition? Hunches?"

"Sometimes." He touched the side of her cheek. "But you know how much I love you. I'd never take a chance with your safety."

"I know. But . . ."

"What is it?"

"I feel like I'm being watched. At first I felt real safe here, but lately I've been very frightened."

He hugged her. "Dana, the past week has been a nightmare for me. It's natural that it affects the way you feel. I'm sorry I lost it, but I'm okay now. We met with the D.A. If we can get evidence enough to arrest Santiago by just following him, we'll put him away."

Kevin left her at four-thirty and, as previously arranged, met Joey and Terry at the airport. He'd obtained the portable radio base system that would go in the aircraft. He and Terry would each carry a handset.

Joey was pissed. "I thought I was going with Terry," he said, "and you with the pilot."

"I'm the principal investigator on the case, and I have a personal interest."

Terry cut in. "Kevin, maybe that's a good reason you shouldn't be the one to put the cuffs on Santiago, if it comes to that. You know how a defense attorney could twist it." She left unsaid that she believed Joey was better at surveillance than he was, and that Kevin hadn't exactly been operating on all cylinders since Flip was killed. And, she admitted to herself, it was fun to be with Joey. He obviously found her attractive and didn't try to bullshit her that there were no other women in his life. He helped keep her mind off Craig Lewis.

Kevin shook his head impatiently. "I've considered all that, but I'm most familiar with the M.O. in all the other cases, and that could be important in establishing probable cause. Remember what Thatcher said about having the evidence excluded if we don't have probable cause. We'll test the radio and other equipment as soon as you're up." Kevin's tone indicated that the discussion was over.

Joey couldn't hide his disappointment. "Hey, partner, take care." He squeezed Terry in a hug and she blushed. "By the way, when I put the transmitter under his bumper, I also slapped a dab of luminous paint on the roof of the Ford. He should be easy to spot from the chopper." Seeing Kevin's frown, he added, "Don't worry. It blends with the color. He'll never notice it."

Terry ran several tests of the radio while Kevin drove to

Raul Santiago's work depot. She hadn't argued with Kevin, but she would have sat around the corner from Santiago's job and let Joey, in the aircraft, tell them when the car moved to avoid giving Santiago any chance to spot them. Kevin said he was doing it so he could swear Santiago was in the car, so subsequent applications for warrants would stand up.

A half hour later she silently acknowledged that their initial observation of Raul getting into his car had gone without a hitch, and noted it on her pad: *At 1810 hours the undersigned and Inspector Kevin McKay, observed the subject, Raul Santiago, enter a green late model Ford sedan in front of his work place at 2567 23rd Ave.* Terry had been afraid Kevin would be so eager, he'd try to keep the Ford in sight, but Joey, in the helicopter, picked the car up right away. Kevin was content to stay back after his initial observation.

"Okay, folks, this is your friendly traffic observer in the sky." Joey mimicked the radio traffic reporter. "As usual, conditions are shit for you slobs on the ground. Traffic is hopeless, so why don't all of you head for the nearest bar for an hour or two? Then you can get home quick, or maybe you won't want to get home at all. The green Ford shows fine both visually and soundwise. He's on Potrero now, probably headed for the freeway."

Terry smiled, but Kevin was too tense to respond to Joey's humor. He gripped the wheel tightly. She grimaced as he almost hit a parked car in his haste to follow Joey's directions.

The radio crackled. "Uh-oh, Kevin, there he goes again. He cut an illegal U-turn. He's coming back toward you."

Kevin quickly pulled the car into a driveway. They sat for a moment, then saw the Ford pass on Potrero. Kevin gave him a minute before pulling back onto the street. The Ford wasn't in sight.

"Okay, guys, our friend is approaching Twenty-third Street. He's making a right now." Joey's voice rose. "Hey, he almost got clipped crossing Mission. It looks like he ran a red light." A while later he said, "He's making a right on Dolores."

Kevin stopped trying to follow the Ford. He turned right on Van Ness, raced to Sixteenth Street and waited on the corner.

Joey came back on the radio. "He's crossing Sixteenth now, heading for Market."

Kevin let the Ford pass them. As soon as it was out of sight, he eased back into traffic.

"He's on Market now, there's a lot of traffic. Yeah, I know. So what else is new?" Joey spoke quickly.

"This seems to be working good, whatcha think, Kevin?" Terry recorded the Ford's evasive movements on her pad.

"So far." Kevin wore a frown, and she wondered what was worrying him.

"He just cut in front of a whole bunch of folks and made an illegal left off Market on Turk." Some static had broken Joey's transmission and he had to repeat it.

"Shit." Kevin hit the wheel in frustration. They were stalled in the traffic. He would have to make a left off Market, which was not only illegal, but very difficult to do, given the heavy traffic. The Ford was a long way from them now.

Kevin's too uptight, Terry thought. The helicopter could get them oriented quickly.

"Okay, our friend is heading toward Union Square now."

Terry saw Kevin's frown deepen as he absorbed Joey's information. Oh God. She got it. There was all kinds of underground parking around Union Square. What happened to the transmitter then? On the other hand, the chopper could hover overhead.

Kevin made an illegal left right in front of a black and white. The police cruiser's red lights flashed on and Kevin slowed, reaching for his badge. He flashed it when the cruiser pulled abreast and got a disgusted wave from the cop behind the wheel. It had slowed them, and now they were again pinned in traffic as they heard Joey transmit.

"He's pulling into the Union Square garage on Geary." The radio went dead for a moment, then Joey came back on the air. "We have zilch now. No visual sight. No sound. And if he abandons the vehicle, we'll never spot him as a pedestrian. We'll stay up here, though. If the Ford comes out, we'll nail him."

"Ten-four," Terry said, acknowledging the message. "We're

on Geary, almost at Union Square." She replaced the mike and felt a twinge of sympathy looking at the tension on Kevin's face. "As far as we know," she said, "Ski Mask never abandoned his car before this far from—"

"The victim's home," Kevin finished for her. "But we can't assume who his target is, or that he doesn't have another car buried." Kevin drummed his fingers on the steering wheel.

"True," Terry said, trying to reassure him, "but so far as we know, he only owns one car. And he's never done an attack without his car being nearby."

"As far as we know. Listen, Terry, I didn't tell you, but Dana's a nervous wreck. She thinks someone has been watching her at my place. She begged me to stay home tonight."

"So that explains it."

"Explains what?" he asked, looking at her.

"How tense you are. Kevin, you're practically jumping out of your skin."

"Maybe I should cruise the garage," he said. "I'd feel a lot better knowing for sure he's parked down there."

That's the problem with being in love, Terry thought. Instead of coolly playing the percentages, you begin to reach. And then you make a mistake. "I don't think it would be a good idea, Kevin. If he pulls out and we're trapped in a line of traffic down on the fifth level trying to get out of the garage, or if he spots us, we lose everything."

Kevin knew she was right. But he remembered Dana pleading with him. Maybe he should have stayed with her. Let Terry and Joey handle it. God, if anything happened to her, he couldn't take it. Not after Flip. He drummed on the steering wheel.

After a half hour Terry said, "Kevin, why don't you turn off the motor? We don't want to run out of gas." She wished she hadn't mentioned gas. The helicopter would have to refuel soon, and she knew Kevin was worried about it.

Kevin turned the motor off. He fidgeted in his seat. Another thirty minutes went by. They were parked in an awkward spot, blocking traffic, but it was the only location from which they could cover the garage's exit. Twice they'd been ordered to move by different police cars and had to flash their badges. The radio crackled.

"Kevin." Joey's voice gave away his concern. "We've been up almost an hour. The pilot says that in fifteen minutes we'll have to head to the airport for refueling. If we go now, we can be back here in fifteen minutes ready to tail him when he gets out. What do you say?"

Terry scrutinized Kevin. He stayed silent so long she thought he hadn't heard the question. The poor guy was in no condition to have to make decisions, she thought.

Finally, he said, "Okay. We've got the front entrance covered. Let us know when you're back. And hurry." He returned the mike to its holder and tried to grin at Terry. She wished he hadn't. "I guess I didn't have to tell them to hurry."

"We're back and have an hour and a half of fuel, guys, do you read me?"

"Ten-four," Terry said, noticing a perceptible relaxation in Kevin, who hadn't taken his eyes off the garage exit.

A car pulled up. "What's going on, McKay?" Captain Fitzgerald got out of a marked police car and leaned in the window next to Kevin. "Are you just trying to fuck up traffic or conducting a romance?" He looked at Terry without a smile.

"He's moving." Joey's voice was excited. Terry quickly turned the radio down, but Fitzgerald had heard.

"You guys got an operation going, patrol is supposed to know. I'm operations commander tonight, and I haven't heard a thing about it."

Terry knew that if Fitzgerald's car hadn't been blocking them, Kevin would have immediately gone after the Ford. "We don't have an operation going, Fitz. Just checking out some complaints of gropers in the department stores," Kevin said.

"Yeah, and what was that I heard on the radio?" Fitzgerald made no effort to hide his disbelief. "You're a real member of the team, McKay. But just keep going. You're digging your own hole in this organization, and a lot of us are going to enjoy watching you go down."

As soon as the police cruiser allowed them to pull away, they checked with Joey and found that the Ford had crossed Market and was approaching the Fourth Street entrance to the freeway. Kevin and Terry were at least five minutes behind.

Chapter Forty-seven

Elena Santiago hummed to herself. It was her mother's birthday, and she was going to make it a special day for her. She was leaving the boys at her cousin's house, and then as a surprise was taking her mother to dinner and shopping at Macy's in Union Square. She had been startled but pleased when Raul agreed to her plan. Ordinarily, he was very possessive about the car, but he'd agreed that it would be a treat for her mother to be driven to dinner and shopping. And it would be convenient for Elena to use the car to pick up the boys after she brought her mother home. By then it would be late, and she didn't like traveling in their neighborhood in the dark.

Elena wanted to get the gift certificate for her mother before taking her to Macy's, and she was afraid that by the time Raul drove home from work, it would be too late to get to Union Square, pay for the gift certificate, drive to her mother's, take her to dinner, and then get to the store before the nine P.M. closing. But Raul was in a good mood. He told her to take a bus to Union Square. He would come from work, park in the underground garage across from Macy's, and meet her in the store. He would give her the keys and tell her where the car was. She could have it all night. He had some business to take care of.

Raul did feel good. He was confident that no one could have followed him. His planning and maneuvers made him smarter and more powerful than the people he'd met in prison. Let silly Elena be happy with the car and her mother. He could easily get to where he was going. To where the cop's bitch would be taught a lesson. Her last lesson. He walked through the door of Macy's enjoying his feeling of power. There was no hurry. Although Elena was waiting for him at the store's business section, which sold gift certificates, he took his time. He took the escalator from floor to floor, lingering in the women's sections, hoping he would see arrogant rich bitches who would sharpen his appetite for what he would do later. He actually sat in a chair in the lingerie department for a while, as if waiting for his wife or girlfriend. Finally, he met Elena.

Raul gave her the parking ticket and carefully explained to her that the car was on the second level in the C section. She flushed with pleasure and kissed his cheek. He could be so sweet at times, she thought.

Elena wondered if the garage cashier had made a mistake. He charged her for an hour and ten minutes. She paid the fee and turned right, leaving the garage just half a block from where Captain Fitzgerald was confronting Kevin McKay and Terry Fisher. Elena had telephoned her mother to tell her she would pick her up in ten minutes at the rear of the housing project where she lived.

Kevin drove furiously after Captain Fitzgerald finally got out of their way, but he and Terry never did catch up to the Ford. They were just entering the Fourth Street ramp when Joey announced, "He's leaving the freeway. It must be the Army Street exit." A couple of minutes later the radio hummed again. "The car's pulling into the housing project on Guerrero."

"That's strange," Kevin said, concentrating on the freeway traffic, "that's a low-income project. Ski Mask never hit in that kind of area."

"Who knows—" Terry stopped as the radio purred.

"The car must have gone under a carport or something,"

Joey said. "We can't spot the luminous paint, but we're getting a broken signal, not like the blank we drew from the parking garage. Try checking around Fourteenth Street."

They cruised by the project on Fourteenth Street and saw that there were indeed carports, but the driveway was a one-way exit in the wrong direction. "I'm going to circle the block. Maybe we'll drive through the entrance on Twenty-second."

Before Kevin could get to the entrance, however, Joey was on the air. "Okay, he's on the move again. The car was stopped less than ten minutes. It probably was the carport. Maybe he just took a peek and spooked like he did when Terry and I followed him. Anyway, he's almost back on the freeway."

Kevin headed toward Potrero and the freeway. "What do you think, Terry?"

"Well, he did a lot of short stops when we followed him. Maybe Joey's right. Maybe he's just peeking or trying to shake a tail."

"The car's getting off at Seventh Street," Joey informed them. "He's not jumping lights, just moving with the traffic, which is pretty light now."

The light ahead of them was changing. Kevin stepped on the gas but had to slow when the car in front of them suddenly got law-abiding and didn't run the light.

Terry spoke into the mike. "Where is he now, Joey?"

"He's crossing Market. He's back near the Union Square garage. Can you guys get there in time to split and follow him on foot if he parks again?"

The light changed and Kevin whipped around the slow-moving car in front. "Damn," Terry said when she saw that a double-parked truck had traffic stopped. Kevin jumped from the car, pulling out his badge. Terry pressed the mike again. "We're blocked by a truck. I don't think we can get there in time. Any chance you can get low enough to see him leave the garage?"

"I have the night glasses," Joey replied. "I'll try, but you know how many ways there are to walk out of that place."

Kevin managed to find the truck driver. The man grumbled, but moved the vehicle, and they quickly picked up the trail.

They were just leaving the freeway when Joey came on the air.

"Here we go again, folks. The car is buried under the park. We're hovering low enough so I could look into the rooms at the St. Francis and be a dirty young man if I tried, but it will be tough to spot him unless we get very lucky. Like he stops to look up at us or something."

"Goddamn," Terry said as Kevin pulled to the curb in the same spot across from the garage. "I guess we just have to sit and wait again."

When Raul left Macy's, he walked a few blocks to a hardware store on Market. He purchased a glass cutter, masking tape, a suction cup, some clothesline, and a knife sharp enough to cut the rope easily. At the last moment he selected a small piece of cheesecloth. He would put it in the bitch's mouth, he thought, so her screams wouldn't alert the neighbors.

Stopping a cab on Market Street, he directed the driver to take him to Pete's Greek restaurant. He wasn't at all hungry, but the restaurant was five blocks from the cop's apartment and his date for the evening.

It wasn't long before he was standing in the doorway where earlier F. Bly had observed Dana. Raul watched Dana's shadow as she sketched in the top-floor room and got excited visualizing the next couple of hours. Her pain wouldn't be over quickly. He had practiced on Dolores Summers. He knew how to do it now.

Finally, he moved into the alley. In the darkness, he positioned himself behind the generator and waited, to be sure that no cops were around. After five minutes he moved silently to the fire escape and pulled down the ladder. His tennis shoes made no sound as he quickly moved up to the rear window. He saw that his guess had been correct. It was a simple window lock. He placed the masking tape in a square above the lock. He would not risk the noise of prying the lock open. He would simply use the glass cutter to make a hole, reach in, and turn the lock. The masking tape would prevent the cut glass from falling to the floor and alerting his date before he was ready to surprise her. There might be some noise when he raised the window, but it would be too late then. In fact, it would be even more fun if she came to investigate. As he placed his tools neatly on the windowsill, Raul pictured her face as she watched him climb through the window.

Chapter Forty-eight

Terry felt badly for Kevin. As time went by and they sat across from the garage, he grew more strained. She thought of Dana alone and scared. Of course Kevin was concerned. So was she. But what else could they do?

"Do you believe in hunches, Terry?"

"Sure," she said, not telling him that she guessed what he wanted to do and disagreed.

"Well, I think something's wrong."

"Kevin, I know this waiting is tough on you, but we have to play the percentages. The odds are, he's going to come back for the car before he tries anything. He's followed the same pattern before, trying to shake us. But he always comes back to the car."

"Yeah, but think about it. Driving down to the garage the first time, he used all of his usual tricks. Driving out to the projects he didn't try anything. Then coming back here, the car made a straight run to the garage."

"Hmm, you're right . . ."

"It could mean someone else is driving the car and Santiago is gone."

"My God!"

"I'm going to check on Dana. Do you want to come or stay here?"

"I'm going with you." She reached for the mike. "I'll let Joey know what's up."

Their tires screeched and she was thrown back in the seat. Kevin stuck the portable red dome light on the roof and hit the siren as they sped into traffic. Terry's worry about him functioning faded as she saw the skill with which he took intersections and the speed of the response as he cut back and forth through the streets, picking the best route to his house.

She didn't know whether to hope he was right or wrong as they hurtled across the city. If he was right and Santiago got to Dana before they did, she was finished. Even if he didn't kill her, she would snap. After Flip was killed, and then with Kevin crashing, Dana was clearly in a fragile state. But even if she wasn't, who could survive this bastard's cruelty?

Terry wanted to blow him away. It would be better that way, she thought, than if Kevin did it. He was in enough trouble, and the lawyers would have a field day claiming it was murder. On the other hand, if they were running off on a wild-goose chase and Ski Mask went back to his car and killed someone, Kevin was liable to crack. Hurry, Kevin, hurry, she said to herself.

Kevin left the car double-parked with the keys in it and the motor running. He took the steps to the front door two at a time, Terry right behind him.

Abruptly, she stopped. Shit, she couldn't leave the car with the keys in it. It would be gone when they got back, and Kevin was in too much hot water already. She dashed back to the car and grabbed the keys. Running back to the house, she took the steps two at a time and rushed into the inner hall. "Oh my God," she said aloud as she found the inner door had locked behind Kevin. She leaned on his bell but there was no answering buzzer to let her in. Frantically, she hit the bell to the other apartment, but no one responded. People had gotten cautious in San Francisco about buzzing back if they weren't expecting company.

"Shit!" She left the hall and went to the stoop. The lights to the apartment on the ground floor were on. Terry climbed up on the ledge and pounded on the window. "Police!" she yelled.

In the upstairs bathroom, Dana ran the water and washed her face. It kept her from hearing Kevin's hoarse whisper, "Dana, Dana, it's Kevin. Open up."

The lack of a response made him desperate. He fumbled through his pants for his keys. He heard the bell ringing inside and guessed that Terry was locked out downstairs, but he didn't have time to deal with that. He didn't want to think of why Dana wasn't answering. He managed the lock. Opening the door, he drew his gun.

The running water covered the sound of the downstairs bell. When Dana turned off the faucet, the ringing had stopped. She left the bathroom just as the front door opened and Kevin jumped forward in a crouch.

She stared at his wild face and the pointed gun. "What?" she gasped.

He stayed frozen for a moment, then stood up. "Are you all right? You didn't answer the bell. We thought . . ." He put his gun away and rushed forward, taking her in his arms. "Dana, Dana, I was so worried. . . ."

He tensed, and she heard it too. A noise from the kitchen like the window being opened.

"Oh," she murmured as he roughly pulled her into the hallway.

He whispered, "Dana, Terry is downstairs. Let her in and tell her to call for help." His gun out again, he moved into the apartment.

"Kevin, please! Don't go in there," she whispered, grabbing at him.

He pushed her away. "I have some unfinished business," he said, and moved off.

"No," Dana sobbed, half running, half falling down the stairs. "Terry! Terry!" she cried.

"Where is he?" Terry had been let in by the scared tenant who lived in the other apartment. She caught Dana by the shoulders on the stairs.

"Someone is coming in the window," Dana blurted. "I tried to stop Kevin, but he went in. He said to tell you to call for help."

"Dana, I'm going to help Kevin." She pointed downstairs. "Get your neighbor to call 911." She ran up the stairs.

Kevin waited outside the kitchen door until he was sure Santiago was in. Then he swung into the room in a crouch, both hands bracing his gun.

Raul Santiago was carefully backing through the window into the apartment.

"Hello, scumbag. We have a little surprise for you this time."

Raul, startled, slipped on the windowsill and his gun fell to the floor. He stumbled into the room and froze.

"Pick it up. You're going to die anyway. You might as well try."

Raul left the gun on the floor. He looked around, dazed. A butcher knife was on the counter. In slow motion he picked it up.

Terry rushed into the room and saw Santiago beyond Kevin with the knife. She leveled her gun, yelling, "Get out of the way, Kevin!"

Kevin never took his eyes off Santiago, who turned toward them with the knife in his right hand. The glass china closet above him reflected Terry behind him and, behind her, Dana, who'd followed Terry in and watched with horror.

Santiago threw the knife to the floor. "I give up," he said, and raised his hands.

"It's too late, you bastard," Terry said. "Kevin, get the hell out of the way." Terry moved, trying to get a clear shot.

Kevin's eyes were riveted to Dana's in the glass. His finger had eased off the trigger when Santiago raised his hands, but he was now fingering the trigger again. He'd never killed anyone, but now he wanted to see Santiago on the floor writhing in pain, his life fading as his heart pumped blood from his wounds. But Dana was shaking her head from side to side, pleading. Surely not for Santiago. No, it was for him. She didn't want him to kill Santiago. Raul turned his back on them, spread his hands on the cabinet and assumed the search position. Kevin sagged against the doorway and his gun arm sank to his side.

Terry pushed him roughly out of the way and raised her gun. "Not in the back, Terry," Kevin said softly.

Tears of frustration in her eyes, she said, "Goddamn you, Kevin, why didn't you get out of my way?"

Chapter Forty-nine

Kevin fumbled with papers on his desk. He was drafting an application for a search warrant for Raul Santiago's apartment. With Santiago in jail on charges of burglary, illegal possession of a firearm, and attempted assault, some of the urgency was gone. Of course, the search warrants were important. The evidence would tie Santiago to enough rapes to put him away for life. But Kevin found it hard to concentrate.

The distraction of nailing the ski mask rapist no longer shielded him from thinking about Flip. The deep pain in the pit of his stomach never left him. Despite Dana's attempts to soothe him during the night, he was unable to sleep. He'd spoken with the Homicide team assigned to Flip's case. They were sympathetic, but told him it was too early to see any leads. They had dummied up when he asked why.

"Got a minute, Kevin?" Barney Brady stood next to Kevin's desk.

"Not right now, B&B. I have to go to the Police Commission meeting in ten minutes."

"I know. That's what I wanted to talk to you about. It's important." B&B's eyes roamed the room and he lowered his voice. "I have to take a leak. Come with me."

Kevin put on his suit jacket and stuck a copy of his memo to the chief on Lieutenant Sherry in his pocket. He gave the applications on the search warrants to Terry to finish and followed B&B to the men's room.

B&B checked the stalls to make sure they were alone. Any other time it would have brought a smile to Kevin's face, but now he watched somberly.

"You look flushed, Kevin." B&B touched his forehead. "Hot. Just as I suspected. You've got the flu. You ought to go home right away."

"What're you talking about? You know I'm due at the Police Commission meeting."

"That's what I mean. I'll go up and tell them you've been sick all day and the lieutenant sent you home. I've already cleared it with Garza. He'll back us up."

"I don't get it, B&B. I'm just going in to tell them I wrote a memo repeating what a dope dealer told me about Lieutenant Sherry. I did what the manual requires. What's the big deal?"

"Look, Kevin, I'm the POA delegate, but I'm also your friend. I'm trying to give you some good advice."

"Well, as you suggested, I contacted the POA. I'm still a member. They didn't sound happy about it, but they're sending Cary Benton, the attorney, to represent me, although I'll be damned if I can see why I need representation."

"Kevin, Kevin . . ." B&B spoke in a near whisper even though they were alone. Kevin found the smell of mints mixed with whatever B&B was consuming unpleasant. He moved back a step, but the fat man closed in on him. "Kevin, I don't like what I hear about this commission meeting. Take my advice. Get the flu and take a few days off."

"Bullshit. I'm trying to wrap up the ski mask case, and then I'll look into what happened to Flip. I don't have time to play games."

The door opened and two uniformed men came in. B&B shook his head. "Think about it. If you change your mind, I'll be at my desk."

Kevin went to the sink and splashed cold water on his face. Drying himself with a paper towel, he saw that the uniformed cops were watching. He nodded, but both of them turned away. Kevin was about to take the cops on, then decided it wasn't worth the effort. He straightened his jacket and went upstairs to the Police Commission's chambers.

The commissioners hadn't taken their places behind the dais yet, but there were four or five people sitting in the audience. He was surprised to see Lieutenant Garza and Terry Fisher in the front row. Lieutenant Glen Sherry was alone on the opposite side of the room.

Kevin sat at the table with Cary Benton, the POA attorney, who squeezed his hand in a reluctant shake and quickly dropped it. The uniformed cop who was acting as a bailiff vanished through the door behind the dais. A couple of minutes later he opened it and the commissioners filed in.

Benton jumped to his feet, and after a moment's hesitation, Kevin stood. Priscilla Stone, a black woman and an attorney, walked to the far seat and was followed by Angelo Ruggieri, the new president of the commission, and also an attorney. Ruggieri, a close friend of the mayor, had taken over the chairmanship when Bill Logan, his predecessor, left to preside over a huge resort development in southern California. Ruggieri's friendship with the mayor, duly sanctioned by appointment to the police board, hadn't hurt his law practice a bit. Every once in a while the newspapers went on a crusade and mentioned that he represented a lot of landlords in the Tenderloin who often hired off-duty cops for security at the topless bars, massage parlors, and sex show joints proliferating in the area, but such conflict-of-interest claims raised more smiles than eyebrows in blasé San Francisco. Within the inner circle of the police department, it was also known that the POA had petitioned the mayor to appoint Ruggieri, who had represented them in a number of labor disputes.

The three remaining members of the commission took their seats to the right of Ruggieri. Intentionally or not, Priscilla Stone was isolated on the dais. She'd been appointed by the previous mayor, and it was rumored throughout the department that when her term was up in three months, she would be replaced by someone less critical of the police administration.

Ruggieri banged the gavel and nodded at the legal stenographer, whose fingers hovered over her machine. "Before we begin, I am announcing that this is a personnel hearing, and as such, is a closed hearing in conformance with the state of California labor laws." He smiled and touched his pencil mustache. "I'm afraid, Lieutenant Garza, that means that you and your secretary will have to leave."

Garza got to his feet, and Kevin could see anger in his face. "Commissioner, this is not my secretary. This is Inspector Terry Fisher, Inspector McKay's partner."

"Nevertheless," Ruggieri replied, "it is a closed hearing and you'll have to leave."

Garza looked at Kevin's lawyer to see if he would object, but Benton stared down at papers on the desk. The other people in the room, with the exception of Lieutenant Glen Sherry, headed for the doors. Garza and Terry followed them.

"Inspector Fisher . . ." Priscilla Stone's voice stopped them at the door. "I'd like to apologize for the ignorance of the chairman in assuming that you were a secretary. Hopefully, someday the police department will provide enough equal opportunity for women so that such comments won't be made. Congratulations on your promotion."

Ruggieri ignored her remarks. When the bailiff locked the doors behind the departing cops, he said: "This hearing concerns a memorandum to the police chief submitted by Inspector McKay. I have the memorandum before me. Officer McKay, will you come forward to the witness chair for the oath?"

After Kevin had been sworn in, Ruggieri handed him the sheet of paper. "Inspector, is this the memo you wrote?"

"Yes."

"The clerk will note that the witness has identified the document, which will be labeled Exhibit A. Now, Inspector McKay, at the time you wrote this memorandum, you were a member of the Narcotics Unit, were you not?"

"Yes."

"Mr. Benton," Priscilla Stone interrupted, "are you not going to review this document before it is labeled as evidence?"

Benton got to his feet, flustered. "Yes, of course." He took the memo, skimmed it, and handed it to the stenographer with a nod.

Priscilla Stone smiled sweetly. "Mr. Benton, as an experienced attorney I'm sure you do not have to be reminded that the stenographer cannot record your body motions, only your words."

"I have no objection to the memo," Benton mumbled.

Ruggieri frowned at Priscilla Stone. "Fine. Now, if Mrs. Stone has no objections . . ." He turned to Kevin. "Tell me, Inspector McKay, what is your present assignment?"

"I have no objections, Mr. Chairman, but I would like the record to state that Inspector McKay's memo is dated six weeks ago, and I hope that the chairman will inform us why it has taken so long to come before us."

Ruggieri scowled at her. "Mrs. Stone, I ask for your cooperation. We will never get through this hearing if you constantly interrupt."

"I draw attention to the fact that the chair has declined to answer my question, but please continue, Mr. Ruggieri, I am most interested that Inspector McKay get his time before this commission."

"Let me try again." Ruggieri turned to Kevin in the witness chair. "Where are you now assigned, Inspector?"

"Sexual Assaults Unit."

"And how long have you been in that assignment?"

"Almost six weeks."

"And was your partner Inspector Flip O'Neil?"

Kevin felt a wave of emotion. He looked down, then found his voice. "Yes."

"And Inspector O'Neil was murdered approximately two weeks ago?"

Kevin felt tears on his cheeks.

"Mr. Chairman, since Mr. Benton is not asking, I must." Priscilla Stone was angry. "What does the murder of Inspector O'Neil have to do with a memo Inspector McKay submitted about possible narcotics corruption?"

"It will be clear momentarily if you can restrain yourself from interrupting."

"I will not restrain myself. This man submitted a memo reporting possible corruption. It is the duty of this commission to investigate reports of misconduct, not harass the witness. He's obviously under great strain after losing a partner, and I want to know why you are asking about it."

"You are quite correct, Commissioner Stone. It is the duty of the commission to investigate, and the duty of the chairman to conduct hearings. This memo alleges quite serious—actually, criminal—behavior by a veteran lieutenant and two other veterans of the department. It is incumbent upon us to determine how much truth there is in the allegations, and that means the credibility of the memo and its author must be examined."

Priscilla Stone turned to look at Cary Benton, who gazed vacantly at Ruggieri.

Kevin's mind was churning with a mixture of rage and fear. Rage that these people would desecrate Flip's memory for their own shoddy purposes of protecting dirty cops. And fear that they were about to disclose some new evidence that Flip was guilty of something.

Ruggieri again fingered his mustache. "Inspector McKay, you were present with Mr. O'Neil when he was shot, were you not?"

Kevin stifled his rage. "Yes."

"Yes? And did you return the gunfire?"

"No." Kevin had trouble speaking.

"I see. But you were there when he was shot."

Priscilla Stone was about to object again, but realized it wouldn't do any good, and instead would just drag out McKay's agony.

"Did you hear the shots?" Ruggieri asked.

"Yes."

"But the man who shot your partner escaped?"

Kevin looked at his lawyer, who was studying his legal pad.

Ruggieri didn't wait for an answer. "How long have you been a policeman?" he asked.

"Fourteen years."

"And you didn't return fire? Did you get a description of the killer?"

Kevin gave Ruggieri a contemptuous look. As the chairman, he had undoubtedly seen the report and knew he'd been injured.

"Were you on duty at the time?" Ruggieri continued.

"Of course."

"I see. And Inspector O'Neil?"

Kevin didn't answer. The knot in his stomach was so intense he felt dizzy, and he could feel his rage at Ruggieri approaching the breaking point.

Priscilla Stone could see it also. "Mr. Chairman, once again I must ask what this tragedy has to do with Inspector McKay's memo?"

Ruggieri didn't miss a beat. "This commission must consider the credibility of the memo's author. Is it not interesting that an experienced policeman would not see the killer of his partner, yet be so alert that he would spot corruption where no one else sees it?"

"Speak for yourself when you say no one else," Priscilla Stone said. "When do we actually get to the memo?"

"In a moment, Mrs. Stone. One more question, Inspector McKay. Was your partner, Inspector O'Neil, also on duty?"

"Yes." Kevin could feel his face reddening.

"In other words, you worked together."

"Yes."

Ruggieri let the silence build. "All day?"

"Yes."

"And the day before."

"We were together most of the day."

"Most? What time was it when you first saw Inspector O'Neil?"

"After lunch." Kevin wiped his sweaty palms on his pants while Ruggieri stared at him. It was the old game, Kevin knew. Ruggieri had him on the ropes and was pausing for effect with the other commissioners.

"Were you and O'Neil working on one case more than another?"

"Yes."

"Would that be the ski mask rapist?"

"Yes."

"You said that you hadn't seen Inspector O'Neil that morning. Is that correct?"

"No. He came in around two P.M."

"But the log of the Sexual Assaults Unit shows you and Inspector O'Neil signed out that morning on the ski mask investigation. Am I right?"

"Yes."

"And who made that entry?"

"I did."

"Yet Inspector O'Neil wasn't with you all morning?"

"No."

"Where was he?"

"I don't know."

"So you made a false entry?"

Kevin thought about trying to explain to these people that it was done all the time. Department management never inquired where anyone was as long as there was a log someplace covering management's ass.

"Let me ask you again, Inspector. Did you sign the log indicating that you and Inspector O'Neil were out of the office investigating the ski mask rapist?"

"Yes."

"Yet you hadn't seen him that day?"

"No."

"Did you know where he was?"

"No."

"Did you know what he was doing?"

"I assumed he was working the case."

"Did Inspector O'Neil ever do the same for you? Sign you out when you weren't present?"

"Sometimes."

"And how often had you done it for him?"

"I don't recall how many times."

"A lot?"

Kevin shrugged.

"Let's consider the two weeks before Inspector O'Neil's death. How many times had you signed the log indicating Inspector O'Neil was working with you on the ski mask case?"

"Ten." Kevin was aware of the scandalized look on the other commissioners' faces. Even Priscilla Stone was frowning.

"Ten? In other words, every workday."

"I trusted Flip. I assumed he was working."

"I see. And you assumed Lieutenant Sherry was guilty on the word of a convicted dope dealer."

"I didn't assume. I just wrote the memo the way I was supposed to."

"But you didn't write a memo reporting Inspector O'Neil's absences the way you were supposed to?"

Kevin hunched forward in the witness chair. He was very thirsty but didn't want to ask for a glass of water.

"You haven't answered. But I don't want Commissioner Stone to think I'm harassing you. Let me sum it up, and if you feel I have misstated anything, please correct me. You falsified the squad log on numerous occasions to indicate that you and your partner were investigating a series rapist, when you had no idea where your partner was. Now let's move on before Commissioner Stone reprimands me again. How long did you work for Lieutenant Sherry?"

"Two years."

"Are you aware that for the four years Lieutenant Sherry has been in command, the Narcotics Unit has made more arrests than ever before?"

"No."

"Do you care?"

"It's not my job to evaluate the number and quality of arrests."

"Quite true. Teams are evaluated by the commander, are they not? And the unit by the Chief of Detectives."

"Yes."

"Your former partner, Joseph Demanto, and you, were compared to the rest of the teams, is that correct?"

"Yes."

"How many teams were there?"

"Fifteen."

"And where was your team in the arrest standings?"

"That's not a fair comparison. We were given long-term investigations requiring prolonged undercover work."

"Do you know where you and Demanto rated in arrests?"

"Yes."

"It was fifteenth, last. Wasn't it?"

"I've already said why."

"Yes you have. Did Lieutenant Sherry ever reprimand you for so few arrests?"

"No. He gave us the long-term cases. He knew we would be last."

"Inspector McKay, if I brought in your fellow workers on the Narcotics Unit, wouldn't they testify that Lieutenant Sherry yelled at you and your partner in the squad room?"

"He sure did when he found out about the memo to the chief."

"But let's talk about before that. He never yelled at you?"

"He yelled at everyone."

"Was the subject the number of your arrests?"

"Yes."

"Did you answer him?"

"Yes. I told him it was unfair to compare us because of the kind of cases he gave us."

"Did Lieutenant Sherry ever give you a written reprimand?"

"No."

"You're sure?"

"Yes."

"I ask you to look at this document."

Kevin took the paper, noticing that his hands were trembling.

"Under the title 'Subject,' what does it say?" Ruggieri sat back in his chair.

"Reprimand for Inspector Kevin McKay. I never saw this." He turned and glared at Sherry, who sat without expression.

"Who signed it?"

"Lieutenant Sherry."

"And is it dated during the time you were in the Narcotics Unit?"

"Yes, but this isn't in my personnel file."

"Let the record show that this document was obtained by the commission from the police department personnel officer." Ruggieri was smug.

"Inspector McKay," Priscilla Stone said, "doesn't the department require that all written reprimands be countersigned by the recipient before being placed in a personnel file?"

"Yes, Commissioner."

"Would you look at that document and tell me if you signed it."

"No. The line for a countersignature is blank."

"Well, I move that it be excluded and that the personnel officer be asked to explain how the document got into a personnel file without the officer's signature."

"Thank you, Mrs. Stone." Ruggieri looked down at Kevin. "Inspector, I believe that the record will show that we gave you every opportunity to speak. However, since Commissioner Stone keeps implying that we have not, I would like to invite you to tell me why you submitted this memorandum alleging criminal conduct by Lieutenant Sherry."

"I believe I was required to report what was very serious misconduct. I can't think of anything more terrible than police officers who arc in a war against drugs actually being involved with the drug trade."

"You feel strongly that everything should be done to keep drugs away from young people in our country."

"Yes."

"Do you like Lieutenant Sherry?"

Kevin hesitated. "No."

"Did your dislike for and criticism by Lieutenant Sherry have anything to do with the memo?"

"No."

Again Ruggieri paused, staring at Kevin, who couldn't keep the anger out of his face as he glared at the chairman. "So, it is your contention that your strong feelings against drug use and your dedication to young people motivated your memo. Do you think Lieutenant Sherry is guilty of what the dope dealer alleged?"

"I have no proof of that. I merely did what the rules required."

"Yes, but we have seen that you are very selective about following the rules and reporting misconduct. I want to move to another subject." Ruggieri held up a photo.

"Before we do, Mr. Chairman," Priscilla Stone cut in, "Inspector McKay, I appreciate that you are unwilling to judge Lieutenant Sherry without further evidence. It was your hope that an investigation would take place, was it not?"

"Yes, Commissioner."

"To your knowledge, did the police department ever investigate your memo?"

"No."

"Do you know of any police department plans to interview Mr. Hallman, who made the allegations to you?"

"That can't be done now."

Priscilla Stone frowned. "Why not, Inspector?"

"His body was found two weeks ago in San Mateo. He had been shot."

"I see. Let me ask you this question. You've been a cop for fourteen years. Would you have submitted that memo if you believed that it was a dope dealer trying to set up an innocent policeman?"

"No. I—"

"Hold on, Inspector." Ruggieri for the first time showed some emotion. "You're an attorney, Commissioner Stone. You know that was an improper question. The clerk will strike the question and answer."

"As an attorney, I'd welcome a judicial review of the transcript of this hearing." Priscilla Stone slapped shut her notebook.

"Inspector McKay . . . " Ruggieri composed himself, stroking his thin mustache. "Do you have knowledge of any evidence that might link the death of Mr. Hallman with your memo?"

"No." Ruggieri had been ostentatiously playing with a photograph, and Kevin realized it had been for his benefit, thinking it would unnerve him.

"Inspector McKay, are you familiar with a police department rule that prohibits members of the force from associating with known criminals?"

"Yes."

"And what is the purpose of that rule?"

"To protect the department's credibility and prevent corruption."

"Well said. Please look at this picture and tell me if you recognize it."

Kevin took the picture and frowned. It was a mug shot of Ronnie Blue taken the day before.

"I take it you know this subject?"

"His name is Ronnie Blue. He's one of the youngsters I coach at Sacred Heart."

"Is he a drug user?"

Kevin felt sick, remembering the recent change in Ronnie's behavior. "Not that I know."

"Not that you know?" Again Ruggieri paused. "You, a policeman for fourteen years and a former member of the Narcotics Unit? Did you know that Lieutenant Sherry suspected Ronnie Blue and the other boys you hung out with of running a drug ring?"

"That's garbage." Kevin realized he'd yelled. He took a deep breath.

"Were you angry when you found out they were under investigation?"

"No one ever told me they were under investigation."

"Was that because they thought you might disclose the investigation?"

"This is getting more ridiculous." Kevin knew he was flushed. "When are we going to talk about my memo?"

"Right now, Inspector." Ruggieri picked up another photo and once again toyed with it. Kevin noticed that Ruggieri's legal techniques had drawn the full attention of the rest of the commission.

Kevin got down from the witness chair and walked to the table where his lawyer sat. He poured water and drank deeply. Some water splashed on the table, and everyone in the room watched. He returned to the witness chair.

"Just one more photo, Inspector."

Kevin took it from Ruggieri's hand. It was the photo he'd noticed the first time he stayed with Dana. The man's face had nagged at him then, but he'd dismissed it as jealousy. The arm around Dana's shoulder had been possessive, but he hadn't asked Dana about it, didn't want to scare her away. When he and Flip went to Dana's apartment to do the photo lineup with Jane Remick, the photo hadn't been visible. He felt bile in his throat now, recalling his childish pleasure that day when he realized it wasn't displayed. Pleasure that distracted him from the question of who had paid for such an expensive apartment.

Ruggieri was pleased with Kevin's surprised reaction. "Now, Inspector McKay, as a member of the Narcotics Unit for several years, you would be aware of any large drug busts in the city, would you not? And of the identity of known large-scale dealers?"

Kevin felt a kind of paralysis setting over him. Almost like his mental break after Flip's murder. How had they gotten the picture? Could Dana have given it to them? And Ruggieri was getting at something. Something he should know . . . but he couldn't focus.

"Does the name Carlos Castellano mean anything to you?" Ruggieri was quite content not to push Kevin to answer. His fellow commissioners were watching a witness unravel on the stand.

Kevin only dimly heard Ruggieri's purring questions. It was coming together for him now, all the mysterious details and loose ends concerning Dana. The photo, the expensive apartment, the sense that she was keeping something from him . . .

Carlos Castellano. Of course. Carlos Castellano had surfaced very briefly, and it had been a federal case. Kevin had only glanced at a mug shot at the time, and the beach photo was poor quality. But it was him. And Dana had never told him. She'd lived with a dealer. Was that why she'd gone out of her way to meet him that first time? Had she done it for Carlos Castellano? Was it a setup? He felt his face flushing again.

"Inspector, are you now living with a woman by the name of Dana Rogers, who previously cohabited for two years with Mr. Castellano, before and after his arrest?"

Kevin, dazed, remained silent.

"How does this square with your previous statement that you reported Lieutenant Sherry because of your strong anti-drug feelings?" Ruggieri asked.

Kevin became aware that even Priscilla Stone had stopped defending him. She looked down at her notes.

Ruggieri had blood in his nostrils now. "I ask you, Inspector McKay, did you knowingly violate the department's rule prohibiting intimate relations with known criminals and their associates?"

Kevin gripped the arms of the witness chair until his knuckles were white. Flip. Dana. B&B's warning that the department was backing Sherry and betraying him. He'd been so blind. Ruggieri's banging gavel exploded against the insides of his head.

"Inspector McKay, you're under oath, and the police department rules require every member of the department to answer questions from this commission." Ruggieri let his voice rise in a dramatic roar.

Kevin stood. He'd been sitting so long that his knee gave out and he stumbled. As he righted himself he heard Ruggieri shouting at him. He walked to the door, oblivious of the consternation behind him. Dana, Dana, he thought, I love you so much, and you never told me. . . .

Chapter Fifty

Father Riordan moved the Eucharist into the tabernacle and locked it with the tiny key. He genuflected and turned away, glancing out beyond the altar rail into the pews, dark and empty at nine P.M. The church is beautiful, in its own way, he reminisced. Simple and old fashioned, not like the newer cathedrals. This church was meant to be filled with the sound of Latin and the smell of incense and the mystery of the sacraments. It had been built sixty years earlier to serve the Irish and Italian working-class neighborhood. The kind of neighborhood that produced the priests, brothers, and nuns to serve future generations. He had spent ten years of his life here among the people he'd grown up with. Baptizing them, marrying them, hearing their confessions, and burying them.

The priest crossed himself and started for the sacristy behind the altar, then stopped. He hadn't noticed the solitary figure sitting quite still in the rear of the church. The outer doors had been locked hours ago. How long had the person been there? Father Riordan walked toward the motionless figure. Dark as it was, there was something familiar about him.

"Kevin." Father Riordan's face lit with a smile. "God be praised. We've gotten you into the church again."

Kevin stood and the priest saw his face. Instinctively, he put his arms around Kevin and patted him on the back. "I'm sorry, Kevin. I spoke too soon. I don't know what new troubles you have, but let me help you all I can."

The gloom they felt after hearing of Kevin's hearing was still with them, but Terry and Joey felt better now, sitting in one of San Francisco's oldest restaurants, Sam's Grill, in the financial district. Joey had taken her here, and now sat across from her in one of the booths along the wall, with the curtains drawn and a buzzer to summon the waiter. He had teased her with stories of legendary San Franciscans' escapades behind these curtains. She thought he was cute, with his long nose and thin Italian face, and making such a big play for her.

"Thankfully, the tourists haven't discovered this place yet," Joey said. "It's still reasonable, and the food is better than in the expensive joints. What are you having?"

"I think I'll have the New York cut." She caught his expression. "What's wrong? It's no good?"

"Everything's top notch here. It's just that it's a seafood place. You order fish in a seafood place. You order steak in a steak house."

"But I feel like a good steak."

"Women." He shook his head, rolled his eyes toward the ceiling and gestured upward with both hands.

She smiled at his theatrics. "Joey, you want fish, have fish. Don't try that male domination crap on me. What are you having?"

"I'm having clams casino to start, and the sand dabs à la Sam's. Delicious. Why don't you try the Dungeness crab?"

She glanced at the drawn curtain and motioned him with her finger. "I want to whisper something to you."

He leaned forward with a grin. She put her lips to his ear and gently ran her tongue around the lobe. When she felt his gasp, she said, "Fuck you, and the seafood, Joey. I want steak."

He leaned back, red-faced. "Hey," he said, and then started laughing. "I should have told you to have steak. Then you would have enjoyed great seafood. But I'll tell you what. We'll share. Okay?"

"Sure."

"No wonder I like you so much."

"Really?"

"Scout's honor."

"No doubt you were an Eagle Scout, Joey."

"Hey, the only thing wops like me were allowed to join growing up in Kansas City was the Mafia or the church."

"You don't act like an altar boy."

"I compromised. I joined the Kansas City Police Department. But I lucked out. Before they officially told me I was too dumb, I came to everybody's favorite city and met the woman of the year." Joey squeezed her hand across the table. This time his Al Pacino smile got a better reaction from Terry than outside the schoolyard.

After dinner, Joey ordered Sambuca for two, coffee beans and all in the glass. He ordered espresso for both of them, gesturing with his hands to see if Terry accepted. She smiled her agreement. When the waiter drew the curtain, Joey moved around to sit beside her. Terry made no objection. "So tell me, how did a nice girl like you end up in a racket like this?" His white teeth flashed at her and his hand felt good on her thigh.

She touched his cheek. "Thanks for bringing me here, Joey. You have a way of cheering me up. I—"

Terry's beeper sounded. She unhooked it from her purse and glanced at the message. "It's Garza. Do you have any change for the phone?"

"What else am I good for?" he said, mocking despair.

Terry touched his cheek again and said, "I hope a lot more than change, Joey."

She was back from the phone quickly. Joey looked at her pale face. "What is it?"

"Santiago's out."

"Jesus Christ! A jail break?"

"You won't believe this. The fucking jail released him by mistake. It was just a screwup over his jail ID number."

"Unbelievable. That's the tenth time this year they let out a righteous felon by mistake. What the hell is wrong with those people?"

"I guess they're not super efficient, like the SFPD. It seems a George Santiago, also in on a burglary charge, was to be released on his own recognizance. Unfortunately, a correction officer let Raul Santiago go instead. They didn't even know about it until the public defender representing George Santiago started screaming. By then it was too late. Garza put out an APB as soon as he heard."

"A lot of good that will do. Raul is probably in Texas or Mexico by now."

"I'm not so sure," Terry said. "When we busted him, he threatened Dana, said she would see him again. Guys like him aren't playing with a full deck in the first place. I think she's still in danger."

"Yeah, maybe you're right. What do you want to do?"

"Well, I've been putting off going to Kevin's to tell Dana that they used her doper boyfriend to do in Kevin at the hearing, but now she has to know Santiago's out. Want to come along?"

"Is the pope a Catholic? I want to hear what else you think I'm good for besides providing change for the phone. Then too, maybe Kevin went home or called her."

"I wouldn't bet on that," Terry said, applying lipstick.

F. Bly had already heard about the suspension of Kevin McKay. He had mixed feelings about it. In one way, it made his job easier. Killing a cop who wasn't a cop anymore would be a snap. The guy wouldn't be surrounded by a blanket of blue, and he would be all screwed up mentally, an easy target. On the other hand, Bly had guessed long ago that the contract on McKay resulted from something he'd done as a cop. Bly wanted to do this job. He didn't want it canceled, even though he got paid twenty-five percent of the fee on canceled contracts. No. He wanted to enjoy killing Kevin McKay, so as soon as he heard of McKay's suspension he parked across the street from his apartment and waited for him. The sooner the better, to avoid a cancellation.

Bly cursed when he saw Terry Fisher and Joey Demanto double-park in front of the house and enter. What the hell was going on? Cops all over the place. And he had sat for hours. Even if McKay came now, he wouldn't be able to touch him. And where the hell was he, anyway? Bly drove away in disgust.

Dana opened the door after Terry announced herself. She

immediately read something wrong in Terry's face and a coolness in her attitude. The cop with Terry walked into the living room, and Terry and Dana went to the front studio room.

"Dana, I have to warn you," Terry said. "We just got notified that Raul Santiago got out of jail on some kind of misidentity. Even though we no longer need you as a key witness, you should know that you may still be in danger."

Dana shrank back from her and her eyes widened. "But you captured him. You said that he would never get out."

"He shouldn't have. I'm sorry, but someone at the jail made a human error. Have you heard from Kevin?"

"No. He hasn't called, and I'm worried." She sank to a chair. "What is it, Terry? There's something in your face, your manner."

"Look, Dana, what's between Kevin and you is none of my business. I just think what you did to him stinks after all he did for you."

"I love him, you know that. I wouldn't hurt him. What are you saying?"

Terry's face was hard. "Kevin was suspended at a police hearing today because of you."

Dana's hand was at her throat. She gasped. "Because of me?"

"Yeah, Dana. It was the little matter of his living with you, the girlfriend of a prominent dope dealer. How come you never told Kevin? You let him go into that hearing unprepared. He cracked up when they sprang it on him. He got off the stand and walked out. It was just what the brass wanted."

Dana sank into a chair, her eyes wet. "What have I done? He never mentioned a hearing." Clutching a handkerchief, she looked at Terry. "I meant to tell him, Terry. I was so afraid of losing him. Can you understand that?"

Terry softened a bit. "I guess, but this is a god-awful mess, Dana. Kevin may have cracked up. We don't know where he is, and you can't stay here. Santiago might come back."

Dana stood abruptly, drying her tears. "I'm going back to my place. I should never have come here."

"It was probably at your place that Santiago first tracked you. Don't you have someplace else to go?"

"I'll call my father from my apartment. He'll help me."

"We'll wait until you pack up, then take you to your place and check it out."

"Thanks, Terry." She rushed toward the bedroom but stopped in the doorway. "Terry, can you tell Kevin I love him? That I'm so sorry?"

Terry's face was grim. "You're the only one who can tell him that, if and when we find him, and if he's capable of listening. I'll let you know when we catch up to him."

Dana opened the door then stood aside so Joey and Terry could enter first and search the apartment.

"Carlos!" Dana exclaimed.

So, this was Carlos. Terry studied the dark, handsome man sitting on the couch. For a moment she felt the pull of his personality as he studied her with a touch of arrogance. But she decided instantly this was a dangerous man. Someone very sure of his own power. If he hadn't killed anyone yet, it was because he hadn't wanted to.

Carlos looked Joey over for a moment, then stood and walked to Dana. "I've missed you so much." He held out his arms.

After a moment's hesitation, Dana went to him.

"It will be all right, Dana." He put his arms around her. "I'll make it that way. I promise. You two officers can go now," he said, with a mocking look in his eyes.

"We'll go when Dana says we go," Joey replied, making no effort to hide his dislike of Carlos.

"Then she'll tell you." Carlos released Dana, turning her so she faced the detectives. "They seem confused, Dana. Tell them they can go now. You're safe. Safer than you were with them." His eyes were hard now, contrasting with the softness of his voice.

After a moment, Dana said, "It's okay, Terry." Her voice had no strength and her shoulders sagged. "I want to thank you for all you've done."

"We're not in any hurry, Dana," Terry said. "If you want, we can stay while you pack."

"That won't be necessary," Carlos said.

"Listen, pal, we don't need your advice," Joey snapped, barely containing his anger.

Dana intervened, saying, "No, please, no fighting. I can't stand it. You can go. I'm all right."

Heading down in the elevator, Joey said, "I hope we didn't just make a mistake leaving her with that bum."

"It wasn't a mistake," Terry replied sadly, "because it wasn't our call, it was hers."

PART FOUR

Danger

Chapter Fifty-one

It was two in the afternoon, an hour before the start of the commuter traffic. Trish Jordan drove too fast across the Golden Gate into Marin County. The fog had come in and the surface of the bridge was slippery, but she didn't care. She lit another cigarette, misjudging the distance to the toll plaza, and skidded wildly before she remembered she didn't have to stop. You got nailed for two bucks going in the other direction, into the "City," as northern Californians referred to San Francisco. She hadn't smoked in twelve years, but since Flip died, she was back to a pack and a half a day. She sometimes pictured him shaking his head and wagging his finger at her in disapproval, but she didn't care much about dangers to her health since he was gone.

She sped past the poorly marked side road leading up to the retreat house in the Marin hills and screeched into an illegal U-turn to go back. On a clear day the view of the ocean would have been beautiful, but today the gray would be an all-day thing. She wasn't into beauty anymore, anyway.

A sickly-looking young man in his twenties at the front desk looked up from a thick book and gave her directions. She found Kevin's room on the south wing of the first floor. When there was no answer to her knock, she slowly opened the door. Kevin was sitting outside in a stainless steel folding chair on a tiny patio. The room was small. A narrow, uncomfortable-looking bed crowded a wooden desk and a chair. The furniture looked like it had come out of San Quentin's workshop.

"Kevin?"

It took a moment, but he turned and looked at her. "Hello, Trish."

She was shocked. She didn't know what she'd expected, but the smiling, energetic young man Flip had once introduced her to had been replaced by someone she didn't know. He was dressed carelessly in a worn, blue SFPD baseball jacket and faded blue jeans. One of his loafers had a hole in the side, and she noticed he wasn't wearing socks. He hadn't shaved in a couple of days. His dark stubble matched the color of the blanket draped across his lap. Trish looked to see the view he'd been staring at and saw only fog. The few feet of grass visible was verdant and dripping, but there wasn't even a shrub, let alone a tree in sight. She shuddered, imagining the scene that riveted his stare.

"How are you, Kevin?" she asked.

He turned back toward the fog without answering and pulled the worn blanket tighter around his waist.

She came and put her hand on his shoulder. "I heard you were hurt. It must have been terrible. Tell me about it."

"We were just going through the motions of questioning an ex-con named Santucci. Neither Flip nor I thought he was Ski Mask. It was a little dumpy room. I walked over and looked in the bathroom. I blew it. The shooter was hiding in the shower stall. I never opened it to look in. No way to see him. Suddenly, Santucci tried to run. I grabbed him from the front, Flip from behind. There were shots . . ." Kevin squeezed her hand.

"Why'd he run, if it wasn't him?"

"I don't know. I didn't even get to see the shooter. Santucci kicked me in the head. He almost got away." Kevin shook his head. "Flip never had a chance. He saw me look in the bathroom. He had no reason to think someone was behind him."

"So you're blaming yourself?"

He gave the slightest nod, and Trish lost it. "You son of a bitch, you didn't even call me!"

"I tried," he said tonelessly. "You were on the road."

"And you couldn't find me. You're some fucking detective."

"The understatement of the year." He looked straight ahead.

"You're so sorry for yourself, you're a basket case. When do you get your wheelchair?"

He reached out and took her hand, but she pulled away and slapped him in the face. He looked at her, but his expression was blank.

"I . . ." He lost whatever he was going to say and looked back into the fog.

She was crying, near hysteria. "You bastard! Flip would tell you you're an asshole for blaming yourself. You didn't have any reason to look in that bathroom, let alone shower, if you weren't busting the guy. You're not even trying to catch your partner's killer. If it was the other way around, Flip wouldn't have slept until he did justice." She rushed out of the room.

He looked after her for a moment before his eyes went back to the fog.

Trish's foot was heavy on the gas pedal. She was driving a new Lexus that Flip had loved. She hit a deep puddle on the freeway and the car hydroplaned. Somehow she kept her foot off the brake and controlled the skid. A six-wheeler rig too close to slow down gave her an angry blast with the air horn, and the Lexus shook in the air wake of the speeding truck. Trembling, she pulled onto the shoulder and sobbed. Her head was on the steering wheel when the CHP cop approached.

"What seems to be the trouble, lady?" His eyes roamed the backseat covered with boxes of sales brochures, advertising, and order forms she carried on the road.

"Trouble? The trouble is I don't understand you. What makes all of you so stupid and cocky you walk up to cars and think you're immune from some nut or crook blowing you away?"

The cop backed up and his eyes probed the nearby fog as if he feared someone might be drawing a bead on him. He unlatched the snap on his holster. "All right, how about you tell me what that's supposed to mean, and while you're telling me, just keep your hands right where they are on the steering wheel."

Trish looked at him for the first time. He was tall and

stocky. His round head and big neck sat on heavy shoulders. No breakaway runner, this one. A tackle. His close-cropped hair was reddish-blond and his hard, gray eyes were surrounded by freckles.

"Have you been drinking, lady?"

"Oh Christ, I had to get stopped by a honky redneck. Where did they recruit you from, Birmingham, Alabama?"

"Okay, lady, suppose you just get out of the car real slow. Don't reach for your purse, or anything else."

She was incredulous. His gun was half out of his holster. "Suppose I don't get out of the car real slow? Suppose you go fuck yourself instead."

Trish reached to start the ignition, but the big man moved fast. Reaching through the open window, he grabbed the keys with his left hand and had the door open with his right. Before she knew it he had dragged her from the car and thrown her roughly up against the hood. He patted her down without getting handsy about it. It was too much. She collapsed on the trunk of the car moaning and sobbing. She heard him transmitting on the radio without bothering to absorb what he said.

Finally she stopped and turned to face him. He kept his distance, and his arms were ready at his sides, but his face didn't show any anger.

"What was it, vodka or pills?" he said softly.

"Oh shit, officer. I haven't been drinking. I'm sorry to unload on you. I guess you're no different than the guy I just lost. He carried a badge too. He got blown away two weeks ago in San Francisco. They gave him a hero's funeral, but we were supposed to get married."

The CHP cop frowned. "You were related to the San Francisco cop? Tell me what happened."

"Who knows? Someone blew him away while he was questioning a rape suspect. The goddamn police department acts like it's not even interested in finding out who did it. It's disgusting."

He took her arm and gently steered her back into the driver's seat of the Lexus. "Sit and relax for a minute."

Trish was emotionally drained. She leaned back and fought

the temptation to fall into a deep sleep. She heard the side door open and felt the seat move as the big man settled into the passenger seat.

"I don't want to preach at you, but you really shouldn't be driving when you're this upset."

She looked at him and nodded. Funny, he had looked like a storm trooper. Now she saw how young he was. Not even thirty. "You're right. I drove out to see his partner. The bastard is sitting in a retreat house like a monk. Not even going after the guy who killed his partner."

"You know, I volunteered. A few of us with the CHP were there with the funeral procession. I don't know all the details, but your boyfriend was well thought of as a cop. It was one of the biggest turnouts they've had for a funeral."

"A lot of good it's doing him now. I didn't mean to hassle you, but I really don't understand how you go out and do it every day. And for what? The public doesn't exactly love you guys. How many civilian review boards did they put in across the country this year? How many pay raises did you get?"

"Sometimes I wonder myself," he said, his eyes looking out the windshield at the heavy fog. "But a couple of years ago I lost a partner. It wasn't like your boyfriend's case. It was a day just like this. Real poor visibility. A family of tourists had broken down in their station wagon. Three kids were screaming. Billy and I were pushing the wagon farther off the roadway. We heard the noise but there was no time to react. Zap! We all went flying. It was a drunk. They got him a few hours later in Sonoma, and he went away for ten years. I tried to get Billy off the highway. The driver from the station wagon helped. Billy had been a star halfback in high school, twenty-nine years old. It was like moving a sack of shit and blood. Everything was broken. I'm glad he didn't live."

Trish saw his eyes were moist. "I've got to have a smoke. Do you mind?" she mumbled.

"Hell no." He reached down to the floor and handed her bag to her. "But what I wanted to say was that I was out of it for six months. I couldn't work, couldn't sleep. I hit the booze, then sleeping pills. My wife left me, and I thought about . . ." He shrugged. "But I didn't. Some good people helped me and I came out of it. What I'm trying to say is that maybe you have to give his partner some time. These things are tough and everybody handles them different."

She sagged in the seat. "You've made me feel like shit."

"God," he said, "that's the last thing I wanted to do. I'm sorry. I was just trying to explain."

"I know. But you're right. I'm being an asshole. I jumped all over Kevin, then you. I'm going to drive back up to the retreat house and apologize to him. He loved Flip too. I can't leave the poor guy brooding over what I said."

"Is it the retreat house five miles back," he gestured, "in the hills?"

"Yes."

"Hold on a minute." He got out and she heard him transmitting on his shoulder radio. Then he came back and leaned in. "Look, I'm going to take you up there and then bring you back. Just lock your car. It will be okay here."

Trish was too tired to argue. She watched him write something on a yellow ticket and put it under her windshield. He held the side door of the cruiser open and closed it softly after she squeezed in next to the shotgun rack.

The CHP officer stayed in the cruiser when they got to the retreat center. This time, however, the young man at the desk asked Trish to wait. Still emotionally drained, she sat on a sagging couch in the lounge. A couple of minutes later a young priest wearing a cassock and white collar approached her.

"You must be Trish Jordan. I'm Father Riordan. I spend a day a week here. I thought it would be a good place for Kevin. I'm truly sorry for your grief."

She shook his extended hand, which was soft and uncallused. So, this was Father Riordan, one of the people Flip had talked about. He was handsome. His unlined face had a certain sensuality. What a waste, she thought. He could make some woman very happy. Then she mocked herself. You never thought that way about all those nuns who brought you up.

"I gave Kevin a hard time, Father. I came back to apologize."

"I know. I saw him a short time ago. He was quite agitated."

Trish hung her head. "I heard about what he went through with Flip, then the suspension. I should have known better, but I lost it."

He took her hand. "Trish, don't blame yourself. It's quite human under the circumstances."

She found his sincerity and concern comforting. He doesn't even know me, she thought, but he cares. "Anyway, I know Kevin isn't ready to return to work yet. It's just that—" Tears welled up in her eyes.

He squeezed her hand. "Trish, it was a terrible thing. It's only natural that you want someone punished. But you're right, Kevin needs healing time. I hope you'll remember that when you go back in to see him. Please call me here any time I can help."

Trish found the door partially open. She entered after knocking. Kevin was sitting in the same position, but he'd shaved and put on fresh clothes. There was a small canvas bag at his feet.

He heard her come in and stood. His eyes focused on her. "I'm ready, Trish." He reached down and picked up the bag.

She was alarmed. "Hold on, Kevin. I came back to apologize. I realize you need more grieving time, just like me."

"No. You were right. It's time I bring in my partner's killer."

Walking out to the parking lot, she said, "Kevin, please be careful. Whoever did that to him is a stone killer. I couldn't bear it if anything happened to you after I pushed you to get into it."

Absently, he said, "Flip was in a good mood that day."

She stopped and looked at him. "He never told you?"

Kevin appeared puzzled. "Told me what?"

"That we were going to get married in a couple of months. Honeymoon in Paris."

Kevin frowned. "No, he didn't tell me."

"He also never told you about the letter and the school."

Kevin was alert now, watching her.

"Flip had been sitting on Sacred Heart because Ferrante got a letter saying a black cop was molesting children."

"What? Ferrante assigned him?"

She shook her head. "Hell, no. Nate gave him the letter, Nate Lincoln. Flip was afraid someone was setting up Sammy Robbins."

"Why the hell didn't he tell me?"

"He thought you were too close to the school."

Kevin shook his head. After a moment he said, "Who's Nate?"

"A cop in the black officer's organization. He lifted the letter from Ferrante's office. It's in my car. I figured you might want it."

Chapter Fifty-two

Frank Clancy sat in front of Ray Bloom's desk for their weekly meeting. He detected an uneasiness in his boss.

"Frank, I have something top-sensitive to tell you," Bloom began, not bothering with the preliminaries. "You're familiar with the satellite intelligence gathering?"

"Just in general."

"Well, it's mostly military and CIA, but they cut us in for a small slice. We should have a much bigger role, but you know how the CIA treats us."

Clancy grinned. "The same way we treat them when we get a chance."

Bloom wasn't in a smiling mood. "In any event, we've been monitoring international phone calls from people on our red hot list of dope dealers abroad. The satellite's ability to pick up transmissions and phone calls is unbelievable. We intercepted something from a yacht in Saint-Tropez—" Bloom's phone rang. "Yes, sir. I'll be right in." He placed the receiver back in the cradle and nodded toward a side door. "The SAC, Frank. Hang on in here. This shouldn't take more than a couple of minutes."

Frank Clancy gazed out the window overlooking San Francisco's beautiful City Hall and wondered what a call from Saint-Tropez had to do with him. He noticed that a stack of monthly activity reports from agents was on Bloom's desk, and he tried to remember if he'd gotten his own report in on time this month. The door opened and Bloom's secretary came in. "Hi, Frank. Mr. Bloom just called from the SAC's office and said it's going to take about fifteen minutes. He said you could go back to your desk or sit and have some coffee."

"If you made it, Judy, I'll have a cup of black. If Ray made it, I'll wait at my desk."

"Ray, God forbid. Stay. I'll bring you a cup."

Clancy picked up the file of monthly activity reports and flipped through to his. Sure enough, there in the margin was a penciled note by Bloom: *Give Frank a buzz about getting his reports in on time.*

God bless the bureaucracy, Clancy thought, returning the folder to the desk. It slipped in his hand and he saw Craig Lewis's sheet. On impulse, he skimmed it, then frowned. The report showed a lot of activity and it looked phony to Clancy. But he expected that. What caught his attention were three references to Subject 99. Each agent was encouraged—to the point of being obligated—to have confidential sources. Some sources were paid, but most weren't. The San Francisco office years earlier had decided that a central registry be used instead of maintaining a list of confidential sources for each agent. Subject 99 had been developed by Frank Clancy, and while there was no directive saying that another agent couldn't happen on to the same source of information, Clancy didn't know whether to be pissed or not that Craig Lewis was on his turf.

Subject 99 was San Francisco Chief of Detectives Vincent Ferrante, who had been quite candid about municipal corruption, when it suited his purposes. The Bureau didn't care about the motivation. It welcomed information from all sources.

Clancy had been designated as local police liaison. On the other hand, he thought, maybe Lewis had simply fabricated the meetings with Subject 99. Clancy returned the report to the pile and sipped the coffee Judy had provided.

"Sorry, Frank." Bloom was back. "What I wanted to tell you was that the satellite picked up a conversation indicating a contract had been put out on a couple of San Francisco cops—Demanto and McKay. The boss thought maybe you should be the one to let them know, given their questionable status in the department."

Clancy frowned. "When did this come down?"

Bloom tapped on his desk. "Um, let's see . . . The transmission itself was about a month ago."

"A month! For Christ's sake, Ray, we've been sitting on this for a month?" Clancy saw through Bloom's finger-tapping ploy.

"Now, Frank, we've talked before about you getting too much into organization decision-making. This satellite is top secret stuff. We don't want any of our hot dope subjects to get wind of it. We've been getting great intelligence. We can't afford to jeopardize the war on drugs by publicizing unconfirmed rumors."

"This rumor concerned the lives of two cops!" With an effort, Clancy controlled his temper. If Bloom or the SAC got the idea he was being critical of the Bureau, he'd be out of his assignment instantly. "Are there any other details I should know, Ray?"

"Um, there is one more thing. The conversation also concerned a local doper named Hallman."

"Hallman!" Clancy couldn't contain himself. "Hallman's body floated up in San Mateo about three weeks ago. Looked like a mob hit. So, finally the Bureau figures maybe we should warn the cops."

"Hold on, Frank. You're getting emotional. There is no evidence that Hallman's killing is connected. You know these guys get knocked off all the time. The Bureau's not always the bad guy either. I'll let you in on something in strict confidence. The SAC had a private conversation with the police chief. McKay is going to be reinstated. By all reports, that Police

Commission hearing was a kangaroo court. That's not to go any further, by the way."

Clancy thought out loud. "McKay's reinstatement could actually reinforce their desire to hit him."

"Who knows? But Frank, when you convey the warning about a hit, you are to keep the Bureau's interest at heart. No mention of the satellite, understand?"

"I understand." Clancy made an effort not to snarl.

"Fine. Tell me, where is McKay? I hear he's unstable—walked out of the hearing and disappeared."

"He's at a retreat house in Marin. He's a solid guy, but his partner just about died in his arms, and then he got jerked around by his own department. He should take some time to get himself together."

"Anything else about him?"

Clancy took a breath. He was being tested. He was sure Bloom and the SAC knew about Carlos Castellano. "Apparently, McKay got too close to a woman. Turned out her boyfriend had been busted a couple of years ago as a multikilo dealer."

Bloom nodded. He had passed the loyalty test, Clancy thought. "All the more reason to keep your distance, Frank, when you're dealing with these local cops."

"Ray, let me ask you this. Has this information led the Bureau to reconsider its decision not to investigate McKay's memo?"

"It's under reconsideration, Frank, but you don't know about it."

"Gotcha." Clancy got up to go.

Bloom walked to the door with him. He put a hand on Clancy's shoulder. "We were in the same Academy class, Frank, and I know the quality work you do. Walk carefully on anything affecting the SFPD." Bloom's face showed concern. "I wouldn't be able to stop your reassignment if someone above thinks you should go." Abruptly, he grinned. "Not that I give a damn. It's just that I'd have to break in someone new."

Clancy rode down on the elevator thinking about what

Bloom had confided. Ray Bloom wasn't the kind of guy to let his hair down, so this was important.

Clancy had learned of Kevin's whereabouts from Terry Fisher, who'd gotten a call from Father Riordan. Now, he decided to visit Terry in the Hall of Justice to discuss the best way of letting Kevin know about the threat.

"I'll buy the coffee, Terry," Clancy said.

"No way, Frank. I've heard about you. You'll be saying it's my turn to buy at some function where it's four bucks a drink. I'll buy. The cafeteria coffee goes for half a buck."

In the police cafeteria, Frank walked to a table in the far corner. Terry shrugged but followed him. "Terry," he said when they were seated, "I'm going to confide in you, but at the moment this is confidential. The Bureau got some information that a contract has been put out on Kevin and his old partner, Joey Demanto."

"Is this bullshit or reliable?"

"I don't know. But the same source mentioned Hallman, and he's dead."

"Jesus! What are the details?"

"I don't know. They gave very limited information. It's top secret. We haven't even told the brass. I'm here to ask your help in notifying Kevin and Demanto."

"Top secret? Two cops are in danger, and the FBI won't give out any information?"

Clancy looked at her angry face and sighed. Maybe he should have been a truck driver. He chose his words carefully. "I don't blame you for being pissed, Terry, but I'm just a messenger boy. As soon as I find out any more, I'll let you know immediately. Apparently, the contract had something to do with their work in Narcotics."

"You mean something to do with the memo on Lieutenant Sherry?"

Clancy held up his hands. "Honestly, Terry, I've told you all I know."

She wasn't appeased. "Have you heard that the Chief of Police suddenly reversed Kevin's suspension this morning? They're carrying him on sick report."

"I did hear that. I'm glad. It was pretty raw, the way they walked over him. How's he doing?"

"I don't know. No one's seen him. He's always been very close to Father Riordan, so hopefully Riordan's helping him. I did give his address to Trish Jordan, Flip O'Neil's girlfriend. She's going to see him. I'll call up there and see if I can speak directly to Kevin."

"Look, I don't mind driving up," Clancy said. "Do you want to come with me?"

"I'd like to, but the ski mask rapist is on the loose again, thanks to the jail. I've got to stay with it. Let me give you Father Riordan's number. You can talk to him and decide if you want to drive up."

In the corridor, Terry hesitated. "Frank, can I ask you a question that's sort of offbeat? Just for my own curiosity."

Clancy smiled. "As long as I don't have to answer it."

She colored. "Did Craig Lewis have to fill for someone doing security checks recently?"

Clancy laughed. "No way. Only two guys from the office are allowed to do them. But it's the softest job in the office. The guys would never let anyone else have a shot at it. Why? Did Craig break a date with you using that excuse?"

"No. Not exactly. It's just that I almost ran him over outside Kevin's place when I was bringing Kevin home after Flip was killed. And when I offered Craig dinner, he said he had to do a security check. He ended up coming with me, but it sounded funny at the time. Just one more lie, I guess."

Chapter Fifty-three

Frank Clancy's car choked as he was pulling out of the garage in the Federal Building. He was headed for an FBI training class for local police held on Coast Guard Island in the East Bay. Clancy pulled to the side and raced the motor until the fuel mix adjusted. A government car without G plates passed him on the left, tires whining. Clancy was tuned in to the FBI emergency radio channel and hadn't heard anything unusual. He glanced at the passing car who was in such a hurry and glimpsed Craig Lewis behind the wheel. On a whim, Clancy followed.

As he kept a discreet distance behind the unmarked Oldsmobile, Clancy chided himself. He wasn't Lewis's supervisor, after all. So Lewis claimed the SFPD Chief of Detectives was his informant, though he'd probably never met Ferrante. Why should he care? Lewis was probably rushing off to see some bimbo, or do something else that had nothing to do with Bureau business. But then, the story Lewis had told Terry Fisher about security checks didn't make sense. What the hell had he been doing around Kevin McKay's house? Did it have something to do with Lewis picking a fight with Kevin?

Craig Lewis parked the Bureau car, opened the trunk, took out a laundry bag, and slung it over his shoulder. Watching it bounce off Lewis's muscular shoulders, Clancy decided it wasn't filled with clothes. Clancy grew even more curious. He drove slowly behind Craig Lewis, who walked two blocks and turned east on California Street. Clancy pulled to the curb as Lewis slowed. He saw the big FBI man enter 19½ California and speak to the security guard at the desk. Lewis showed the guard his ID and appeared to give him something. Then Lewis got on the elevator and the guard left the building. What the hell could Lewis be up to now? Clancy wondered.

Craig Lewis got off the elevator on the sixth floor and walked to Jane Remick's apartment. He'd already determined that she hadn't been staying there for the past two days. In fact, the security guard downstairs told him she'd left town altogether, for a long vacation at an unspecified location. She was frightened, after all, and who could blame her?

Lewis put the bag down and fumbled for keys. He'd taken wax impressions of her keys lying on the foyer table the night Terry Fisher had so fortuitously brought him along. While the two women had been talking in the living room, Lewis, gazing at the keys, had begun to plan.

Once inside the apartment, he went immediately to the phone and dialed.

"McKay."

"Kevin, this is Craig Lewis. Look, you and I have had our differences in the past, to put it mildly. In fact, you cold-cocked me in Charley's. I just want you to know there's no hard feelings on my part."

"What do you want, Lewis?"

Craig Lewis smiled at Kevin's hostile tone. "This is totally professional. I'm over in Jane Remick's apartment, and I think I'm on to something that will help locate Raul Santiago."

"How are you involved, Lewis?"

"Terry Fisher brought me into it before we broke up. You and me didn't hit it off, McKay, but I used to be a homicide dick before I joined the Bureau, and it pisses me off to see guys like Santiago get away with what they do. It's a goddamn revolving door. Anyway, I think there's something here in the apartment that may well be a lead to where he's holing up."

"What is it?"

Craig Lewis hesitated. This was the tricky part. "I'm not sure. I think you have to see it. He apparently scratched some message inside one of the cabinets."

"I'm not interested in running over there because you have a wild hunch."

"Believe me, it's not just a hunch. I had one of the technicians in the Bureau look at it, and he thinks I'm right. Unfortunately, we can't find Jane Remick to ask her about it." Craig lowered his voice. "It hasn't been easy calling you, McKay, but I thought you'd be professional enough to put aside your feelings about me and look at this stuff. You're the principal investigator on the ski mask case and you know more about it than anyone else. This guy has to be taken off the street. It's only a matter of time before he strikes again."

Kevin's voice was gruff. "All right. I'm on my way to a meeting, anyway. I'll stop at the apartment in about twenty minutes."

Craig Lewis hung up and jumped to his feet. "Hot dog!" He took his tool bag back to the elevator. He had learned all about elevators during the special FBI training he'd received as part of an antiterrorist, hostage rescue team. It took him only a couple of minutes to open the elevator door and fix the controls. Then he closed the door and took the other elevator to the basement. In the basement control room, he summoned the elevator whose door control he had tampered with to the bottom of the shaft and disconnected its fuse. It would remain where it was in the basement six stories below the door he'd rigged.

Lewis took the other elevator to the lobby and was pleased to see that the security guard was still gone. He must have made a powerful impression on the man, he thought, and chuckled to himself. A hundred-dollar bill would do that for most watchmen. The man had been so eager to leave it hadn't even occurred to him to lock the lobby doors.

Lewis placed an OUT OF ORDER sign on the door of the elevator he'd tinkered with and took the working elevator to the sixth floor, grateful that the building was inhabited by so many people who were away at work during the day.

He returned to Jane's apartment and took a black case from his laundry bag. Carefully, he filled a hypodermic-type device with a nervous system depressant. He'd appropriated the device after seeing it demonstrated during a training course designed to teach agents about weapons of the cold war, and was anxious to try it out. He attached it to his right wrist, and it fitted perfectly into the palm of his hand.

Slapping someone on the back activated a needle that injected the serum. If done right, the victim didn't feel more than the friendly slap, and within minutes was sound asleep. Of course, it was highly dangerous. People could die from an allergic reaction. Or, if you loaded it with too much of the serum, it could shock the heart into cardiac arrest. Lewis had loaded it to the hilt. The main thing was that it worked quickly and left no trace in the body. Perfect for this particular job.

He sat back in a chair waiting for McKay, reflecting on how easy his FBI status had made his second career as F. Bly. Early on, he'd perceived the limited advantages of being a detective in Cleveland. He applied for the FBI and was quickly picked under the Bureau's program of hiring experienced police investigators. He'd enjoyed the FBI basic training at Quantico, but found boredom setting in again as a field agent in Chicago. By nature, he was a loner, not given to conversation or socializing with his colleagues, whom he found dull. The restrictive rules of the Bureau chafed at him, and he disregarded them as much as possible.

On one occasion he and his partner were to make one of their periodic visits to Paulie Triste, head of the West Side Mafia in Chicago. Lewis's partner was delayed in a meeting, so he ignored Bureau procedure and went alone to see Paulie Triste. The interviews were bullshit. Typical FBI ass-covering, or simple harassment of mobsters, therefore he hadn't seen any necessity to be late for a dinner date with a model. He walked into the crowded saloon where Triste held court in the backroom. The bartender and patrons picked up on him right away, of course, and the bar fell silent. Lewis ignored the patrons and walked to the door of the rear room, where a bull-necked, 250-pound goon stood guard.

"FBI." He flashed his credentials.

The goon gave him the bad eye. "So what? Unless you got a warrant, we don't give a shit who you are."

"Really?" Lewis looked sharply to his right, and the goon's eyes swung the same way. Before the man knew what had happened, Lewis shoved him out of the way and opened the door. He saw Paulie Triste sitting behind a small bare table in the middle of a large, empty room. The gangster was reading a novel. Triste, in his sixties, was small, and his brown eyes regarded Lewis as if the FBI man were an interesting species of butterfly.

"FBI, Triste." Cold eyes didn't bother Craig Lewis.

"Boss, he pushed right past me." The goon waved a .45 automatic.

Triste's eyes shifted to the goon, who fell silent.

"I want to ask you a couple of questions, Triste."

The small man put down his novel. "You're alone?" the mafioso said softly.

"Very astute of you, Triste. No wonder you got to be boss. Are you now, or have you ever been, a member of the Cosa Nostra?"

"What is your name? I've never seen you before." Triste folded his hands like a schoolteacher putting a pupil through his lessons.

Lewis looked at his watch, ignoring the .45 pointed at his back. "Look, Triste, I don't have all fucking day. Just answer the questions and I'll get out of here before this moron shoots himself in the balls."

"No FBI agent has ever come here alone before. You have no fear?"

"It would be stupid of you to kill me, even if Junior could do it, and I'm not at all sure he can. It would produce a lot of heat."

"On the other hand, it doesn't have to be a killing. We could teach you some respect. You would still be alive, and all of the witnesses outside would testify that you broke in and assaulted us."

"Forget it. You'd have to kill me, or I'd come back and kill you," Lewis said.

The briefest of smiles flitted across Triste's face. "The FBI doesn't shoot first. And, *there is* a gun pointed at you."

Lewis took his service weapon out and bounced it in the palm of his hand. He looked away from Triste at the goon pointing the .45. Triste watched with interest. Slowly, Lewis raised his weapon and sighted on the goon's face. The man stared impassively at him, waiting for an order from Triste. Lewis squeezed the trigger and the man's face shattered. The sound of the shot reverberated around the empty room. The goon sank to the floor, dead. Lewis sighted on Triste, who looked at him without expression. Doors opened and people burst in.

Lewis didn't take his eyes off Triste. "Tell them to clear out or you're next," he said.

Triste raised his right hand to the people watching. "Go. It's all right."

When the doors closed, Lewis smiled. "Do you still think the FBI doesn't shoot first? I'm going to kill you too. And you know what? They're going to give me a medal."

Triste continued to look at him without fear. "Before you squeeze any further, let me offer you something in addition to the medal you'll get for him." He motioned toward the body.

"Trying to bribe an FBI man, Triste?"

"No. I've done that before. I'm trying to hire one. You are very interesting. I believe we could be of great service to each other."

And they had, Lewis reflected, although Triste's lack of a sense of humor disappointed Craig. When the Mafia boss had asked him what code name he preferred, he'd said F. Bly, in perfect imitation of a Chinese restaurant owner's pronunciation of the FBI. If Triste got it, he didn't let on. Lewis's earnings as F. Bly had made him rich. He had adopted his good old boy, stud image as the perfect cover. Who could imagine the married man with three kids, the boisterous, public braggart, Craig Lewis, as anything deeper than the buffoon they saw? Lewis secretly laughed at his colleagues' talk of their pensions and hopes of getting some soft security job in private industry after retirement. He was already a millionaire and saw no reason to stop until he had accumulated enough money to disappear. The government could keep his pension.

On his first two jobs for the mob, he'd opened the dead men's mouths with gloved hands and placed rolls of silver dollars in their throats. Ridiculous, he thought. Boys will be boys. They try to live up to the movies about themselves. But they were paying. He'd do it their way. On the other hand, Kevin McKay, after the encounter in Charley's, was his pleasure. He should pay *them* for letting him arrange an accidental fall down the elevator shaft.

Chapter Fifty-four

Talking to Craig Lewis, Kevin had doodled on his pad, scratching the FBI man's name, *Jane R.—19½ California.* He disliked Craig Lewis and didn't believe the man was sharp enough to spot a mysterious clue to Raul Santiago's whereabouts. Still, he was on his way to join Terry Fisher at Bert Thatcher's office. The D.A. wanted to confer one more time on what the search warrant on Santiago had produced before presenting the evidence to the grand jury. It would only take ten minutes to stop at Jane Remick's apartment.

Before leaving, Kevin once more tried Ronnie Blue's home phone number. B&B was off on a week's fishing vacation with some other cops, but he'd left Kevin a note saying it was urgent to call Ronnie. Kevin read again B&B's cryptic note: *You'll understand when I see you why I didn't put the kid's message in writing.* B&B and his melodrama, Kevin thought, hanging up after the tenth ring. Ronnie's mother was a receptionist who worked during the day. There was no way he could leave a message. He paused at Lieutenant Garza's office to let him know where he was going, but the lieutenant wasn't in.

Terry had presented Thatcher with a list of the credit cards and jewelry recovered from Raul Santiago's apartment and locker at work. She and Thatcher argued halfheartedly about whether they had sixteen cases or fourteen.

"Look, Terry, he's dead in the water on these fourteen cases, why bring in two dubious ones? You know the witnesses aren't that solid, and the credit cards and jewelry were found in Mrs. Santiago's dresser. She won't testify, and I can't compel her. He'll get at least ten years on each count. Do you really care whether he gets 160 years or 140?"

"So you say, Bert. How about five or six years down the road he wins an appeal on some of these cases, and the next thing, the ACLU springs him?"

Thatcher squared his shoulders. "I beg your pardon, young detective. They do not win appeals on my cases, with the exception of instances where I allow my better judgment to be overcome by cops and push on weak cases."

Terry grinned. "Forgive me, I forgot I was dealing with Clarence Darrow."

"Darrow lost. Compare me to Justice Holmes or someone more appropriate."

"Okay, Holmes. You know, I'm wondering where Kevin is. He wanted to be here for the kill total."

"How is he, Terry? He's one of the most skilled cops I ever worked with, but lately he seems to have a storm cloud over his head."

"Telling the P.D. the truth about itself doesn't make you popular. And then, there's the issue of—" Terry stopped herself, deciding not to tell Bert about Kevin, Dana, and Carlos Castellano.

"We don't get many like Kevin," Thatcher said. "I hope he makes it."

"I better call to see what's up."

Terry used a vacant phone and dialed Kevin's number. SOP was that if a dick wasn't there, someone picked up his call and took a message. No one did that for Kevin. Or for me either, she thought. She dialed the lieutenant's number.

"Garza."

"Lieutenant, this is Terry. I'm trying to get hold of Kevin."

"Hold on. I'll see if I can find him."

A moment later Garza was back on the line. "No one knows where he is. I *did* ask Kevin to keep me informed, for his own protection, but he's a hard head. Unfortunately, I was upstairs getting my ass chewed for a while. He was gone when I got back."

"He did want to meet with Thatcher," Terry told him, "but we finished fifteen minutes ago. I guess I'll just come back to the office."

"You know," Garza said, "he had some scribbles on his pad. *Craig Lewis, Jane R., 19½ California.* What do you make of that?"

Terry swallowed the bile in her throat at the mention of Craig Lewis. "Well, that's Jane Remick's address."

"And Craig Lewis is the FBI guy Kevin decked. Look, on your way back, stop over there. I don't want him getting in any more fights."

Across town from Jane Remick's apartment, Ronnie Blue and the other boys were playing basketball in the schoolyard, but it wasn't the same without Kevin. After the workout, Ronnie decided to skip study period. He'd been doing it a lot during the past couple of months, and Kevin had gotten on his case. A couple of times, he'd smoked joints with some kids who lived in his housing project. Ronnie was convinced there was no way Kevin could know about it, yet Kevin had started questioning him about whether he was messing with dope.

Ronnie was sorry now that he'd given Kevin a hard time. He'd found out how bad Kevin felt when his partner was killed. There weren't many white guys who got that upset when a brother was blown away. In fact, Ronnie wanted to see Kevin so he could tell him about what he'd seen happen to the dude who supplied their smokes. And about the cop who was spreading grass in the project. Of course, the dude who got zapped had supplied everything else too, but Ronnie was too smart to mess with crack or smack. That shit fucked people up. He was going to the NBA. A little grass never hurt, but the other shit took hold of you. Pretty soon you could forget about a slam dunk. You'd be lucky not to get hit by a cable car.

He'd told the fat cop about it, and the guy had gotten tough with him, saying, "How do you know the guys who ripped the man off were cops?" Shit, anyone who didn't know who was a cop and who wasn't didn't grow up in his neighborhood. But beating the brother with guns was too much. They laughed when they were putting the dealer down. And the man was simply gone. No one had seen him since. Ugly talk was around that the cops had buried him. Kevin would know what to do. Ronnie wondered why he hadn't heard from him.

He jumped a fire hydrant and broke into an easy lope, feeling the flow get into his legs. He was moving now, and the power of his body brought a grin to his face. He went full-out and sprang into a long graceful leap over the five-foot fence outside his apartment building. He sprinted the last fifty yards and hit the outer door full stride, which was why he didn't see the three Asian boys standing in the dark corner of the hallway. He was about to take the steps to the third floor where he lived with his mother.

"Hey, Ronnie."

Ronnie stopped and peered into the corner. The huge flash and noise of the shotgun blast were simultaneous, and Ronnie felt himself picked up and slammed down into the terrible, permanent darkness.

As usual, Kevin considered Craig Lewis an aggravating asshole. He brushed off the overly familiar slap on the back of the neck with which Lewis greeted him.

"Hey, Kevin." Lewis wore a sympathetic look on his face. "I heard about that bullshit hearing those guys saddled you with. I'm glad to hear that they took you off suspension."

"Yeah. What was it that you wanted me to see?"

But the FBI man was in no hurry. He just stood there, blocking Kevin's way into the apartment. "How are they treating you since you're back? Still jacking you around?"

Kevin shrugged and rubbed the back of his neck. "I'm working. That's all I care about." He brought his hand down and stared at a spot of blood. He looked at the FBI man's easy grin. "Did you cut me with your ring just now?"

"Hey, no way. I learned once not to mess with you."

Kevin was puzzled. On the phone, Craig Lewis had sounded urgent to get him over here. Now, after patting him on the back, Lewis wore a big, shit-eating grin on his face. Kevin felt warm. He hadn't had lunch today, and he had need to watch fluctuations in his blood sugar, particularly since he'd been stressed-out recently. "Wh-What did you want me to see?" he said, surprised at hearing himself stutter. He never stuttered.

"In the other room." Lewis pointed, but remained in his path.

Kevin didn't feel much like moving, but he brushed past the FBI man and went into the living room. He'd come into this room for something, but he couldn't remember what. He was aware that Lewis had followed him. It had something to do with Lewis. A question.

"What was it, Lewis?" Kevin heard thickness in his voice and wasn't really sure what the question meant. He opened his tie and shirt collar. He was really warm now.

"Look at the painting. What do you think?" Lewis's voice was low, soothing. He pointed at a landscape hanging above the couch.

The trees in the painting were swaying. Kevin was confused and dizzy. He heard himself say, "I think it's the wind."

"Go on." Lewis nodded encouragingly.

Nausea hit Kevin. His head was spinning. He needed to lie down. But a sudden panic hit him. *Danger!* "You bastard." He staggered past Lewis, who let him get to the outer door.

"Hold on, hero. That's far enough." Lewis gripped him lightly by the belt.

Kevin knew this was bad. He needed to get away, but he couldn't raise his arms. I should have told Garza who I was meeting, he thought. No one knows I'm with him. Lewis is going to get away with this. He tried to walk, but his legs wouldn't move. He wanted to smash Craig Lewis's smile. It took all of his willpower to try to raise his arm. It moved about four inches before he collapsed to the floor, unconscious.

"I must say that it was most cooperative of you to come back to the door by yourself," Lewis said to Kevin as if he were awake. "I don't think anyone's really going to give a shit about you going down the elevator shaft, but it would have taken me another few minutes to drag you across the carpet and then erase the drag marks. The hallway has all kinds of heel marks. Yours will blend in nicely."

The FBI man gripped Kevin under the shoulders and grunted, moving his dead weight so he could open the apartment door. He opened the door a crack. The hall was clear. The phone rang, and Craig Lewis wondered if McKay had told someone where he was going. Well, it didn't matter now.

Lewis walked to the working elevator and put his ear to the door. Nothing. There was no time to lose now. He put his gloves back on and quickly opened the door of the elevator he'd disabled. He glanced down the six-story shaft and was only dimly able to make out the top of the elevator. It would appear that a distracted McKay had the bad luck to step into an open elevator shaft. Suspicious, of course. But there wouldn't be any other possible explanation. And such freak accidents did happen a few times a year across the country. There wouldn't be any evidence to prove otherwise, and a lot of people would be glad that Kevin McKay wasn't causing any more trouble.

He dragged Kevin to the open door, being as careful as he could to keep the detective's heels from marking the floor. "So long, copper," he muttered to himself, reaching down for a more secure grip so he could throw the body into the center of the shaft.

"Craig!"

Lewis dropped Kevin and stood dumbfounded. Terry Fisher was in the staircase doorway. She'd seen the OUT OF ORDER sign downstairs after entering through the unlocked lobby doors and had assumed both elevators weren't working. Lewis hadn't heard her coming up the stairs.

"What the hell is going on?" She stared at Kevin's inert body.

Craig Lewis amazed himself with the quickness of his recovery. "It's Kevin. He fainted. Terry, help me."

Terry rushed forward. Only when she was bending over

Kevin did she notice the open elevator shaft. She stood up. "What the hell?"

"So long, beautiful." She was off balance, and Craig's unexpected push sent her into the terrifyingly empty space. She screamed and desperately grabbed at the slender steel beam ledge on the far wall of the shaft. Her left hand slipped on grease but her right held as her body swung outward. Her body slammed back into the wall, and this time she was able to grasp the beam with her left hand as well. The full weight of her body was agony on her arms. Her right toe found a crevice, which helped a bit as her other foot searched for purchase.

Lewis's smile changed to a frown. "Now don't be difficult. Let go. Your arms will fail soon anyway."

But Terry's other foot found a hole in the wall, and with a surge of adrenaline she pushed upward, reversed her hands, and deftly swung around so that half her butt rested on the narrow beam while her hands gripped it tightly. She had done the same maneuver a hundred times on parallel bars. This was the first time on top of a six-story abyss.

Lewis smiled again. "Now, don't go away, angel. I'll be right back."

As quickly as she dared, Terry moved on the beam toward the hall, where she could see her purse lying next to Kevin. Her gun was in it. Lewis was a psycho, she thought. He'd snapped. She had to get her gun before he returned.

Frank Clancy was still watching the lobby when Kevin McKay arrived. These two guys hate each other, he thought, and considered going in. This was a mystery. He had no idea of what was going on. But Clancy was a chess player. He liked to see what was on the board and make a calculated move. He stayed behind the wheel.

As he continued watching, Terry Fisher arrived and went into the building. That reassured him. Terry was solid. She would know how to cool those two guys off in case they started at each other again. Clancy got out of his car and slowly walked over to see what sign Lewis had taped to the elevator. OUT OF ORDER. He stared at it a moment, trying to figure out what Lewis could be up to, then walked to the stairwell. He had to take a look. And if something was funny with one elevator, he didn't feel like trusting the other. He would walk up and check each floor.

Until he got to the sixth floor, he saw nothing unusual; in fact, nothing at all. The building was quiet. But when he opened the sixth-floor door a crack and peered down the hallway, he saw a motionless body twenty-five feet away. What the hell? He eased his gun from its holster. An apartment door opened at the end of the corridor, and Clancy watched Craig Lewis hurry forward carrying a heavy walking stick. Only when Lewis began talking into the elevator shaft did Clancy realize that the door was open and someone was in the shaft. He strained to hear.

Terry had worked herself close to the door to the corridor, but she scampered back when Craig Lewis reappeared.

He held up the walking stick. "The upper class keeps such useful brickbats around. You were the best, baby. I mean it. No one else even came close for me. I'm sorry, but business is business. Your partner here was about to take the plunge." Craig twirled the walking stick. "If you'd just been along a minute later, everything would have been okay."

Abruptly, he lunged at Terry. The walking stick missed her head by about six inches. She looked down six stories and felt a wave of dizziness. Frantic, she overcame the vertigo and, supporting herself with tired arms, backed farther away from him.

"I guess that's what makes you such a great fuck. You never give up. And you're so strong. I loved how long you could stay on top of me." He'd moved one foot out onto the beam. Without warning he swung the stick. Again it came so close that she felt the swish of air as it went by her head. She'd reached the end of the beam now. Lewis moved a little more into the shaft, too close to miss this time. He raised the stick, and Terry closed her eyes.

He was off balance as he started his swing, and Frank Clancy's push from behind was so hard that it sent Lewis crashing into the far wall of the shaft. As he slipped down, the walking stick flew back into the hallway. Lewis, frantic, was able to grab the steel beam on which Terry half sat. She watched in horror as he flexed his powerful arms and pulled himself steadily up. In the hallway, Clancy scowled and reached for the gun he'd holstered.

"Help me, baby." Lewis's smile was wide. "Give me your left hand."

Terry reached out with her left hand. Lewis's own hand moved up toward her. When it was halfway, Terry kicked him hard in his unprotected forehead. Lewis shot backward and plunged down the shaft. It seemed forever to Terry before she heard the body crash into the top of the elevator in the basement six floors below.

She didn't look down and sat without moving as Kevin began stirring in the hallway. Thank God, she thought. He's alive.

"Are you okay, Terry?" Clancy asked. "Or do you want me to call for help to get you out of there?"

"I'm okay, Frank."

They heard excited voices from the lobby.

"Give me a hand, Frank," Terry said, reaching for Clancy.

When Terry had reached the safety of the hallway, Clancy put his hands under one of Kevin's shoulders and Terry took the other.

"It's unfortunate that these elevator accidents occur from time to time," Clancy said. "This is the first time I can remember an agent having such bad luck."

Terry looked at him. "Does it have to be a line-of-duty funeral, Frank?"

He sighed. " 'Fraid so. What other choice do we have?"

"None. Not a goddamned one," Terry Fisher said, thinking of the impossibility of convincing people of the truth.

Chapter Fifty-five

Joey Demanto and Richard Garza listened intently as Terry Fisher related the story of Craig Lewis's freak accident. They were in Lieutenant Garza's office.

"Fucking unbelievable," Joey said.

You got that right, Terry thought. But she'd been surprised at their lack of skepticism about the account Frank Clancy had invented.

"Let me see if I got this straight," Garza said. "You got to Jane Remick's place, and Kevin, and the Fee Bees, Clancy and Lewis, are talking about the ski mask case. How did they get involved?"

"I brought Craig Lewis there a few weeks ago. The Bureau is getting into series crimes more and more. And Kevin had conferred with Brenda Phillips, the agent who does psychological profiling. Clancy is local police liaison."

Garza snorted. "Funny, suddenly the FBI wants to be cops. They're lucky to catch the flu, let alone rapists. Anyway, you're in the apartment, and then, without warning, Kevin gets sick, has a dizzy spell, and passes out. You and Lewis rush to the elevator to go to the M.D., whose office is on the first floor. Clancy is supposed to call 911 to get an ambulance. But he yells to you just as the elevator door is opening. And Lewis walks right into space?"

"I know it's weird," Terry said. "I guess, like me, he was looking back at Clancy. He heard the door open and stepped forward. The fuse had blown in the downstairs control box, so the elevator stayed in the basement. There's a safety system

331

that's supposed to prevent the floor doors from opening when the elevator's not there. But it didn't work for some reason."

"Why did Clancy call you back?" Garza asked.

"He was having second thoughts about calling 911. Kevin seemed to be coming out of it. Clancy was thinking Kevin didn't need any more publicity."

"That's for sure. The guy must be under some kind of jinx. How's he doing now?"

Terry thought it over before answering. "He's in shock. Not as bad as when Flip was killed. They're giving Kevin a complete medical to see what made him pass out. But he can't believe what happened to Craig."

"Neither can I," Joey said. "If you and Clancy weren't eyewitnesses, no one would believe it."

Garza's eyes fixed on her. "Clancy was close to Kevin. He wouldn't have had anything to do with Lewis going down that shaft, would he?"

"Lieutenant, I swear on my life, Kevin McKay was unconscious when Craig Lewis fell."

"Well, both the Bureau and our own tech crews went over the scene, and I haven't heard about anyone shooting holes in your story." He shook his head. "Now we get to another problem. Kevin is still rocky. Who's going to tell him about the kid getting blown away? What's his name—Ronnie Blue. I understand he was Kevin's favorite. Homicide thinks he was dealing and got wiped out. Kevin doesn't need any more bad news, but someone has to tell him." Garza looked at Terry and Joey, who both sat still.

The lieutenant motioned at Terry. "You're his partner."

"Only for two weeks. Joey's much closer. They were partners for years."

"That was in Narcotics, ancient history," Joey said. "Usually, notifications are made by the guy's commanding officer."

Garza swiveled in his chair and looked at the wall behind his desk as if it was a window offering a scenic view of the bay. He swung back and faced them. "On the other hand, Kevin is very close to that priest, Father Riordan. It's good procedure to involve the clergy in these things. Terry, give Father Riordan a call and see if he'll break the news to Kevin. Unless either of you has a better idea?"

Both detectives remained silent.

Two days later there was anxiety in the squad room. Kevin McKay was due back from his latest sick leave. The other detectives were curious to see how he was holding up after all that had happened. The guy was a walking disaster. McKay had reported to the Homicide Unit at nine A.M. At ten after eleven he walked into the Sexual Assaults Unit office.

The other inspectors studied him out of the corner of their eyes. He was pale and had lost weight. His eyes were red from sleeplessness, and his body language signaled a guy on a tight wire.

"Kevin, how are you, lad?" B&B rose to greet him. "It's good to have you back."

Kevin walked past B&B's outstretched hand and sat at his desk. An uncomfortable silence settled over the squad room. The detectives wondered what the Homicide dicks had said that got Kevin so out of shape. B&B pulled back his outstretched hand and returned to his own desk. His face was redder than usual. He opened the right drawer where he kept his flask, but quickly closed it when he realized people were watching.

Lieutenant Garza, with his partially open door, was sensitive to changes in the squad room tempo. He came out and took in the scene. Kevin sat staring at B&B, whose unease was evident. Garza went back into his office and quietly closed the door.

"What are you looking at? What's wrong with you anyway, Kevin?" B&B asked, his voice climbing.

There was almost total silence in the room. The only noise was the murmur of a detective on the phone at a desk in the corner. And his eyes never left Kevin and B&B, whose hand unconsciously reached for the right drawer again; he snatched it back as if the drawer handle was hot. B&B's face had lost its customary ruddiness, and he mopped sweat from it with a handkerchief. The detectives close to him could see a trembling in his jowls. B&B began shuffling papers on his desk, trying not to look at Kevin, who continued to stare at him.

Five tense minutes had gone by before Kevin's monotone broke the silence. "You really did it. Didn't you? You pathetic son of a bitch." There was a weariness in his voice that no one had ever heard before.

B&B looked up. "Did what? What are you talking about? Get hold of yourself, Kevin." His consternation wasn't pleasant to see, and several cops looked down at their desks. B&B's eyes roamed the room without settling anywhere. He put his shaking hands under the desk.

"No one expects us to be angels." Kevin's voice was still flat, exhausted. His eyes bore into B&B. "There aren't that many rules for detectives, B&B. We more or less do what we want. But one rule is sacred." Kevin rose from his desk and slowly walked toward the fat man, who sat frozen. "Every detective protects his snitch. How could you do it, B&B? How could you burn the boy, Ronnie? He was going to be an NBA great. He came to me because he trusted me. But he ended up telling you about some dirty cops, and you killed him as sure as if you pulled the trigger. You repeated what he said, and signed his death warrant." Tears were streaming down Kevin's face. The other detectives found the tension almost unbearable, but no one moved in their seats. They were as frozen as B&B.

"Who was it you told, B&B?" Kevin asked, his voice breaking. "The president of the association? The association attorney? Or did you go direct to Sherry himself?" Kevin was leaning on B&B's desk now, his tear-streaked face only inches away from B&B's.

The fat detective stood up and came around the desk. He was crying. "Kevin, I swear it wasn't like that. I'm a rep. I got a duty. I have to tell the association attorney so he can protect us. I'm sure it had nothing to do with the kid being killed. It happens all the time with these kids. If someone came in and said something about you, I'd tell. Can't you understand?" He took Kevin by the shoulders and for a moment the two big, crying men were locked in B&B's embrace.

Kevin drew away. "No, B&B, I can't understand."

B&B turned in frantic appeal to the rest of the room. "You guys understand, don't you? I'm a POA rep. We have to back cops."

No one looked at him.

"Kevin?" B&B turned back and reached out a hand, pleading.

Kevin turned his back and walked to his desk. B&B stood alone for a moment, then hunched his shoulders and shuffled toward the door, his usual cop's half swagger gone.

Chapter Fifty-six

In the week that followed, Terry Fisher learned a lot about being a detective, and a lot more about Kevin McKay than she'd known before. As a uniformed officer, she'd only known Kevin at a distance. She had thought he was a nice guy, and more sensitive than the other bozos in the Bureau of Investigations, but was never overly impressed by the bureau's reputation for quality investigations, which she thought was largely self-invented. The bureau was riddled with dead wood, the inevitable result of San Francisco politics and bureaucratic politics within the police department. She realized that in her early weeks as a detective, she'd seen Kevin only as a wounded sparrow, limping from one disaster to another. Now she saw a soaring eagle, every bit the predator, meticulously hunting his prey.

Sitting next to him, she gazed at B&B's empty desk. He hadn't returned since his confrontation with Kevin. Nor had

Kevin been much use the day of his confrontation with B&B, but the next day he was at work before she arrived at ten minutes to eight. His desk was filled with investigator supplemental reports, and he was sorting them into three stacks. One on Flip, one on Raul Santiago, and the smaller stack on Ronnie Blue. Kevin had requested that they be relieved of all other cases, and Lieutenant Garza had readily agreed. The only catch was that their work on the homicides was off the record.

Somehow, Kevin had put all the personal stuff out of his mind and was indoctrinating her as his new partner into the nitty gritty of detective work. He divided their time roughly in thirds. They were pulling out all stops in trying to find Raul Santiago, and spending an equivalent effort in pursuing the murder of Flip O'Neil. Kevin was also skimming information on the murder of Ronnie Blue. Terry realized that Kevin saw things in the case files that went right by her. For example, he had obtained a copy of the homicide investigation file on Flip, and she'd gone through it without seeing anything exceptional. But on Kevin's notepad she read: *Where are room and bathroom latent prints?* On the other case she saw his question: *Where are background reports on supposed drug ring of Ronnie Blue?* Terry realized she still had skills to learn.

And at the same time Kevin pored over the files, she found that he had contacts everywhere and was systematically using them. Even within the police department, where Kevin was still taking a beating for writing the memo on Sherry, many working cops respected him and were more than willing to help. One of his old narc friends called and said he had wondered if Santiago hadn't been dealing for an operation moving in and out of the Mission District. Kevin made a note to follow up. And Terry had discovered that one of the crime-scene technicians was more than willing to talk to her out of respect for Kevin. In fact, he preferred to talk to her. Kevin was hot. The tech had promised to call her as soon as fingerprint and blood evidence at the scene of Flip's murder were processed.

At Kevin's suggestion, they established a routine of summing up the day's developments at seven P.M. every night at

Fung's on Stockton. It was a medium-sized restaurant on the fringes of Chinatown. Fung gave them a large table in the corner, and Terry enjoyed brainstorming with Kevin over won ton soup and cashew chicken.

"You look like you have enough work for a while, Kevin," Frank Clancy said when he stopped by the squad room.

"More than enough, Frank." Kevin pushed aside a uniformed cop's field interview with a kid in Ronnie Blue's housing project.

"Terry bought the last time I was here," Clancy said, "which means I guess I have to pay for that muck your cafeteria calls coffee."

"We don't have the tax powers of Uncle Sam at our disposal, Frank," Terry said. Her desk was as full as Kevin's. "So we can't afford the huge gourmet cafeteria you guys have in the Federal Building."

"Gourmet?" Clancy said. "Federal inmates eat better than we do. Anyway, I'm here from Washington to help you locals, as you know. So I'll buy you guys coffee. You're on your own for any doughnuts."

When they were alone in the cafeteria, Kevin blew on his coffee and gave them a level gaze. "You two didn't consult me when you dreamed up the story of Craig Lewis's demise, so I guess I'm stuck with it like everyone else. But you'll never win an Edgar Award from the Mystery Writers of America with that tale."

"You weren't exactly in condition to contribute, you know." Clancy made a face after tasting his coffee.

"What the hell was the stuff he used? And how did he dope me?"

"This is all hypothetical, of course," the FBI man said, "but Craig Lewis went through a lot of specialized training in terrorism, cold war cloak-and-dagger stuff, and hostage rescues. Craig had a back-slapping device that injects poison. Fortunately, he used knockout stuff, or maybe you're just too damned ornery to die."

"I felt like I was dead. I gather that all the stuff Craig Lewis brought into the building with him vanished?"

Clancy nodded. "What choices did we have, Kevin? You were out of it, and we didn't really know what went on."

"I'm not complaining, but I take it this wasn't just revenge for the bar fight?"

"I don't think we'll ever know."

"But if you had to guess, Frank?" Kevin pushed.

Clancy heaved a sigh. "Well, you know there was a contract out on you."

Terry nodded. "A new twist to your line, Frank, 'We're here from Washington to help you.' Even if it's an occasional hit."

"Is the Bureau going to look into what Craig Lewis was up to?" Kevin asked.

"No. The best I could do was prevent them from giving him an Attorney General's medal."

Terry laughed. A medal from the Attorney General was the highest recognition available to an FBI agent. "He deserved an Oscar. He fooled a lot of people." She realized her cheeks were flushed, but the men were looking at each other. "How did you stop the medal?" she asked Frank.

Clancy was uncomfortable. The Bureau was being ridiculed. "I pointed out that absentmindedly falling down an elevator shaft and getting a medal would cause a lot of laughter in FBI offices across the country."

Kevin spoke slowly: "So the Bureau will take a pass. It's like this department and Flip's murder."

"Boys will be boys. And boys' organizations will be boys' organizations," Terry said.

Clancy looked unhappy. "I'm not sure that's fair, Terry."

"But as Jimmy Carter said before he stopped you guys from doing any more Abscam stings on Congress, 'Life is not fair.' "

When Clancy got off the elevator with them, he waited until the hallway cleared, then said, "Watch your back, Kevin. I'm doing the best I can to see what's behind this contract on you, but in the meantime you have to assume it's still on."

Back in their office, Terry and Kevin found Joey Demanto

sitting with his feet up on Kevin's desk. He was grinning. "Inspectors McKay and Fisher, it's time for you to welcome the new member of your team, Inspector Joseph Demanto." He jumped to his feet. "It's all right. You don't need to applaud."

"Hey, that's great, Joey!" Terry hugged and kissed him. Then slapped him as he put his tongue in her ear.

Kevin smiled. "That's good news, Joey. We sure need the help."

"Did Ferrante break down and admit we needed more people?" Terry asked.

"No," Joey said. "B&B put in for a disability retirement. High blood pressure. With his contacts in the POA, it's a foregone conclusion. So Ferrante paid me off to keep my mouth shut about the school assignment. He gave me the vacancy. I was easy to bribe." He stopped, puzzled at the somber look that came over Terry and Kevin when he mentioned B&B.

Terry helped Joey get settled into what had been B&B's desk. A few minutes later Kevin came over. "I'm going to check with the lieutenant to see if I can lay out work schedules for us. Our first priority is to put Raul Santiago behind bars, but I think we can also start working on Flip and Ronnie Blue." Kevin picked up a pile of papers and headed for Garza's office.

"Terry, when Kevin and I were narcs, we put in a lot of hours, but he set up an exercise routine for us that helped," Joey said. "Do you think you'd want to join?"

"You bet. Maybe that's what's helping him cope now. And I sure would like to get back in shape."

"Okay. We meet at six A.M. at the Breakers in Golden Gate Park."

"Six A.M.! You got to be joking."

"Nope. We run five miles, then do a short calisthenics session. Then to the gym for showers. Of course, if it's too much for a woman—"

"I'll be there, asshole." And she was, but afterward, sitting at her desk the next morning sipping coffee, Terry wondered if she was going to get through the day.

She and Joey had talked. They decided they had to broach the subject of Carlos with Kevin. Neither wanted to tell him that Dana had rushed into Carlos's arms when they brought her back to her apartment, but Kevin had to know what was going on to work the ski mask case.

"Kevin, could you come over here for a sec?" Terry knew that if they didn't get Kevin away from his desk, his eyes would keep returning to the case reports.

He stretched and walked to her desk. "What's up?"

She pointed to the unlined sheet of paper on her desk. She had printed: *Dana, Carlos, Raul.* "Joey and I took Dana home. Carlos was there. She's living with him now at a new apartment. Nevertheless, we're not sure she's safe. Remember Raul's threat when we took him out of your place?"

Kevin nodded. Both Terry and Joey had been uneasy, but Kevin was calm. "So?"

"Well . . ." Joey stopped.

"Oh, hell, Kevin. We're not sure she wanted to stay with Carlos," Terry exclaimed. "In fact, damn it, I think she loves you. You ought to go see her."

Kevin's expression darkened. "Let's keep this professional, Terry. If you want, I'll go with you to make sure she's alert to her danger, but the personal stuff is off limits." He returned to his desk.

"You sure have a delicate touch, Terry," Joey said.

"I? You . . . you just stood there sucking your thumb. Why didn't you say something?" She was furious.

Later that afternoon, Terry was still simmering when she and Kevin drove to Dana's new residence. It had been two weeks since they'd taken Dana home to find Carlos waiting.

The apartment was on Mason on the downward slope of Nob Hill, just a block from the exclusive Fairmont Hotel, sitting on the crest. The spectacular view of the city and bay, and the expensive area, brought no comment from Kevin. Terry swallowed her caustic remarks about the money dope dealers seemed to abound in. She was still cautious about Kevin's mental state concerning this meeting and didn't want to set him off.

A doorman stopped them, but they flashed badges and brushed past his halfhearted efforts to announce them to whoever they were going to see. Joey had obtained the address without disclosing to Terry how he'd done it. She hoped it was the right apartment. But it was Carlos who opened the door.

"Carlos, I'm Kevin McKay. I believe you've already met Inspector Fisher. We came to speak with Dana."

The same arrogance was there, Terry thought, watching Carlos look her over and probe with his eyes to see if he set off a spark. He was used to seeing women react to him. She kept her glance bland, hiding a sudden intense desire to grab Carlos by the hair and slam him into a search position.

Carlos turned to Kevin. "I'll see if she's interested in talking to you." Abruptly he tried to close the door, but Kevin was too quick, pushing it open.

For a brief moment Carlos leaned against the door, but quickly realized the futility of pitting his strength against Kevin's. Kevin stepped inside, and Terry followed. Spots of color appeared in Carlos's cheeks, but he said nothing, quietly closing the door and disappearing down the hallway into an interior room.

Kevin scored a point, Terry calculated. They were inside. He hadn't left Carlos any options. She surveyed the expensively furnished living room with a real fireplace and steps down into a paneled den lined with bookshelves, and wondered what Dana would look like. Terry was rooting for her to rush out wan-faced and throw herself into Kevin's arms, as she had with Carlos. But when Dana appeared, she was beautiful, composed, and Carlos was a step behind her. She wore black slacks with low-heel pumps and a black cotton turtleneck that emphasized her attractive figure. Somehow, Terry knew Dana didn't have to run five miles with the guys as she did to maintain it. There were traces of paint on her hands, and all signs of apprehension were gone.

For a moment Terry envied her. Plenty of money, clothes, jewelry, and spending her days painting in what no doubt was a beautiful room with a magnificent view. Then she saw the way Dana looked at Kevin, and she felt sympathy for her.

"Hello, Dana," Kevin said. "How are you?"

"I'm fine, Kevin." His cool greeting killed the glow of hope in her eyes, and her voice trembled.

A small smile played on Carlos's face. Terry realized he was enjoying this.

What Terry didn't know was that the passion that had once been there, between Dana and Carlos, was gone, though Dana clung to him during the night. She had told Carlos about Raul and his escape and how frightened she was. He reassured her that he would watch over her, and she accepted that.

In fact, Carlos had not been disturbed to hear that Raul had escaped. He hadn't told Dana, but he'd made immediate plans to take care of Raul once and for all. As much as he wanted to kill Raul himself, Carlos knew he couldn't afford the risk. The Nguyen brothers would kill Raul, as soon as they could find him. They told Carlos they'd traced him to Watsonville. Dana would never know the details, but she would appreciate that he'd protected her. In a short time, she would not have to worry about Raul. And then, he thought, he would not have to worry about this fool McKay.

Now, Carlos sat savoring the uneasiness between Dana and Kevin. The cop had failed her, as he had been bound to, with his civil service poverty and puny badge and gun. McKay was no match for him. The coded message last week from Alphonse on the Mentor's yacht saying F. Bly was no longer doing the contract and that the Mentor would like Carlos to place a "new order" pleased Carlos. It had taken too long, and McKay and Demanto were back on duty.

It gave Carlos pleasure that they would be dead by tomorrow night, including this woman cop who thought she was tough. The Mentor had agreed with Carlos's assessment that the Sherry situation had gotten so severe that they had to act immediately. The Mentor had approved of his plan to use a teenage gang as a cover.

Carlos had made arrangements with the team he'd used before. They were bloody, but had never failed. They had dispatched Ronnie Blue twelve hours after a panicky Lieutenant Sherry had informed Carlos of Blue's conversation with B&B.

Yes, Cong Nguyen and his brothers would serve him well in eliminating three troublesome cops, Carlos decided, as well as eliminating Raul. The brothers had followed McKay, and learned of the detectives' habit of meeting at Fung's at seven P.M. each evening. The heat would be enormous, but Carlos also planned to kill Cong and his brothers after their work was done tomorrow night. No one would connect him with what would appear to be a Vietnamese gang vendetta against cops.

"Dana." Kevin's face was expressionless.

He was a cop as he spoke to her, Dana realized sadly. He hadn't forgiven her. Somehow, he had erased his love for her, and wouldn't see that she couldn't change her love for him. Of course, seeing her with Carlos was the final straw. But what else could she have done, with Raul Santiago hunting for her while he was gone? She listened to Kevin, hoping for a sign that something remained between them.

Kevin cleared his throat. This was more difficult than he'd expected. "We're looking everywhere for Raul Santiago, but he's still a danger to you."

"I disagree, policeman," Carlos said.

"I'm not here for a debate, Carlos," Kevin replied. "I think we both have the same interest in keeping Dana safe."

Carlos had sat down, but now abruptly stood up and glared at Kevin, who gazed back impassively.

"You had a chance to do justice, and you didn't have the courage. Dana would not be in danger if you had been a man."

Kevin's face tinged with red, but he stepped away from Carlos's anger. "Dana, you know where to reach Terry or me twenty-four hours a day. Don't hesitate to call." He paused, still ignoring Carlos. "Are you all right now?" he asked her.

Dana couldn't stand the tension between the men, or Kevin's coldness to her, or Carlos's anger, so mean and so dangerous.

"Please go now, Kevin," she said, turning away from their confrontation. For an instant Terry saw something in Kevin's face as he recognized Dana's pain, but he merely nodded and turned away.

Terry drove, and Kevin hunched his shoulders and looked

out the window. Terry didn't think he was seeing the tourists who had lost their way, uneasily walking through the long lines of homeless men at St. Anthony's kitchen in the Mission District. "You were cold, Kevin. She would have left him in an instant if you had asked."

His voice was muffled. "I couldn't protect her before," he said, "and I can't now, Terry. Carlos was right."

"You should have let me—" She stopped, remembering Carlos's cutting remark to Kevin about not shooting Raul.

Picking up on what she'd begun to say, Kevin said, "I couldn't let you kill Raul, Terry. That's what makes us different from Carlos. No one pulls that trigger without changing. I've seen a lot of cops who thought they were doing the right thing at the time crack afterward. We don't hire out our souls to the department, just our bodies.

"All the neighborhood people want us to be the jury and executioner, but when we go before the grand jury to explain what we did, we're all alone." As she pulled into the Bryant Street police garage, he added, "And we're most alone when we try to justify to ourselves what we did."

Chapter Fifty-seven

"Kevin?" Joey hesitated.

Kevin was engrossed in an interview report. He put his finger on a sentence and looked up. "Yeah?"

"Remember our great stakeout of Tim's joint, looking for Big Billy?"

"Remember? You joking?"

"Yeah. The day we made the first buy from Hallman and my career began to end. Anyway, I found out something. Big

Billy was in the can on a DUI, and Sherry knew it when he assigned the stakeout."

"I'm sure the Chief of Detectives will be outraged, Joey. Have you told him yet?"

"Screw you and the chief. I'm trying to tell you something. Big Billy is back in circulation."

"We're not in Narcotics anymore, Joey."

"God, you can be thick. I was thinking—"

"Congratulations," Terry Fisher said.

"Yeah. Well, one of us has to remain conscious. Look, Big Billy sold to a number of locations in the area. Including the bus depot where Santiago worked. One of my narc buddies saw him apparently hand off some dope to Santiago the day after the Corrections Department let him go by mistake."

Kevin put the report he was reading to the side. "Hmm. Is it your feeling that we might remind Big Billy of his civic duty to help the police apprehend the ski mask rapist?"

"No shit, Sherlock. You're getting to be a real detective."

"It's a long shot, but what the hell." Kevin reached for his car keys. "We don't seem to have any other hot leads at the moment. Maybe Big Billy knows something about Santiago that will help us find him. Let's give it a try."

Watching Tim's Bar and Grill, Kevin fought off a nasty feeling of déjà vu. Of course, this time Terry was with them. Maybe she would change their luck.

"It would help a lot if we caught Big Billy dirty," Kevin thought out loud.

"Why don't I check out the bar to see if he's in there?" Joey sat hunched in the backseat.

"Want me to come with you to make sure they don't mistake you for a dicky waver?" Terry sat up front next to Kevin.

"Yuck-yuck. Who writes the lines for you two? Butt-head? I think I should go by myself. Tim's isn't exactly a family joint."

"Okay. We have the front and side doors covered in case he makes you." Kevin said. "Don't let him split through the parking lot."

"He ain't going to make me. I'll be right back." Joey got out of the car and walked a half block to Tim's. He strode through the front entrance and headed for the men's room without displaying any awareness he was being looked over by the bartender and customers. But in workman's clothes, Joey didn't raise an eyebrow among the bar crowd. It was the seventh inning. Almost payoff time for their bets. People turned back to the TV sets.

At the far end of the bar Big Billy paused in a whispered conversation with the waitress. He watched Joey out of the corner of his eye. Joey passed him without a blink and entered the men's room. He hummed to himself at the urinal. Ordinarily he would have stopped for a shot and a beer to establish his credentials, but this wasn't an ordinary narc case. Big Billy moved frequently and suddenly on his rounds. They didn't want to miss him.

Joey's quick exit produced a couple of frowns. Protocol was that you at least had a beer when you came in to take a leak. These street bums didn't have any class.

"He's there. At the end of the bar doing a deal with the waitress," Joey told Kevin and Terry when he was back in the car. "We better cover the doors. He doesn't stick in any one place long."

"Okay," Kevin said. "I'll cover the front entrance. Joey, you take the side street exit. Terry, take the parking lot door. Whoever spots him buzzes the others on their handsets. Let's move before he takes off."

Terry leaned against a car in the parking lot and ignored the questioning glances of the attendant. One of the things she liked about Kevin was his direct approach. He knew Big Billy was most likely to use the parking lot exit, but he gave it to her because she was less likely to get made as a cop by the attendant. No bullshit about trying to protect her.

Two minutes later Big Billy hurried out of the bar toward his car. Terry started to speak into her headset, but Big Billy spotted her and broke into a run. There was no time to transmit. She ran diagonally across the lot to cut him off. Big Billy had her by about forty pounds, but he was puffing. Terry, thanks to the morning workouts, was fit. She slammed a shoulder into the portly drug dealer. He slipped and banged against a pickup truck.

"Police, Billy. Freeze right where you are or you're going to be real sorry."

Big Billy, trying to catch his breath, saw Terry poised on the balls of her feet and tried to decide whether or not to take her on.

Terry held her left hand out and wiggled her fingers. Big Billy looked at the bright red nail polish. "Break a nail, go to jail, Billy," she warned him. Terry opened her jacket, letting him see the Magnum strapped to her waist. With her left hand she took her handset and pressed the transmitter. "We're in the rear of the lot," she said.

A moment later Terry smiled. Joey had torn around the corner and then stopped self-consciously when he saw Terry standing quietly with Big Billy. Kevin joined them. Big Billy recognized Joey from the bar but said nothing. He stared straight ahead, but his attention was fixed on Kevin.

Kevin studied the drug dealer. He was puffing, so clearly he'd run from Terry. He was holding, or his car was dirty. Otherwise he would have been making speeches about his rights.

Kevin nodded at the man. "Billy, I'm McKay, and this is Demanto. We used to be narcs. You've already met our new partner, Fisher. We aren't interested in drugs at the moment. We're working rape cases. We thought you might be able to help us a little, and we can help you a little."

Big Billy was puzzled but was listening.

"Look, Andy"—Joey used Big Billy's real name—"we can toss you and that old piece of shit Buick you drive. But as my partner said, we ain't into the drug war right now. We're looking for an asshole by the name of Raul Santiago on a rape case."

"I don't know no rapists," Big Billy said.

"Wrong answer, Billy." Joey leaned close. "You got one felony conviction already. Even if you're only holding small amounts right now, you're looking at a long jolt with your record."

"His name is Raul Santiago, and we know you know him.

He's a bus mechanic." Kevin rested a hand lightly on Big Billy's shoulder.

"I . . ." Big Billy hesitated. Kevin had spoken quietly, but Big Billy suddenly thought better of his routine stonewalling.

The three detectives stood silently. The dope dealer was either going to open up or clam up.

"Of course, it's only what I heard, and I wouldn't want it to get around that we even talked about it." The man's eyes scanned the parking lot, momentarily empty of people.

"No problem, Billy," Joey said. "Tell us what you heard."

"He's supposed to be working in the big truck repair place in Watsonville. The one that does farm stuff too."

Kevin watched Big Billy, wondering. After a moment he said, "What kind of hours does he work?"

Big Billy fidgeted. He was anxious not to be seen with them. "I think he finishes like at two or three in the afternoon."

"Okay," Kevin said. "We're going to cut you loose now, Billy. That was part of the deal, but if you're sending us on a wild-goose chase all the way to Watsonville . . ."

"I only know what he told me . . . I mean what I heard."

Kevin nodded to Terry, and she moved out of Big Billy's way. It took him a moment, but once he realized he'd been released, he hurried away without a backward look.

"Think he's being straight with us?" Terry asked.

"He slipped just then. He didn't mean to tell us that Santiago himself told him about the Watsonville job. And it figures. Santiago was a mechanic. One way or the other, you and Joey will have the scenic journey to Watsonville first thing in the morning. It's too late to catch him at work today. And if he is in Watsonville, we don't want to spook him by having you guys hanging around."

Chapter Fifty-eight

Frank Clancy kept missing Ray Bloom. Bloom had requested to see him two days earlier, but Clancy hadn't returned to headquarters until nearly six P.M., and by then Bloom was gone. The next day, Bloom attended a conference in Los Angeles. Finally, Clancy caught up to him as the elevator door was closing the next morning. Bloom hit the open button and stepped back into the corridor outside the FBI's eleventh-floor office in the Federal Building. "Frank, I've been trying to get hold of you," Bloom said.

Clancy diplomatically refrained from pointing out that Bloom, not he, had been unavailable.

Bloom put his hand on Clancy's shoulder and steered him away from a group waiting for the elevator. "Unfortunately, Frank, I'm late for a meeting with the U.S. Attorney, so we can't sit down right now."

"Do you want me to ride on the elevator with you?" Clancy said.

"No, but listen—this is for your ears only. We got another satellite intercept. A Vietnamese teenage gang we think has being doing these home invasions and murders has been given a contract to hit three people in Fung's restaurant. The code was confusing, but one part was clear. No hit was to take place if there was a uniformed cop in the vicinity. That's what I wanted to tell you. Because of time constraints, we contacted Ferrante directly. He's having a radio car in front of the place, and one of the cops inside just to make sure." Bloom glanced at his watch.

"I'll go and look the setup over," Clancy said. "Who's the hit on?"

"That, we're not sure of." Bloom moved toward the elevator.

"Ray, I know you're in a hurry, but since we don't know the potential victims, shouldn't we just pick these jerks up and scare the shit out of them? Let them know we're aware and that they better not try anything?"

Bloom moved away from the elevators, realizing once again that there was no such thing as a quick conversation with Frank Clancy.

"Frank, we're hoping this satellite will give us the biggest seizure since the war on drugs started. We don't dare alert the bad guys that we're listening to conversations they think are safe. Ferrante gave us his word that he'd cover the restaurant. That will buy us time. By all means go and look the place over, but whatever you do, don't burn our intelligence source. I've got to run, but pin me down later. We can flesh out the details."

Ray Bloom got on the elevator forgetting to mention that the satellite transmission had been picked up from the same yacht in Saint-Tropez that had generated the contract on Kevin McKay and Joey Demanto.

Clancy went back to his desk. It looked like he was going to have lunch at a new restaurant today, he thought. But he was due for Chinese food anyway. It was less fattening, unless he went for the deep-fried stuff. He rubbed his hands. Bloom would have to approve his expense chit.

In Chinatown, Cong Nguyen gave last-minute instructions to his team. He had decided that his younger brother, Sahn, would be the primary shooter. The youngest, fifteen-year-old Hung Thai, would be the second shooter. He, Cong, was the leader. He would be in the rear, like a general. Ready to take care of any trouble, ready to guard their flanks, to improvise if necessary.

Inside Fung's restaurant, Terry Fisher spread out papers on their rear corner table while Joey fiddled with his chopsticks. Kevin sipped tea.

"Okay," she said, "summing up as of tonight. As a result of

the narc of the year coming up with an intelligence gem," she winked at Joey, "we traced Raul Santiago to a drug operation. It turns out he's been developing into a low-level dealer in Watsonville. Joey and I will check it out tomorrow. You with me, Kevin?" She paused when it appeared Kevin was dreaming into his cup of tea.

"I'm sorry, Terry. Go on."

"I don't know, Kevin. You seem out of it." Terry shuffled the papers.

"Go on."

"Okay." She looked at Joey fiddling with the chopsticks, his eyes hungrily following the waiters coming out of the kitchen. "Maybe I should wait until you get your pot stickers and Kevin comes back to earth?"

Joey waved his index finger. "Inspector Fisher, you are apparently unaware that Inspector McKay and I were busting big-time crooks before your badge was even printed."

"You mean stamped in a metal plant, asshole." She glared at Joey, who only smiled back and pursed his lips in a kiss.

Terry laughed. "Okay. It turns out that one of our friendly narcs observed Raul the day after his escape from jail that wasn't an escape. Raul showed up at the drug operation. Our narc, in the best traditions of the department, decides the drug war is more important than arresting a series rapist, murderer, fugitive, which might blow his surveillance of the dopers. So he lets Raul vanish."

Joey said, "It's SOP on drug surveillances that you don't stop what you're doing for every other little violation of the penal code that you see. We'd never have a dope surveillance or undercover operation otherwise."

"Thanks, Joey. You couldn't have said that better than the former drug czar, Bill Bennett. I wonder what you guys would do if the victims of rape were men? Anyway, that plus Big Billy's info means you and me get to visit the garden spot of Watsonville first thing tomorrow morning, right, Kevin?"

A few blocks from Fung's, Cong Nguyen gave ammunition to his brothers. The three teenage killers loaded fifteen-round magazines into their Uzi machine pistols and walked toward the restaurant.

On the street outside Fung's, Captain Jack Fitzgerald swore. His car had been blocked in traffic for ten minutes. He was ready to cite whoever was responsible. But when he got to the bottleneck, it turned out that it was a black and white double-parked, and a cop behind the wheel, reading a newspaper, oblivious to the curses and dirty looks motorists were throwing his way. The police car left just enough room for another vehicle to squeeze by. The captain saw it was parked outside Fung's and assumed the other cop was probably inside picking up their dinner.

"Brady!"

The cop looked across at an angry Fitzgerald. "Hi, Captain," he said, wondering what the boss was sore about.

"Lunkhead. Do you have any idea that you have traffic backed up all the way past Bush? I've been stuck ten minutes just trying to get here."

The cop looked sheepish. "Sorry, Captain. But we got an order from Chief Ferrante—"

"Ferrante?" Fitzgerald was furious. It was outrageous. The Chief of Detectives using his uniformed men to pick up Chinese food. Fitzgerald didn't dare cancel the order, but he snarled at Brady. "You work for me, not Ferrante. Get that goddamn car parked at the curb, now!"

Brady shrugged. Bosses. You couldn't please them. His orders were to stay right in front of Fung's, but he wasn't about to argue with Captain Fitzgerald. He pulled to the far end of the block, where there was an open space at a fire hydrant. He could still see the front of Fung's, and his partner, Piggy Waldron, was in uniform inside, sitting at the end of the bar and watching the front door. Of course, no one had told them what they were watching for, but that was par for the course.

Piggy Waldron had been in the men's room relieving himself when the three inspectors took their table in the rear. Piggy returned to the corner stool he'd selected without looking around the restaurant, and he wasn't visible from the rear table. He sat sipping club soda and picking his bets for the next day's sporting events. He had decided to back the Giants because Gordon was starting pitcher and he always did well against the Dodgers. And Piggy liked Devil's Paw in the fifth race at Bay Meadows. He'd probably make a couple more picks, he thought, if they weren't ordered someplace else before midnight, but he knew in police work you could never count on staying in one place very long.

He decided to get his two bets to his bookie before some supervisor decided they were needed elsewhere. His partner, Arnie, was double-parked outside. The police presence was visible, so Piggy ambled back to the public phone he'd noticed near the rest rooms. Neither Piggy nor his partner had any way of knowing that the well-armed Nguyen brothers would approach the restaurant from the opposite street and not see the police car. Nor would the brothers have any way of knowing that a uniformed cop who was supposed to be visible at the bar was calling his bookie instead.

"Kevin, something has put you in the dumps," Terry said. "Hey, where are you going?"

Kevin was on his feet. "I'm sorry. I lost track of the time. I have an appointment to see Ronnie Blue's mother. I'll catch you guys in the morning for our run."

Sahn Nguyen was advancing slowly as Kevin shrugged off Terry's protests that he hadn't eaten. Sahn never noticed officer Piggy Waldron coming back from the telephone. Sahn now had his targets in sight. One man was standing, the other sitting with the woman. Just as they had been described. They would go down in one burst, but he would make sure with subsequent shots. His brothers would not be required. He reached for the Uzi machine pistol under his jacket. Suddenly he was pulled from behind.

"Fool," his brother Cong whispered. "Have you no eyes?" He nodded toward the uniformed cop getting onto the bar stool.

Kevin McKay walked past the three Vietnamese boys

without really seeing them. He was thinking of his interview with Ronnie's mother.

Chapter Fifty-nine

Kevin took the case file on Ronnie Blue with him to the housing project. His first stop was to see Ronnie's mother.

"Come in, Kevin. Ordinarily I'd be working all day, but my boss insisted that I take time off. I'm not sure it's the best thing." She looked around the small, dark apartment. "I see him everywhere. How could this happen? He was a good boy, wasn't he?"

Corrine Blue was forty. She had left Ronnie's father when Ronnie was a baby, after she could no longer tolerate the man's alcoholism and beatings. She found solace in her church. And in her son's life. Her tear-reddened eyes questioned Kevin.

"He was a good boy, Corrine." Kevin hugged her, then stepped back, holding onto her shoulders. "Never let anyone tell you different."

"Are you just saying that? The other detectives asked about Ronnie and drugs."

"I checked, Corrine. Ronnie never dealt drugs."

Corrine Blue didn't say anything.

"He was a boy growing up, Corrine. He smoked some pot. I got on him about it. But most of the kids try it. It's not like crack or the other drugs. Ronnie wasn't hooked and he wasn't dealing."

"Then why?"

"I'm not sure." Kevin didn't want to add to her grief. "But that's what I'm here to find out. Have you heard any gossip?"

Corrine Blue went to the kitchen. "I'll make us some coffee. How do you take it?"

"Black."

They sat at the small kitchen table. "There has been some talk that it was a teenage gang."

Kevin frowned. Perhaps he'd been wrong about B&B and information leaking that had burned Ronnie as an informant.

"Were there any descriptions?" he asked.

"No one around here wants to talk much. You know that. But some say it was Vietnamese boys. Very young. What in the name of God is this country coming to, Kevin? Little boys shooting and killing."

"Corrine, would you take me to your neighbors? Anyone who might have seen the boys? They'll never talk to me alone."

Two hours later Kevin returned to headquarters with descriptions of the killers who had waited in the hallway for Ronnie Blue and a story that a tall, red-haired man had been dealing drugs to boys in the project. None of the people who spoke to him were willing to look at photo lineups or come to court to testify. It was going to be a tough case. It took Kevin several hours and a number of conversations with other detectives in the Juvenile Assaults Unit before he became convinced that three brothers named Nguyen were the killers. He was still puzzled as to the motive. He dialed Dermat McGloughlin in the Intelligence Unit and offered to buy him a drink.

McGloughlin was from County Cork and had a thick brogue. He was an improbable choice for the Intelligence Unit, where he was supposed to become an expert on the various ethnic and racial gangs frequenting the San Francisco Bay area. He had surprised everyone except himself by becoming a walking encyclopedia. The best authority on gangs the department had ever developed.

"How are you, Kevin? I've heard you've had some rough times." The thick-shouldered Irishman sipped at a Guinness stout. They sat at the bar in the Double Play on Sixteenth Avenue. The aroma of good food tempted Kevin.

Kevin smiled. "Of course, Derry, you, the intelligence man, hear everything. I guess I don't have to answer your question."

McGloughlin held up the glass of stout. "I'm easily corrupted. But I may weasel an answer or two out of you later."

"I coached a young black boy named Ronnie Blue. He would have been a basketball great. He was killed last week in the Ford Housing Project. Two shotguns."

Derry McGloughlin nodded.

"Homicide didn't seem interested. Dismissed it as a kid dealing dope, but I'm sure Ronnie never dealt."

"I skimmed the report. It did look like a dope hit. You know, Kevin, sometimes the bad guys make mistakes. They aren't as clever as the police." McGloughlin's eyes twinkled. Then he became serious. "It's possible the lad was hit in error."

"Maybe. It's a whodunit right now. I got some information that three Vietnamese brothers by the name of Nguyen did it. The IDs won't hold up in court, but I wanted to know what you think."

"Ah . . ." The husky detective pulled a pipe out of his jacket and began to fill it. "They're a bad lot, the three of them. Father was military. Just escaped the Saigon disaster with the wife before it fell. We think he worked some of the residential robbery and killings. Are you familiar with the home invasions?"

Kevin nodded. "The ones that worked the circuit from Oregon to Houston and California?"

"The same. Anyway, a couple of years ago San Jose cops got some information and made a case. Old man Nguyen was murdered before it came to trial. I heard he had turned to save himself." He sucked on his pipe. "The boys are chips off the old block. Cong, the oldest, is seventeen. Let's see, the other two are Sahn and Hung Thai. I forget which is which, but they would be sixteen and fifteen. They ran with a Chinatown gang called the Red Dragons. The gang broke up when five of them were found shot to death in a garage on Stockton. We believe that the brothers wiped them out and kept the proceeds of the robbery of the Mandarin restaurant. Not one of the fifty people robbed would give a statement. The take from the customers and the office was supposed to be well into six figures." Mc-Gloughlin shook his head. " 'Tis a sad world, Kevin, when so many people refuse to talk."

"What have the brothers been up to lately?"

"That's interesting. They've been into low-level dealing and some muscle for the ring we hear is taking over cocaine in the city and area. Very big. Might even have had some ties to that fellow you wrote the memo on, Hallman. Don't quote me on any of this, Kevin."

"Of course not," Kevin said sarcastically. "We have to preserve the integrity of the Intelligence Unit. Isn't that the way you guys put it to avoid testifying?"

"That slur will cost you another Guinness."

Kevin sipped at his beer and signaled the bartender to bring another Guinness. He watched McGloughlin closely. The intelligence man had carefully avoided mention of Lieutenant Sherry and his detectives, but he was certainly aware of it.

McGloughlin shrugged and relit his pipe while Kevin digested what he had said and hadn't said. The Homicide Unit hadn't gotten anywhere on the Hallman hit, but it looked like a mob hit on an informer. Could the same people have hit Ronnie? Kevin wondered. Both Hallman and Ronnie had a connection—him. It was easy enough to see Sherry getting rid of Hallman, but Ronnie?

"Derry, don't say anything unless you think I'm wrong. But is it possible that these kids hit both Hallman and Ronnie because they gave information to me?"

McGloughlin blew out a cloud of smoke and smiled at Kevin. Why would a dope ring be hitting people to cover up for a rogue lieutenant and his team? The FBI information about a contract on him and Joey had come shortly before Hallman was hit. Of course, he and Joey had busted a number of dealers. The contract could have been from one of them. Yet, there had been no warning. No outburst by the prisoners or promises of revenge. He would have to get back to Frank Clancy on the details of the contract.

* * *

In Chinatown, Cong gathered his clan. "We must be more alert tomorrow, my brothers," he said. "Remember, our orders were not to act if the police were present."

Sahn shrugged. "I would have killed the fat cop. No problem."

Cong spoke quickly. "We are being paid well. We must follow discipline. Those who pay us said not to shoot if uniformed police were there. That is the way it will be. It is not likely the fat cop will have dinner there two nights in a row. Tomorrow, we will succeed, and Carlos will pay us twenty thousand dollars in cash afterward."

Chapter Sixty

The phone rang and Terry came out of a deep dream and fumbled for it on the third or fourth ring. "Hello."

"Terry?"

"Yes?"

"Kevin. I guess I don't have to ask why you guys aren't here to run."

"Run? What time is it?"

"Six-twenty."

"Oh, sorry, Kevin." She was half asleep.

"Well, I hope I'll see you later at work."

"Sure thing, Kevin," Terry said, hanging up. In the dim light she made out Joey's slender ass in bed. Then it registered. "Holy shit!" She'd answered Joey's phone. Looking at him snoring, she reached over and slapped his rump, hard.

"What? What?" Sleepily, he sat up, staring at her.

"What? You just announced to our partner that we're sleeping together."

"I did?"

"Yeah, you slept right through the phone ringing." Terry grinned, then jumped on top of him. "So you might as well make it worthwhile."

"Oh God," he groaned. "Again?"

When Joey and Terry arrived at the squad room carrying coffee cups, Kevin greeted them with a smile. "I had a good workout this morning, but to each his own, I guess."

Terry, paying no attention, sat down and sipped her coffee. "Kevin, that wasn't fair yesterday, you jumping up and leaving the restaurant, telling us over your shoulder you were going to see Mrs. Blue."

"I'm sorry. I lost track of time. I suddenly realized I was late for the appointment. I didn't know it was going to cause you guys a sleepless night."

Terry blushed and Joey chuckled.

"That will be enough of that, Joey Demented," Terry said, stopping Joey in the middle of a laugh by using the nickname that inevitably pissed him off.

Kevin was amused by Joey's sudden discomfort. "Equal time, Joey?" he inquired.

Joey made a face and remained silent.

Terry, serious now, said to Kevin, "Joey and I are going to Watsonville, but tonight at Fung's we want you to tell us what you've been up to."

Carlos had used the front door chain lock so he would know when Dana arrived. She always used the front door to the spacious apartment he'd rented on Nob Hill. However, on this day Dana was burdened with paint supplies and decided to use the rear kitchen entrance so she wouldn't have to carry the supplies all the way through the apartment to the studio. As she went down the corridor from the kitchen, she heard an angry voice and looked through the open door to the den. She saw a red-faced man with a flushed birthmark shaking his finger at Carlos.

"You told me McKay would be taken care of by now."

Dana shrank back out of sight.

"The first attempt apparently misfired," Carlos said. "This time I took control. It will be done."

Dana felt a pain in her chest. Kevin. She had hoped that by living with Carlos she could somehow help Kevin, that perhaps Carlos would no longer be angry at him. But she'd seen the way Carlos looked at Kevin when the detectives had come to warn them about Raul Santiago.

"Yeah, well, we don't have all year. The State Investigation Commission hearings start next week."

"And what of all your plans to discredit McKay?"

Dana heard the contempt in Carlos's voice even as he feigned respect.

"The wimps had no balls. The stuff we gave them at the hearing worked fine. For some reason, they let him off suspension."

Dana realized the other man must be a policeman.

"I remember that you were also going to make it appear that his basketball players were all users."

"I did. Brennan did what I told him. The kids were rolling in grass. It helped smear McKay at the hearing. Lucky for me I found out that McKay's pet went to headquarters and ratted on Brennan."

"Yes. Fortunately, I was able to act in time after you told me. He was taken out before McKay came back on duty."

Dana was terrified. She felt faint. Carlos had been responsible for someone getting killed. She heard the fury in Carlos's voice and waited for the sound of him attacking the other man.

"Yeah, Carlos." The other man was equally angry. "But unlike you, I get things done. Maybe I should take care of McKay the way I did Hallman."

"Sherry . . ." Dana heard the conciliatory tone in Carlos's voice and realized how hard he was trying to control his fury. "The same people who took care of the basketball player will take care of McKay."

"When?" the policeman asked.

"Tonight."

"Where?"

"Is there a reason for you to know that?"

"You bet your ass. Suppose I happened to be nearby? Someone might suspect me."

Carlos sighed. "Stay out of Chinatown."

"It better work. I'm not going to wait forever for you yo-yos. I been doing my part. I even got McKay smeared for letting his partner get killed and the shooter escape. People think he froze in the hallway."

"What about the investigation?"

Sherry laughed. "I dropped an anonymous letter on Ferrante so that someone would see McKay goofing off at Sacred Heart. The letter said a black cop was molesting kids and that the basketball players were dopers. Since O'Neil was killed, I dropped a word here and there that he was the child molester. There ain't much investigation going on."

"What does all of this mean, Sherry?"

"It means that the department ain't breaking its ass to finish the case and bring in the shooter. And when McKay goes down, there'll be more cheers than tears."

Dana heard Sherry stand up. "I gotta get going. I'll be in touch."

Dana raced back down the hallway and crouched in the back doorway. When she heard the front door close, she eased back out of the apartment, trying not to rustle the bags containing her art supplies. She couldn't let Carlos discover her inside the apartment. She heard Sherry's heavy footsteps heading toward the elevators, then waited until the elevator arrived and the door closed.

Dana tried to stop shaking. She had decided to wait a few minutes and then make a noisy entrance through the front door. But at that moment she heard Carlos inside the kitchen, approaching the rear entrance. Her knees were weak. Frightened that he might find her and think she'd been hiding, she turned her key in the lock and pushed the door open. Carlos stood a few feet away, staring at her.

"Carlos, you frightened me."

"What are you doing?" His eyes were hard.

Dana forced herself to turn away. "Can't you see I have my hands filled with supplies? You might at least help."

He advanced slowly and reached for her. Dana thought her heart was about to stop. Casually, she shoved a bag of brushes at him. He grabbed it roughly and looked inside, then looked inside the other two packages. It took all of her willpower to pretend she hadn't noticed his suspicions. She walked to her studio. As soon as he left, she was determined to call Kevin and warn him.

But Carlos followed her to the studio and sat in a chaise lounge where he often watched her paint. Dana put her supplies away, hiding her trembling hands by turning her back on him.

"You just arrived home?" he asked.

"Hmm." Carlos had just seen her at the door, so she would have to ask why he was asking such a senseless question. But knowing he was too astute to fool, she ignored the question and took her time putting the supplies away in various drawers. When it became apparent that he wasn't going to move, Dana started for her bedroom.

Carlos leaped to his feet and put his arms around her, kissing her aggressively.

"Carlos . . ." She tried to push him gently away. "I'm tired. I've been shopping all day. I need a shower."

He smiled. "I'll join you."

She hid her revulsion. "You have more energy than I have. You took the afternoon off."

"No, my sweet. I actually took care of some important business. But I hope you're not too tired, I made dinner reservations for us at Ernie's."

"Oh, Carlos. I don't think I'm up to it tonight."

"But I insist. It's a celebration. I'm turning over a new leaf tomorrow. I'll hire some people and begin to take more time off to spend with you. How would you like to spend a week in Mexico?"

"Your moods change like lightning, Carlos." Dana walked to her bedroom knowing that he was not going to leave her alone even long enough to make a phone call.

Chapter Sixty-one

Frank Clancy finally got to see Ray Bloom in his office. He'd chatted with Judy at her desk while Bloom finished a phone call. Clancy took a cup of coffee in with him.

"Hi, Frank," Bloom said. "It's been hectic this week, but we need to talk. Did you spot the uniformed cops at Fung's?"

"No. I was scheduled to be in Oakland last night. I did have lunch there. Great food. Try the pot stickers."

"Too bad. We could have covered dinner for you. The contract specified dinner, so you're on your own for the lunch tab."

Clancy had to study Bloom's straight face for a moment before he knew he was being kidded. He smiled. "The setup looked okay to me, and I guess since we don't have any dead bodies, the cops were there. Any more info on who the targets might be?"

"None. There was some interference. A storm or meteor or something. Only part of the message was received."

"Ray, have you given any more thought to bringing in those kids and shaking them up?"

"These kids are badasses, Frank. SFPD Intelligence thinks they were the ones who did the Mandarin restaurant robbery and wiped out the Red Dragons. Bringing them in won't faze them, and it could burn our satellite. Why don't you go over there for dinner tonight, see if you spot any likely subjects?"

Clancy winced. "Ray, I've been out three nights so far this week. Gloria is pretty good about it, but—"

"She should be. At least she knows with the shape you're in it's not another woman. Anyway, do what you think best, but remember mum's the word on the satellite." Bloom's phone buzzed. "Okay, right boss." He shrugged at Clancy and got up to go into the SAC's office, once again forgetting to mention that the interception had come from Saint-Tropez.

"Do what I think best," Clancy muttered to himself. Sure, and if something went down, he thought, it was his ass. He went back to his desk to call Gloria and tell her they wouldn't be going to the movies tonight after all.

It had taken Kevin a day of discreet effort to find Nate Lincoln, the cop who had passed a copy of the anonymous letter to Flip concerning a black, child-molesting cop. Trish had mentioned that he was a patrol officer on temporary disability in Ferrante's office. Kevin didn't want the brass to hear he was sniffing around the Chief of Detectives' office. He found out that Nate was due for the swing shift at Mission Station and caught him in the briefing room before his tour began. Nate was slender and dark black.

"Nate, I'm Kevin McKay, Flip O'Neil's partner," he said, holding out his hand. "Do you have a minute?"

Nate ignored his outstretched hand. "You have the nerve to call yourself his partner?"

Kevin, surprised at the hostility, looked at Nate questioningly. When the other man remained silent, he said, "Trish told me about the anonymous letter."

"What are you going to do, report me to the chief?"

Kevin flushed. "It's nothing like that. I just wanted to know what Flip said about the letter."

"Well, thanks to you, he ain't around to answer questions, and I don't have anything to say to you," Nate Lincoln said, then spun around and walked out of the room.

Cong and his brothers loaded their weapons. It was time to go to Fung's. The three diminutive teenagers made their way through the crowded sidewalk. Cong was anxious to get this job finished. Carlos had paid them good money so far. He would be proud of their work tonight. He had promised they would be promoted upward in the organization. They would have status. They would no longer need to do dangerous robberies. The drug trade was safe and more profitable if one was given status. Right now they were just hires, workers. But after tonight they would be known and respected.

George Anthony, Ferrante's administrative captain, looked at his watch. It was ten after six and Chief Ferrante was not back yet. Nor had he called. George knew where he was. The chief had a squeeze, and George had her number. But he was under orders to use it only in an emergency. He was reluctant to call. Ferrante had been in a bad mood all day, and had almost taken his head off three times during the morning. George didn't think it was an emergency, and Jack Fitzgerald had been breaking his balls about putting those uniformed cops in front of Fung's. If it had been anything important, the chief would have let him know what it was about. If he went ahead and ordered the same coverage on his own tonight and the Patrol Bureau bitched, it would be just like Ferrante to say, as he always did, "George, just do what I say. When you use your own judgment, you're on thin ice." If Ferrante didn't call within the next twenty minutes, George decided, he was going home to have dinner on time for a change.

The phone didn't ring, and at six-thirty George turned out the lights, locked up, and left.

Carlos never left her alone, even in the restaurant, and Dana wondered if she was his alibi. She could hardly touch her food, and felt Carlos watching her. She had to get a warning to Kevin. Finally, she could stand it no longer and excused herself to go to the rest room.

The phones were located between the men's and ladies' bathrooms. Quickly, she dialed, then swore and hung up. She'd called Kevin's beeper, and of course she couldn't leave a number for him to call. Then she called his work number, knowing he wouldn't be there, but at least she could leave a message. Instinctively, she put the phone down while it was ringing and peeked around the corner. Carlos was rising, coming to check on her. She rushed back to the phone. Kevin's number was ringing. Hurry! Hurry! she said to herself. Finally, Kevin's voice came on saying to leave a message after the beep. Dana whispered a warning into the phone, hung up, and dashed for the ladies' room. By the time Carlos turned the corner, she was smoothing her dress and on the way back to the dining room. She raised her eyebrows. Carlos shrugged and nodded toward the men's room. Dana noticed, however, that he waited for her to get back to the table before he entered.

Terry summed up her and Joey's frustrating trip to Watsonville. They finally got the garage owner to admit that Raul Santiago had worked for him up until two days ago, when he got paid. "Didn't see him since then, or so he says," Terry told Kevin. "Joey and I think we should drop back tomorrow during Raul's working hours just to be sure. Whatcha think, Kevin?"

"You're right. We have APBs out everywhere. If you come up blank, stop and tell the Watsonville cops what we know."

"Okay, Dr. McKay. Would you like to enlighten us on any of your activities, or are we supposed to guess, as usual?" Terry asked as Fung himself placed chopsticks for them.

"Joey, I'm not sure you're having the right effect on her." Kevin shook his head, and paused until Fung left. "Anyway, I went to talk to Nate Lincoln. You remember I mentioned to you that Trish said Nate had gotten Flip to do some surveillance based on an anonymous letter. Well, Nate told me to get fucked, that I had gotten Flip killed." He paused, and when neither of them said anything, continued, "Last night was more interesting. I talked to Ronnie's mother. She told me that the story around the neighborhood was Ronnie was killed by a Vietnamese gang."

Joey scowled. "What? The Homicide dicks never said anything about that."

"They didn't know. I got descriptions and a tentative ID on three brothers named Nguyen. I bought Derry McGloughlin a couple pints of Guinness and found out that these kids are killers. They may be working for a dope ring."

Terry sipped tea. "So it was a dope hit. That's sad for Ronnie's mother."

"I'm pretty sure Ronnie wasn't into dope dealing . . ." Kevin paused. ". . . but I can't figure it out. There's some talk that a white guy started supplying dope to the kids in the project a few weeks ago." Kevin stopped while they gave their orders to the waitress. When she left, he added, "That's another reason why I wanted to talk to Nate, to see if Flip had mentioned dope."

Frank Clancy wondered why no police car was parked outside of Fung's. He decided it might be wise to have a glass of chardonnay at the bar while he discreetly cased the restaurant. After reading the menu, he decided on a Jordan, a Napa Vineyard selection that had won a gold medal. Clancy swirled the glass and absorbed the fragrance. There was supposed to be a uniformed cop visible at the bar. It was five minutes to seven.

Clancy went to the phone and called Ferrante's office. No one answered. He dialed Ray Bloom at home. No one answered. He went back to the bar, swirled his glass some more, and thought the wine had a promising, deep fruity aroma. Clancy blinked. Joey Demanto was heading down the hall toward the men's room. Some of the chardonnay splashed onto Clancy's jacket. Something was weird. Clancy didn't wait to taste the wine. Joey had come from the back of the restaurant. Unconsciously, Clancy shifted the glass of wine to his left hand and slowly walked to the tables in the rear. His back was turned when Cong Nguyen entered the front door and stepped aside for his two brothers.

Terry looked up and saw Clancy, wineglass in hand, staring at them. "Well, the FBI never sleeps." She laughed. "Join the party, Frank."

"What is it, Frank?" Kevin read the FBI man's face and began to slide out of the booth.

"Why are you three here?" Clancy's mind was racing. What was the connection? A hit on three people? A previous contract on Kevin and Joey? The Nguyen brothers.

Cong Nguyen looked over the bar and peered into the part

of the restaurant that was visible. No uniforms. He nodded to his brothers, and they moved toward the rear table where the three victims would be dining.

"We've been having dinner here and debriefing every night. Don't tell me there's a federal law against it." Terry grinned at Clancy. He was really square tonight.

Ten feet behind Clancy, Sahn Nguyen, the primary shooter, saw the woman and two men at the table. Just as they'd been told. He eased the Uzi from under his coat.

"Do you know the Nguyen brothers?" Clancy still hadn't sipped his wine.

Kevin looked over his shoulder at the Vietnamese youngster gazing at them. Nguyen? Kevin's eyes dropped. He saw the Uzi being raised.

"Jesus! Look out, Frank."

Clancy tossed his chardonnay to the side and dove to the floor, drawing his .45 as he fell. Kevin was already on the ground reaching for his gun. Terry was squeezing out of the booth. All three watched as Joey Demanto came from the side hall. Sahn Nguyen never saw him. Joey grabbed the barrel of the Uzi and slammed Sahn Nguyen in the side of the head with his right fist. The slender boy fell unconscious as two rounds from the Uzi exploded into the ceiling. People screamed. Kevin started to his feet as Joey, without a second's hesitation, whirled and savagely kicked Hung Thai Nguyen in the balls before he could bring his weapon to bear. Kevin was sprinting forward just as Cong, the leader, fired wildly. The Uzi climbed on him, raking the ceiling with bullets. Cong panicked and ran out the front door. Kevin rushed past Joey, who was trying to grab both Uzis at once. Clancy brushed by Joey and slapped handcuffs on Sahn. Terry put her cuffs on Hung Thai.

"I'm going after Kevin," she said, running for the front door.

Kevin had bolted through the door a few steps behind Cong and was slowly gaining on the slender youth as they jostled people on the sidewalk. They were almost to the corner. Kevin saw that Cong still had the Uzi in his hand. He knew he should stop and let the SWAT team handle it, but he reached for Cong and missed him. The boy turned around and attempted to level the Uzi. Kevin slammed into him like a middle linebacker blitzing an unprotected quarterback. They both went down heavily. The Uzi clattered down the sidewalk, and a moment later Kevin handcuffed the stunned Cong. He dragged Cong to his feet while Terry picked up the machine pistol.

"There's nothing like a nice, tranquil Chinese dinner with you, McKay," she said.

Chief of Detectives Vincent Ferrante tried with some success to clamp a news blackout over the incident at Fung's. He didn't want McKay looking good.

Late into the night, while Kevin, Joey, and Terry wrote reports, Lieutenant Garza sat calmly through a session with Chief Ferrante and Lieutenant Benedetti of Homicide and was not at all surprised when the Chief of Detectives dismissed him and Ralph Benedetti without complimenting him on his team apparently breaking Ronnie Blue's homicide. Benedetti didn't even say good night to Garza when they left Ferrante's office. The Homicide Unit's turf had been fucked over. The fact that the case had been solved didn't matter.

Garza went home to bed. Kevin, Terry, and Joey imposed on Ralph, the owner of Liverpool Lil's bar and restaurant near the Presidio, to give them a back table and to keep the booze and food coming. Ralph reopened the kitchen and put together the sandwiches himself. At one A.M., Terry and Joey headed for his apartment and Kevin went home. Lieutenant Garza had given all of them, including himself, the next day off. They had thanked him without mentioning that department regulations required the time off.

PART FIVE

Cop Justice

Chapter Sixty-two

When Kevin checked his voice mail the next morning, he frowned over the message from Dana. It was whispered and sounded stressed. "Kevin, a man named Sherry is dangerous to you. Be careful of Chinatown. I have to go. Don't call me. I will call you again." What the hell? Chinatown? The Nguyen brothers?

He looked up. Nate Lincoln stood in front of his desk. "I owe you an apology." Nate gave an embarrassed smile.

Kevin waved him to a chair. "Don't worry about it."

"No." Nate leaned forward. "I was an asshole. I should know better than to believe the gossip. Lucky I called Trish. She straightened me out. You're clean on Flip getting shot."

"I should have checked the bathroom better, Nate."

"Bullshit. You guys had no reason to suspect anything on a routine parole questioning. What I heard was that you stayed in the hallway. Never bothered to go after the shooter. I talked to Bernie Andrews, the uniformed cop who took you to the hospital. He told me he never saw anything like it. You were unconscious but holding a gun on Santucci, lucky you're alive. I'm sorry I gave you a ration of shit." He held out his hand.

Kevin was puzzled. Where in the world had the rumor come from that he'd stayed in the hall? He decided not to discuss it with Nate. There were more important questions. "No problem." Kevin shook his hand. "What I wanted was anything you can tell me about that letter."

"Can't tell you much. I was told to file it. When I read it, I decided to give a copy to Flip. Ferrante played some dirty tricks when we filed the affirmative-action suit. I just wanted Flip to check to make sure he wasn't up to something."

Kevin shook his head. "The molestation stuff is weird. And the drugs . . . I don't know what to make of it. I coach those kids in basketball. None of them ever used, but just after the letter, some of them were smoking grass. Now I hear rumors from some of the people that a white guy was giving them the dope."

"Maybe that's what Sherry was doing in Ferrante's office the day before."

"Sherry? Hmm. Nate, did Flip say anything to you?"

"Yeah. He called me a few days before he got shot. Said he had looked over the school for days. Didn't think there was anything to the child molesting. And the drugs . . . how'd he put it? No way those kids could run like they do and be doing much drugs."

Kevin spent a few more minutes with Nate without learning anything more. But after the patrol officer had left, Kevin again read the anonymous letter. Then he dug into his file drawer and pulled out a copy of the phony letter of reprimand from Sherry that Ruggieri had clotheslined him with during the hearing.

"Goddamn!" Both letters had a distinctive defect in the lowercase letter *e*. Also, the uppercase letter *d* was filled with ink. The anonymous letter on child molesting and drug use by the basketball kids had come from the same typewriter. It hit him like a right to the jaw. One of Corrine Blue's friends had said a red-haired man had been with the boys. He'd thought it was merely a polite way of saying that a white man had been giving the kids grass. Now the vision of Brennan came to him. Had Sherry sent Brennan to give the kids drugs so it could be used against him in the hearing? Ronnie had come to tell him about it the day Flip was killed, and B&B, giving a friendly little warning to Brennan or the POA attorney, had led to Ronnie being hit.

Kevin felt a white-hot hatred of Sherry. First, Sherry had tried to destroy him and Joey for reporting the drug rip-offs. When that didn't work, he'd somehow engineered a contract on them. He'd even tried to smear Flip, and himself as a coward, but taking the life of an innocent, gifted youngster like Ronnie ... Kevin vowed that Sherry wasn't going to beat this rap.

Kevin faced Frank Clancy over the FBI man's desk in the Federal Building on Golden Gate Avenue. "Unbelievable, Frank. How the hell could the Bureau be so careless as to not tell you that the message on the Nguyen brother's contract on us came from the same source as the previous one?"

Clancy held a finger to his lips and looked at the ceiling. "What do you say about having lunch? There's a pretty good place over on Van Ness, in Opera Plaza."

As they walked to the restaurant, Kevin said, "I thought the cold war was over. What's all the paranoia about?"

"The cold war may be over, but the bureaucratic war never ends." Clancy smiled. "I've been threatened with exile if I mention the satellite interception, so I'm not telling you about it. It's the newest secret weapon that's supposed to win the drug war."

"Well, I'm not holding my breath until victory is declared."

"Me neither. Nor until the politicians stop bullshitting about how we're winning." Clancy pointed to Max's. "Good food and fine women walking around. Too bad you guys are in a slum over on Bryant."

"We don't have the time or expense account that you have, Frank. But I still think it's incredible that the Bureau would withhold information about a contract on cops."

"We never really withheld it, Kevin. But, you know, shit happens."

When they were seated, Kevin resumed their conversation, saying, "I wonder if you'd be so philosophical, Frank, if it had been a contract on you."

"Wait a minute, Kevin. You're not equating a threat against the life of a federal agent with a contract on local cops, are you?"

Kevin laughed. "All right, Frank, I know it wasn't your

fault. But all this bullshit about protecting the source of intelligence while people are getting knocked off is ridiculous."

"I won't argue with that. But at least the Nguyen brothers are out of operation."

"For how long? And whoever gave them the contract is still at large. They didn't say a word, and we questioned them for hours." Kevin put his menu down.

"You may not like this, but I hear the U.S. Attorney is moving to deport the kids to Vietnam. They were never citizens."

"Deport them! They killed five Red Dragons, attempted to murder us, and almost caused a bloodbath at Fung's, and all we're going to do is deport them?"

"It's not my idea, but the only other alternative is to try them as youthful offenders under California law. You have no evidence to charge them with the Red Dragon homicides, so it will be just what happened at Fung's. Their lawyer will probably argue that they were disadvantaged youths just doing some fireworks and we don't understand their culture. How safe is it going to be with them walking away from some Youth Authority ranch?"

Clancy looked at the menu as the waitress approached. "Great burgers and fries, Kevin," he said, then ordered, along with Kevin.

"Do you believe in justice, Frank?" Kevin asked afterward.

"Depends. What are you talking about?"

"More than two months ago I submitted a memo on Lieutenant Glen Sherry. Since then, my partner was killed, the police department has treated me like public enemy number one, I was almost killed by Craig Lewis, Ronnie Blue tried to give me information on Sherry and got killed, and last night my two new partners were almost killed along with me."

"Don't overlook me," Clancy said.

"Feds are expendable. To continue the story. We break the ski mask case, and a series rapist murderer goes to jail for a few hours until they release him by mistake. Now all we have to do is capture him again after he kills a few more people."

"Don't forget that your girlfriend left you for a dope pusher."

"Thanks, Frank. I really needed that."

"I'm sorry, buddy, but when I hear cops start to talk about doing justice themselves, I usually find an excuse to leave the room. You've had a rough time, but self-pity isn't going to get you anyplace."

"You think that's what I'm talking about?"

"I don't know what you're talking about, and I don't want to know."

"Clean hands, Frank? Aren't they the same hands that helped throw Craig Lewis down an elevator shaft so your beloved Bureau wouldn't have its dirty laundry washed in public?" Kevin's face was red.

"I've known you a long time, Kevin," Clancy said. "I never saw you like this before." He hesitated. "You're a good investigator, terrific at analyzing cases, interviewing suspects and witnesses. I always felt we needed more people like you in law enforcement. Now I'm not sure. You're changing. I think for your own sake you ought to get out."

The food they'd ordered arrived. As the waitress moved off, Clancy said, "You're bright, Kevin. People like you. Except the dirt-bags. You could be a success in the private sector no matter what you went into. Maybe you're jinxed in this business. But if that was an implicit threat you tossed at me before, we part ways here."

"I'm not threatening you, Frank, but sometimes all that crap you spout about the organization is too righteous. The fact is, Glen Sherry and his narc pals are worse than the people we put away. The Nguyen brothers are just as bad, and I think for some reason they got the contract on me after Craig Lewis failed. The dope ring must be trying to protect Sherry and putting out contracts on people he says are dangerous to him."

"That's intriguing." Clancy continued eating his sandwich. "I have tried to get the Bureau to investigate your memo, you know."

"I know. But it's not in the organization's interests just now."

Clancy frowned and took another bite of his hamburger. He sipped his coffee. "You're headed someplace, Kevin, and I'm not sure I want to hear where it is."

"Fine, Frank." Kevin tapped his spoon on the table. "Seen any good movies lately? What do you think of the Forty-niners' chances for another Super Bowl championship?"

"God, you can really ruin a lunch. I suppose it wouldn't do any harm to listen to you."

Kevin sipped a Diet Pepsi. "Well, my guess is that Sherry is working with the dope ring. Some funny things went on when Joey and I were narcs. We came up empty on a couple of our raids. We always wondered if they were warned. Of course, it could come from anywhere, the D.A. and his staff works on warrants for us, and so do the court personnel. But Sherry seemed to get fantastic information. The squad—or, I should say, Sherry and his three favorites—made big busts. Great media stuff. Half the time they would get the police chief and Ferrante in front of the TV cameras. Their snitches were always secret, which is standard, but the cases were funny. The volume of dope seized was always exaggerated. Of course, that's normal drug war bullshit, for the media's benefit. Yet, time and again, the stuff involved would be so stepped on that even a hype couldn't get high on it. And the crook arrested was always some jerk who was low-level. It was news to us that they had gotten up to kilo levels. Some of them claimed that they were set up. I listened to the tape recordings of the buys. They were guilty, all right, but their rise to become big dealers seemed to come an hour before their arrest."

"The pattern is unusual," Clancy agreed, "big arrests and seizures, but the suspects are low-level and the stuff seized doesn't have much dope in it."

"Right. In addition, we saw one distribution ring get stronger because of Sherry's arrests, and I'm pretty sure that Carlos Castellano is in it up to his eyeballs."

"Hmm. The path of true love is never smooth, Kevin, but how sure are you about Carlos?"

"I checked with DEA. They say Carlos has really moved up the ladder the last few years. They only had one case on him. And get this—Neil Brennan booked the dope into the SFPD property room. It turned up missing and Carlos walked."

"So you suspect foul play. It does stink, and I confess even I heard some whispers about Sherry. He does show good stats, though."

"Of course that's standard in drug enforcement. We seem to do little more than guarantee the survival of the strongest of the species. The solid distribution network prospers while we knock off their competition for them. But if Sherry was in with them, they had it made."

Clancy signaled for the check. "So, it's possible that Sherry might have gotten information from some dopers to knock others out of business?"

"Right. And remember, there were a lot of stories about a cop robbery team."

"How could Sherry survive so long?"

"Survive? The department loves him. He's got the best arrest and seizure stats ever. He gets Ferrante and the police chief on television every few months with some seizure or bust. Of course, no one looks at the quality of either the collars or the dope seized. As long as the media is happy, the chief is happy. One other thing is strange. Sherry and his team have never made any cash seizures."

"Given the extraordinary amount of cash in drugs, that may be the most suspicious item of all," Clancy said. "So, what's really on your mind?"

Kevin shook off the waitress's suggestion of some coffee. When she left, he leaned toward Clancy. "The M.O. of the dope robbers is that they get very good specific information on when a dope operation is going to have a lot of cash on hand. Then they crash in and rob the dopers. You with me so far?"

Clancy nodded.

"Now, the M.O. of the Nguyen brothers in the residential robberies is quite similar. They got very good information on Vietnamese people in this country who had gold and cash stashed in their homes. Some of the victims were shaky, of course. The money had been smuggled out of Vietnam. But others were legitimate business people who didn't trust banks or were playing games with the IRS. So, it's kind of ironic to think that the Nguyen brothers are doing a contract to protect robbery teams just like them, except this robbery team happens to be made up of cops."

"And what you're telling me is that under the law, we can't do much about either the teenage killers or the dirty cops?" Clancy said.

"You disagree?" Kevin raised his eyebrows.

Clancy grunted. "Not really. It's your solution to it all that I may have a problem with."

"Why, Frank, as far as we know, Sherry and his team have never met the Nguyen brothers. All I want to do is have these nice people meet each other. The party could be fascinating." Kevin smiled.

"Somehow, it's hard to imagine either group responding to your invitation, Kevin."

"True, but with a little help from your illustrious organization, it could be arranged."

Chapter Sixty-three

As a result of Frank Clancy's efforts, the Nguyen brothers were taken to an INS hearing on deportation. The court-appointed attorney routinely requested time to study the case. The brothers were too young to be lodged in cells, so they sat in a large room with about twenty other people under INS guard. A thin boy who didn't appear much older than Cong introduced himself as Min Diem. He bowed with respect.

"I have heard of your work."

Cong was suspicious. "What have you heard?"

"In Chinatown the Nguyen brothers are known as the lions who eat Red Dragons."

Nguyen sneered. "Silly talk. We work as laborers for the food trucks." But he was pleased. They were gaining status.

"As you say, wise Nguyen." Min Diem glanced around. "But I have a friend who knows of a wealthy one. A communist who brought much gold out of the homeland and now lives in San Francisco like a king."

"I have no interest," Cong said, "and as you can see, we are not free to meet your friend."

"But they will be releasing all of us in this room momentarily. This is INS, not jail authorities."

Cong said nothing. Min Diem might be released, but they would be taken back to juvenile detention. Suddenly, the door opened and a white man in a blue uniform appeared. "The commissioner will resume hearings at two o'clock," he said. "You must all return to this room. If you are not here, warrants will be issued for you."

Sahn and Hung Thai looked at Cong inquiringly. Cong dipped his head toward the door. If the fools were so careless, the Nguyen brothers would take advantage.

Leaving the building, Min Diem edged closer. "Remember, Cong, my friend's name is Earl Wilson, a fat white man, but quite reliable. That is his car, if you wish a ride to Chinatown." Diem pointed to a white Cadillac at the curb.

Cong wanted to get away before the authorities realized their mistake in releasing them. There would be no harm in getting a ride. Cong and Sahn sat in the backseat with the white man. Hung Thai, being the youngest, sat up front next to the Mexican driver.

Min Diem introduced them. "As I mentioned, worthy Cong, this is the fat man, Earl Wilson. You can trust him."

The large man in the backseat glared at Min Diem. "Begone, worthless one. I will deal with you later."

Min Diem bowed and smiled. He turned quickly and walked away from the car as it slowly left the curb.

"It will be worth your while, Cong, to visit this place at nine P.M. tonight," Earl Wilson said, wheezing as he spoke. "I will share half of what you obtain, but I will also help you to travel to Hong Kong, where you will not be bothered by cops. You will have plenty of money. I promise you." The big man handed Cong an unsealed envelope.

"Why do you do this for us?" Cong scrutinized the big man.

The fat man wheezed and chuckled. "For you? No. For me. You can make us both rich tonight, and I have heard of your reliable work."

Status. It is so easy when one has status, Cong thought. He smiled, taking the slip of paper with an address from within the envelope.

"Just one thing," the fat man added. "Be very alert when these people arrive home. They are armed and very careful since they keep such wealth hidden."

"Lieutenant?" Detective Neil Brennan sat on the edge of Glen Sherry's desk.

"What's up, Neil?" Sherry said.

"Maybe something good for us. Look at this FBI report."

Brennan dropped it on the desk, and Sherry read it quickly, then looked up. "How'd you come by this?"

"I stole it. You know how unconscious those guys are. I was over there for a drug task force meeting, and the Fee Bee next to me went to take a leak. This was right there on top of his file."

Sherry frowned. "Will he know you took it?"

"No. I moved to the other side of the room. He had a whole bunch of papers with him. He just shoved them in a briefcase."

"This looks very good for us," Sherry said, tapping the report on his desk with a finger. "A money transfer tonight at a dope operation. You think the Bureau has it staked out?"

Brennan covered a look of disgust. Sherry was so dumb. "No. See the final paragraph, where they say they're planning to renew surveillance next week. It was called off because of manpower shortages."

"Where?" Sherry searched the report. "Oh," he said when Brennan pointed to the paragraph with a finger. "Okay, tell your partner to get ready for some fun tonight." Sherry smiled. "We'll follow the usual procedures."

* * *

Cong didn't have time to locate new automatic pistols, so he retrieved the shotguns. He would have preferred their Uzis since they carried fifteen rounds and were easily concealed. However, the shotguns had been effective against Ronnie Blue, and there would be no reason for concealment. The fat man had indicated that the apartment would be unoccupied until the victims returned home at nine P.M. Reportedly, the rear fire-escape window had a simple lock. The brothers would wait inside the apartment. They would have the element of surprise on their side. And, as the fat man said, it would be desirable to be in Hong Kong until the American police forgot them; desirable because tonight's treasures would be added to what they had already accumulated. The Nguyen brothers would be rich people in Hong Kong, Cong mused. They would have status.

After the Cadillac dropped the Nguyen brothers in Chinatown, it drove to Liverpool Lil's. Kevin and Frank Clancy sat with Min Diem, otherwise known as Jimmy Young, Burglary Squad detective. He and Kevin had graduated from the Police Academy together and had been patrol partners before becoming detectives.

Jimmy was arguing violently with Frank Clancy, showing no trace of the Asian accent he had used when speaking to Cong Nguyen. "You're crazy, Frank. Notre Dame is so overrated. I've got twenty bucks that says Cal rolls them over."

"Nothing any good ever came out of Berkeley. They shouldn't even be playing on the same level as Notre Dame. How many Heisman winners from Cal compared to Notre Dame?" Clancy said as the fat man entered the bar and glanced around. Conversation in the bar stopped as people turned to look at him. Earl Wilson tugged at the ivory-colored safari hat on his head. Slowly, he approached the table at which the law enforcement group was gathered.

The three men looked up. The fat man leaned on the table and whispered, "Min Diem, you inscrutable asshole. Your accent wouldn't stand up to a bright Girl Scout. And if you refer to me again as the fat man, I'm going to turn your yellow ass in for DWA."

"DWA?" Clancy raised his eyebrows.

"Driving While Asian," the fat man said.

Jimmy Young looked at Kevin. "I know you were desperate, Kevin, but this guy is too much. You know, the only requirement to serve in the Intelligence Unit is to be inarticulate. That way you keep your mouth shut and people think you know something. When this guy had to talk today, it strained his brain. You better give him some alcohol before he collapses of overwork."

"Sit down, Harry," Kevin said to Harry Long, Dermat McGloughlin's partner in the Intelligence Unit. "How did it go?"

"Well, we ain't exactly dealing with a criminal genius. And if they have time to think about the phony scheme Clancy here set up with the INS, who knows? But I suppose the three little fuckers know how to pull the trigger."

"Sometimes," Frank Clancy said. "They didn't do so good the other night. Of course, they were up against an FBI agent."

"Yeah, I heard about it," Jimmy Young said. "They probably got paralyzed laughing at the sight of you trying to draw a gun."

Clancy swallowed some chardonnay, then said to Kevin, "What makes you think Sherry and his guys won't just blow the kids away?"

"I wouldn't exactly call Sherry a genius either," Kevin said, "and he and his crew have been getting away with it for so long they're cocky. All the other times, they surprised people. This time the Nguyen brothers will be waiting for them. And if I'm wrong," he said, thinking of Ronnie Blue, "it won't break my heart."

The apartment on the third floor of a run-down building on Howard Street seemed like a strange place for a rich person to live, but Cong knew many such people hid their wealth. He and his associates had been quite successful in getting people to disclose where things were hidden. Cong had learned how to inflict pain, and to use the fear of pain to get information. He did not anticipate difficulty tonight.

He sat on a folding chair to the left of the front door, his loaded Remington shotgun across his knees. He had positioned his brothers three feet away from him on each side. He would cover the middle. Sahn would take anyone on the right, and Hung Thai anyone on the left. Once people entered the door it would be too late. They would be covered by shotguns.

They waited silently. Cong had forbid any conversation. At ten minutes after nine they heard a slight rustling sound at the front door. Cong brought his shotgun up to cover the door. His brothers did the same.

Suddenly, the door shattered and Sherry charged in, yelling, "Police! Freeze where you are." He jumped into a firing crouch. Neil Brennan was a step behind him to the right and also yelling. The third member of the team was to the left, also in a firing crouch. Sherry swung his weapon toward Cong and spotted the shotgun. He squeezed the trigger at the same time as Cong. The other brothers had the detectives lined up, and they fired as the policemen emptied their guns. The apartment filled with noise and the smell of gunpowder.

Sherry was blown backward and killed instantly, but not before he got off three shots, the second of which struck Cong Nguyen between the eyes. Cong collapsed lifeless a second after Sherry. The other two detectives were dead from the shotgun blasts.

Sahn and Hung Thai saw that Cong was dead. They dropped their shotguns and ran out the door. Hung Thai reached the downstairs street door first and stopped. He cautiously looked into the street to make sure there were no police waiting and turned to signal Sahn that it was clear. But Sahn stood still with a puzzled look on his face. He looked down at his hands, holding his stomach. They were covered with blood. In the excitement, he had not even felt being hit. Now his eyes widened and he sank to the ground. Hung Thai took one look at his motionless form and ran in full flight back toward Chinatown.

Chapter Sixty-four

Dana and Carlos returned to the apartment at five minutes to ten. Carlos went to the television set and turned on an early news channel. Dana felt dizzy, not sure she could bring herself to watch.

The program came on with the announcement of a breaking story. Three policemen had been killed. Dana staggered and had to steady herself by holding onto the sofa. Carlos smiled, his attention totally on the screen. The camera flashed to a residential neighborhood. Carlos's smile turned to a scowl. The reporter solemnly announced that three veteran policemen had apparently died in a gun battle with a teenage gang.

Dana realized she'd been clenching her arm so tightly that the circulation had stopped. She felt tears in her eyes. Suddenly, she was confused. Carlos jumped to his feet and swore. There, on the television screen, was the face of the man she'd seen in the den. He and his men had been killed, not Kevin. Dana eased out of the room. She had to get away from Carlos. But she stopped to listen. Carlos had gone to the phone.

"I have some work for you." His voice was barely controlled. "Immediately. I'll meet you in an hour."

Dana stayed where she was, and heard the front door slam. Carlos didn't even say good-bye. She needed to escape, but where could she go? Kevin's apartment was out. With all that was going on, he was unlikely to be there anyway. And it had been at his apartment that Raul Santiago threatened her as he was being led away in handcuffs. But she needed a phone number to leave on Kevin's beeper. She would go to the old apartment on Russian Hill, she decided. Carlos had kept the lease. She had two thousand dollars in cash there, in her closet safe. She would go to New York after warning Kevin. Carlos would never look for her in the apartment, and she could wait for Kevin's call. She dialed, and when his beeper signal came on, punched in the phone number of the Russian Hill apartment.

Lieutenant Garza beckoned Kevin to his office. Garza was holding his bag and fumbling with a black band. News had just reached headquarters of the death of Sherry, Brennan, and the third narc Sherry had used. It was late, and there weren't many people in the Bureau of Investigations, but those who were working overtime or night duty reached into their desks for the black elastic bands that cops placed over their badges on days when a cop had been killed. Garza looked at the unadorned badge attached to Kevin's belt.

"You heard?"

"Yeah."

Garza nodded thoughtfully. He opened his drawer, tossed the black ribbon into the desk, and closed the drawer. He replaced his badge in the holder without the black ribbon. "Anything you want to tell me?"

"No, Lieutenant."

"Well, I got news for you. They identified the prints in the bathroom as belonging to Santucci's brother. It looks like he's the shooter. They're going to put out an APB tomorrow."

"I heard they had the ID two days ago. Why delay the APB?"

Garza sighed. "I don't know, Kevin. I don't know what the fuck they're doing upstairs. And maybe it's just as well."

Kevin returned to his desk, surprised to find Nate Lincoln standing there. He was in uniform, and Kevin noticed that there was no black ribbon on his badge.

"Hello, Nate."

"Kevin." The uniformed man nodded. "I guess you heard what just went down out there."

"Yeah."

Nate looked away from Kevin's undraped badge. "A couple

of days ago the Officers for Justice announced a ten thousand dollar reward for Flip's killer. I put the word out on the street that we were looking for Santucci's brother. It seemed like no one was surprised to hear that."

"That's what I heard too. I also heard Santucci split to San Diego."

"He's back. The ten grand got results."

Kevin nodded. "Good."

"I'm going out to pay my respects."

"No SWAT team?"

"Nope. Just me. And you, if you want in."

"Thanks, Nate." Kevin unlocked his desk drawer and stared at a 9mm fifteen-round Beretta and a Smith & Wesson Magnum that carried six rounds. He picked up the Magnum and strapped the holster to his belt. He locked the desk and slung his coat jacket over his arm.

"Magnum's got more stopping power," Nate agreed. "Got a vest?" Nate tapped his uniform shirt, which covered a bullet-proof vest.

"In the trunk. You going in uniform?"

"Right. I want to make sure Santucci doesn't have any doubts about what's happening."

Two uniformed cops in the elevator noticed that Nate and Kevin weren't wearing black ribbons.

"You guys want a ribbon? I got a couple of extra," the older cop said.

"No thanks. Not this time." Nate smiled, and the two uniformed cops looked hard at him and Kevin as they walked toward their cars.

Nate drove without hurrying. Kevin sat next to him behind the dark computer terminal. He didn't ask why Nate wasn't logged in.

"How'd you meet Flip?" Kevin asked.

"I was looking for a job. Turned down twice by the SFPD. Eye problems."

Kevin noticed Nate was driving without glasses.

"Nothing wrong with my eyes," Nate said. "But around that

time Flip got the folks in the local NAACP to come with him to a Board of Supervisors meeting. They raised hell about only two percent of the force being black. I got hired the next week. Funny thing, my eyes felt just the same. Flip was founding the Officers for Justice. I joined. Never been on the board or anything, but I go to meetings and pay my dues. This is the place."

Nate had parked a few yards from a pool hall. They couldn't be seen from the front entrance. Kevin looked at the neon lights blinking on and off while Nate unlocked the shotgun rack and pulled the Remington from its holder. He locked the car as carefully as if he were going to a homeowners' crime prevention meeting. Kevin, wearing a flak jacket labeled PO-LICE on both sides, walked next to him as Nate slowly approached the pool hall. Inside, a fat man sitting on a stool next to the cash register looked up. His mouth fell open when he saw Nate and the shotgun. The cigar he was smoking fell out of his mouth and hit his shirt with a shower of sparks. He caught the cigar with one hand and brushed the sparks away from his shirt with the other. His eyes never left Nate. Three young black men looked sullenly at Nate and Kevin.

"Myself and this gentleman are going to walk into the back-room, and we don't want to be announced in any way." Nate jacked two rounds into the shotgun. It was pointed directly at the fat man's stomach.

"Yes sir. I mean, no sir," he said.

Nate slowly twisted so that the gun in turn covered each of the young men. There was no sullenness now. One by one they nodded in earnest agreement.

Without another word, Nate and Kevin walked toward a curtained-off area. The pool hall was empty except for the men in the front. Two long drapes blocked the view of the backroom. Nate stopped and gently pushed the drapes slightly open with the barrel of the shotgun. Kevin recognized Vincent Santucci from his mug shot. He was sitting behind a table, engrossed in a horse-racing sheet. Nate nodded at Kevin, and both men moved through the drapes and sideways away from each other.

Santucci looked up. His eyes focused on Nate's uniform.

"Hello, motherfucker," Nate said.

Santucci's hand darted under the race sheet. The room filled with the blast of the shotgun and hammering of the Magnum. Kevin thought his first shot splashed blood from Santucci's eye just a hair of a second before the shotgun blast lifted him from the chair and threw him against the wall. He wasn't sure whether his second two shots hit him or not. Not that it made any difference. Santucci's body slumped in the corner. The Colt automatic he'd grabbed sailed upward, and it seemed to fall down almost in slow motion, hitting the table and bouncing to the floor with a clatter.

"That the same gun?" Nate asked.

"Doesn't matter. They found his prints in the bathroom shower."

Nate squinted at Kevin. "How come you didn't mention that before?"

"Guess I forgot."

"Or maybe you thought I might wait a bit to see if he surrendered and you'd get the first shot in."

"Nate, you're devious enough to be a detective."

"I wouldn't go that far, McKay."

Chapter Sixty-five

Dana was certain that Carlos had been on the phone arranging another attempt on Kevin's life after he saw the television news about Sherry. Because of that, she'd been in the Russian Hill apartment for two hours, waiting for Kevin's call. She knew she couldn't stay much longer. The two thousand dollars in cash was in her purse, and she had keys to her father's condo in Laguna Beach. She decided she'd take a shower, and if Kevin hadn't called by then, she would stop at headquarters and leave him a note before leaving San Francisco.

She was in the shower when Carlos entered the apartment and went to the bedroom closet to remove two suitcases. He heard the shower running, and startled, rushed into Dana's room. Her clothes were spread neatly on the bed. What did it mean, he wondered, her returning to this apartment? Perhaps it was a good sign.

Carlos slipped out of his loafers and sank back into a comfortable lounge chair. He heard Dana finish her shower. During happier days it had been their custom for Dana to sit nude brushing her hair for twenty minutes while he sat like this and watched. Often, they had made passionate love afterward.

He heard the hair dryer's buzz. A few minutes later Dana came out, nude. Halfway to the dressing table and her hairbrush she saw him. Without a word, she turned and went into the walk-in closet, coming out a minute later wearing a silk dress. Then, still silent, she sat brushing her hair. Their eyes met in the mirror, Dana's reflecting quiet determination.

"Are you angry, Dana?" Carlos asked. He could see his own face next to her reflected beauty in the mirror. He was tense. Had she, the artist, seen deeper? Seen the killings he'd had to order? The deaths that were necessary?

"I'm sorry, Carlos. I have no desire to hurt you, but I should not have come back. I'm going to get my own place. I need to be alone for a while."

He felt a flash of anger. Women, so ungrateful, so ignorant of the pressures of the real world. So full of romance and illusion. He remembered his earlier decision to give her space and respect her moods, and controlled himself.

"If that is what you want, Dana. Why don't you stay here until you find a place? I'll have the locks changed tomorrow. I'll leave you alone. You can have the only keys."

"Are you sure, Carlos?" She was afraid to tell him that she was leaving him forever and had no intention of returning to the apartment.

"I have two suitcases stored here. I'll take them with me. There will be no need for me to come here."

Dana nodded, and Carlos wondered what her reaction would be if she knew the two suitcases contained four million dollars in cash. He had been forced to sell everything. His hopes of keeping a million in reserve had been dashed by the organization. Everything he had was on the line.

The day he had been mistakenly let out of jail, Raul Santiago started to go home to pick up cash. Then he remembered that the cops had searched his place and taken credit cards, jewelry, and the money. He went instead to the main bus depot and waited for Big Billy. From time to time Billy had given him packages to deliver. As he hoped, he caught Big Billy hurrying toward Tim's Bar. The drug dealer was nervous. He knew Raul was a fugitive. He quickly gave him two hundred dollars and a small amount of PCP to get rid of him. Big Billy did not need the kind of heat Raul could bring.

Raul had traveled by bus to Watsonville. He had shaved his mustache, gotten a short haircut, and wore glasses. His appearance had changed enough to blend into Watsonville, where thousands of Mexican nationals concealed their identities and lived and worked without green cards. A large truck repair garage was happy to hire a skilled mechanic who couldn't produce identification. They could pay him substandard cash wages, and it saved them payroll taxes, health, and other benefits. Raul pretended not to understand English, but that was no problem in Watsonville, and he was a competent mechanic.

But after two weeks he saw a potential to market the PCP from the garage. The profit was so great that in a few months it would give him a stake to flee to Mexico. He might never return. He borrowed a pickup truck from the garage and drove back to San Francisco.

Big Billy once again decided it wiser to get rid of Raul quickly. He took the two hundred dollars Raul had garnered from selling the PCP and provided him powdered cocaine, several bags of grass, and more PCP on consignment. Neither Raul nor Big Billy were aware that a San Francisco narc observed them, and that eventually the information would reach Kevin McKay.

To Raul's delight, he sold everything within a couple of days. He had made a thousand dollars profit.

The garage owner had told him that two cops had come looking for him when he was out on a towing job. The owner, not wanting to be caught employing illegal aliens, had covered for him and told them Raul had disappeared two days ago. Raul figured the cops would not have any reason to come back, making the garage a safe haven for the time being, and he began to think about renewing his drug supply.

It was early morning when Raul drove toward San Francisco in a borrowed pickup truck.

By the time Raul reached San Jose, he'd begun fantasizing about Dana. It was time to teach the cop and his bitch the power of Ski Mask. He was careful to obey the speed limit and traffic regulations, but as he approached San Francisco's freeway exits, he'd all but forgotten about the drugs he'd intended to purchase from Big Billy.

He knew she wouldn't be in the Victorian house. No, she would return to the fancy place on Russian Hill. He had followed her from there to the Victorian, so he knew where it was. He laughed. All the fancy security, but anyone in a workingman's uniform could pass unobserved. And, of course, the rich fools thought it cool to have a back door to their apartments. This time there wouldn't be any cops, like at the Victorian. This time he would show his full power. He touched the crowbar next to him. He would break through the door with it. Let her hear the noise and be terrified.

Carlos was trying to get Dana to agree to a future meeting when Raul Santiago left the freeway and drove cautiously toward Dana's apartment. After a while Carlos saw he was wasting his time. He would let her cool off for a couple of weeks before he came back.

"Good-bye, Dana." Carlos kissed her lightly on the lips. She didn't draw away, nor did she return the kiss. "Call me anytime at this number," he said, handing her a slip of paper as Raul Santiago made his way up in the service elevator. "If I'm not there, they can page me." Carlos picked up the suitcases, and Dana went to the door with him. She watched him walking slowly toward the tenant's elevator with the heavy luggage.

When the elevator came and went, Dana closed and locked the door.

Meanwhile, the service elevator lurched to a stop. Raul frowned. He still had three floors to go. Something was wrong. He abandoned the elevator and made his way up the fire stairs. He was careful, peering around corners to make sure no one observed his ascent.

Dana heard the doorbell ring. She looked out the peephole and saw Carlos. She opened the door.

"I'm sorry," he said, "I forgot to tell you the place to have new keys made. Give them my name. I have an account." He searched for a slip of paper.

"Come in," she said.

Carlos placed the two suitcases inside the apartment and closed the door. He followed Dana toward the kitchen. Both stopped as they heard the crowbar wrenching the wooden frame of the back door. Carlos started forward and stopped when Raul Santiago rushed into the room. Raul's eyes gleamed when he saw Dana. The crowbar was clenched in his right hand. Suddenly, he became aware of Carlos.

"You pig!" Carlos's eyes burned into Raul, immobilizing him. Carlos pointed a small pearl-handled gun at Raul, who dropped the crowbar and stood quite still. Carlos stepped forward and slapped him in the face. "Where I come from, peasants like you died if they even looked at a lady."

The two men were a foot apart. Neither noticed Dana walk past them into the kitchen. She took a carving knife from its rack and, slipping it into the long pocket in her dress, started back toward where Raul Santiago stood paralyzed by Carlos's contempt. The phone rang then. No one answered it. After two rings Dana's prerecorded message came on. A moment later, following the beep, they heard Kevin's voice saying he was returning her call.

"Ah . . ." Carlos's face twisted. "Your friend the cop. That gives me an idea. It would be much better with the police if you killed this animal." He held out the gun to Dana.

She just stared at him.

"Yes. Take it, Dana." Carlos moved closer to her, taking her hand and putting the gun into it. He pointed her hand so the weapon was aimed at Raul Santiago's chest. Raul was sweating heavily, his eyes fixed on the muzzle of the gun.

Carlos stepped back. "Just squeeze it as many times as you can, Dana."

She looked at Carlos, and as she turned, the gun moved with her to point at Carlos's stomach.

"Point it at him, not me," Carlos said sharply. Then, confused by the look in her eyes, he said, "Dana," softly, and moved toward her.

She remembered him assuring the man with the birthmark that Kevin would be taken care of. Remembered his smile watching the TV newsflash on the policemen being killed, and his disappointment when he discovered it hadn't been Kevin. Carlos took another step, and Dana squeezed the trigger.

There was an explosion, and Carlos clutched his stomach, looking at her in disbelief. He lurched forward then, grabbing for the gun, and wrestled it from her as she fired twice more. Then, abruptly, Carlos collapsed to the floor, still holding the gun.

Raul Santiago snatched up the crowbar. "And now, bitch, you're all mine," he said, a terrible smile on his unshaven face. "There's no one to save you." He moved toward her.

Dana stood erect. She had envisioned this scene with Kevin when they discussed the attack on Jane Remick. She remembered his reaction when she had said she'd die before giving in to the rapist. Female strength and determination in the face of a threatening male had even crept into her new paintings. He might kill her, but he'd never control her. She watched him advance and saw the cruelty in his face. He paused, and she realized he was puzzled by her reaction. Quickly, she feigned fear. Unless she timed this perfectly, he'd hit her with the crowbar and she'd be helpless. She turned aside so Raul couldn't see the knife she'd taken from her pocket.

"Please don't hurt me," she said, backing toward the kitchen.

"If you satisfy me and beg, perhaps I'll be nice to you." His eyes were insane.

The crowbar was still cocked. She needed to distract him. "I'll do whatever you want, just don't hurt me."

"Call me Raul, the Powerful. Tell me what a great lover I am." He had paused just out of her reach. The crowbar was still raised, but he was staring at her face now.

"Raul," she said, "you're so powerful. Your dick is so big. You're the greatest lover."

He moved a step closer. Dana wanted to run screaming into the other room. Somehow she stayed still.

"Go on, bitch, try to talk me out of killing you after I'm through fucking you."

"Raul, you are so strong. I've never know a man with a dick so big." She glanced down at his swollen groin. "Don't hurt me. I want to fuck you. Please?"

She had backed into the kitchen, with Raul following. He licked his lips. He was shaking with anticipation. Raul touched her hair with his left hand and she began to shake. The crowbar was still positioned to crush her skull. She tightened her grip on the knife.

"I promise to let you live if you please me." Raul smiled and turned his head to place the crowbar on the kitchen counter.

While his head was turned, she slashed through his cotton pants. The knife was so sharp that at first he didn't feel the razor slash across his testicles into his thigh. His mouth fell open in astonishment as the blade severed his femoral artery and bright red blood gushed upward.

Dana watched. Raul clutched at his groin, jamming his hand over the artery so that the blood stopped spurting. He glared at her and reached for her. Dana poised the bloody knife and plunged it into his stomach to the hilt. His hands went up too late. He stepped backward and fell to the floor with his hands grabbing the knife handle.

Dana felt faint. There was blood everywhere. It was all over her, but she wasn't leaving until she was sure he was dead.

Finally, his eyes glazed over and he stopped moving. Dana walked into the other room and looked at Carlos's unseeing eyes, then went to the phone and dialed.

"McKay."

"Kevin, I need you right away. Come to my apartment on Russian Hill." She hung up and started for the hallway. She couldn't stay there. She stumbled over one of Carlos's suitcases. Righting herself, she unlocked the dead bolt. Then, taking a deep breath, she closed the door again and returned to the suitcase she'd tripped on. She knelt and opened it. For a moment she simply stared at the stacks of green hundred-dollar bills. "My God," she gasped.

She locked the suitcase and, in her bloody dress, dragged it to the elevator. She returned to the apartment and with great effort brought the second suitcase out into the hall as well. She took them in the elevator to the basement garage, where she managed to wrestle them into the trunk of her car. A car was leaving the garage, but amazingly, no one saw her.

Exhausted, she took the elevator to the lobby and went out onto the sidewalk just as Kevin's car screeched to the curb. He jumped out and ran to her, taking in her bloodstained dress as he embraced her and stroked her hair.

"I love you, Kevin," she said, putting her head on his chest. "Never leave me."

Chapter Sixty-six

Returning to the apartment, Dana told Kevin how Carlos and Raul had died. She was surprisingly calm as she spoke, but he sensed her shock and hysteria under the surface.

Kevin knelt over Carlos in the living room and felt in vain for a pulse. Approaching the kitchen, he saw the splattered bloodstains on the cabinets and counter space from Raul's open artery and the huge globs of blood congealing in the vicinity of the body. God! What a sight. Poor Dana. Without entering the kitchen, he studied the broken door and the scattered wood. Returning to the studio, where he'd left Dana, he took her hand and led her to the phone. She leaned against him while he dialed.

"Garza."

"Lieutenant, this is Kevin. I'm with Dana Rogers at her Russian Hill apartment. Raul Santiago broke through the kitchen door. Dana was here with Carlos Castellano. Carlos pulled a gun on Santiago. He was giving the gun to Dana to hold on Santiago while he called 911, but Santiago rushed them. The gun went off, killing Carlos."

Surprised, Dana stepped back.

"Santiago then attacked Dana," Kevin went on. "She defended herself with a kitchen knife. He's dead."

"Good. Was she hurt?"

"No. She's in shock, though."

"Have you called Homicide?"

"No. I thought maybe you could do it. Dana's on the edge. I don't want some dumb Homicide bull to cause a breakdown."

"Yeah. I'll call Benedetti myself, and I'll come over there.

One thing, Kevin, when she gives her statement, you've got to keep your mouth buttoned. Okay? You know how Benedetti feels about you."

"No problem."

When Kevin hung up, Dana said to him, "I heard Carlos on the phone. He was going to have you killed." She put her arms around him. "I couldn't let him go on. I love you too much. Won't they understand?"

Kevin led her to a chair. "Dana, in a few minutes this place will be full of cops. Listen closely to me now. You need to be careful what you say. I won't be able to say anything."

She looked concerned. "I don't understand. What did I do wrong?"

He hesitated. "Nothing, but what you said to me at first about shooting Carlos . . . it's better to describe it the way I did on the phone. Just remember that you were all struggling when the gun went off, killing Carlos. You're not too clear what happened. You were perfectly within your rights to defend yourself against Santiago. It's just that some cops suspect everything and may try to get you to say something you shouldn't. Stick to the way I told it. Watch me before you answer any question. If I shake my head no, tell the detective you won't answer that question without your lawyer being present. He won't like that, but don't pay any attention to him."

"I still don't understand. Carlos had turned evil."

He touched her cheek. "The law can be strange, Dana. Stick to what you heard me say on the phone. The other area where you need to be careful is if they ask about Carlos's business. Remember, you don't know anything, and if they try to browbeat you, just say what I told you about the lawyer."

"I see." She tried to stop her hands from shaking.

"None of this may happen, Dana. I'm just being super careful. One other thing. The knife is in Santiago's chest but the blood didn't come from there."

"No. I stuck it in him after I sliced his groin to make sure he would die."

"Okay, I understand, but when you talk to the detectives, say that he was still threatening you. That's why you stabbed him in the chest. Don't volunteer anything. Just answer the questions and don't say that you wanted to kill either of them. If they ask why you called me and not 911, just say that you knew me from volunteering at Sacred Heart and you were all confused. If they start getting into the details of our relationship, tell them you don't feel well and want to see your doctor and lawyer. I know you don't understand this now, but just do what I say and it will be okay."

"I'll try. Can I change my dress before they get here?"

Kevin hesitated. He kissed her lightly on the cheek. "I think it would be better if you didn't. When they see the blood all over your dress, they'll know how terrible it was."

"God." She looked at her herself. "It's awful."

"I'll be with you. You can't stay here. Will you come with me tonight?"

"Forever. If you ask."

He smiled. "One more thing, Dana. There's going to be ugly publicity. After the questions, I'm going to take you out the back exit. We don't want any pictures. Don't even tell the cops where you'll be. Give your father's address if they ask."

"Publicity!" Dana was horrified. "All I did was try to save you and kill an animal who violated women and was going to do it again and kill me. You know that."

"Yes." He held her hand. "But Santiago was the ski mask rapist. And you were involved with Carlos and me. I'm the notorious cop who was suspended. The media will turn it into a circus. The best thing is to disappear and let the story die."

Kevin had left the front door ajar. They heard the elevator stop. "You'll be fine. Just hang in there for a while." Kevin went to the door. Lieutenants Garza and Benedetti led a pack of cops from the first elevator. The second elevator discharged crime-scene technicians.

"Only the photographers in the room until the coroner declares them DOA," Benedetti said. "He should be here any minute. In the meantime, you guys stay put, except for Klein and Lee, who have the case. You can interview the woman in the other room." He pointed to the studio. "I'll personally interview you, McKay."

Kevin started to say something, but Garza held up his hand. "Hold on, Ralph," he said to Benedetti. "Kevin is principal investigator on the ski mask cases. I want him present when your guys interview Dana Rogers."

Benedetti frowned, trying to guess how Vincent Ferrante would rule on this. Finally, he turned to Kevin. "Okay, but I warn you, McKay, you open your mouth once during this interview and you're out of the room. Got it?"

Kevin nodded.

William Lee, the soft-spoken Chinese-American inspector, interviewed Dana, while his partner, Andy Klein, took notes. They were both slender and in their mid-thirties. They had done a walk-through of the apartment and conferred briefly before Lee introduced himself and his partner to Dana. Kevin knew them only from passing in the hallways of the Bureau of Investigations. Neither man showed any reaction to Kevin sitting behind them during the interview.

Lee informed Dana that he would be recording the conversation, and placed a small cassette recorder in front of her. Kevin wished he'd remembered to tell Dana that the other detective had a similar recorder in his pocket. If occasion suggested it, Lee would ostentatiously turn off the recorder while his partner activated the hidden one. Some suspects made the mistake of getting more talkative when they thought they were not being recorded. Lee routinely gave Dana the Miranda warnings before beginning. She blinked at the warnings, but since Kevin gave no sign, agreed to answer questions.

"Miss Rogers, in your own words, tell us what happened. I may interrupt occasionally to try to understand better. Please don't let that disturb you."

Dana told how she and Carlos had arrived at the apartment, how Carlos had left, but came back with the address to have keys made.

Lee smiled apologetically. "Miss Rogers, forgive me for interrupting so soon, but could you please explain. You weren't staying here?"

"No. I was staying with Carlos at his other place."

"I see. But you were moving back. Why couldn't he just give you the keys?"

"I had decided I wanted to be by myself. He said I could have the locks changed."

"Pardon me, miss, but did you have a fight with your boyfriend?" Lee smiled understandingly.

Behind him Kevin shook his head, no.

Dana looked Kevin in the eye as she ignored his advice to say nothing. "No. It was not a fight. I told him that I had decided to end our relationship."

"Did that make him angry?" Lee's voice was soft, encouraging.

Again Kevin shook his head. Again Dana answered.

"No. He was not angry. He was resigned. He'd seen it coming."

"Really? For how long?"

"Perhaps a year. This is personal, Inspector. What does it have to do with what happened here?"

"Nothing, I'm sure, Miss Rogers, but my superiors would chastise me if I skipped anything that might somehow later be questioned." Lee's smile encouraged empathy, and Dana understood why Kevin had wanted to warn her. "Please continue."

Dana related how at first Raul had been frightened of Carlos and how the ringing phone had apparently broken the spell.

"Miss Rogers . . ." Lee gently held up his hand. "Please help me to understand this. Carlos is armed with a gun. Yet he gets close to a big, violent man holding a crowbar and slaps him in the face. Why didn't Santiago attack him then?"

Dana shrugged. "You have to understand the culture, Inspector. Carlos was from an upper-class background in Lima. He regarded Santiago as a peasant. For some reason, Santiago was intimidated. He attacked later when Carlos was looking at me."

"Lima, Peru?"

Dana nodded.

"What business was he in?"

"He's dead. Is that important?"

Lee smiled. "I'm just trying to understand, Miss Rogers."

"Well, I'm afraid I can't help. Carlos was in some sort of shipping."

Lee sat waiting. Behind him Kevin had again signaled Dana not to continue.

"Go on, Miss Rogers," Lee finally said, when it became obvious that his interrogator's ploy of silently expecting the witness to say more was unproductive.

"When the two men confronted each other, I went into the kitchen and picked up the knife."

"Excuse me, Miss Rogers, I meant go on about what kind of shipping business Carlos was in."

"I told you all I know. I'm exhausted, Inspector. Would it be all right if I left and my lawyer gave you all of the information you need?"

Lee smiled. "I appreciate how you must feel. It will only take a few more minutes, and I'll try not to interrupt again. Of course, as I said at the beginning, you have a right to have a lawyer present anytime you wish." Lee never forgot that his words were also being recorded.

Dana continued her story, and Lee did not interrupt.

When she stopped talking, Lee said, "You were very brave, Miss Rogers. I truly admire your ability to stay so calm when he came next to you in the kitchen. May I ask why you slashed at his groin instead of stabbing him?"

"I wanted him to leave me alone. If he was wounded there, he couldn't rape me."

"Yes. That is true. When the blood spurted from his artery, why did you feel it was necessary to stab him in the chest?"

"He was reaching for the crowbar. I was afraid he would hit me."

Lee glanced at his partner. "Andy, can you think of any questions I missed?"

Kevin acknowledged that Lee was good. The witness was exhausted. If there was something she was hiding, now was the time to get it. His question to Klein was a subterfuge to make Dana think the interview was over so she would lower her defenses.

"No, Bill, just what Miss Rogers did then."

Lee said, "Of course, just tell us what you did after stabbing Santiago in the chest."

"I went and called Inspector McKay."

"You did not call 911?" Kevin was sure Lee and Klein already knew that, but it was standard to put the witness through the paces.

"He was someone I knew from doing volunteer work at the Sacred Heart school. I thought it would be faster than trying to explain to some 911 operator."

Lee nodded. "Any other reason?"

"No."

Lee turned off the recorder and stood. Kevin noticed that he gave Klein time to reach in his jacket and switch on his recorder.

"Thank you, Miss Rogers," Lee said. "You have been most helpful. What did you do after you spoke to Inspector McKay?"

Dana had stood, obviously relieved that the interview was over. She frowned when Lee asked another question. Kevin wanted to tell her this question was okay, to tell them she'd gone downstairs and waited for him. But Dana was bothered.

"I don't remember," she snapped at Lee, and went into the bathroom.

Lee held up his hands to his partner, who had surreptitiously turned off the cassette in his pocket. "She's had enough of us after what she's been through, and I don't blame her, Andy." Lee smiled, and turned to Kevin as if seeing him for the first time. "How are you, Kevin?" He held out his hand.

Kevin shook hands with both detectives.

Lee looked in the direction Dana had gone. "Quite a lady. Looks like she saved the state a lot of money in not having to try Santiago."

"Yeah," Klein said, "and this time the dirt-bag won't be let out by Corrections."

Both men looked at Kevin, but he remained silent, wondering which one had a recorder going.

"You've got some blood on your suit, Kevin." Lee pointed to stains on Kevin's jacket.

"I know." Kevin shrugged.

"Was it from when you checked their pulses?"

Lee had seen blood all over Dana's dress. He knew an experienced cop like Kevin would not have gotten blood on him from the bodies.

"When I got here, the victim was almost hysterical down on the street. I put my arms around her to comfort her."

Neither detective said anything. After it became clear that Kevin wasn't going to add anything, they went into the other room.

Dana changed while Kevin recorded a statement for Lieutenant Garza on a cassette, relating how he'd received a call from Dana and responded immediately. Garza had apparently talked Benedetti into letting him take Kevin's statement. Kevin didn't mention his coaching session with Dana.

After giving his statement, Kevin said to Dana, "These people will be here for hours. My car's in front of the building. Why don't I pull it into the basement and come up and get you?"

"My car is in the basement," she said. "I'd like to take it with me."

"No problem. We'll go in your car, and I'll have Terry or Joey pick up my car."

Kevin carried Dana's two small bags to the basement after letting Inspector Lee see what she was taking.

"I'm going to hire someone to move my things," Dana said. "I never want to come back here."

"It will take a day or two before the crime scene is officially released," Kevin told her.

When they got to her car, Kevin carried the bags to the trunk, but Dana opened the car door. "Could you put them in the backseat, please?"

Kevin frowned at the bloodstains on the rear bumper and trunk lock. He put the bags in the rear seat. "I'll drive, if you like," he said.

"Thank you. I'm exhausted." She handed him her key ring.

Kevin looked at the keys. There was a small dried bloodstain on the trunk key. He sighed and scraped it off with his thumbnail. She watched him without a word. He started the car, remembering her waiting in front for him covered in blood, and her agitation at Inspector Lee's question on what she'd done after she called him.

Chapter Sixty-seven

They stopped for a red light, and Dana reached out and touched Kevin's hand. "I didn't tell you everything." She brushed her hair back from her forehead. "After I called you, I rushed to get out of the apartment. I knocked over one of Carlos's suitcases." She paused, seeing Kevin's frown. "I'm not telling this well. But as I said to Inspector Lee, I had told Carlos that I wanted to end our relationship. He didn't really accept it, of course, but for reasons of his own, he didn't argue. Probably thought I didn't mean it." She squeezed his hand. "But I did. I was so devastated when you went away after Flip was killed, so frightened, I went with Carlos, but I knew immediately it was a mistake."

"You only told me what happened in the apartment. We didn't have time to talk before the crime team got there."

"I know, Kevin. I can understand why you're confused now by my mention of Carlos's suitcases. He told me that he had stored suitcases there, and after he took them, I could have the apartment locks changed. I was afraid to tell him the truth, that I would never see him again. In any event, what I told Lee is true to a point. Carlos left with the suitcases, but when he returned to give me the address to have keys made, he placed them near the door. Rushing out after all the bloodshed, I tripped over one of them. Then I thought, if it's full of drugs, I might get in trouble. I opened the suitcases."

"I hope I'm not driving with a couple of kilos of dope in the trunk." He stopped in front of his house and turned off the ignition.

"No. There are no drugs. Bring the bags upstairs. I want you to see what's inside, but not here in the street."

Kevin opened the door to his apartment and took the suitcases in. Dana carried her two smaller bags. Upstairs, he put his arms around her. "I told you once before that you could talk to me, Dana. It caused a lot of pain when you didn't. Don't hold anything back now."

She nuzzled his neck. "I was such a fool. I'm telling you everything. Open the suitcases and you'll see why I didn't want to say anything to Lee."

Kevin opened a case. "Jesus! How much money is it?"

"I don't know. I swear I didn't even think about it until I tripped over the case. I know it's hard to believe that, Kevin, but my life with Carlos was compartmentalized. I knew he was into drugs, but I told him I didn't want to know the details. You're a cop. You probably have strong feelings, but I don't. People are going to use drugs. In Paris, we all experimented. I stopped only because I felt it was interfering with my painting."

Kevin knelt and opened the other case. He held up a manila envelope that had been on top of the money. "What's in this?"

"Carlos's papers. It seems he was liquidating property he owned. I got a number of his phone calls from sales people. Those appear to be some of the records."

"Dana, there must be millions of dollars here. I don't know what you're thinking, but the people he worked for would never let anyone disappear with this much of their money."

"I'm sure none of it belonged to them, Kevin. You can check those papers, of course, maybe I'm wrong."

They went to the couch and sat holding hands. "I didn't know what to do," she said. "Impulsively, I put the bags in my car. I wanted you to make the decision and not have to do it in front of a bunch of cops."

He spoke slowly. "The law is clear. The proceeds of drug profits are subject to seizure. If it could be proved that Carlos obtained the money through drugs, the San Francisco Police Department would get the money. On the other hand, Carlos's relatives could protest and maybe keep the dough."

"Carlos had no relatives. His father was killed in Peru years ago."

"I suppose, then, you could claim it." He laughed. "But your lawyer fees fighting in court to keep it would eat it all up."

"I'm not sure I want it, Kevin," she said. "Don't misunderstand me. I'm an artist. I don't take the moral position that you do—that this is dirty money from poisoning people. All the customers were quite willing. It's just . . ."

"What?"

"Well, Carlos changed from when I knew him in Paris. Here in San Francisco, I gradually began to see another side of him. A toughness. He never did anything overt in front of me. I can't say that. It's just that I began to suspect that he and the people he worked with were violent."

"Violence is inevitable at a certain level of the drug trade," Kevin said. "A lot of middle-class people get in and find out too late. Others adapt and prosper."

"Carlos prospered. In fact, he said something had happened when he was away. You know, when he returned from that long trip, Carlos hinted that he was on to something big. I cut him off. As I mentioned, I didn't want to know details, and also I didn't want to encourage him into thinking he was doing it for our future. What should we do?"

"For now, let's put the cases in the closet." He grinned at her. "Let's celebrate being together again." He took Dana's hand and led her into the bedroom.

Later, they drove to Van Ness, where Kevin spotted a parking space a block from the restaurant. They sat in a plush booth and sipped wine.

"You haven't stopped grinning at me," she said.

"I'm sorry. I know you've been through a bloody mess. I'm just so happy we're back together. Your problems with Carlos and Raul are over, and I haven't thought of my crap in the police department in hours." He laughed. "It seems our only problem is to decide what to do with a few million bucks in cash."

She laughed with him. "I know I'll probably wake up screaming during the night, but right now I feel happy for the first time since you left."

"I know what to do for you if you wake up screaming."

"You certainly do, Kevin. And there are all kinds of screams," she said. Her face sobered then, and she asked, "What will the police department do with the money?"

"Use it for buy money. Overtime for narcs." He thought of Hallman, Simp Jiminez, Sherry and his team. "It will be used for the drug war."

"I couldn't take any of it, Kevin. I'm not rich, but my mother left me a trust. And I do make some money from my work. I know you well enough to know you wouldn't take any of it."

"You're right." He grinned. "I'm cursed with an honest streak in a dishonest world."

She touched his hand. "I like that."

"On the other hand . . ."

"What?"

"If you were so inclined, just think of all the wonderful people who we could make deliriously happy with anonymous donations of cash. Like Ronnie Blue's mother, who never had a decent shot at life. Like those kids on the basketball team, and the ones who can't even make the team."

"Don't forget," Dana said, "the school doesn't have an art budget for the students. And what about all the kids who never get a trip to the museum, and the single mothers who could get job training if there was money for child care, and . . ."

Kevin just sat smiling at her. The waiter had to cough twice to get his attention so they could order dinner.

Investigate Joseph D. McNamara's gripping novels.

THE FIRST DIRECTIVE

A rich man's teenage daughter has
disappeared, and for some reason people
in high places are getting nervous. Sergeant
Fraleigh, a homicide cop, is put on the
case but promptly violates the first directive
of police work: He gets involved with a
beautiful suspect.

FATAL COMMAND

Fraleigh, the high-tech boomtown's unorthodox new chief of detectives, had supervised a quiet stakeout. Now the mayor's aide has been gunned down, and an innocent young woman is near death. Life in Silicon City is filled with menace.

THE BLUE MIRAGE

Fraleigh is the new acting police chief of the turbulent Silicon City police force. But between a bungled SWAT strike and his high-profile affair with a female politician, Fraleigh would rather disappear.

Instead, he goes to the seedy Blue Mirage. And he ends up in New York City, confronting his cop brother—and a life-threatening scandal.

JOSEPH D. McNAMARA

Unsparing, authentic cop stories.